HALO®
THE FALL OF REACH

NOVELS IN THE *NEW YORK TIMES* BESTSELLING HALO® SERIES

Halo®: The Fall of Reach by Eric Nylund
Halo®: The Flood by William C. Dietz
Halo®: First Strike by Eric Nylund
Halo®: Ghosts of Onyx by Eric Nylund
Halo®: Contact Harvest by Joseph Staten
Halo®: The Cole Protocol by Tobias S. Buckell
Halo®: Evolutions: Essential Tales of the Halo Universe
by various authors/artists

HALO®
THE FALL OF REACH

ERIC NYLUND

A TOM DOHERTY ASSOCIATES BOOK
NEW YORK

This is a work of fiction. All of the characters, organizations, and events portrayed in this novel are either products of the author's imagination or are used fictitiously.

HALO®: THE FALL OF REACH

Originally published by Del Rey, The Random House Publishing Group

Cover and interior art by Gabriel "Robogabo" Garza

A Tor Book
Published by Tom Doherty Associates, LLC
175 Fifth Avenue
New York, NY 10010

www.tor-forge.com

ISBN 978-0-7653-2832-8

First Tor Trade Paperback Edition: August 2010

Printed in the United States of America

11

For Syne Mitchell.
She watched my six, patched me up, and
provided transportation to my DZ everyday—
no soldier could ever ask for better support
in the field . . . or a better wife.

ACKNOWLEDGMENTS TO THE 2010 EDITION

None of this would have been possible without Microsoft staffers Jacob Benton, Nicolas "Sparth" Bouvier, Alicia Brattin, Gabriel "Robogabo" Garza, Jon Goff, Kevin Grace, Tyler Jeffers, Frank O'Connor, Jeremy Patenaude, Kenneth Scott, and Kiki Wolfkill.

Nor without the efforts of the staff at Tor Books: Tom Doherty, Eric Raab, Whitney Ross, Seth Lerner, Megan Barnard, Teresa DeLucci, Jim Kapp, Lauren Hougen, Heather Saunders, Nathan Weaver, Justin Golenbock, and Patty Garcia.

343 Industries would like to thank Bungie Studios, Scott Dell'Osso, Nick Dimitrov, David Figatner, Nancy Figatner, Josh Kerwin, Bryan Koski, Eric Nylund, Bonnie Ross-Ziegler, Phil Spencer, and Carla Woo.

This edition features early drafts of the new cover art, which have been included periodically throughout the book. These images give a small insight into the process of creating the new cover from artists within 343 Industries.

FORE WORLD

When Bungie, Eric Nylund, and Microsoft teamed up to create the novel *Halo: The Fall of Reach,* it was one of those *things*—an interesting and sudden opportunity—the kind of thing where you simply don't think about what's coming next. You react (Eric cranked that thing out in record time) and sit back, or rather, move on to other business. We were launching and supporting not only a game, but an entire business, a console that would go on to be the home base for Halo for another ten years.

The Fall of Reach wasn't the first novelization of a video game; there had been several, in fact, before that. All had differing layers and measures of success. But *Fall of Reach* did something unexpected.

I won't bother talking about sales or success as it relates to dollars and numbers, or bestsellers' lists, but it reached a level of success that was unprecedented and would continue for years to come with Eric and other authors thriving in this "new" space.

It bridged the invisible gulf between story, universe, game, and imagination. It was a brilliantly executed matrix of material that connected these disparate elements and cohesively pulled it all together, making Halo, a game built on suddenness and mystery, feel immediately like it had been around forever, and that we the player were just tuning in, catching a universe in motion at a particularly exciting moment.

The idea started when Nancy Figatner, then part of the Halo franchise team, and Jordan Weisman (founder of Shadowrun creators FASA, among other things) decided that book publishing was something that Microsoft's nascent console business ought to be attached to. They worked to find a good publishing partner and writers to germinate the idea, and ended up working with Eric Trautmann, Eric Nylund (of course), and Bungie to begin the novel.

Eric did something remarkable. He fleshed out, in just a few short weeks, a nascent universe that we've continued to build on, and continued to connect the dots between those disparate stars, some of which were planted in the Halo firmament in *The Fall of Reach*.

Reach wasn't just a piece of deliberate universe-building, but a careful exercise in crisis avoidance. Eric had the challenge of not only creating believable characters with history and impact, but ensuring they didn't step on the toes of a story that's still in motion. This is not an enviable task—and it takes a patient, understanding, imaginative type of writer to create grand fiction with those kinds of restrictions.

And yet Eric was somehow able to use those restrictions not as training wheels or prison bars, but rather as a high-tensile springboard from which to launch a whole new aspect of the universe—one grounded in the dirt and blood of the Spartan program as it existed—rather than the mystery and awe of the universe where the Master Chief is the last standing Spartan.

It seems absurd on its face to talk about the scale of those two facets of the Halo universe, but in some ways *Fall of Reach* is smaller and more personal, while at the same time deeper and denser than the wide-open enigmas and vistas of the game.

Whereas Halo is all about loneliness and exploration, *Fall of*

Reach is about a different kind of journey—that of childhood to adulthood and that of innocence to war, for both its protagonist and the species he champions.

And the process itself was almost as grueling as the Spartan training. Eric had very limited access to Bungie—hard at work finishing the game—and basically had to rely on a large drop of information (the seeds of the fabled story bible) from Jason Jones and Bungie, while his writing partner and co–heavy lifter at the time, Eric Trautmann, consolidated feedback and information from the team and filtered it to and with Eric Nylund. And again, all this in a hypercompressed timeline to take advantage of a narrow window of opportunity.

The book went from conception to final print in a staggering four months.

It was a collaborative effort, but often blindly so. In the riot of noise for the launch of the game, the book took a backseat, but only for a short drive. As the game exploded in popularity, people became curious about the backstory of this deliberately obfuscated protagonist. Putting yourself in the Master Chief's MJOLNIR boots was probably one of the most satisfying experiences gamers ever had, but curiosity about a universe you're inserted into, literally midbattle, propelled sales of the novel. And it just continued to sell.

We've made a lot of Halo novels since then, with a broad range of writers, and one thing remains the same, from Eric Nylund to Karen Traviss to Greg Bear and beyond: the Halo sandbox of characters, events, and emotions is a perfect playground for prose.

And this is literally just the beginning.

Frank O'Connor
Redmond, WA 2010

HALO®
THE FALL OF REACH

TRIUMPH

PROLOGUE

0500 HOURS, FEBRUARY 12, 2535 (MILITARY CALENDAR) / LAMBDA SERPENTIS SYSTEM, JERICHO VII THEATER OF OPERATIONS

"Contact. All teams stand by: enemy contact, my position."

The Chief knew there were probably more than a hundred of them—motion sensors were off the scale. He wanted to see them for himself, though; his training made that lesson clear: "Machines break. Eyes don't."

The four Spartans that composed Blue Team covered his back, standing absolutely silent and immobile in their MJOLNIR combat armor. Someone had once commented that they looked like Greek war gods in the armor . . . but his Spartans were far more effective and ruthless than Homer's gods had ever been.

He snaked the fiber-optic probe up and over the three-meter-high stone ridge. When it was in place, the Chief linked it to his helmet's heads-up display.

On the other side he saw a valley with eroded rock walls and a river meandering through it . . . and camped along the banks as far as he could see were Grunts.

The Covenant used these stocky aliens as cannon fodder. They stood a meter tall and wore armored environment suits that replicated the atmosphere of their frozen homeworld. They reminded the Chief of biped dogs, not only in appearance, but because their speech—even with the new translation software—was an odd combination of high-pitched squeaks, guttural barks, and growls.

They were about as smart as dogs, too. But what they lacked in brainpower, they made up for in sheer tenacity. He had seen them hurl themselves at their enemies until the ground was piled high with their corpses . . . and their opponents had depleted their ammunition.

These Grunts were unusually well armed: needlers, plasma pistols, and there were four stationary plasma cannons. Those could be a problem.

One other problem: there were easily a thousand of them.

This operation had to go off without a hitch. Blue Team's mission was to draw out the Covenant rear guard and let Red Team slip through in the confusion. Red Team would then plant a HAVOK tactical nuke. When the next Covenant ship landed, dropped its shields, and started to unload its troops, they'd get a thirty-megaton surprise.

The Chief detached the optics and took a step back from the rock wall. He passed the tactical information along to his team over a secure COM channel.

"Four of us," Blue-Two whispered over the link. "And a thousand of them? Piss-poor odds for the little guys."

"Blue-Two," the Chief said, "I want you up with those Jackhammer launchers. Take out the cannons and soften the rest of them. Blue-Three and Five, you follow me up—we're on crowd control. Blue-Four: you get the welcome mat ready. Understood?"

Four blue lights winked on his heads-up display as his team acknowledged the orders.

"On my mark." The Chief crouched and readied himself. "Mark!"

Blue-Two leaped gracefully atop the ridge—three meters straight up. There was no sound as the half ton of MJOLNIR armor and Spartan landed on the limestone.

She hefted one launcher and ran along the ridge—she was the fastest Spartan on the Chief's team. He was confident those Grunts wouldn't be able to track her for the three seconds she'd be exposed. In quick succession, Blue-Two emptied both of the Jackhammer's tubes, dropped one launcher, and then fired the other rockets just as fast. The shells streaked into the Grunts' formation and detonated. One of the stationary guns flipped over, engulfed in the blast, and the gunner was flung to the ground.

She ditched the launcher, jumped down—rolled once—and was back on her feet, running at top speed to the fallback point.

The Chief, Blue-Three, and Blue-Five leaped to the top of the ridge. The Chief switched to infrared to cut through the clouds of dust and propellant exhaust just in time to see the second salvo of Jackhammers strike their targets. Two consecutive blossoms of flash, fire, and thunder decimated the front ranks of the Grunt guards, and most importantly, turned the last of the plasma cannons into smoldering wreckage.

The Chief and the others opened fire with their MA5B assault rifles—a full automatic spray of fifteen rounds per second. Armor-piercing bullets tore into the aliens, breaching their environment suits and sparking the methane tanks they carried. Gouts of flame traced wild arcs as the wounded Grunts ran in confusion and pain.

Finally the Grunts realized what was happening—and where this attack was coming from. They regrouped and charged *en masse*. An earthquake vibration coursed through the ground and shook the porous stone beneath the Chief's boots.

The three Spartans exhausted their AP clips and then, in unison, switched to shredder rounds. They fired into the tide of creatures as they surged forward. Line after line of them dropped. Scores more just trampled their fallen comrades.

Explosive needles bounced off the Chief's armor, detonating as they hit the ground. He saw the flash of a plasma bolt—side stepped—and heard the air crackle where he had stood a split second before.

"Inbound Covenant air support," Blue-Four reported over the COM link. *"ETA is two minutes, Chief."*

"Roger that," he said. "Blue-Three and -Five: maintain fire for five seconds, then fall back. Mark!"

Their status lights winked once, acknowledging his order.

The Grunts were three meters from the wall. The Chief tossed two grenades. He, Blue-Three, and Blue-Five stepped backward off the ridge, landed, spun, and ran.

Two dull thumps reverberated through the ground. The squeals and barks of the incoming Grunts, however, drowned out the noise of the exploding grenades.

The Chief and his team sprinted up the half-kilometer sandstone slope in thirty-two seconds flat. The hill ended abruptly—a sheer drop of two hundred meters straight into the ocean.

Blue-Four's voice crackled over the COM channel: *"Welcome mat is laid out, Chief. Ready when you are."*

The Grunts looked like a living carpet of steel-blue skin, claws, and chrome weapons. Some ran on all fours up the slope. They barked and howled, baying for the Spartans' blood.

"Roll out the carpet," the Chief told Blue-Four.

The hill exploded—plumes of pulverized sandstone and fire and smoke hurtled skyward.

The Spartans had buried a spiderweb pattern of Lotus antitank mines earlier that morning.

Sand and bits of metal pinged off of the Chief's helmet.

The Chief and his team opened fire again, picking off the remaining Grunts that were still alive and struggling to stand.

His motion detector flashed a warning. There were incoming projectiles high at two o'clock—velocities at over a hundred kilometers per hour.

Five Covenant Banshee fliers appeared over the ridge.

"New contacts. All teams, open fire!" he barked.

The Spartans, without hesitation, fired on the alien fliers. Bullet hits pinged from the fliers' chitinous armor—it would take a very lucky shot to take out the antigrav pods on the end of the craft's stubby meter-long "wings."

The fire got the aliens' attention, however. Lances of fire slashed from the Banshees' gunports.

The Chief dove and rolled to his feet. Sandstone exploded where he had stood only an instant before. Globules of molten glass sprayed the Spartans.

The Banshees screamed over their heads—then banked sharply for another pass.

"Blue-Three, Blue-Five: Theta Maneuver," the Chief called out.

Blue-Three and-Five gave him the thumbs-up signal.

They regrouped at the edge of the cliff and clipped onto the steel cables that dangled down the length of the rock wall.

"Did you set up the fougasses with fire or shrapnel?" the Chief asked.

"Both," Blue-Three replied.

"Good." The Chief grabbed the detonators. "Cover me."

The fougasses were never meant to take down flying targets; the Spartans had put them there to mop up the Grunts. In the field, though, you had to improvise. Another tenet of their training: adapt or die.

The Banshees formed into a "flying V" and swooped toward them, almost brushing the ground.

The Spartans opened fire.

Bolts of superheated plasma from the Banshees punctuated the air.

The Chief dodged to the right, then to the left; he ducked. Their aim was getting better.

The Banshees were one hundred meters away, then fifty meters. Their plasma weapons might recycle fast enough to get another shot . . . and at this range, the Chief wouldn't be dodging.

The Spartans jumped backward off the cliff—guns still blazing. The Chief jumped, too, and hit the detonators.

The ten fougasses—each a steel barrel filled with napalm and spent AP and shredder casings—had been buried a few meters from the edge of the cliff, their mouths angled up at thirty degrees. When the grenades at the bottom of the barrels exploded, it made one hell of a barbecue out of anything that got in their way.

The Spartans slammed into the side of the cliff—the steel cables they were attached to twanged taut.

A wave of heat and pressure washed over them. A heartbeat later five flaming Banshees hurtled over their heads, leaving thick trails of black smoke as they arced into the water. They splashed down, then vanished beneath the emerald waves. The Spartans hung there a moment, waiting and watching with their assault rifles trained on the water.

No survivors surfaced.

They rappelled down to the beach and rendezvoused with Blue-Two and -Four.

"Red Team reports mission objective achieved, Chief," Blue-Two said. "They send their compliments."

"It's hardly going to balance the scales," Blue-Three muttered, and kicked the sand. "Not like those Grunts when they slaughtered the 105th Drop Jet Platoon. They should suffer just as much as those guys did."

The Chief had nothing to say to that. It wasn't his job to make things suffer—he was just here to win battles. Whatever it took.

"Blue-Two," the Chief said. "Get me an uplink."

"Aye aye." She patched him into the SATCOM system.

"Mission accomplished, Captain de Blanc," the Chief reported. "Enemy neutralized."

"Excellent news," the Captain said. He sighed, and added, *"But we're pulling you out, Chief."*

"We're just getting warmed up down here, sir."

"Well, it's a different story up here. Move out for pickup ASAP."

"Understood, sir." The Chief killed the uplink. He told his team, "The party's over, Spartans. Dust-off in fifteen."

They jogged double-quick up the ten kilometers of the beach, and returned to their dropship—a Pelican, scuffed and dented from three days' hard fighting. They boarded and the ship's engines whined to life.

Blue-Two took off her helmet and scratched the stubble of her brown hair. "It's a shame to leave this place," she said, and leaned against the porthole. "There are so few left."

The Chief stood by her and glanced out as they lifted into the air—there were wide rolling plains of palmgrass, the green expanse of ocean, a wispy band of clouds in the sky, and setting red suns.

"There will be other places to fight for," he said.

"Will there?" she whispered.

The Pelican ascended rapidly through the atmosphere, the sky darkened, and soon only stars surrounded them.

In orbit, there were dozens of frigates, destroyers, and two massive carriers. Every ship had carbon scoring and holes peppering their hulls. They were all maneuvering to break orbit.

They docked in the port bay of the UNSC destroyer *Resolute*. Despite being surrounded by two meters of titanium-A battle plate and an array of modern weapons, the Chief preferred to have his feet on the ground, with real gravity, and real atmosphere to breathe—a place where he was in control, and where his life wasn't held in the hands of anonymous pilots. A ship just wasn't home.

The battlefield was.

The Chief rode the elevator to the bridge to make his report, taking advantage of the momentary respite to read Red Team's after-action report in his display. As predicted, the Spartans of Red, Blue, and Green Teams—augmenting three divisions of battle-hardened UNSC Marines—had stalled a Covenant ground advance. Casualty figures were still coming in, but—on the ground, at least—the alien forces had been completely stonewalled.

A moment later the lift doors parted, and he stepped on the rubberized deck. He snapped a crisp salute to Captain de Blanc. "Sir. Reporting as ordered."

The junior bridge officers took a step back from the Chief. They weren't used to seeing a Spartan in full MJOLNIR armor up close—most line troops had never even seen a Spartan. The ghostly iridescent green of the armor plates and the matte black layers underneath made him look part gladiator, part machine. Or perhaps to the bridge crew, he looked as alien as the Covenant.

The view screens showed stars and Jericho VII's four silver moons. At extreme range, a small constellation of stars drifted closer.

The Captain waved the Chief closer as he stared at that cluster of stars—the rest of the battlegroup. "It's happening again."

"Request permission to remain on the bridge, sir," the Chief said. "I . . . want to see it this time, sir."

The Captain hung his head, looking weary. He glanced at the Master Chief with haunted eyes. "Very well, Chief. After all you've been through to save Jericho Seven, we owe you that. We're only thirty million kilometers out-system, though, not half as far as I'd like to be." He turned to the NAV Officer. "Bearing one two zero. Prepare our exit vector."

He turned to face the Chief. "We'll stay to watch . . . but if those bastards so much as twitch in our direction, we're jumping the hell out of here."

"Understood, sir. Thank you."

Resolute's engines rumbled and the ship moved off.

Three dozen Covenant ships—big ones, destroyers and cruisers—winked into view in the system. They were sleek, looking more like sharks than starcraft. Their lateral lines brightened with plasma—then discharged and rained fire down upon Jericho VII.

The Chief watched for an hour and didn't move a muscle.

The planet's lakes, rivers, and oceans vaporized. By tomorrow, the atmosphere would boil away, too. Fields and forests were glassy smooth and glowing red-hot in patches.

Where there had once been a paradise, only hell remained.

"Make ready to jump clear of the system," the Captain ordered.

The Chief continued to watch, his face grim.

There had been ten years of this—the vast network of human colonies whittled down to a handful of strongholds by a merciless, implacable enemy. The Chief had killed the enemy on the ground—shot them, stabbed them, and broken them with his own two hands. On the ground, the Spartans *always* won.

The problem was, the Spartans couldn't take their fight into space. Every minor victory on the ground turned into a major defeat in orbit.

Soon there would be no more colonies, no human settlements—and nowhere left to run.

SECTION I

REVEILLE

VIGILANCE

CHAPTER ONE

0430 HOURS, AUGUST 17, 2517 (MILITARY CALENDAR)
SLIPSTREAM SPACE—UNKNOWN COORDINATES NEAR ERIDANUS STAR SYSTEM

Lieutenant Junior Grade Jacob Keyes awoke. Dull red light filled his blurry vision and he choked on the slime in his lungs and throat.

"Sit up, Lieutenant Keyes," a disembodied male voice said. "Sit. Take a deep breath and cough, sir. You need to clear the bronchial surfactant."

Lieutenant Keyes pushed himself up, peeling his back off the formfitting gel bed. Wisps of fog overflowed from the cryogenic tube as he clumsily climbed out. He sat on a nearby bench, tried to inhale, and doubled over, coughing until a long string of clear fluid flowed from his open mouth.

He sat up and drew his first full breath in two weeks. He tasted his lips and almost gagged. The cryo inhalant was specially designed to be regurgitated and swallowed, replacing nutrients lost in the deep sleep. No matter how they changed the formula, though, it always tasted like lime-flavored mucus.

"Status, Toran? Are we under attack?"

"Negative, sir," the ship's AI replied. "Status normal. We will enter normal space near the Eridanus System in forty-five minutes."

Lieutenant Keyes coughed again. "Good. Thank you, Toran."

"You're welcome, Lieutenant."

Eridanus was on the border of the Outer Colonies. It was

just far enough off the beaten path for pirates to be lurking . . . waiting to capture a diplomatic shuttle like the *Han*. This ship wouldn't last long in a space action. They *should* have an escort. He didn't understand why they had been sent alone—but Junior Lieutenants didn't question orders. Especially when those orders came from FLEETCOM HQ on planet Reach.

Wake-up protocols dictated that he inspect the rest of the crew to make sure no one had run into problems reviving. He looked around the sleep chamber: rows of stainless steel lockers and showers, a medical pod for emergency resuscitations, and forty cryogenic tubes—all empty except the one to his left.

The other person on the *Han* was the civilian specialist, Dr. Halsey. Keyes had been ordered to protect her at all costs, pilot this ship, and generally stay the hell out of her way. They might as well have asked him to hold her hand. This wasn't a military mission; it was baby-sitting. Someone at Fleet Command must have him on their blacklist.

The cover of Dr. Halsey's tube hummed open. Mist rippled out as she sat up, coughing. Her pale skin made her look like a ghost in the fog. Matted locks of dark hair clung to her neck. She didn't look much older than him, and she was lovely—not beautiful, but definitely a striking woman. For a civilian, anyway.

Her blue eyes fixed upon the Lieutenant and she looked him over. "We must be near Eridanus," she said.

Lieutenant Keyes almost saluted reflectively, but checked the motion. "Yes, Doctor." His face reddened and he looked away from her slender body.

He had drilled in cryogenic recovery a dozen times at the Academy. He'd seen his fellow officers naked before—men and women. But Dr. Halsey was a civilian. He didn't know what protocols applied.

Lieutenant Keyes got up and went to her. "Can I help you—"

She swung her legs out of the tube and climbed out. "I'm fine, Lieutenant. Get cleaned up and dressed." She brushed past him and strode to the showers. "Hurry. We have important work to do."

Lieutenant Keyes stood straighter. "Aye, aye, ma'am."

With that brief encounter, their roles and the rules of conduct crystallized. Civilian or not—like it or not—Lieutenant Keyes understood that Dr. Halsey was in charge.

The bridge of the *Han* had an abundance of space for a vessel of its size. That is, it had all the maneuvering room of a walk-in closet. A freshly showered, shaved, and uniformed Lieutenant Keyes pulled himself into the room and sealed the pressure door behind him. Every surface of the bridge was covered with monitors and screens. The wall on his left was a single large semicurved view screen, dark for the moment because there was nothing in the visible spectrum to see in Slipspace.

Behind him was the *Han*'s spinning center section, containing the mess, the rec room, and the sleep chambers. There was no gravity on the bridge, however. The diplomatic shuttle had been designed for the comfort of its passengers, not the crew.

It didn't seem to bother Dr. Halsey. Strapped into the navigator's couch, she wore a white jumpsuit that matched her pale skin, and had tied her dark hair into a simple, elegant knot. Her fingers danced across four keypads, tapping in commands.

"Welcome, Lieutenant," she said without looking up. "Please have a seat at the communication station and monitor the channels when we enter normal space. If there's so much as a squeak on nonstandard frequencies, I want to know instantly."

He drifted to the communication station and strapped himself down.

"Toran?" she asked.

"Awaiting your orders, Dr. Halsey," the ship AI replied.

"Give me astrogation maps of the system."

"Online, Dr. Halsey."

"Are there any planets currently aligned with our entry trajectory and Eridanus Two? I want to pick up a gravitational boost so we can move in-system ASAP."

"Calculating now, Doctor Hal—"

"And can we have some music? Rachmaninov's Piano Concerto Number Three, I think."

"Understood, Doctor—"

"And start a preburn warm-up cycle for the fusion engines."

"Yes, Doc—"

"And stop spinning the *Han*'s central carousel section. We may need the power."

"Working . . ."

She eased back. The music started and she sighed. "Thank you, Toran."

"You're welcome, Dr. Halsey. Entering normal space in five minutes, plus or minus three minutes."

Lieutenant Keyes shot the doctor an admiring glance. He was impressed—few people could put a shipboard AI through its paces so rigorously as to cause a detectable pause.

She turned to face him. "Yes, Lieutenant? You have a question?"

He composed himself and pulled his uniform jacket taut. "I was curious about our mission, ma'am. I assume we are to reconnoiter something in this system, but why send a shuttle, rather than a prowler or a corvette? And why just the two of us?"

She blinked and smiled. "A fairly accurate assumption and analysis, Lieutenant. This *is* a reconnaissance mission . . . of sorts. We are here to observe a child. The first of many, I hope."

"A child?"

"A six-year-old male, to be precise." She waved her hand. "It may help if you think of this purely as a UNSC-funded physiological study." Every trace of a smile evaporated from her lips. "Which is precisely what you are to tell anyone who asks. Is that understood, Lieutenant?"

"Yes, Doctor."

Keyes frowned, retrieved his grandfather's pipe from his pocket, and turned it end over end. He couldn't smoke the thing—igniting a combustible on the flight deck was against every major regulation on a UNSC space vehicle—but sometimes he just fiddled with it or chewed on the tip, which helped him think. He stuck it back into his pocket, and decided to push the issue and find out more.

"With all due respect, Dr. Halsey, this sector of space is dangerous."

With a sudden deceleration, they entered normal space. The main view screen flickered and a million stars snapped into focus. The *Han* dove toward a cloud-swirled gas giant dead ahead.

"Stand by for burn," Dr. Halsey announced. "On my mark, Toran."

Lieutenant Keyes tightened his harness.

"Three . . . two . . . one. *Mark.*"

The ship rumbled and sped faster toward the gas giant. The pull of the harness increased around the Lieutenant's chest, making breathing difficult. They accelerated for sixty-seven seconds . . . the storms of the gas giant grew larger on the view screen—then the *Han* arced up and away from its surface.

Eridanus drifted into the center of the screen and filled the bridge with warm orange light.

"Gravity boost complete," Toran chimed. "ETA to Eridanus is forty-two minutes, three seconds."

"Well done," Dr. Halsey said. She unlocked her harness and floated free, stretching. "I hate cryo sleep," she said. "It leaves one so cramped."

"As I was saying before, Doctor, this system is dangerous—"

She gracefully spun to face him, halting her momentum with a hand on the bulkhead. "Oh yes, I know how dangerous this system is. It has a colorful history: rebel insurrection in 2494, beaten down by the UNSC two years later at the cost of four destroyers." She thought a moment, then added, "I don't believe the Office of Naval Intelligence ever found their base in the asteroid field. And since there have been organized raids and scattered pirate activity nearby, one might conclude—as ONI clearly has—that the remnants of the original rebel faction are still active. Is that what you were worried about?"

"Yes," the Lieutenant replied. He swallowed, his mouth suddenly dry, but he refused to be cowed by the doctor—by a *civilian*. "I need hardly remind you that it's my job to worry about our security."

She knew more than he did, much more, about the Eridanus System—and she obviously had contacts in the intelligence community. Keyes had never seen an ONI spook—to the best of his knowledge anyway. Mainline Navy personnel had elevated such agents to near-mythological status.

Whatever else he thought of Dr. Halsey, he would assume from now on that she knew what she was doing.

Dr. Halsey stretched once more and then strapped herself back onto the navigation couch. "Speaking of pirates," she said with her back now to him, "weren't you supposed to be monitoring communication channels for illegal signals? Just in case someone takes undue interest in a lone, unescorted, diplomatic shuttle?"

Lieutenant Keyes cursed himself for his momentary lapse and snapped to. He scanned all frequencies and had Toran cross-check their authentication codes.

"All signals verified," he reported. "No pirate transmissions detected."

"Continue to monitor them, please."

An awkward thirty minutes passed. Dr. Halsey was content to read reports on the navigational screens, and kept her back to him.

Lieutenant Keyes finally cleared his throat. "May I speak candidly, Doctor?"

"You don't need my permission," she said. "By all means, speak candidly, Lieutenant. You've been doing a fine job so far."

Under normal circumstances, among normal officers, that last remark would have been insubordination—or worse, a rebuke. But he let it pass. Normal military protocol seemed to have been jettisoned on this flight.

"You said we were here to observe a child." He shook his head dubiously. "If this is a cover for real military intelligence work, then, to tell the truth, there are better-qualified officers for this mission. I graduated from UNSC OCS only seven weeks ago. My orders had me rotated to the *Magellan*. Those orders were rescinded, ma'am."

She turned and scrutinized him with icy blue eyes. "Go on, Lieutenant."

He reached for his pipe, but then checked the motion. She would probably think it a silly habit.

"If this is an intel op," he said, "then . . . then I don't understand why I'm here at all."

She leaned forward. "Then, Lieutenant, I shall be equally candid."

Something deep inside Lieutenant Keyes told him he would regret hearing whatever Dr. Halsey had to say. He ignored the feeling. He wanted to know the truth.

"Go ahead, Doctor."

Her slight smile returned. "You are here because Vice Admiral Stanforth, head of Section Three of UNSC Military Intelligence Division, refused to lend me this shuttle without at least one UNSC officer aboard—even though he knows damn well that I can pilot this bucket by myself. So I picked one UNSC officer. You." She tapped her lower lip thoughtfully and added, "You see, I've read your file, Lieutenant. All of it."

"I don't know—"

"You *do* know what I'm talking about." She rolled her eyes. "You don't lie well. Don't insult me by trying again."

Lieutenant Keyes swallowed. "Then why me? *Especially* if you've seen my record?"

"I chose you precisely *because* of your record—because of the incident in your second year at OCS. Fourteen ensigns killed. You were wounded and spent two months in rehabilitation. Plasma burns are particularly painful, I understand."

He rubbed his hands together. "Yes."

"The Lieutenant responsible was your CO on that training mission. You refused to testify against him despite overwhelming evidence and the testimony of his fellow officers . . . and friends."

"Yes."

"They told the board of review the secret the Lieutenant had entrusted to you all—that he was going to test his new theory to make Slipspace jumps more accurate. He was wrong, and you all paid for his eagerness and poor mathematics."

Lieutenant Keyes studied his hands and had the feeling of falling inward. Dr. Halsey's voice sounded distant. "Yes."

"Despite continuing pressure, you never testified. They threatened to demote you, charge you with insubordination and refusing a direct order—even discharge you from the Navy.

"Your fellow officer candidates testified, though. The review board had all the evidence they needed to court-martial your CO. They put you on report and dropped all further disciplinary actions."

He said nothing. His head hung low.

"That is why you are here, Lieutenant—because you have an ability that is exceedingly rare in the military. You can keep a secret." She drew in a long breath and added, "You may have to keep many secrets after this mission is over."

He glanced up. There was a strange look in her eyes. Pity? That caught him off guard and he looked away again. But he felt better than he had since OCS. Someone trusted him again.

"I think," she said, "that you would rather be on the *Magellan*. Fighting and dying on the frontier."

"No, I—" He caught the lie as he said it, stopped, then corrected himself. "Yes. The UNSC needs every man and woman patrolling the Outer Colonies. Between the raiders and insurrections, it's a wonder it all hasn't fallen apart."

"Indeed, Lieutenant, ever since we left Earth's gravity well, we've been fighting one another for every cubic centimeter of vacuum—from Mars to the Jovian Moons to the Hydra System Massacres and on to the hundred brushfire wars in the Outer Colonies. It has always been on the brink of falling apart. That's why we're here."

"To observe one child," he said. "What difference could a child make?"

One of her eyebrows arched. "This child could be more useful to the UNSC than a fleet of destroyers, a thousand Junior Grade Lieutenants—or even *me*. In the end, the child may be the only thing that makes *any* difference."

"Approaching Eridanus Two," Toran informed them.

"Plot an atmospheric vector for the Luxor spaceport," Dr. Halsey ordered. "Lieutenant Keyes, make ready to land."

CHAPTER TWO

1130 HOURS, AUGUST 17, 2517 (MILITARY CALENDAR)
ERIDANUS STAR SYSTEM, ERIDANUS II, ELYSIUM CITY

The orange sun cast a fiery glow on the playground of Elysium City Primary Education Facility No. 119. Dr. Halsey and Lieutenant Keyes stood in the semishade of a canvas awning and watched children as they screamed and chased one another and climbed on steel lattices and skimmed gravballs across the repulsor courts.

Lieutenant Keyes looked extremely uncomfortable in civilian clothes. He wore a loose gray suit, a white shirt, and no tie. Dr. Halsey found his sudden awkwardness charming.

When he had complained the clothes were too loose and sloppy, she had almost laughed. He was pure military to the core. Even out of uniform, the Lieutenant stood rigid, as if he were at perpetual attention. "It's nice here," she said. "This colony doesn't know how good they've got it. Rural lifestyle. No pollution. No crowding. Climate-controlled weather."

The Lieutenant grunted an acknowledgment as he tried to smooth the wrinkles out of his silk jacket.

"Relax," she said. "We're supposed to be parents inspecting the school for our little girl." She slipped her arm through his, and although she would have thought such a feat impossible, the Lieutenant stood even straighter.

She sighed and pulled away from him, opened her purse, and retrieved a palm-sized pad. She adjusted the brim of her wide straw hat to shade the pad from the noon glare. With a tap of her finger, she accessed and scanned the file she had assembled of their subject.

Number-117 had all the genetic markers she had flagged in her original study—he was as close to a perfect subject for her purposes as science could determine. But Dr. Halsey knew it would take more than theoretical perfection to make this project work. People were more than the sum of their genes. There were environmental factors, mutations, learned ethics, and a hundred other factors that could make this candidate unacceptable.

The picture in the file showed a typical six-year-old male. He had tousled brown hair and a sly grin that revealed a gap between his front teeth. A few freckles were speckled across his cheeks. Good—she could match the patterns to confirm his identity.

"Our subject." As she angled the pad toward the Lieutenant so he could see the boy, Dr. Halsey noticed that the picture was four months old. Didn't ONI realize how fast these children changed? Sloppy. She made a note to request updated pictures on a regular basis until phase three started.

"Is that him?" the Lieutenant whispered.

Dr. Halsey looked up.

The Lieutenant nodded to a grassy hill at the end of the playground. The crest of that hill was bare dirt, scuffed clean of all vegetation. A dozen boys pushed and shoved one another—grabbed, tackled, rolled down the slope, and then got up, ran back, and started the process over.

"King of the hill," Dr. Halsey remarked.

One boy stood on the crest. He blocked, pushed, and strong-armed all the other children.

Dr. Halsey pointed her data pad at him and recorded this incident for later study. She zoomed in on the subject to get a better look. This boy smiled and showed the same small gap between his front teeth. A split-second freeze frame and she matched his freckles to the picture on file.

"That's our boy."

He was taller than the other children by a full head, and—if his performance in the game was any indicator—stronger as well. Another boy grabbed him from behind in a headlock. Number-117 peeled the boy off, and—with a laugh—tossed him down the hillside like a toy.

Dr. Halsey had expected a specimen of perfect physical proportions and stunning intellect. True, the subject was strong and fast, but he was also dirty and rude.

Then again, unrealistic and subjective perceptions had to be confronted in these field studies. What did she really expect? He was a six-year-old boy—full of life and unchecked emotion and as predictable as the wind.

Three boys ganged up on him. Two grabbed his legs and one threw his arms around his chest. They all tumbled down the hill. Number-117 kicked and punched and bit his attackers until they let go and ran away to a safe distance. He rose and tore back up the hill, bumping another boy and shouting that he was king.

"He seems," the Lieutenant started, "um, very animated."

"Yes," Dr. Halsey said. "We may be able to use this one."

She glanced up and down the playground. The only adult was helping a girl get to her feet after falling down and scraping her elbow; she marched her towards the nurse's office.

"Stay here and watch me, Lieutenant," she said, and passed him the data pad. "I'm going to have a closer look."

The Lieutenant started to say something, but Dr. Halsey walked away, then half jogged across the painted lines of hopscotch squares on the playground. A breeze caught her sundress and she had to clutch the hem with one hand, grabbing the brim of her straw hat with the other. She slowed to a trot and halted four meters from the base of the hill.

The children stopped and turned.

"You're in trouble," one boy said, and pushed Number-117.

He shoved the boy back and then looked Dr. Halsey squarely in the eyes. The other children looked away; some wore embarrassed smirks, and a few slowly backed off.

Her subject, however, stood there defiantly. He was either confident she wasn't going to punish him—or he simply wasn't afraid. She saw that he had a bruise on his cheek, the knees of his pants were torn, and his lip was cracked.

Dr. Halsey took three steps closer. Several of the children took three involuntary steps backward.

"Can I speak with you, please?" she asked, and continued to stare at her subject.

He finally broke eye contact, shrugged, and then lumbered down the hill. The other children giggled and made tsking sounds; one tossed a pebble at him. Number-117 ignored them.

Dr. Halsey led him to the edge of the nearby sandpit and stopped.

"What's your name?" she asked.

"I'm John," he said. The boy held out his hand.

Dr. Halsey didn't expect physical contact. The subject's father must have taught him the ritual, or the boy was highly imitative.

She shook his hand and was surprised by the strength in his miniscule grip. "It's very nice to meet you." She knelt so she was at his level. "I wanted to ask you what you were doing."

"Winning," he said.

Dr. Halsey smiled. He was unafraid of her . . . and she doubted that he'd have any trouble pushing her off the hill, either.

"You like games," she said. "So do I."

He sighed. "Yeah, but they made me play chess last week. That got boring. It's too easy to win." He took a quick breath. "Or—can we play gravball? They don't let me play gravball anymore, but maybe if you tell them it's okay?"

"I have a different game I want you to try," she told him.

"Look." She reached into her purse and brought out a metal disk. She turned it over and it gleamed in the sun. "People used coins like this for currency a long time ago, when Earth was the only planet we lived on."

His eyes fixed on the object. He reached for it.

Dr. Halsey moved it away, continuing to flip it between her thumb and index finger. "Each side is different. Do you see? One has the face of a man with long hair. The other side has a bird, called an eagle, and it's holding—"

"Arrows," John said.

"Yes. Good." His eyesight must be exceptional to see such detail so far away. "We'll use this coin in our game. If you win, you can keep it."

John tore his gaze from the coin and looked at her again, squinted, then said, "Okay. I always win, though. That's why they won't let me play gravball anymore."

"I'm sure you do."

"What's the game?"

"It's very simple. I toss the coin like this." She flicked her wrist, snapped her thumb, and the coin arced, spinning into the air, and landed in the sand. "Next time, though, before it lands, I want you to tell me if it will fall with the face of the man showing or with the eagle holding the arrows."

"I got it." John tensed, bent his knees, and then his eyes seemed to lose their focus on her and the coin.

Dr. Halsey picked up the quarter. "Ready?"

John gave a slight nod.

She tossed it, making sure there was plenty of spin.

John's eyes watched it with that strange distant gaze. He tracked it as it went up, and then down toward the ground—his hand snapped out and snatched the quarter out of the air.

He held up his closed hand. "Eagle!" he shouted.

She tentatively reached for his hand and peeled open the tiny fist.

The quarter lay in his palm: the eagle shining in the orange sun.

Was it possible that he saw which side was up when he grabbed it . . . or more improbably, could have picked which side he wanted? She hoped the Lieutenant had recorded that. She should have told him to keep the data pad trained on her.

John retracted his hand. “I get to keep it, right? That’s what you said.”

“Yes, you can keep it, John.” She smiled at him—then stopped.

She shouldn’t have used his name. That was a bad sign. She couldn’t afford the luxury of *liking* her test subjects. She mentally stepped away from her feelings. She had to maintain a professional distance. She had to . . . because in a few months Number-117 might not be alive.

“Can we play again?”

Dr. Halsey stood and took a step back. “That was the only one I had, I’m afraid. I have to leave now,” she told him. “Go back and play with your friends.”

“Thanks.” He ran back, shouting to the other boys, “Look!”

Dr. Halsey strode to the Lieutenant. The sun reflecting off the asphalt felt too hot, and she suddenly didn’t want to be outside. She wanted to be back in the ship, where it was cool and dark. She wanted to get off this planet.

She stepped under the canvas awning and said to the Lieutenant, “Tell me you recorded that.”

He handed her the data pad and looked puzzled. “Yes. What was it all about?”

Dr. Halsey checked the recording and then sent a copy ahead to Toran on the *Han* for safekeeping.

“We screen these subjects for certain genetic markers,” she said. “Strength, agility, even predispositions for aggression and intellect. But we couldn’t remote test for everything. We don’t test for luck.”

"Luck?" Lieutenant Keyes asked. "You believe in luck, Doctor?"

"Of course not," she said with a dismissive wave of her hand. "But we have one hundred and fifty test subjects to consider, and facilities and funding for only half that number. It's a simple mathematical elimination, Lieutenant. That child was one of the lucky ones—either that or he is extraordinarily fast. Either way, he's in."

"I don't understand," Lieutenant Keyes said, and he started fiddling with the pipe he carried in his pocket.

"I hope that continues, Lieutenant," Dr. Halsey replied quietly. "For your sake, I hope you never understand what we're doing."

She looked one last time at Number-117—at John. He was having so much fun, running and laughing. For a moment she envied the boy's innocence; hers was long dead. Life or death, lucky or not, she was condemning this boy to a great deal of pain and suffering.

But it had to be done.

CHAPTER THREE

2300 HOURS SEPTEMBER 23, 2517 (MILITARY CALENDAR) / EPSILON ERIDANI SYSTEM, REACH MILITARY COMPLEX, PLANET REACH

Dr. Halsey stood on a platform in the center of the amphitheater. Concentric rings of slate-gray risers surrounded her—empty for now. Overhead spotlights focused and reflected off her white lab coat, but she still was cold.

She should feel safe here. Reach was one of the UNSC's largest industrial bases, ringed with high-orbit gun batteries, space docks, and a fleet of heavily-armed capital ships. On the planet's surface were Marine and Navy Special Warfare training grounds, OCS schools, and between her underground facilities and the surface were three hundred meters of hardened steel and concrete. The room where she now stood could withstand a direct hit from an 80-megaton nuke.

So why did she feel so vulnerable?

Dr. Halsey knew what she had to do. Her duty. It was for the greater good. All humanity would be served . . . even if a tiny handful of them had to suffer for it. Still, when she turned inward and faced her complicity in this—she was revolted by what she saw.

She wished she still had Lieutenant Keyes. He had proven himself a capable assistant during the last month. But he had begun to understand the nature of the project—at least seen the edges of the truth. Dr. Halsey had him reassigned to the *Magellan* with a commission to full Lieutenant for his troubles.

"Are you ready, Doctor?" a disembodied woman's voice asked.

"Almost, Déjà." Dr. Halsey sighed. "Please summon Chief Petty Officer Mendez. I'd like you both present when I address them."

Déjà's hologram flicked on next to Dr. Halsey. The AI had been specifically created for Dr. Halsey's SPARTAN project. She took the appearance of a Greek goddess: barefoot, wrapped in the toga, motes of light dancing about her luminous white hair. She held a clay tablet in her left hand. Binary cuneiform markings scrolled across the tablet. Dr. Halsey couldn't help but marvel at the AI's chosen form; each AI "self-assigned" a holographic appearance, and each was unique.

One of the doors at the top of the amphitheater opened and Chief Petty Officer Mendez strode down the stairs. He wore a black dress uniform, his chest awash with silver and gold stars and a rainbow of campaign ribbons. His close-shorn hair had a touch of gray at the temples. He was neither tall nor muscular; he looked so ordinary for a man who had seen so much combat . . . except for his stride. The man moved with a slow grace as if he were walking in half gravity. He paused before Dr. Halsey, awaiting further instructions.

"Up here, please," she told him, gesturing to the stairs on her right.

Mendez mounted the steps of the platform and then stood at ease next to her.

"You have read my psychological evaluations?" Déjà asked Dr. Halsey.

"Yes. They were quite thorough," she said. "Thank you."

"And?"

"I'm forgoing your recommendations, Déjà. I'm going to tell them the truth."

Mendez gave a nearly inaudible grunt of approval—one of the most verbose acknowledgments Dr. Halsey had heard from him. As a hand-to-hand combat and physical-training DI,

Mendez was the best in the Navy. As a conversationalist, however, he left a great deal to be desired.

"The truth has risks," Déjà cautioned.

"So do lies," Dr. Halsey replied. "Any story fabricated to motivate the children—claiming their parents were taken and killed by pirates, or by a plague that devastated their planet—if they learned the truth later, they would turn against us."

"It is a legitimate concern," conceded Déjà, and then she consulted her tablet. "May I suggest selective neural paralysis? It produces a targeted amnesia—"

"A memory loss that may leak into other parts of the brain. No," Dr. Halsey said, "this will be dangerous enough for them even with intact minds."

Dr. Halsey clicked on her microphone. "Bring them in now."

"Aye aye," a voice replied from the speakers in the ceiling.

"They'll adapt," Dr. Halsey told Déjà. "Or they won't, and they will be untrainable and unsuitable for the project. Either way I just want to get this over with."

Four sets of double doors at the top tier of the amphitheater swung open. Seventy-five children marched in—each accompanied by a handler, a Naval drill instructor in camouflage pattern fatigues.

The children had circles of fatigue around their eyes. They had all been collected, rushed here through Slipstream space, and only recently brought out of cryo sleep. The shock of their ordeal must be hitting them hard, Halsey realized. She stifled a pang of regret.

When they had been seated in the risers, Dr. Halsey cleared her throat and spoke: "As per Naval Code 45812, you are hereby conscripted into the UNSC Special Project, codenamed SPARTAN-II."

She paused; the words stuck in her windpipe. How could they possibly understand this? *She* barely understood the justifications and ethics behind this program.

They looked so confused. A few tried to stand and leave, but their handlers placed firm hands on their shoulders and pushed them back down.

Six years old . . . this was too much for them to digest. But she had to make them understand, explain it in simple terms that they could grasp.

Dr. Halsey took a tentative step forward. "You have been called upon to serve," she explained. "You will be trained . . . and you will become the best we can make of you. You will be the protectors of Earth and all her colonies."

A handful of the children sat up straighter, no longer entirely frightened, but now interested.

Dr. Halsey spotted John, subject Number-117, the first boy she had confirmed as a viable candidate. He wrinkled his forehead, confused, but he listened with rapt attention.

"This will be hard to understand, but you cannot return to your parents."

The children stirred. Their handlers kept a firm grip on their shoulders.

"This place will become your home," Dr. Halsey said in as soothing a voice as she could muster. "Your fellow trainees will be your family now. The training will be difficult. There will be a great deal of hardship on the road ahead, but I know you will all make it."

Patriotic words, but they rang hollow in her ears. She had wanted to tell them the truth—but how could she?

Not all of them would make it. "Acceptable losses," the Office of Naval Intelligence representative had assured her. None of it was acceptable.

"Rest now," Dr. Halsey said to them. "We begin tomorrow."

She turned to Mendez. "Have the children . . . the trainees escorted to their barracks. Feed them and put them to bed."

"Yes, ma'am," Mendez said. "Fall out!" he shouted.

The children rose—at the urging of their handlers. John-117

stood, but he kept his gaze on Dr. Halsey and remained stoic. Many of the subjects seemed stunned, a few had trembling lips—but none of them cried.

These were indeed the right children for the project. Dr. Halsey only hoped that she had half their courage when the time came.

"Keep them busy tomorrow," she told Mendez and Déjà. "Keep them from thinking about what we've just done to them."

SECTION II

BOOT

SUPPORT

CHAPTER FOUR

0530 HOURS, SEPTEMBER 24, 2517 (MILITARY CALENDAR) / EPSILON ERIDANI SYSTEM, REACH MILITARY COMPLEX, PLANET REACH

"Wake up, trainee!"

John rolled over in his cot and went back to sleep. He was dimly aware that this wasn't his room, and that there were other people here.

A shock jolted him—from his bare feet to the base of his spine. He yelled in surprise and fell off the cot. He shook off the disorientation from being nearly asleep and got up.

"I said *up,* boot! You know which way *up* is?"

A man in a camouflage uniform stood over John. His hair was shorn and gray at his temples. His dark eyes didn't look human—too big and black and they didn't blink. He held a silver baton in one hand; he flicked it toward John and it sparked.

John backed away. He wasn't afraid of anything. Only little kids were afraid . . . but his body instinctively moved as far away from the instrument as possible.

Dozens of other men roused the rest of the children. Seventy-four boys and girls screamed and jumped out of their cots.

"I am Chief Petty Officer Mendez," the uniformed man next to John shouted. "The rest of these men are your instructors. You will do exactly as we tell you at all times."

Mendez pointed to the far end of the cinderblock barracks. "Showers are aft. You will all wash and then return here to dress."

He opened a trunk at the foot of John's cot and pulled out a matching set of gray sweats.

John leaned closer and saw his name stenciled on the chest: JOHN-117.

"No slacking. On the double!" Mendez tapped John between his shoulder blades with the baton.

Lightning surged across John's chest. He sprawled on the cot and gasped for breath.

"I mean it! Go Go GO!"

John moved. He couldn't inhale—but he ran anyway, clutching his chest. He managed a ragged breath by the time he got to the showers. The other kids looked scared and disoriented. They all stripped off their nightshirts and stepped onto the conveyor, washed themselves in lukewarm soapy water, then rinsed in an icy cold spray.

He ran back to his bunk, got into underwear, thick socks, pulled on the sweats and a pair of combat boots that fit his feet perfectly.

"Outside, trainees," Mendez announced. "Triple time . . . *march!*"

John and the others stampeded out of the barracks onto a strip of grass.

The sun hadn't risen yet, and the edge of the sky was indigo. The grass was wet with dew. There were dozens of rows of barracks, but no one else was up and outside. A pair of jets roared overhead and arced up into the sky. Far away, John heard a metallic crackle.

Chief Petty Officer Mendez barked, "You will make five equal-length rows. Fifteen trainees in each." He waited a few seconds as they milled about. "Straighten those rows. You know how to count to fifteen, trainee? Take three steps back."

John stepped into the second row.

As he breathed the cold air he began to wake up. He started to remember. They had taken him in the middle of the night.

They injected him with something and he slept for a long time. Then the woman who had given him the coin told him he couldn't go back. That he wouldn't see his mother or father—

"Jumping jacks!" Mendez shouted. "Count off to one hundred. Ready, go." The officer started the exercise and John followed his lead.

One boy refused—for a split-second. An instructor was on him instantly. The baton whipped into the boy's stomach. The kid doubled over. "Get with the program, boot," the trainer snarled. The boy uncurled and started jumping.

John had never done so many jumping jacks in his life. His arms and stomach and legs burned. Sweat trickled down his back.

"Ninety-eight—99—100." Mendez paused. He drew in a deep breath. "Sit-ups!" He dropped onto the grass. "Count off to one hundred. No slacking."

John threw himself on the ground.

"The first crewman who quits," Mendez said, "gets to run around the compound twice—and then comes back here and does two hundred sit-ups. Ready . . . count off! One . . . two . . . three. . . ."

Deep squats followed. Then knee bends.

John threw up, but that didn't buy him any respite. A trainer descended on him after a few seconds. John rolled back over and continued.

"Leg lifts." Mendez continued like he was a machine. As if they all were machines.

John couldn't go on—but he knew he'd get the baton again if he stopped. He tried; he had to move. His legs trembled and only sluggishly responded.

"Rest," Mendez finally called. "Trainers: get the water."

The trainers wheeled out carts laden with water bottles. John grabbed one and gulped down the liquid. It was warm and slightly salty. He didn't care. It was the best water he'd ever had.

He flopped on his back in the grass and panted.

The sun was up now. It was warm. He rolled to his knees and let the sweat drip off him like a heavy rain.

He slowly got up and glanced at the other children. They crouched on the ground, holding their sides, and no one talked. Their clothes were soaked through with perspiration. John didn't recognize anyone from his school here.

So he was alone with strangers. He wondered where his mother was, and what—

"A good start, trainees," Mendez told them. "Now we run. On your feet!"

The trainers brandished their batons and herded the trainees along. They jogged down a gravel path through the compound, past more cinderblock barracks. The run seemed to go on forever—they ran alongside a river, over a bridge, then by the edge of a runway where jets took off straight into the air. Once past the runway, Mendez led them on a zigzagging path of stone.

John wanted to think about what had happened, how he got here, and what was going to happen next . . . but he couldn't think straight. All he could feel was the blood pounding through him, the ache in his muscles, and hunger.

They ran into a courtyard of smooth flagstones. A pole in the center flew the colors of the UNSC, a blue field with stars and Earth in the corner. At the far end of the yard was a building with a scalloped dome and white columns and dozens of wide steps leading to the entrance. The words NAVAL OFFICERS ACADEMY were chiseled into the arch over the entrance.

A woman stood on the top step and beckoned to them. She wore a white sheet wrapped around her body. She looked old to John, yet young at the same time. Then he saw the motes of light orbiting her head and knew she was an AI. He had seen them on vids. She wasn't solid, but she was still real.

"Excellent work, Chief Petty Officer Mendez," she said in a

resonant, silk-smooth voice. She turned to the children. "Welcome. My name is Déjà and I will be your teacher. Please come in. Class is about to start."

John groaned out loud. Several of the others grumbled, too.

She turned and started to walk inside. "Of course," she said, "if you prefer to skip your lessons, you may continue the morning calisthenics."

John double-timed it up the steps.

It was cool inside. A tray with crackers and a carton of milk had been laid out for each of them. John nibbled on the dry stale food, then gulped down his milk.

John was so tired he wanted to lay his head down on the desk and take a nap—until Déjà started to tell them about a battle and how three hundred soldiers fought against thousands of Persian infantry.

A holographic countryside appeared in the classroom. The children walked around the miniature mountains and hills and let the edge of the illusionary sea lap at their boots. Toy-sized soldiers marched toward what Déjà explained was Thermopylae, a narrow strip of land between steep mountains and the sea. Thousands of soldiers marched toward the three hundred who guarded the pass. The soldiers fought: spears and shields splintered, swords flashed and spilled blood.

John couldn't take his eyes off the spectacle.

Déjà explained that the three hundred were Spartans and they were the best soldiers who had ever lived. They had been trained to fight since they were children. No one could beat them.

John watched, fascinated, as the holographic Spartans slaughtered the Persian spearmen.

He had eaten his crackers but he was still hungry, so he took the girl's next to him when she wasn't looking, and munched them down as the battle raged on. His stomach still growled and grumbled.

When was lunch? Or was it dinnertime already?

The Persians broke and ran and the Spartans stood victorious on the field.

The children cheered. They wanted to see it again.

"That's all for today," Déjà said. "We'll continue tomorrow and I'll show you some wolves. Now it's time for you to go to the playground."

"Playground?" John said. That was perfect. He could finally just sit on a swing, relax, and think for a moment.

He ran out of the room, as did the other trainees.

Chief Petty Officer Mendez and the trainers waited for them outside the classroom.

"Time for the playground," Mendez said, and waved the children closer. "It's a short run. Fall in."

The "short run" turned into two miles. And the playground was like nothing John had ever seen. It was a forest of twenty-meter tall wooden poles. Rope cargo nets and bridges stretched between the poles; they swayed, crossed and crisscrossed one another, a maze suspended in the air. There were slide poles and knotted climbing ropes. There were swings and suspended platforms. There were ropes looped through pulleys and tied to baskets that looked sturdy enough to hoist a person.

"Trainees," Mendez said, "form three lines."

The instructors moved in to herd them, but John and the others made three rows without comment or fuss.

"The first person in every row will be team number one," Mendez said. "The second person in each row will be team number two . . . and so on. If you do not understand this, speak up now."

No one spoke.

John looked to his right. A boy with sandy hair, green eyes, and darkly tanned skin gave him a weary smile. Stenciled on his sweat top was SAMUEL-034. In the row beyond Samuel was a girl. She was taller than John, and skinny, with a long mane of hair dyed blue. KELLY-087. She didn't look too happy to see him.

"Today's game," Mendez explained, "is called 'Ring the Bell.'" He pointed to the tallest pole on the playground. It stood an additional ten meters above the others and had a steel slide pole next to it. Hung at the very top of that pole was a brass bell.

"There are many ways to get to the bell," he told them. "I leave it up to each team to find their own way. When every member of your team has rung the bell, you are to get groundside double time and run back here across this finish line."

Mendez took his baton and scratched a straight line in the sand.

John raised his hand.

Mendez glared at him for a moment with those black unblinking eyes. "A question, trainee?"

"What do we win?"

Mendez cocked one eyebrow and appraised John. "You win dinner, Number-117. Tonight, dinner is roast turkey, gravy and mashed potatoes, corn on the cob, brownies, and ice cream."

A murmur of approval swept though the children.

"But," Mendez added, "for there to be winners there must be a loser. The last team to finish goes without food."

The children fell silent—and then looked at each other warily.

"Make ready," Mendez said.

"I'm Sam," the boy whispered to John and the girl on their team.

She said, "I'm Kelly."

John just looked at them and said nothing. The girl would slow him down. Too bad. He was hungry and he wasn't about to let them make him lose.

"Go!" Mendez shouted.

John ran through the pack of children and scrambled up a cargo net onto a platform. He raced across the bridge—jumped onto the next platform, just in time. The bridge flipped and sent five others into the water below.

He paused at the rope tied to the large basket. It ran up through a pulley and then back down. He didn't think he was strong enough to pull himself up in it. Instead, he tackled a knotted climbing rope and scrunched his body up. The rope swung wildly around the center pole. John looked down and almost lost his grip. It looked twice as far down as it had looked from the ground. He saw all the others, some climbing, others floundering in the water, getting up and starting over. No one was as close to the bell as he was.

He swallowed his fear and kept climbing up. He thought of the ice cream and chocolate brownies and how he was going to win.

John got to the top, grabbed the bell, and rang it three times. He then clasped the steel pole and slid all the way to the ground, falling into a pile of cushions.

He got up and ran smiling all the way to the Chief Petty Officer. John crossed the finish line and gave a victory cry. "I was first," he said, panting.

Mendez nodded and made a check on his clipboard.

John watched as the others made it and up rang the bell, then raced across the finish line. Kelly and Sam had trouble. They got stuck in a line to get to the bell as everyone bunched up at the end.

They finally rang the bell, slid down together . . . but they crossed the finish line last. They glared at John.

He shrugged.

"Good work, trainees," Mendez said, and he beamed at them all. "Let's get back to the barracks and chow down."

The children, covered in mud and leaning on each another, cheered.

"—all except team three," Mendez said, and looked at Sam, Kelly, and then John.

"But I won," John protested. "I was first."

"Yes, *you* were first," Mendez explained, "but your team came in last." He then addressed all the children. "Remember this: *you* don't win unless your team wins. One person winning at the expense of the group means that you lose."

John ran in a stupor all the way back to the barracks. It wasn't fair. He had won. How can you win and still lose?

He watched as the others stuffed themselves with turkey, white meat dripping with gravy. They spooned down mountains of vanilla ice cream and left the mess hall with chocolate encrusting the corners of their mouths.

John got a liter of water. He drank it, but it didn't have any taste. It did nothing to fill his hunger.

He wanted to cry, but he was too tired. He collapsed in his bunk, thinking of ways to get even with Sam and Kelly for messing him up—but he couldn't think. Every muscle and bone ached.

John fell asleep as soon as his head hit the flat pillow.

The next day was the same—calisthenics and running all morning, then class until the afternoon.

Today Déjà taught them about wolves. The classroom became a holographic meadow, and the children watched seven wolves hunt a moose. The pack worked together, striking wherever the giant beast wasn't facing. It was fascinating and horrifying to watch the wolves track down, and then devour, an animal many times their size.

John avoided Sam and Kelly in the classroom. He stole a few extra crackers when no one was looking, but they didn't dull his hunger.

After class, they ran back to the playground. Today it was different. There were fewer bridges and more complicated rope-and-pulley systems. The pole with the bell was now twenty meters taller than any of the others.

"Same teams as yesterday," Mendez announced.

Sam and Kelly walked up to John. Sam shoved him.

John's temper flared—he wanted to hit Sam in the face, but he was too tired. He'd need all his strength to get to the bell.

"You better help us," Sam hissed, "or I'll push you off one of those platforms."

"And I'll jump on top of you," Kelly added.

"Okay," John whispered. "Just try not to slow me down."

John examined the course. It was like doing a maze on paper, only this one twisted and turned into and out of the page. Many bridges and rope ladders led to dead ends. He squinted—then found one possible route.

He nudged Sam and Kelly, then pointed. "Look," he said, "that basket and rope on the far side. It goes straight to the top. It's a long pull, though." He flexed his biceps, uncertain if he could make it in his weakened state.

"We can do it," Sam said.

John glanced at the other teams; they were searching the course as well. "We'll have to make a quick run for it," he said. "Make sure no one else gets there first."

"I'm fast," Kelly said. "Real fast."

"Trainees, get ready," Mendez shouted.

"Okay," John said. "You sprint ahead and hold it for us."

"Go!"

Kelly shot forward. John had never seen anyone move like her. She ran like the wolves he had seen today; her feet seemed barely to touch the ground.

She got to the basket. John and Sam were only halfway there.

One boy beat them to the basket. "Get out," he ordered Kelly. "I'm going up."

Sam and John ran up and pushed him back. "Wait your turn," Sam said.

John and Sam joined Kelly in the basket. Together they pulled on the rope and raised themselves up. There was a lot of rope—for every three meters they pulled, they only rose one meter. A breeze made the basket sway and bounce into the pole.

"Faster," John urged.

They pulled as one person, six hands working in unison, and accelerated into the sky.

They didn't get there first. They were third. Each of them got to ring the bell, though—Kelly, Sam, and John.

They slid down the pole. Kelly and Sam waited for John to land, and then together they ran across the finish line.

Chief Petty Officer Mendez watched them. He didn't say anything, but John thought he saw a smile flicker across his face.

Sam clapped John and Kelly on their backs. "That was good work," Sam said. He looked thoughtful for a moment, then said, "We can be friends . . . I mean, if you want. It'd be no big deal."

Kelly shrugged and replied, "Sure."

"Okay," John said. "Friends."

CHAPTER FIVE

0630 HOURS, JULY 12, 2519 (MILITARY CALENDAR) / EPSILON ERIDANI SYSTEM, REACH MILITARY WILDERNESS TRAINING PRESERVE, PLANET REACH

John held on tight as the dropship accelerated up and over a jagged snowcapped mountain range. The sun peeked over the horizon and washed the white snow with pinks and oranges. The other members of his unit pressed their faces to the windows and watched.

Sam sat next to him and looked outside. "Nice place for a snowball fight."

"You'll lose," Kelly said. She leaned over John's shoulder to get a better look at the terrain. "I'm a dead aim with snowballs." She scratched the stubble of her shorn hair.

"Dead is right," John muttered. "Especially when you load them with rocks."

CPO Mendez stepped from the cockpit into the passenger compartment. The trainees stood and snapped to attention. "At ease, and sit down." The silver at Mendez's temples had grown to a band across the side of his closely shaved hair, but if anything he had gotten stronger and tougher since John had first laid eyes on him two years ago.

"Today's mission will be simple for a change." Mendez's voice easily penetrated the roar of the dropship's engines. He handed a stack of papers to Kelly. "Pass these out, recruit."

"Sir!" She saluted smartly and handed one paper to each of the seventy-five children in the squad.

"These are portions of maps of the local region. You will be set down by yourselves. You will then navigate to a marked extraction point and we will pick you up there."

John turned his map over. It was just one part of a much larger map—no drop or extraction point marked. How was he supposed to navigate without a reference point? But he knew this was part of the mission, to answer that question on his own.

"One more thing," Mendez said. "The last trainee to make it to the extraction point will be left behind." He glanced out a window. "And it's a very long walk back."

John didn't like it. He wasn't going to lose, but he didn't want anyone else to lose, either. The thought of Kelly or Sam or any of the others marching all the way back made him uneasy . . . if they *could* make it all the way back alone over those mountains.

"First drop in three minutes," Mendez barked. "Trainee 117, you're up first."

"Sir! Yes, sir!" John replied.

He glanced out the window and scanned the terrain. There was a ring of jagged mountains, a valley thick with cedars, and a ribbon of silver—a river that fed into a lake.

John nudged Sam, pointed to the river, then jerked his thumb toward the lake.

Sam nodded, then pulled Kelly aside and pointed out the window. Kelly and Sam moved quickly down the line of seated trainees.

The ship decelerated. John felt his stomach rise as they dropped toward the ground.

"Trainee 117: front and center." Mendez stepped to the rear of the compartment as the ship's tail split and a ramp extended. Cold air blasted into the ship. He patted John on the shoulder. "Watch out for wolves in the forest, 117."

"Yes, sir!" John looked over his shoulder at the others.

His teammates gave him an almost imperceptible nod. Good, everyone got his message.

He ran down the ramp and into the forest. The dropship's engines roared to life and it rose high into the cloudless sky. He zipped up his jacket. He wore only fatigues, boots, and a heavy parka—not exactly the gear he'd pack for a prolonged stay in the wilderness.

John started toward one particularly sharp peak he had spotted from the air; the river lay in that direction. He'd follow it downstream and meet the others at the lake.

He marched through the woods until he heard the gurgling of a stream. He got close enough to see the direction of the flow, then headed back into the forest. Mendez's exercises often had a twist to them—stun mines on the obstacle course, snipers with paint pellet guns during parade drills. And with the Chief up in that dropship, John wasn't about to reveal his position unless he had a good reason.

He passed a blueberry bush and took the time to strip it before he moved on.

This was the first time in months he had been alone and could just think. He popped a handful of berries into his mouth and chewed.

He thought about the place that had been his home, his parents . . . but more and more that seemed like a dream. John knew it wasn't, and that he had once had a different life. But this was the life he wanted. He was a soldier. He had an important job to train for. Mendez said they were the Navy's best and brightest. That they were the only hope for peace. He liked that.

Before, he never knew what he would be when he grew up. He never really thought about anything other than watching vids and playing—nothing had been a challenge.

Now every day was a challenge and a new adventure.

John knew more things, thanks to Déjà, than he ever thought he could have learned at his old school: algebra and trigonometry, the history of a hundred battles and kings. He could string a trip line, fire a rifle, and treat a chest wound. Mendez had shown him how to be strong . . . not only with his body, but strong with his head, too.

He had a family here: Kelly, Sam, and all the others in his squad.

The thought of his squadmates brought him back to Mendez's mission—one of them was going to be left behind. There had to be a way to get them all home. John decided he wasn't going to leave if he couldn't figure it out.

He arrived at the edge of the lake, stood, and listened.

John heard an owl hooting in the distance. He marched toward the sound. "Hey, owl," he said when he was close.

Sam stepped out from behind a tree and grinned. "That's 'Chief Owl' to you, trainee."

They walked around the circumference of the lake, gathering the rest of the children in the squad. John counted them to make sure: seventy-four.

"Let's get the map pieces together," Kelly suggested.

"Good idea," John said. "Sam, take three and scout the area. I don't want any of the Chief's surprises sneaking up on us."

"Right." Sam picked Fhajad, James, and Linda, and then the four of them took off into the brush.

Kelly collected the map pieces and settled in the shade of an ancient cedar tree. "Some of these don't belong, and some are copies," she said, and she laid them out. "Yes, here's an edge. Got it—this is the lake, the river, and here . . ." She pointed to a distant patch of green. "That's got to be the extraction point." She shook her head and frowned. "If the legend on this map is right, it's a full day's hike, though. We better get started."

John whistled and a moment later Sam and his scouts returned.

"Let's move out," John said.

No one argued. They fell into line behind Kelly as she

navigated. Sam blazed the trail ahead. He had the best eyes and ears. Several times he stopped and signaled everyone to freeze or hide—but it turned out to be just a rabbit or a bird.

After several miles of marching, Sam dropped back. He whispered to John, "This is too easy. It's not like any of the Chief's normal field exercises."

John nodded. "I've been thinking that, too. Just keep your eyes and ears sharp."

They stopped at noon to stretch and eat berries they had gathered along the trail.

Fhajad spoke up. "I want to know one thing," he said. He paused to wipe the sweat off his dark skin. "We're going to get to the extraction point at the same time. So who's getting left behind? We should decide now."

"Draw straws," someone suggested.

"No," John said, and stood. "No one's being left behind. We're going to figure a way to get *all* of us out."

"How?" Kelly asked, scratching her head. "Mendez said—"

"I know what he said. But there's got to be a way—I just haven't thought of one yet. Even if it has to be me that stays behind—I'll make sure everyone gets back to the base." John started marching again. "Come on, we're wasting time."

The others fell in behind him.

The shadows of the trees lengthened and melted together and the sun turned the edge of the sky red. Kelly halted and motioned for everyone else to stop. "We're almost there," she whispered.

"Me and Sam will scout it out," John said. "Everyone fall out . . . and keep quiet."

The rest of the children silently followed his orders.

John and Sam crept through the underbrush and then hunkered down at the edge of a meadow.

The dropship sat in the center of the grassy field; her

floodlights illuminated everything for thirty meters. Six men sat on the open launch ramp, smoking cigarettes and passing a canteen between themselves.

Sam motioned to drop back. "You recognize them?" he whispered.

"No. You?"

Sam shook his head. "They're not in uniform. They don't look like any soldiers I've ever seen. Maybe they're rebels. Maybe they stole the dropship and killed the Chief."

"No way," John said. "Nothing can kill the Chief. But one thing's for sure: I don't think we can just walk up there and get a free ride back to the base. Let's go back."

They crept back into the woods and then explained the situation to the others.

"What do you want to do?" Kelly asked him.

John wondered why she thought he had an answer. He looked around and saw everyone was watching him, waiting for him to speak. He shifted on his feet. He had to say something.

"Okay . . . we don't know who these men are or what they'll do when they see us. So we find out."

The children nodded, seeming to think this was the right thing to do.

"Here's how," John told them. "First, I'll need a rabbit."

"That's me," Kelly said, and sprang to her feet. "I'm the fastest."

"Good," John said. "You go to the edge of the meadow—and then let them see you. I'll go along and hide nearby and watch. In case anything happens to you, I'll report back to the others."

She nodded.

"Then you lure a few back here. Run right past this spot. Sam, you'll be out in the open, pretending like you've broken your leg."

"Gotcha," Sam said. He walked over to Fhajad and had him scrape his shin with his boot. Blood welled from the wound.

"The rest of you," John said, "wait in the woods in a big circle. If they try to do anything but help Sam . . ." John made a fist with his right hand and slammed it into his open palm. "Remember the moose and the wolves?"

They all nodded and grinned. They had seen that lesson many times in Déjà's classroom.

"Get some rocks," John told them.

Kelly stripped off her parka, stretched her legs and knees. "Okay," she said, "let's do this."

Sam lay down, clutching his leg. "Oooh—it hurts, help me."

"Don't overdo it," John said, and kicked some dirt on him. "Or they'll know it's a setup."

John and Kelly then crept toward the meadow and halted a few meters from the edge. He whispered to her, "If you want me to be the rabbit . . ."

She slugged him in the shoulder—hard. "You think I can't do my part?"

"I take it back," he said, rubbing his shoulder.

John moved off ten meters to her flank, took cover, and watched.

Kelly emerged at the edge of the meadow, stepping into the illumination from the dropship's floodlights.

"Hey!" she said, and waved her arms over her head. "Over here. You got any food? I'm starving."

The men slowly stood and pulled out stun batons. "There's one," John heard them whisper. "I'll get her. The rest of you stay here and wait for the others."

The man cautiously approached Kelly, a stun baton held behind his back so she couldn't see it. She stayed put and waited for him to get closer.

"Hang on a sec," she said. "I dropped my jacket back there. I'll be right back." She turned and ran. The man leaped after her, but she had already vanished into the shadows.

"Stop!"

"This will be too easy," one of the other men said. "Kids won't know what hit them." Another remarked, "Fish in a barrel."

John had heard enough. He ran after Kelly, but realized that neither he nor the other man had a chance to catch her. He halted when he got close to where Sam lay.

The man stopped. He looked around, his eyes not quite adjusted to the dark, then spotted Sam on the ground holding his bloody leg.

"Please, help me," Sam whimpered. "It's broken."

"I got your broken leg right here, kid." The man raised his baton.

John picked up a rock. He threw it, but missed.

The man spun around. "Who's there?"

Sam rolled to his feet and darted away. There was a rustling in the forest, then a hail of stones whistled through the trees, pelting the man.

Kelly appeared and sidearmed a rock as hard as she could—and hit the man dead center in the forehead.

He toppled and slammed into the ground.

The other children moved in. "What do we do with him?" Sam asked.

"It's just an exercise, right?" Fhajad said. "He has to be with Mendez."

John rolled the man over. A trickle of blood snaked from his head into his eye socket.

"You heard him," John whispered. "You saw what he was going to do to Sam. Mendez or our trainers would never do that to us. Ever. He's got no uniform. No insignias. He's not one of us."

John kicked the man in the face and then the ribs. The man reflexively curled into a ball. "Get his baton."

Sam grabbed the weapon. He kicked him, too.

"Now we go back and get the others," John told them. "Kelly, you be the rabbit again. Just get them to the edge of the clearing. Duck out, and let us do the rest."

She nodded and started back to the meadow. The rest of the squad fanned out, collecting rocks along the way.

After a minute Kelly stepped onto the grassy field and shouted, "That guy fell and hit his head. Over here!"

The five remaining men stood and ran toward her.

When they were close enough, John whistled.

The air suddenly swarmed with stones. The men held up their hands and tried to protect themselves. They dropped and covered their heads.

John whistled again and seventy-five children charged screaming toward the bewildered men. The men got up to defend themselves. They looked stunned—like they couldn't believe what they were seeing.

Sam smashed his baton over a man's head. Fhajad was hit squarely in the face by one man's fist, and he fell.

The men were overwhelmed by a wave of flesh, beaten to the ground with fists and stones and boots until they no longer moved.

John stood over their bleeding bodies. He was mad. They would have hurt him and his squad. He wanted to kick in their skulls. He took a deep breath and then exhaled. He had better things to do and bigger problems to figure out—anger would have to wait.

"Want to call Mendez now?" Sam asked as he pulled Fhajad shakily to his feet.

"Not yet," John told him. He marched onto the dropship. No one else was on board.

John accessed the COM system and opened the mail link. He linked up with Déjà. Her face appeared, a scratchy hologram hovering over the terminal.

"Good evening, Trainee 117," she said. "Do you have a homework question?"

"Kind of," he replied. "One of CPO Mendez's assignments."

"Ah." After a moment's pause she said, "Very well."

"I'm in an Albatross dropship. There's no pilot, but I need to get home. Teach me to fly it, please."

Déjà shook her head. "You are not rated to fly that craft, trainee. But I *can* help. Do you see the winged icon in the corner of your screen? Tap it three times."

John tapped it and a hundred icons and displays filled the screen.

"Touch the green arrows at nine o'clock twice," she told him.

He did and then the words *autopilot activated* flashed on-screen.

"I have control now," Déjà said. "I will get you home."

"Hang on a second," John said and ran outside. "Everyone onboard—double time!"

The children ran onto the ship.

Kelly paused and asked, "Who's getting left behind?"

"No one," John said. "Just get in." He made sure he was the last on the ship, then said, "Okay, Déjà, get out us out of here."

The dropship's jets roared to life and it rose into the sky.

John stood at attention in Chief Petty Officer Mendez's office. He had never been in here. No one had. A trickle of sweat dripped down his back. The dark wood paneling and the smell of cigar smoke made him feel claustrophobic.

Mendez glowered at John as he read the report on his clip-board.

The door opened and Dr. Halsey walked in. Mendez stood, gave her a curt nod and then sat back in his padded chair.

"Hello, John," Dr. Halsey said. She sat across from Mendez, crossed her legs, and then adjusted her gray skirt.

"Dr. Halsey," John replied instantly. He saluted. None of the other grown-ups called him by his first name, ever. He didn't understand why she did.

"Trainee 117," Mendez snapped. "Tell me again why you stole

UNSC property . . . and why you attacked the men I had assigned to guard it."

John wanted to explain that he was just doing what had to be done. That he was sorry. That he would do anything to make it up. But John knew the Chief hated whiners, almost as much as he hated excuses.

"Sir," John said. "The guards were out of uniform. No insignia. They failed to identify themselves, sir!"

"Hmm," Mendez mused over the report again. "So it seems. And the ship?"

"I took my squad home, sir. I was the last onboard—so if anyone should have been left—"

"I didn't ask for a passenger list, Crewman." His voice softened to a growl and he turned to Dr. Halsey. "What are we going to do with this one?"

"Do?" She pushed her glasses higher on her nose and examined John. "I think that's obvious, Chief. Make him a Squad Leader."

CHAPTER SIX

1130 HOURS MARCH 09, 2525 (MILITARY CALENDAR) / EPSILON ERIDANI SYSTEM, OFFICE OF NAVAL INTELLIGENCE MEDICAL FACILITY, IN ORBIT AROUND PLANET REACH

"I want that transmission decoded now," Dr. Halsey snapped at Déjà.

"The encryption scheme is extremely complex," replied Déjà with a hint of irritation in her normally glass-smooth voice. "I don't even know why they bothered. Who else but Beta-5 Division even has the resources to use this data?"

"Spare me the banter, Déjà. I'm not in the mood. Just concentrate on the decryption."

"Yes, Doctor."

Dr. Halsey paced across the antiseptic white tile of the Observation Room. One side of the room was filled with floor-to-ceiling terminals that monitored the vital signs of the children—*test subjects,* she corrected herself. They displayed drug uptake rates and winking green, blue, and red status indicators: EKGs, pulse rates, and a hundred other pieces of medical data.

The other side of the observation room overlooked dozens of translucent domes, windows into the surgical bays on the level below. Each bay was a sealed environment staffed with the best surgeons and biotechnicians that the Office of Naval Intelligence could drum up. The bays had been scrubbed and irradiated and were in the final preparation stages to receive and hold the special biohazardous materials.

"Done," Déjà announced. "The file awaits your inspection, Doctor."

Dr. Halsey stopped her pacing and sat. "On my glasses, please, Déjà."

Her glasses scanned retinal and brain patterns, and the security barrier of the file lifted. With a blink of her eyes, she opened the file.

It read:

UNITED NATIONS SPACE COMMAND PRIORITY TRANSMISSION 09872H-98

ENCRYPTION CODE: RED

PUBLIC KEY: FILE /EXCISED ACCESS OMEGA/

FROM: ADMIRAL YSIONRIS JEROMI, CHIEF MEDICAL OFFICER, UNSC RESEARCH STATION HOPEFUL

TO: DR. CATHERINE ELIZABETH HALSEY M.D., PH.D., SPECIAL CIVILIAN CONSULTANT (CIVILIAN IDENTIFICATION NUMBER: 10141-026-SRB4695)

SUBJECT: MITIGATING FACTORS AND RELATIVE BIOLOGICAL RISKS ASSOCIATED WITH QUERIED EXPERIMENTAL MEDICAL PROCEDURES

CLASSIFICATION: RESTRICTED (BGX DIRECTIVE)

/START FILE/

CATHERINE,

I AM AFRAID FURTHER ANALYSIS HAS YIELDED NO VIABLE ALTERNATIVES TO MITIGATE THE RISKS IN YOUR PROPOSED "HYPOTHETICAL" EXPERIMENTATION. I HAVE, HOWEVER, ATTACHED THE SYNOPSIS OF MY TEAM'S FINDINGS AS WELL AS ALL RELEVANT CASE STUDIES. PERHAPS YOU WILL FIND THEM USEFUL.

I HOPE IT IS A HYPOTHETICAL STUDY . . . THE USE OF BONOBOS IN YOUR PROPOSAL IS TROUBLESOME. THESE ANIMALS ARE EXPENSIVE AND RARE NOW SINCE THEY ARE NO LONGER BRED IN CAPTIVITY. I WOULD HATE TO SEE SUCH

VALUABLE SPECIMENS WASTED IN SOME SECTION THREE PROJECT.

BEST,

Y.J.

She winced at the veiled rebuke in the Admiral's communiqué. He had never approved of her decision to work with the Office of Naval Intelligence, and made his disappointment with his star pupil evident every time she visited *Hopeful.*

It was hard enough to justify the morality of the course she was about to embark upon. Jeromi's disapproval only made her decision more difficult.

Dr. Halsey gritted her teeth and returned to the report.

SYNOPSIS OF CHEMICAL/BIOLOGICAL RISKS

WARNING: THE FOLLOWING PROCEDURES ARE CLASSIFIED LEVEL-3 EXPERIMENTAL. PRIMATE TEST SUBJECTS MUST BE CLEARED THROUGH UNSC QUARTERMASTER GENERAL OFFICE CODE: OBF34. FOLLOW GAMMA CODE BIOHAZARD DISPOSAL PROTOCOL.

1. *CARBIDE CERAMIC OSSIFICATION:* ADVANCED MATERIAL GRAFTING ONTO SKELETAL STRUCTURES TO MAKE BONES VIRTUALLY UNBREAKABLE. RECOMMENDED COVERAGE NOT TO EXCEED 3 PERCENT TOTAL BONE MASS BECAUSE SIGNIFICANT WHITE BLOOD CELL NECROSIS. SPECIFIC RISK FOR PRE- AND NEAR-POSTPUBESCENT ADOLESCENTS: SKELETAL GROWTH SPURTS MAY CAUSE IRREPARABLE BONE PULVERIZATION. SEE ATTACHED CASE STUDIES.

2. *MUSCULAR ENHANCEMENT INJECTIONS:* PROTEIN COMPLEX IS INJECTED INTRAMUSCULARLY TO INCREASE TISSUE DENSITY AND DECREASE LACTASE RECOVERY TIME. RISK: 5 PERCENT OF TEST SUBJECTS EXPERIENCE A FATAL CARDIAC VOLUME INCREASE.

3. *CATALYTIC THYROID IMPLANT:* PLATINUM PELLET CONTAINING HUMAN GROWTH HORMONE CATALYST IS IMPLANTED IN THE THYROID TO BOOST GROWTH OF SKELETAL AND MUSCLE TISSUES. RISK: RARE INSTANCES OF ELEPHANTIASIS. SUPPRESSED SEXUAL DRIVE.

4. *OCCIPITAL CAPILLARY REVERSAL:* SUBMERGENCE AND BOOSTED BLOOD VESSEL FLOW BENEATH THE RODS AND CONES OF SUBJECT'S RETINA. PRODUCES A MARKED VISUAL PERCEPTION INCREASE. RISK: RETINAL REJECTION AND DETACHMENT. PERMANENT BLINDNESS. SEE ATTACHED AUTOPSY REPORTS.

5. *SUPERCONDUCTING FIBRIFICATION OF NEURAL DENDRITES:* ALTERATION OF BIOELECTRICAL NERVE TRANSDUCTION TO SHIELDED ELECTRONIC TRANSDUCTION. THREE HUNDRED PERCENT INCREASE IN SUBJECT REFLEXES. ANECDOTAL EVIDENCE OF MARKED INCREASE IN INTELLIGENCE, MEMORY, AND CREATIVITY. RISK: SIGNIFICANT INSTANCES OF PARKINSON'S DISEASE AND FLETCHER'S SYNDROME.

/END FILE/

PRESS **ENTER** TO OPEN LINKED ATTACHMENTS.

Dr. Halsey closed the file. She erased all traces of it—sent Déjà to track the file pathways all the way back to *Hopeful* and destroy Admiral Jeromi's notes and files relative to this incident.

She removed her glasses and pinched the bridge of her nose.

"I'm sorry," Déjà said. "I, too, had hoped there would be some new process to lower the risks."

Dr. Halsey sighed. "I have doubts, Déjà. I thought the reasons so compelling when we first started project SPARTAN. Now? I . . . I just don't know."

"I have been over the ONI projections of Outer Colony stability three times, Doctor. Their conclusion is correct: massive rebellion within twenty years unless drastic military action is taken. And you know the 'drastic military action' the brass would like. The SPARTANS are our only option to avoid overwhelming civilian losses. They will be the perfect pinpoint strike force. They can prevent a civil war."

"Only if they survive to fulfill that mission," Dr. Halsey countered. "We should delay the procedures. More research needs to be done. We could use the time to work on MJOLNIR. We need time to—"

"There is another reason to proceed expeditiously," Déjà said. "Although I am loath to bring this to your attention, I must. If the Office of Naval Intelligence detects a delay in their prize project, you will likely be replaced by someone who harbors . . . fewer doubts. And regrettably for the children, most likely someone less qualified."

"I hate this." Dr. Halsey got up and strode to the fire exit. "And sometimes, Déjà, I hate you, too." She left the observation room.

Mendez was waiting for her in the hallway.

"Walk with me, Chief," she said.

He followed without a word as they took the stairs to the pre-op wing of the hospital.

They entered room 117. John lay in bed and an IV drip was attached to his arm. His head had been shaved and incision vectors had been lasered onto his entire body. Despite these indignities, Dr. Halsey marveled at what a spectacular physical specimen he had grown into. Fourteen years old and he had the body of an eighteen-year-old Olympic athlete, and a mind the equal of any Naval Academy honors graduate.

Dr. Halsey forced the best smile she could muster. "How are you feeling?"

"I'm fine, ma'am," John replied groggily. "The nurse said the sedation would take effect soon. I'm fighting it to see how long I can stay awake." His eyelids fluttered. "It's not easy."

John spotted Mendez and he struggled to sit up and salute, but failed. "I know this is one of the Chief's exercises. But I don't know what the twist is. Can you tell me, Dr. Halsey? Just this time? How do I win?"

Mendez looked away.

Dr. Halsey leaned closer to John as he closed his eyes and started to breathe deeply.

"I'll tell you how to win, John," she whispered. "You have to survive."

CHAPTER

SEVEN

0000 HOURS MARCH 30, 2525 (MILITARY CALENDAR) / UNSC CARRIER *ATLAS* EN ROUTE TO THE LAMBDA SERPENTIS SYSTEM

"And so we commit the bodies of our fallen brothers to space."

Mendez solemnly closed his eyes for a moment, the ceremony completed. He pressed a control and the ash canisters moved slowly into the ejection tubes . . . and the void beyond.

John stood rigidly at attention. The carrier's missile launch bays—normally cramped, overcrowded, and bustling with activity—were unusually quiet. The *Atlas'* firing deck had been cleared of munitions and crew. Long, unadorned black banners now hung from the bay's overhead gantries.

"Honors . . . *ten hut*!" Mendez barked.

John and the other surviving Spartans saluted in unison.

"Duty," Mendez said. "Honor and self-sacrifice. Death does not diminish these qualities in a soldier. We shall remember."

A series of thumps resounded through the *Atlas'* hull as the canisters were hurled into space.

The view screen flickered and displayed a field of stars. The canisters appeared one by one, quickly falling behind the carrier as it continued on its course.

John watched. With each of the stainless-steel cylinders that drifted by, he felt that he was losing a part of himself. It felt like leaving his people behind.

Mendez's face might as well been chiseled from stone, for all the emotion it showed. He finished his protracted salute and then said, "Crewmen, dismissed."

Not everything had been lost. John glanced around the launch chamber; Sam, Kelly, and thirty others still stood at attention in their black dress uniforms. They had made it unharmed through the last—"mission" wasn't quite the right word. More or less.

There were a dozen others, though, who had lived . . . but were no longer soldiers. It hurt John to look at them. Fhajad sat in a wheelchair, shaking uncontrollably. Kirk and René were in neutral-buoyancy gel tanks, breathing through respirators; their bones had been so twisted they no longer looked human. There were others, still alive, but with injuries so critical they could not be moved.

Orderlies pushed Fhajad and the other injured toward the elevator.

John strode toward them and stopped, blocking their path. "Stand fast, Crewman," he demanded. "Where are you taking my men?"

The orderly halted and his eyes widened. He swallowed and then said, "I, sir . . . I have my orders, sir."

"Squad Leader," Mendez called out. "A moment."

"Stay," John told the orderly, and marched to face Chief Mendez. "Yes, sir."

"Let them go," Mendez said quietly. "They can't fight anymore. They don't belong here."

John inadvertently glanced at the view screen and the long line of canisters as they shrank in the distance. "What will happen to my men?"

"The Navy takes care of its own," Mendez replied, and lifted his chin a little higher. "They may no longer be the fastest or the strongest soldiers—but they still have sharp minds. They can still plan missions, analyze data, troubleshoot ops . . ."

John exhaled a sigh of relief. "That's all any of us ask for, sir: a chance to serve." He turned to face Fhajad and the others. He snapped to attention and saluted. Fhajad managed to raise one shaking arm and return the salute.

The orderlies wheeled them away.

John looked at what remained of his squad. None of them had moved since the memorial ceremony. They were waiting for their next mission.

"Our orders, sir?" John asked.

"Two days full bed rest, Squad Leader. Then microgravity physical therapy aboard the *Atlas* until you recover from the side effects of your augmentation."

Side effects. John flexed his hand. He was clumsy now. Sometimes he could barely walk without falling. Dr. Halsey had assured him that these "side effects" were a good sign. "Your brain must relearn how to move your body with faster reflexes and stronger muscles," she told him. But his eyes hurt, and they bled a little in the morning, too. He had constant headaches. Every bone in his body ached.

John didn't understand any of this. He only knew that he had a duty to perform—and now he feared he wouldn't be able to. "Is that all, sir?" he asked Mendez.

"No," the Chief replied. "Déjà will be running your squad through the dropship pilot simulator as soon as they are up to it. And," he added, "if they are up for the challenge, she wanted to cover some more organic chemistry and complex algebra."

"Yes, sir," John replied, "we're up to the challenge."

"Good."

John continued to stand fast.

"Was there something else, Squad Leader?"

John furrowed his brow, hesitated, and then finally said, "I was Squad Leader. The last mission was therefore my responsibility . . . and members of my squad *died*. What did I do wrong?"

Mendez stared at John with his impenetrable black eyes. He

glanced at the squad, then back to John. "Walk with me." He led John to the view screen. He stood and watched as the last of the canisters vanished into the darkness.

"A leader must be ready to send the soldiers under his command to their deaths," Mendez said without turning to face John. "You do this because your duty to the UNSC supersedes your duty to yourself or even your crew."

John looked away from the view screen. He couldn't look at the emptiness anymore. He didn't want to think of his teammates—friends who were like brothers and sisters to him—forever lost.

"It is acceptable," Mendez said, "to spend their lives if necessary." He finally turned and met John's gaze. "It is not acceptable, however, to waste those lives. Do you understand the difference?"

"I . . . believe I understand, sir," John said. "But which was it on this last mission? Lives spent? Or lives wasted?"

Mendez turned back toward the blackness of space and didn't answer.

0430 HOURS, APRIL 22, 2525 (MILITARY CALENDAR) / UNSC CARRIER *ATLAS* ON PATROL IN THE LAMBDA SERPENTIS SYSTEM

John oriented himself as he entered the gym.

From the stationary corridor, it was easy to see that this section of the *Atlas* rotated. Like other ships of this age, acceleration gave the circular walls a semblance of gravity.

Unlike the other portions of the dated carrier, however, this section wasn't cylindrical, but rather a segmented cone. The outer portion was wider and rotated more slowly than the narrower inner portion—simulating gravitational forces from one quarter to two gravities along the length of the gym.

There were free weights, punching and speed bags, a boxing ring, and machines to stretch and tone every muscle group. No one else was up this early. He had the place to himself.

John started with arm curls. He went to the center section, calibrated at one gee, and picked up a twenty-kilogram dumbbell. It felt wrong—too light. The spin must be off. He set the weights down and picked up a forty-kilogram set. That felt right.

For the last three weeks the Spartans had gone through a daily routine of stretching, isometric exercises, light sparring drills, and lots of eating. They were under orders to consume five high-protein meals a day. After every meal they had to report to the ship's medical bay for a series of mineral and vitamin injections. John was looking forward to getting back to Reach and his normal routine.

There were only thirty-two other soldiers left in his squad. Thirty candidates had "washed out" of the Spartan program; they died during the augmentation process. The other dozen, suffering from side effects of the process, had been permanently reassigned within the Office of Naval Intelligence.

He missed them all, but he and the others had to go on—they had to recover and prove themselves all over again.

John wished Chief Mendez had warned him. He could have prepared. Maybe that was the trick to the last mission—to learn to be prepared for anything. He wouldn't let his guard down again.

He took a seat at the leg machine, set it to the maximum weight—but it felt too light. He moved to the high-gee end of the gym. Things felt normal again.

John worked every machine, then moved to a speed bag, a leather ball attached to the floor and ceiling by a thick elastic band. There were only certain allowed frequencies at which the bag could be hit, or it gyrated chaotically.

His fist jabbed forward, cobra-quick, and struck. The speed bag moved, but slowly, like it was underwater . . . far too slowly considering how hard he had hit it. The tension on the line must be turned way down.

He twanged the line and it hummed. It was tight.

Was everything broken in this room?

He pulled a pin from the locking collar on the bench press. John walked to the center section—supposedly one gee. He held the pin a meter off the deck and dropped it. It clattered on the deck.

It looked as if it had fallen normally . . . but somehow it also looked slow to John.

He set the timer on his watch and dropped the pin again. Forty-five-hundredths of a second.

One meter in about a half second. He forgot the formula for distance and acceleration, so he ran through the calculus and rederived the equation. He even did the square root.

He frowned. He had always struggled with math before.

The answer was a gravitational acceleration of nine point eight meters per second squared. One standard gee.

So the room *was* rotating correctly. *He* was out of calibration.

His experiment was cut short. Four men entered the gym. They were out of uniform, wearing only shorts and boots. Their heads were cleanly shaven. They were all heavily muscled, lean, and fit. The largest of the four was taller than John. Scars covered one side of his face.

John could tell they were Special Forces—Orbital Drop Shock Troopers. The ODSTs had the traditional tattoos burned onto their arms: DROP JET JUMPERS and FEET FIRST INTO HELL.

"Helljumpers"—the infamous 105th. John had overheard mess hall chatter about them. They had a reputation for success . . . and for brutality, even against fellow soldiers.

John gave them a polite nod.

They just brushed past him and started on the high-gravity free weights. The largest ODST lifted the bar of the bench press.

He struggled and the bar wavered unsteadily. The iron plates on the right end slid off and fell to the deck. The opposite end of the bar tilted, and he dropped the weight, almost crushing his spotter's foot.

Startled by the noise, John jumped up.

"What the—" The big ODST stood and glared at the locking collar that had slipped off. "Someone took the pin." He growled and turned to John.

John picked up the pin. "The error was mine," he said and stepped forward. "My apologies."

The four ODSTs moved as one toward John. The big guy with the scars stood a hand's breadth away from John's nose. "Why don't you take that pin and shove it, meat?" he said, grinning. "Or better yet, maybe I should make you eat it." He nodded to his friends.

John only knew three ways to react to people. If they were his superior officers, he obeyed them. If they were part of his squad, he helped them. If they were a threat, he neutralized them.

So when the men surrounding him moved . . . he hesitated.

Not because he was afraid, but because these men could have fallen into any of John's three categories. He didn't know their rank. They were fellow servicemen in the UNSC. But, at the moment, they didn't seem friendly.

The two men flanking him grabbed John's biceps. The one behind him tried to slip an arm around his neck.

John hunched his shoulders and tucked his chin to his chest so he couldn't be choked. He whipped his right elbow over the hand holding him, pinned it to his side, and then straight punched the man and broke his nose.

The other three reacted, tightening their grips and stepping closer—but like the dropped pin, they moved slowly.

John ducked and slipped out of the unsuccessful headlock. He spun free, breaking the grasp of the man on his left at the same time.

"Stand down!" A booming voice echoed across the gym.

A sergeant stepped into the gym and strode toward them. Unlike Mendez, who was fit and trim and was always serious, this man's stomach bulged over his belt, and he looked bemused.

John snapped to attention. The others stood there and continued to glare at John.

"Sarge," the man with the bleeding nose said. "We were just—"

"Did I ask you a question?" the Sergeant barked.

"No, Sergeant!" the man replied.

The Sergeant eyed John, then the ODSTs. "You're all are so eager to fight, get in the ring and go to it."

"Sir!" John said. He went to the boxing ring, slipped through the ropes, and stood there waiting.

This was starting to make sense. It was a mission. John had received orders from a superior officer, and the four men were now targets.

The big ODST pushed through the ropes and the others gathered to watch. "I'm going to rip you to pieces, meat," he grunted through clenched teeth.

John sprang off his back foot and launched his entire weight behind his first strike. His fist smashed into the man's wide chin. John's left hand followed and impacted on the soldier's jaw.

The man's hands came up; John stepped in, pinned one of the man's arms to his chest, and followed through with a hook to his floating ribs. Bones broke.

The man staggered back. John took a short step, brought his heel down on the man's knee. Three more punches and the man was against the ropes . . . then he stopped moving, his arm and leg and neck tilted at unnatural angles.

The three other men moved. The one with the bloody nose grabbed an iron bar.

John didn't need orders this time. Three attackers at once—he had to take them out before they surrounded him. He might be faster, but he didn't have eyes in the back of his head.

The man with the iron bar swung a vicious blow at John's ribs; John sidestepped, grabbed the man's hand, and clamped it to the bar. He twisted the bar and crushed the bones of his attacker's wrist.

John snapped a side kick toward the second man, caught him in the groin, crushing the soft organs and breaking his target's pelvis.

John pulled the bar free—whipped around and caught the third man in the neck, hitting him so hard the ODST was propelled over the ropes.

"At ease, Number-117," Chief Petty Officer Mendez barked.

John obeyed and dropped the bar. Like the pin, it seemed to take too long for the impromptu weapon to hit the deck.

The ODSTs lay crumpled on the ground, either unconscious or dead.

Mendez, at the far end of the gym, strode toward the boxing ring.

The Sergeant stood with his mouth open. "Chief Mendez, sir!" He snapped a crisp salute. "What are you—" He turned to John, his eyes widened, and he murmured, "He's one of *them*, isn't he?"

"Medics are on their way," Mendez said calmly. He stepped closer to the Sergeant. "There are two intel officers waiting for you in Ops. They'll debrief you . . ." He stepped back. "I suggest you report to them immediately."

"Yes, sir," the Sergeant said. He almost ran out of the gym. He looked once over his shoulder at John; then he moved even faster.

"Your workout is over for today," Mendez told John.

John saluted and left the ring.

A team of medics entered with stretchers and rushed toward the boxing ring.

"Permission to speak, sir?" John said.

Mendez nodded.

"Were those men part of a mission? Were they targets or teammates?"

John knew that this *had* to be some sort of mission. The Chief had been too close for it to be a coincidence.

"You engaged and neutralized a threat," Mendez replied. "That action seems to have answered your question, Squad Leader."

John wrinkled his forehead as he thought it through. "I followed the chain of command," he said. "The Sergeant told me to fight. I was threatened and in imminent danger. But they were still UNSC Special Forces. Fellow soldiers."

Mendez lowered his voice. "Not every mission has simple objectives or comes to a logical conclusion. Your priorities are to follow the orders in your chain of command, and then to preserve your life and the lives of your team. Is that clear?"

"Sir," John said. "Yes, sir." He glanced back at the ring. Blood was seeping into the canvas mat. John had an odd feeling in the pit of his stomach.

He hit the showers and let the blood rinse off him. He felt strangely sorry for the men he had killed.

But he knew his duty—the Chief had even been unusually verbose in order to clarify the matter. Follow orders and keep himself and his team safe. That's all he had to focus on. John didn't give the incident in the gym another thought.

CHAPTER

EIGHT

0930 HOURS, SEPTEMBER 11, 2525 (MILITARY CALENDAR) / EPSILON ERIDANI SYSTEM, REACH UNSC MILITARY COMPLEX, PLANET REACH

Dr. Halsey reclined in Mendez's padded chair. She considered pilfering one of the Sweet William cigars from the box on his desk—see why he considered them such a treat. The stench wafting from the box, however, was too overwhelming. How did he stand them?

The door opened and CPO Mendez halted in the doorway. "Ma'am," he said, and stood straighter. "I wasn't informed that you would be visiting today. In fact, I had understood that you were out of the system for another week. I would have made arrangements."

"I'm sure you would have." She folded her hands in her lap. "Our situation has changed. Where are my Spartans? They are not in their barracks, nor on any of the ranges."

Mendez hesitated. "They can no longer train here, ma'am. We have had to find them . . . other facilities."

Dr. Halsey stood and smoothed the pleats in her gray skirt. "Maybe you should explain that statement, Chief."

"I could," he replied, "but it will be easier to show you."

"Very well," Dr. Halsey said, her curiosity piqued. Mendez escorted her to his personal Warthog parked outside his office. The all-terrain combat vehicle had been refitted; the heavy chain-gun on the back had been removed and replaced with a rack of Argent V missiles.

Mendez drove them off the base and onto winding mountain roads. "Reach was first colonized for its rich titanium deposits," Mendez told her. "There are mines in these mountains thousands of meters deep. The UNSC uses them for storage."

"I presume you do not have my Spartans taking inventory today, Chief?"

"No, ma'am. We just need the privacy."

Mendez drove the Warthog past a manned guardhouse and into a large tunnel that sloped steeply underground.

The road wound down in a spiral, deeper into solid granite. Mendez said, "Do you remember the Navy's first experiments with powered exoskeletons?"

"I'm not sure I see the connection between this place, my Spartans, and the exoskeleton projects," Dr. Halsey replied, frowning, "but I'll play along a bit further. Yes, I know all about the Mark I prototypes. We had to scrap the concept and redesign battle armor from the ground up for the MJOLNIR project. The Mark Is consumed enormous energy. Either they had to be plugged into a generator or use inefficient broadcast power—neither option is practical on a battlefield."

Mendez decelerated slightly as he approached a speed bump. The Warthog's massive tires thudded over the obstacle.

"They used the units that weren't scrapped," Dr. Halsey continued, "as dock loaders to move heavy equipment." She cocked one eyebrow. "Or might they have been dumped in a place like this?"

"There are dozens of the suits here."

"You haven't put *my* Spartans in some of those antiques?"

"No. Their trainers are using them for their own safety," Mendez replied. "When the Spartans recovered from microgravity therapy, they were eager to get back to their routine. However, we experienced some—" He paused, searching for the right word, ". . . difficulties."

He glanced at his passenger. His face was grim. "Their first day back, three trainers were accidentally killed during hand-to-hand combat exercises."

Dr. Halsey cocked an eyebrow. "Then they are faster and stronger than we anticipated?"

"That," Mendez replied, "would be understating the situation."

The tunnel opened into a large cavern. There were lights scattered on the walls, overhead a hundred meters up on the ceiling and along the floor, but they did little to dissipate the overwhelming darkness.

Mendez parked the Warthog next to a small, prefabricated building. He jumped out and helped Dr. Halsey step from the vehicle. "This way, please." Mendez gestured to the room. "We'll have a better view from inside."

The building had three glass walls and several monitors marked MOTION, INFRARED, DOPPLER, and PASSIVE. Mendez pushed a button and the room climbed a track along the wall until they were twenty meters off the floor.

Mendez keyed a microphone and spoke: "Lights."

Floodlights snapped on and illuminated a section of the cavern the size of a football field. In the center stood a concrete bunker. Three men in the primitive Mark I power armor stood on top. Six more stood evenly spaced around the perimeter. A red banner had been planted in the center of the bunker.

"Capture the flag?" Dr. Halsey asked. "Past all that heavy armor?"

"Yes. The trainers in those exoskeletons can run at thirty-two KPH, lift two tons, and have a thirty-millimeter minigun mounted on self-targeting armatures—stun rounds, of course. They're also equipped with the latest motion sensors and IR scopes. And needless to say, their armor is impervious to standard light weapons. It would take two or three platoons of conventional Marines to take that bunker."

Mendez spoke again in the microphone, and his voice echoed off the cavern walls: "Start the drill."

Sixty seconds ticked by. Nothing happened. One hundred twenty seconds. "Where are the Spartans?" Dr. Halsey asked.

"They're here," Mendez replied. Dr. Halsey caught a glimpse of motion in the dark: a shadow against shadows, a familiar silhouette.

"Kelly?" she whispered.

The trainers turned and fired at the shadow, but it moved with almost supernatural quickness. Even the self-targeting systems couldn't track it.

From above, a man free-rappelled down from the girders and gantries overhead. The newcomer landed behind one of the perimeter guards, quiet as a cat. He punched the guard's armor twice, denting the heavy plates, then dropped low and swept the target's legs out from under him. The guard sprawled on the ground.

The Spartan attached his rappelling line to the trainer. A moment later the writhing guard shot upward, into the darkness.

Two other guards turned to attack.

The Spartan dodged, rolled, and melted into the shadows.

Dr. Halsey realized the trainer's exoskeleton wasn't being pulled up—it was being used as a counterweight.

Two more Spartans, dangling from the other end of that rope, dropped unnoticed into the center of the bunker. Dr. Halsey immediately recognized one of them, although he was dressed entirely in black, save his open eye slits—Number-117. John.

John landed, braced, and kicked one guard. The man landed in a heap . . . eight meters away.

The other Spartan jumped off the bunker; he flipped end over end, evading the stun rounds that filled the air. He threw himself at the farthest guard and they skidded together into the shadows. The guard's gun strobed once, and then it was dark again.

On top of the bunker, John was a blur of slashing motions. A second guard's exosuit erupted in a fountain of hydraulic fluid and then collapsed under the armor's weight.

The last guard on the bunker turned to fire at John. Halsey gripped the edge of her chair. "He's at point-blank range! Even stun rounds can kill at that distance!"

As the guard's gun fired, John sidestepped. The stun rounds slashed through the air, a clean miss. John grabbed the weapon's armature—twisted—and with a screech of stressed metal, wrenched it free of the exoskeleton. He fired directly into the man's chest and sent him tumbling off the bunker.

The remaining quartet of perimeter guards turned and sprayed the area with suppression fire.

A heartbeat later, the lights went out.

Mendez cursed and keyed the mike. "Backups. Hit the backup lights now!"

A dozen amber floods flickered to life.

Not a Spartan was in sight, but the nine trainers were either unconscious or lay immobile in inert battle armor.

The red flag was gone.

"Show me that again," Dr. Halsey said unbelievingly. "You recorded all that, didn't you?"

"Of course." Mendez tapped a button, but the monitors played back—static. "Damn it. They got to the cameras, too," he muttered, impressed. "Every time we find a new place to hide them, they disable the recording devices."

Dr. Halsey leaned against the glass wall staring at the carnage below. "Very well, Chief Mendez, what else do I need to know?"

"Your Spartans can run at bursts of up to fifty-five KPH," he explained. "Kelly can run a little faster, I think. They will only get quicker as they adjust to the 'alterations' we've made to their bodies. They can lift three times their body weight—which, I might add, is almost double the norm due to their increased muscle density. And they can virtually see in the dark."

Dr. Halsey pondered this new data. "They should not be performing so well. There must be unexplained synergistic effects brought on by the combined modifications. What are their reaction times?"

"Almost impossible to chart. We estimate it at twenty milliseconds," Mendez replied. He shook his head, then added, "I believe it's significantly faster in combat situations when their adrenaline is pumping."

"Any physiological or mental instabilities?"

"None. They work like no team I've ever seen before. Damn near telepathic, if you ask me. They were dropped in these caves yesterday, and I don't know where they got black suits or the rope for that maneuver, but I can guarantee they haven't left this room. They improvise and improve and adapt.

"And," he added, "they *like* it. The tougher the challenge, the harder the fight . . . the better their morale becomes."

Dr. Halsey watched as the first trainer stirred and struggled to get out of his inert armor. "They might as well have been killed," she murmured. "But can the Spartans kill, Chief? Kill on purpose? Are they ready for real combat?"

Mendez looked away and paused before he spoke. "Yes. If we ordered them to, they would kill quite efficiently." His body stiffened. "May I ask what 'real combat' you mean, ma'am?"

She clasped her hands and wrung them nervously. "Something has happened, Chief. Something ONI and the Admiralty never expected. The brass wants to deploy the Spartans. They want to test them in a real combat mission."

"They're as ready for that as I can make them," Mendez said. He narrowed his dark eyes. "But this is far ahead of your schedule. What happened? I've heard rumors there was some heavy action near Harvest colony."

"Your rumors are out-of-date, Chief," she said, and a chill crept into her voice. "There's no more fighting at Harvest. There *is* no more Harvest."

Dr. Halsey punched the descent button, and the observation room slowly lowered to the floor.

"Get them out of this hole," she said crisply. "I want them ready to muster at 0400. We have a briefing at 0600 tomorrow aboard the *London*. We're taking them on a mission ONI has been saving for the right crew and the right time. This is it."

"Yes, ma'am," Mendez replied.

"Tomorrow we see if all the pain they've been through has been worth it."

CHAPTER NINE

0605 HOURS, SEPTEMBER 12, 2525 (MILITARY CALENDAR) / UNSC DESTROYER *PIONEER*, EN ROUTE TO ERIDANUS SYSTEM

John and the other Spartans stood at ease.

The briefing room aboard the UNSC Destroyer *Pioneer* made him uncomfortable. The holographic projectors at the fore end of the triangular room showed the field of stars visible off the bow of the ship. John wasn't used to seeing so much space; he kept expecting the room to decompress explosively.

The stars flickered and faded and the overhead lights warmed. Chief Petty Officer Mendez and Dr. Halsey entered the room.

The Spartans snapped to attention.

"At ease," Mendez said. He clasped his hands behind his back and clenched his jaw muscles. The Chief looked almost . . . nervous.

That made John nervous, too.

Dr. Halsey walked to the podium. The overhead light reflected off her glasses. "Good morning, Spartans. I have good news for you. The word has come down. Command has decided to test your unique abilities. You have a new mission: an insurgent base in the Eridanus System."

A star map appeared on the wall and zoomed in to show a warm orange sun ringed with twelve planets. "In 2513, an armed insurrection in this system was suppressed by the UNSC force—Operation: TREBUCHET."

An intersystem tactical map appeared, and tiny icons representing destroyers and carriers winked on. They engaged a force of a hundred smaller ships. Pinpoints of fire appeared against the dark.

"The insurrection was put down," Dr. Halsey continued. "However, elements of the rebel forces escaped and regrouped in the local asteroid belt."

The map tilted and moved into the circle of debris around the star.

"Billions of rocks," Dr. Halsey said, "where they hid from our forces . . . and continue to hide to this day. For some time ONI believed that the rebels were disorganized, and were lacking in leadership. That appears to have changed.

"We believe that one of these asteroids has been hollowed out, and that a formidable base has been constructed within. UNSC explorations into the belt have met either with no contact or with an ambush by superior forces."

She paused, pushed up her glasses, and added, "The Office of Naval Intelligence has also confirmed that FLEETCOM has discovered a security breach within their organization—a rebel sympathizer leaking information to these forces."

John and the other Spartans shifted uneasily. A leak? It was possible. Déjà had shown them many historical battles that had been won and lost because of traitors or informants. But it never occurred to him that it could happen in the UNSC.

A flat picture flashed over the star map: a middle-aged man with thinning hair, a neatly trimmed beard, and watery gray eyes.

"This is their leader," Dr. Halsey said. "Colonel Robert Watts. The original photo was taken after Operation: TREBUCHET and has been computer aged.

"Your mission is to infiltrate the rebel base, capture Watts, and return him—alive and unharmed—to UNSC-controlled space. This will deprive the rebels of their new leadership. And it will provide ONI a chance to interrogate Watts and root out traitors within FLEETCOM."

Dr. Halsey stepped aside. "Chief Mendez?"

Mendez exhaled and unclasped his hands. He strode to the podium and cleared his throat. "This operation will be different from your previous missions. You will be engaging the enemy using live rounds and lethal force. They will be returning the favor. If there is any doubt, any confusion—and make no mistake: in combat, there will be confusion—take *no* chances. Kill first, ask questions later.

"Support on this mission will be limited to the resources and firepower of this destroyer," Mendez continued. "This is to minimize the chance of a leak in the command structure."

Mendez walked to the star map. The face of Colonel Watts snapped off and blueprints for a Parabola-class freighter appeared.

"Although we don't know the location of the rebel base, we believe they receive periodic shipments from Eridanus Two. The independent freighter *Laden* is due to leave space dock in six hours for a routine recertification of her engines. She is being loaded with enough food and water to supply a small city. Additionally, her captain has been identified as a rebel officer thought to have been killed during Operation: TREBUCHET.

"You will slip aboard this freighter and hopefully hitch a ride to the rebel base. Once there, infiltrate the installation, grab Watts, and get off of that rock any way you can."

Chief Mendez gazed at them all. "Questions?"

"Sir," John said. "What are our extraction options?"

"You have two options: a panic button that will relay a distress signal to a preestablished listening ship. Also, the *Pioneer* will stay on-station . . . briefly. Our window here is thirteen hours." He tapped the star map on the edge of the asteroid belt and it glowed with a blue NAV marker. "I'll leave the extraction choice up to you. But let me point out that this asteroid belt has a circumference of more than a billion kilometers . . . making it impossible to canvass with ONI surveillance craft. If things get hot, you will be on your own.

"Any other questions?"

The Spartans sat, silent and immobile.

"No? Well, listen up, recruits," Mendez added. "This time I've told you all the twists that I know of. Be prepared for anything." His gaze fixed on John. "Squad Leader, you are hereby promoted to the rank of Petty Officer Third Class."

"Sir!" John snapped to attention.

"Assemble your team and equipment. Be ready to muster at 0300. We'll drop you off at the Eridanus Two docks. You're on your own from there."

"Yes, sir!" John said.

Mendez saluted. He and Dr. Halsey then left the room.

John turned to face his teammates. The other Spartans stood at attention. Thirty-two—too many for this operation. He needed a small team: five or six maximum.

"Sam, Kelly, Linda, and Fred, meet me in the weapons locker in ten minutes." The other Spartans sighed and their gazes dropped to the deck. "The rest of you fall out. You'll have the more difficult part of this mission: you'll have to wait here."

The weapons locker of the *Pioneer* had been stocked with a bewildering array of combat equipment. On a table were guns, knives, communication gear, body armor explosives, medical packs, survival gear, portable computers, even a thruster pack for maneuvering in space.

More important than the equipment, however, John assessed his team.

Sam had recovered from the augmentation faster than any of the other Spartans. He paced impatiently around the crates of grenades. He was the strongest of them all. He stood taller than

John by a head. He had grown out his sandy hair to three centimeters. Chief Mendez had warned him that he was going to look like a civilian soon.

Kelly, in contrast, had taken the longest to recover. She stood in the corner with her arms crossed over her chest. John had thought she wasn't going to make it. She was still gaunt and her hair had yet to grow back. Her face, however, still had its rough, angular beauty. She scared John a little, too. She was fast before . . . now no one could touch her if she didn't allow it.

Fred sat cross-legged on the deck, twirling a razor-edged combat knife in glittering arcs. He always came in second in all the contests. John thought he could have come in first, but he just didn't like the attention. He was neither too short nor too tall. He wasn't overly muscled or slim. His black hair was shot with streaks of silver—a feature he hadn't had before the augmentation. If anyone in the group could blend into a crowd, it would be him.

Linda was the quietest member of the group. She was pale, had close-cropped red hair, and green eyes. She was a crack shot, an artist with a sniper rifle.

Kelly circled the table once, and then selected a pair of grease-stained blue coveralls. Her name had been sloppily embroidered on the chest. "These our new trainee uniforms?"

"ONI provided them," John said. "They're supposed to match what the crew of the *Laden* wears."

Kelly held the coveralls up and frowned. "They don't give a girl much to work with."

"Try this on for size." Linda held a black bodysuit up to Kelly's long slender frame.

They had used these black suits before. They were formfitting, lightweight polymer body armor. They could deflect a small-caliber round and had refrigeration/heating units that would mask infrared signatures. The integrated helmet had encryption and communications gear, a heads-up display, and thermal and motion detectors. Sealed tight, the unit had a fifteen-minute reserve of oxygen to let the wearer survive in a vacuum.

The suits were uncomfortable, and they were tricky to repair in the field. And they always needed repairs.

"They're too tight," Kelly said. "It'll limit my range of motion."

"We wear them for this op," John told her. "There are too many places between here and there with nothing to breathe but vacuum. As for the rest of your equipment, take what you want—but stay light. Without recon data on this place, we're going to be moving fast . . . or we'll be dead."

The team started selecting their weapons first.

"Three-ninety caliber?" Fred asked.

"Yes," John replied. "Everyone take guns that use .390-caliber ammunition so we can share clips if we have to. Except Linda."

Linda gravitated to a matte-black long-barreled rifle—the SRS99C-S2 AM. The sniper rifle system had modular sections: scopes, stocks, barrels, even the firing mechanism could be swapped. She quickly stripped the rifle down and reconfigured it. She assembled a flash-and-sound suppression barrel, and then to compensate for the lower muzzle velocity, she increased the ammunition caliber to .450. She ditched all the sights and scopes and settled for an integrated link to her helmet's heads-up display. She pocketed five extended ammunition clips.

John also chose an MA2B, a cut-down version of the standard MA5B assault rifle. It was tough and reliable, with electronic targeting and an ammo supply indicator. It also had a recoil-reduction system, and could deliver an impressive fifteen rounds per second.

He picked up a knife: twenty-centimeter blade, one serrated edge, nonreflective titanium carbide, and balanced for throwing.

John grabbed the panic button—a tiny single-shot emergency beacon. It had two settings. The red setting alerted the *Pioneer* that it had hit the fan, and to come in guns blazing. The green setting merely marked the location of the base for later assault by the UNSC.

He took a double handful of ammo clips—then paused. He set them down and pocketed five. If they got into a firefight where he'd need that much firepower, their mission was over anyway.

Everyone took similar equipment, with a few variations. Kelly selected a small computer pad with IR links. She also had their field medical kit.

Fred packed a standard-issue lockbreaker.

Linda selected three NAV marker transmitters, each the size of a tick. The trackers could be adhered to an object and would broadcast that object's location to the Spartans' heads-up displays.

Sam hefted two medium-size backpacks—"damage packs." They were filled with C-12, enough high explosives to blow through three meters of battleship armor plate.

"You have enough of that stuff?" Kelly asked him wryly.

"You think I should take more?" Sam replied, and smiled. "Nothing like a little fireworks to celebrate the end of a mission."

"Everyone ready?" John asked.

Sam's smile disappeared and he slapped an extended clip into his MA2B. "Ready!"

Kelly gave him John a thumbs-up.

Fred and Linda nodded.

"Then let's go to work."

CHAPTER

TEN

1210 HOURS, SEPTEMBER 14, 2525 (MILITARY CALENDAR) / ERIDANUS SYSTEM, ERIDANUS II SPACE DOCK, CIVILIAN CARGO SHIP, *LADEN* (REGISTRY NUMBER F-0980W)

"Spartan-117: in position. Next check-in at 0400." John clicked off the microphone, encrypted the message, and fed it into his COM relay. He triggered a secure burst transmission to the *Athens*, the ONI prowler ship on station a few AUs distant.

He and his teammates climbed onto the upper girders. In silence, the team rigged a web of support nets so they could rest in relative comfort. Below them lay a hundred thousand liters of black water, and surrounding them, two centimeters of stainless steel. Sam rigged the fill sensor so the reservoir's computer wouldn't let any more water flow into the storage tank. The lights in their helmets cast a pattern of crossing and crisscrossing reflection lines.

A perfect hiding spot—all according to plan, John thought, and allowed himself a small grin of triumph. The tech specs that ONI had procured on the *Laden* showed a number of hydroponic pods mounted around the ship's carousel system, something not uncommon for this class. The massive water tanks used gravity feed to irrigate the ship's space-grown crops.

Perfect.

They had easily slipped past the lone guard in the *Laden*'s main cargo bay and into the nearly deserted center section. The water tank would mask their thermal signatures, and block any motion sensors.

The only risky element entered the picture if the center section stopped spinning . . . things could get very messy inside the tank, very fast. But John doubted that would happen.

Kelly set up a tiny microwave relay outside the top hatch. She propped her data pad on her stomach and linked to the ship's network. "I'm in," she reported. "There's no AI or serious encryption . . . accessing their system now." She tapped the pad a few more times and activated the intrusion software—the best that ONI could provide. A moment later the pad pulsed to indicate success.

"They've got a NAV trajectory to the asteroid belt. ETA is ten hours."

"Good work," John said. "Team: we'll sleep in shifts." Sam, Fred, and Linda snapped off their flashlights.

The tank reverberated as the *Laden*'s engines flared to life. The water tilted as they accelerated away from the orbital docking station.

John remembered Eridanus II—vaguely recalled that it once was home. He wondered if his old school, his family, were still there—

He squelched his curiosity. Speculation made for a fine mental exercise, but the mission came first. He had to stay alert—or failing that, grab some sleep so he would be alert when he needed to be. Chief Mendez must have told them a thousand times: "Rest can be as deadly a weapon as a pistol or grenade."

"I've got something," Kelly whispered, and handed him her data pad.

It displayed the cargo manifest for the *Laden*. John scrolled down the list: water, flour, milk, frozen orange juice, welding rods, superconducting magnets for a fusion reactor . . . no mention of weapons.

"I give up," he said. "What am I looking for?"

"I'll give you a hint," Kelly replied. "The Chief smokes them."

John flicked back through the list. There: Sweet William cigars. Next to them on the manifest was a crate of champagne, a Procyon vintage. There were fast-chilled New York steaks, and Swiss chocolates. These items were stored in a secure locker. They had the same routing codes.

"Luxury items," Kelly murmured. "I bet they're headed straight for a special delivery to Colonel Watts or his officers."

"Good work," John replied. "We'll tag this stuff and follow it."

"Won't be that easy," Fred said from the darkness. He flicked on his flashlight and peered back at John. "There are a million ways this can go wrong. We're going in without recon. I don't like it."

"We only have one advantage on this mission," John said. "The rebels have never been infiltrated—they'll feel relatively safe and won't be expecting us. But every extra second we stay . . . that's another chance for us to be spotted. We'll follow Kelly's hunch."

"You questioning orders?" Sam asked Fred. "Scared?" There was a slight hint of challenge in his voice.

Fred thought for a moment. "No," he whispered. "But this is no training mission. Our targets won't be firing stun rounds." He sighed. "I just don't want to fail."

"We're not going to fail," John told him. "We've accomplished every mission we've been on before."

That wasn't entirely true: the augmentation mission had wiped out half of the Spartans. They weren't invincible.

But John wasn't scared. A little nervous, maybe—but he was ready.

"Rotate sleep cycles," John said. "Wake me up in four hours."

He turned over and quickly nodded off to the sound of the

sloshing water. He dreamed of gravball and a coin spinning in the air. John caught it and yelled, "Eagle!" as he won again.

He always won.

Kelly nudged John's shoulder and he was instantly awake, hand on his assault rifle.

"We're decelerating," she whispered, and pointed her light into the water below. The liquid tilted at a twenty-degree inclination.

"Lights off," John ordered.

They were plunged into total darkness.

He popped the hatch and snaked the fiber-optic probe—attached to his helmet—through the crack. All clear.

They climbed out, then rappelled down the back of the ten-meter-tall tank. They donned their grease-stained coveralls and removed their helmets. The black suits looked a little bulky beneath the work clothes, but the disguise would hold up to a cursory inspection. With their weapons and gear in duffel bags, they'd pass as crew . . . from a distance.

They crept through a deserted corridor and into the cargo bay. They heard a million tiny metallic pings as gravity settled the ship. The *Laden* must be docking to a spinning station or a rotating asteroid.

The cargo bay was a huge room, stacked to its ceiling with barrels and crates. There were massive tanks of oil. Automated robot forklifts scurried between rows, checking for items that might have come loose in transit.

There was a terrific clang as a docking clamp grabbed the ship.

"Cigars are this way," Kelly whispered. She consulted her data pad, then tucked it back into her pocket.

They moved out, clinging to the shadows. They stopped every few meters, listened, and made sure their fields of fire were clear.

Kelly held up her hand and made a fist. She pointed to the secure hatch on the starboard side of the hold.

John signaled Fred and Kelly and motioned them to go forward. Fred used the lockbreaker on the door and it popped open. They entered and closed it behind them.

John, Sam, and Linda waited. There was a sudden motion and the Spartans snapped their weapons to firing positions—

A robot forklift passed down an adjacent aisle.

The massive aft doors of the cargo hold parted with a hiss. Light spilled into the hold. A dozen dockworkers dressed in coveralls entered.

John gripped his MA2B tighter. One man looked down the aisle where they crouched in the shadows. He stooped, paused—

John raised his weapon slowly, his hands steady, and sighted on the man's chest. "Always shoot for center mass," Mendez had barked during weapons training. The man stood, stretched his back, and moved on, whistling quietly to himself.

Fred and Kelly returned, and Kelly opened and closed her hand, palm out—she had placed the marker.

John grabbed his helmet from his duffel bag and slipped it on. He pinged the navigation marker and saw the blue triangle flash once on his heads-up display. He returned Kelly's thumbs-up and removed the helmet.

John stowed his helmet and MA2B and motioned for the rest of the team to do the same. They casually walked out of the *Laden*'s aft cargo hold and onto the rebel base.

The docking bay was hewn from solid rock. The ceiling stretched a kilometer high. Bright lights overhead effectively illuminated the place, looking like tiny suns in the sky. There were hundreds of ships docked within the cavern—tiny single craft, Mako-class corvettes, cargo freighters, and even a captured UNSC Pelican dropship. Each craft was held by massive cranes that traveled on railroad tracks. The tracks led toward a series of large airlock doors. That's how the *Laden* must have gotten inside.

There were people everywhere: workers and men in crisp white uniforms. John's first instinct was to seek cover. Every one of them was a potential threat. He wished he had his gun in hand.

He remained calm and strode among these strangers. He had to set the right example for his team. If his recent encounter with the ODSTs in the gym of the *Atlas* had been any indication, he knew his team wouldn't interact well with the natives.

John made his way past dockworkers and robotic trams full of cargo and vendors selling roasted meat on sticks. He walked toward a set of double doors set in the far rock wall, marked: PUBLIC SHOWERS. He pushed through and didn't look back.

The place was almost empty. One man was singing in the shower, and there were two rebel officers undressing near the towel dispensers.

John led his team to the most distant corner of the locker room and hunkered down on one of the benches. Linda sat with her back to them, on lookout duty.

"So far so good," John whispered. "This will be our fallback position if everything falls apart and we get separated."

Sam nodded. "Okay—we have a lead on how to find the Colonel. Anyone have any ideas how to get off this rock once we grab him? Back into the *Laden*'s water tank?"

"Too slow," Kelly said. "We've got to assume that when Colonel Watts goes missing, his people are going to look for him."

"There was a Pelican on the dock," John said. "We'll take it. Now let's figure out how to operate the cranes and airlocks."

Sam hefted his pack of explosives. "I know just the way to politely knock on those airlock doors. Don't worry."

Sam tapped his left foot. He only did that when he was eager to move. Fred's hands were clenched into fists; he might be nervous, but he had it under control. Kelly yawned. And Linda sat absolutely still. They were ready.

John got his helmet, donned it, and checked the NAV marker.

"Bearing 320," he said. "It's on the move." He picked up his gear. "And so are we."

They left the showers and strode through the dock, past massive drop doors and into a city. This part of the asteroid looked like a canyon carved into the rock; John could barely make out the ceiling far overhead. There were skyscrapers and apartment buildings, factories, and even a small hospital.

John ducked into an alley, slipped on his helmet, and pinpointed the blue NAV marker. It overlay a cargo tram that silently rolled down the street. There were three armed guards riding in the back.

The Spartans followed at a discreet distance.

John checked his exit routes. Too many people, and too many unknowns. Were the people here armed? Would they all engage if fighting started? A few of the people gave him strange looks.

"Spread out," he whispered to his team. "We look like we're on a parade ground."

Kelly stepped up her pace and pulled ahead. Sam fell behind. Fred and Linda drifted to the right and left.

The cargo tram turned and made its way slowly through a crowded street. It stopped at a building. The structure was twelve stories tall, with balconies on every floor.

John guessed these were barracks.

There were two armed guards in white uniforms at the front entrance. The three men in the tram got out and carried the crate inside.

Kelly glanced at John. He nodded, giving her the go-ahead.

She approached the two guards, smiling. John knew her smile wasn't friendly. She was smiling because she was finally getting a chance to put her training to the test.

Kelly waved to the guard and pulled open the door. He asked her to stop and show her identification.

She stepped inside, grabbed his rifle, twisted, and dragged him inside with her.

The other guard stepped back and leveled his rifle. John sprang at him from behind, grabbed his neck and snapped it, then dragged his limp body inside.

The entry room had cinderblock walls and a steel door with a swipe-card lock. A security camera dangled limply over Kelly's head. The guard she had dragged in lay at her feet. She was already running a cracking program on the lock, using her data pad.

John retrieved his MA2B and covered her. Fred and Linda entered and slipped out of their coveralls, then donned their helmets.

"NAV marker is moving," Linda reported. "Mark 270, elevation ten meters, twenty . . . thirty-five and holding. I'd say that's the top floor."

Sam entered, pulled the door shut behind him, and then jammed the lock. "All clear out there."

The inner door clicked. "Door's open," Kelly said.

John, Kelly, and Sam slipped out of their coveralls as Fred and Linda covered them. John activated the motion and thermal displays in his helmet. The target sight glowed as he raised his MA2B.

"Go," John said.

Kelly pushed open the door. Linda stepped in and to the right. John entered and took the left.

Two guards were seated behind the lobby's reception desk. Another man, without a uniform, stood in front of the desk, waiting to be helped; two more uniformed men stood by the elevator.

Linda shot the three near the desk. John eliminated the targets by the elevator.

Five rounds—five bodies hit the floor.

Fred entered and policed the bodies, dragging them behind the counter.

Kelly moved to the stairwell, opened the door, and gave the all-clear signal.

The elevator pinged and its doors opened. They all wheeled, rifles leveled . . . but the car was empty.

John exhaled, then motioned them to take the stairs; Kelly took point. Sam brought up the rear. They silently went up nine double flights of stairs.

Kelly halted on an upper landing. She pointed to the interior of the building, then pointed up.

John detected faint blurs of heat on the twelfth floor. They'd have to pick a better route, a way in that no one would expect.

John opened the door. There was an empty hallway. No targets.

He went to the elevator doors and pried them open. Then he turned on his black suit's cooling elements to mask his thermal signature. The others did the same . . . and faded from his thermal imaging display.

John and Sam climbed up the elevator cable. John glanced down: a thirty-meter plunge into darkness. He might survive that fall. His bones wouldn't break, but there would be internal damage. And it would certainly compromise their mission. He tightened his grip on the cable and didn't look down again.

When they had climbed up the last three floors, they braced themselves in the corners by the closed elevator door. Kelly and Fred snaked up the cable after them. They braced in the far corners to overlap their fields of fire. Linda came up last. She climbed as far as she could, hooked her foot on a cross brace, and hung upside down.

John held up three fingers, two, then one, and then he and Sam silently pulled open the elevator doors.

There were five guards standing in the room. They wore light body armor and helmets and carried older-model HMG-38 rifles. Two of them turned.

Kelly, Fred, and Linda opened fire. The walnut paneling behind the guards became pockmarked with bullet holes and was spattered with blood.

The team slid inside the room, moving quickly and quietly. Sam policed the guards' weapons.

There were two doors. One led to a balcony; the other featured a peephole. Kelly checked the balcony, then whispered over the channel in their helmets: "This overlooks the alley between buildings. No activity."

John checked the NAV marker. The blue triangles flashed a position directly behind the other door.

Sam and Fred flanked the door. John couldn't get any reading on motion or thermal. The walls were shielded. There were too many unknowns and not enough time.

The situation wasn't ideal. They knew there were at least three men inside—the ones who had carried the crate upstairs. And there might be more guards . . . and to complicate the situation, their target had to be taken alive.

John kicked the door in.

He took in the entire situation at a glance. He was standing on the threshold of a sumptuous apartment. There was a wet bar boasting shelves of amber-filled bottles. A large, round bed dominated the corner, decorated with shimmering silk sheets. Windows on all sides had sheer white curtains—John's helmet automatically compensated for the glare. Red carpet covered the floor. The crate with the cigars and champagne sat in the center of the room. It was black and armored, sealed tight against the vacuum of space.

There were three men standing behind the armored crate, and one man crouched behind them. Colonel Robert Watts—their "package."

John didn't have a clear shot. If he missed, he could hit the Colonel.

The three men, however, didn't have that problem. They fired.

John dove to his left. He caught three rounds in his side—knocking the breath from his body. One bullet penetrated his black suit. He felt it ping off his ribs and pain slashed through him like a red-hot razor.

He ignored the wound and rolled to his feet. He had a clear line of fire. He squeezed the trigger once—a three-round burst caught the center guard in the forehead.

Sam and Fred wheeled around the door frame, Sam high, Fred low. Their silenced weapons coughed and the remaining pair of guards went down.

Watts remained behind the crate. He brandished his pistol. "Stop!" he screamed. "My men are coming. You think I'm alone? You're all dead. Drop your weapons."

John crawled to the wet bar and crouched there. He willed the pain inside his stomach to go away. He signaled Sam and Fred and held up two fingers, then pointed the fingers over his head.

Sam and Fred fired a burst of rounds over Watts. He ducked.

John vaulted over the bar and leaped onto his quarry. He grabbed the pistol and wrenched it out of his hand, breaking the man's index finger and thumb. John snaked his arm around Watts's neck and choked the struggling man into near-unconsciousness.

Kelly and Linda entered. Kelly took out a syringe and injected Watts—enough polypseudomorphine to keep him sedated for the better part of a day.

Fred fell back to cover the elevator. Sam entered and crouched by the windows, watching the street below for any signs of trouble.

Kelly went to John and peeled back his black suit. Her gloves were slick with his blood. "The bullet is still inside," she said, and bit her lower lip. "There's a lot of internal bleeding. Hang on." She dug a tiny bottle from her belt and inserted the nozzle into the bullet hole. "This might sting a little."

The self-sealing biofoam filled John's abdominal cavity. It also stung like a hundred ants crawling through his innards. She pulled the bottle out and taped up the hole. "You're good for a few hours," she said, and then gave him a hand up.

John felt shaky, but he'd make it. The foam would keep him from bleeding to death and stave off the shock . . . for a while, at least.

"Incoming vehicles," Sam announced. "Six men entering the building. Two taking up position outside . . . but just the front."

"Get our package inside that crate and seal it up," John ordered.

He left the room, got his duffel, and went to the balcony. He secured a rope and tossed it down twelve stories into the alley. He rappelled down, took a second to scan the alley for threats, then clicked his throat mike once—the all-clear signal.

Kelly snapped a descent rig on the crate and pushed it off the balcony. It zipped down the line and thudded to a halt at the bottom.

A moment later the rest of the team glided down the rope.

They quickly donned their coveralls. Sam and Fred carried the crate as they entered the adjacent building. They exited on the street a half block down and walked as quickly as they could back to the docks.

Dozens of uniformed men ran from the dock toward the city. No one challenged them.

They reentered the now-deserted public showers.

"Everyone check your seals," John said. "Sam, you go ring the doorbell. Meet us on the dropship."

Sam nodded and sprinted out of the building, both packs of C-12 looped around his shoulder.

John took out the panic button. He triggered the green-mode

transmission and tossed it into an empty locker. If they didn't make it out, at least the UNSC fleet would know where to find the rebel base.

"Your suit is breached," Kelly reminded John. "We better get to the ship now, before Sam sets off his fireworks."

Linda and Fred checked the seals on the crate then carried it out. Kelly took point and John brought up the rear.

They boarded the Pelican dropship and John sized up her armaments—dented and charred armor, a pair of old, out-of-date 40mm chain guns. The rocket pods had been removed. Not much of a warhorse.

There was a flash of lightning at the far end of the dock. The thunder roiled through the deck, and then through John's stomach.

While John watched, a gaping hole materialized in the airlock door amid a cloud of smoke and shattered metal. Black space loomed beyond. With an earsplitting roar, the atmosphere held in the docks abruptly transformed into a hurricane. People, crates, and debris were blasted out of the ragged tear.

John pulled himself inside the dropship and prepared to seal the main hatch.

He watched as emergency doors descended over the breached airlock. There was a second explosion, and the drop door paused, then fell and clattered to the deck, crushing a light transport vessel underneath.

Behind them, large bay doors closed, sealing the docks off from the city. Dozens of workers still on the docks ran for their lives, but didn't make it.

Sam sprinted across the deck, perfectly safe inside his sealed black suit. He cycled through the Pelican's emergency airlock.

"Back door's open," he said with a grin.

Kelly fired up the engines. The Pelican lifted, maneuvered through the dock, and then out through the blasted hole and into open space. She pushed the throttle to maximum burn.

Behind them, the insurgent base looked like any other rock in the asteroid belt . . . but this rock was venting atmosphere and starting to rotate erratically.

After five minutes at full power, Kelly eased the engines back. "We'll hit the extraction point in two hours," she said.

"Check on our prisoner," John said.

Sam popped open the crate. "The seals held. Watts is still alive and has a steady pulse," he said.

"Good," John grunted. He winced as the throbbing pain in his side increased.

"Something bothering you?" Kelly asked. "How's that bio-foam holding up?"

"It's fine," he said without even looking at the hole in his side. "I'll make it."

He knew he should feel elated—but instead he just felt tired. Something didn't sit right about the operation. He wondered about all the dead dockworkers and civilians back there. None of them were designated targets. And yet, weren't they all rebels on that asteroid?

On the other hand, it was like the Chief said—he had followed his orders, completed his mission, and gotten his people out alive. What more did he want?

John stuffed his doubts deep in the back of his mind.

"Nothing's wrong," he said, and squeezed Kelly's shoulder. John smiled. "What could be wrong? We won."

CHAPTER

ELEVEN

0600 HOURS, NOVEMBER 2, 2525 (MILITARY CALENDAR) / EPSILON ERIDANI SYSTEM, REACH UNSC MILITARY COMPLEX, PLANET REACH

John wondered who had died. The Spartans had been called to muster in their dress uniforms only once before: funeral detail.

The Purple Heart awarded to him after his last mission glistened on his chest. He made sure it was polished to a high sheen. It stood out against the black wool of his dress jacket. Occasionally, John would look at it, and make sure it was still there.

He sat in the third row of the amphitheater and faced the center platform. The other Spartans sat quietly on the concentric rings of risers. Spotlights flicked on the empty stage.

He had been in Reach's secure briefing chamber before. This is where Dr. Halsey had told them they were going to be soldiers. This is where his life had changed and he had been given a purpose.

Chief Mendez entered the room and marched to the center platform. He, too, wore his black dress uniform as well. His chest was covered with Silver and Bronze Stars, three Purple Hearts, the Red Legion of Honor award, and a rainbow of campaign ribbons. He had recently shaved his head.

The Spartans rose and stood at attention.

Dr. Halsey entered. She looked older to John, the wrinkles at the corners of her eyes and mouth more pronounced, streaks of gray in her dark hair. But her blue eyes were as sharp as ever.

She wore gray slacks, a black shirt, and her glasses hung about her neck on a gold chain.

"Vice Admiral on deck," Mendez announced.

They all snapped straighter.

A man six years Dr. Halsey's senior strode to the stage. His short silver hair looked like a steel helmet. His gait had a strange lope to it—what crewmen called "space walk"—from spending too much time in microgravity. He wore a simple, unadorned black dress UNSC uniform. No medals or campaign ribbons. The insignia on the forearm of his jacket, however, was unmistakable: the rank of a Vice Admiral.

"At ease, Spartans," he said. "I'm Vice Admiral Stanforth."

The Spartans took their seats in unison.

Dust swirled onstage and collected into a robed figure. Its face was obscured within the shadows of its hood. John could discern no hands at the end of its sleeves.

"And this is Beowulf," Vice Admiral Stanforth said as he gestured to the ghostly creature. Stanforth's voice was calm, but distaste was evident on his face. "He is our AI attaché with the Office of Naval Intelligence."

He turned away from the AI. "We have several important issues to cover this morning, so let's get started."

The lights dimmed. An amber sun appeared in the center of the room, with three planets in close orbit.

"This is Harvest," he said. "Population of approximately three million. Although on the periphery of UNSC-controlled space, this world is one of our more productive and peaceful colonies."

The holographic view zoomed in on the surface of the world and showed grasslands and forests and a thousand lakes swarming with schools of fish.

"As of military calendar February 3, at 1423 hours, the Harvest orbital platform made long range radar contact with this object."

A blurry outline appeared over the stage. "Spectroscopic

analysis proved inconclusive," Vice Admiral Stanforth said. "The object is constructed of material unknown to us."

A molecular absorption graph appeared on a side screen, spikes and jagged lines indicating the relative proportions of elements.

Beowulf raised a cloaked arm and the image darkened. The words CLASSIFIED—EYES ONLY appeared over the blackened data.

Vice Admiral Stanforth shot a glare at the AI.

"Contact with Harvest," he continued, "was lost shortly thereafter. The Colonial Military Administration sent the scout ship *Argo* to investigate. That ship arrived in-system on April 20, but other than a brief transmission to confirm their exit Slipstream position, no further reports were made.

"In response, Fleet Command assembled a battlegroup to investigate. The group consisted of the destroyer *Heracles*, commanded by Captain Veredi, as well as the frigates *Arabia* and *Vostok*. They entered the Epsilon Indi System on October seventh and discovered the following."

The holograph of the planet Harvest changed. The lush fields and rolling hills transformed, morphing into a cratered, barren desert. Thin gray sunlight reflected off a glassy crust. Heat wavered from the surface. Isolated regions glowed red.

"This is what was left of the colony." The Vice Admiral paused for a moment to stare at the image, and then continued. "We assume that all inhabitants are lost."

Three million lives lost. John couldn't fathom the raw force it had taken to kill so many—for a moment he was torn between horror and envy. He glanced at the Purple Heart pinned to his chest and remembered his lost comrades. How did one simple bullet wound compare with so many wasted lives? He was suddenly no longer proud of the decoration.

"And this is what the *Heracles* battlegroup found in orbit," Vice Admiral Stanforth told them.

The blurry outline that was still visible, hanging in the air, sharpened into crisp focus. It looked smooth and organic, and the hull possessed an odd, opalescent sheen—it looked more like the carapace of an exotic insect than the metal hull of a spacecraft. Recessed into the aft section were pods that pulsed with a purple-white glow. The prow of the craft was swollen like the head of a whale. John thought it possessed an odd, predatory beauty.

"The unidentified vessel," the Vice Admiral said, "launched an immediate attack against our forces."

Blue flashes strobed from the ship. Red motes of light then appeared along its hull. Bolts of energy coalesced into a fiery smear against the blackness of space. The deadly flashes of light impacted on the *Arabia*, splashed across its hull. Its meter of armor plating instantly boiled away, and a plume of ignited atmosphere burst from the breach in the ship's hull. "Those were pulse lasers," Vice Admiral Stanforth explained, "and—if this record is to be believed—some kind of self-guided, superheated plasma weapon."

The *Heracles* and *Vostok* launched salvos of missiles toward the craft. The enemy's lasers shot half before they reached their target. The balance of the missiles impacted, detonated into blossoms of fire . . . that quickly faded. The strange ship shimmered with a semitransparent silver coating, which then vanished.

"They also seem to have some reflective energy shield." Vice Admiral Stanforth took a deep breath and his features hardened into a mask of grim resolve. "The *Vostok* and *Arabia* were lost with all hands. The *Heracles* jumped out of the system, but due to the damage she sustained, it took several weeks for Captain Veredi to make it back to Reach.

"These weapons and defensive systems are currently beyond our technology. Therefore . . . this craft is of nonhuman origin." He paused, then added, "The product of a race with technology far in advance of our own."

A murmur buzzed through the chamber.

"We have, of course, developed a number of first contact scenarios," the Vice Admiral continued, "and Captain Veredi followed our established protocols. We had hoped that contact with a new race would be peaceful. Obviously, this was not the case—the alien vessel did not open fire until our task force attempted to initiate communications."

He paused, considering his words. "Fragments of the enemy's transmissions were intercepted," he continued. "A few words have been translated. We believe they call themselves 'The Covenant.' However, before opening fire, the alien ship broadcast the following message in the clear."

He gestured at Beowulf, who nodded. A moment later, a voice thundered from the amphitheater's speakers. John stiffened in his seat when he heard it; the voice from the speakers sounded odd, artificial—strangely calm and formal, but laden with rage and menace.

"Your destruction is the will of the Gods . . . and we are their instrument."

John was awestruck. He stood.

"Yes, Spartan?" Stanforth said.

"Sir, is this a translation?"

"No," the Vice Admiral replied. "They broadcast this to us in our language. We believe they used some kind of translation system to prepare the message . . . but it means they've been studying us for some time."

John took his seat.

"As of November 1, the UNSC has been ordered to full alert," Stanforth said. "Vice Admiral Preston Cole is mobilizing the largest fleet action in human history to retake the Epsilon Indi System and confront this new threat. Their transmission made one thing perfectly clear: they're looking for a fight."

Only years of military discipline kept John rooted to his seat—otherwise he would have stood up and asked to volunteer on the spot. He would have given anything to go and fight. This was the threat he and the other Spartans had been training for all their lives—he was certain of it. Not scattered rebels, pirates, or political dissidents.

"Because of this UNSC-wide mobilization," Vice Admiral Stanforth continued, "your training schedule will be accelerated to its final phase: Project MJOLNIR."

He stepped away from the podium and clasped his hands behind his back. "To that end, I'm afraid I have another unpleasant announcement." He turned to the Chief. "Chief Petty Officer Mendez will be departing us to train the next group of Spartans. Chief?"

John grabbed the edge of the riser. Chief Mendez had always been there for them, the only constant in the universe. Vice Admiral Stanforth might as well have told him that Reach was leaving the Epsilon Eridani System.

The Chief stepped to the podium and clasped its edges.

"Recruits," he said, "soon your training will be complete, and you will graduate to the rank of Petty Officer Second Class in the UNSC. One of the first things you will learn is that change is part of a soldier's life. You will make and lose friends. You will move. This is part of the job."

He looked to his audience. His dark eyes rested on each one of them. He nodded, seemingly satisfied with what he saw.

"The Spartans are the finest group of soldiers I have ever encountered," he said. "It has been a privilege to train you. Never forget what I've tried to teach you—duty, honor, and sacrifice for the greater good of humanity are the qualities that make you the best."

He was silent a moment, searching for more words. But finding none, he stood at attention and saluted.

"Attention," John barked. The Spartans rose as one and saluted the Chief.

"Dismissed, Spartans," Chief Mendez said. "And good luck." He finished his salute.

The Spartans snapped down their arms. They hesitated, and then reluctantly filed out of the amphitheater.

John stayed behind. He had to talk to Chief Mendez.

Dr. Halsey spoke briefly with the Chief and the Vice Admiral, then she and the Vice Admiral left together. Beowulf backed toward the far wall and faded away like a ghost.

The Chief gathered his hat, spotted John, and walked to him. He nodded to the hologram of the scorched colony, Harvest, still rotating in the air. "One final lesson, Petty Officer," he said. "What tactical options do you have when attacking a stronger opponent?"

"Sir!" John said. "There are two options. Attack swiftly and with full force at their weakest point—take them out quickly before they have a chance to respond."

"Good," he said. "And the other option?"

"Fall back," John replied. "Engage in guerrilla actions or get reinforcements."

The Chief sighed. "Those are the correct answers," he said, "but it may not be enough to be correct this time. Sit, please."

John sat, and the Chief settled next to him on the riser.

"There's a third option." The Chief turned his hat over in his hands. "An option that others may eventually consider. . . ."

"Sir?"

"Surrender," the Chief whispered. "That, however, is never an option for the likes of you and me. We don't have the luxury of backing down." He glanced up at Harvest—a glittering ball of glass. "And I doubt that an enemy like this will *let* us surrender."

"I think I understand, sir."

"Make sure you do. And make sure you don't let anyone else give up." He gazed into the shadows beyond the center platform. "Project MJOLNIR will make the Spartans into something . . . new. Something I could never forge them into. I can't fully explain—that damned ONI spook is still here listening—just trust Dr. Halsey."

The Chief dug into his jacket pocket. "I was hoping to see you before they shipped me out. I have something for you." He set a small metal disk on the riser between them.

"When you first came here," the Chief said, "you fought the trainers when they took this away from you—broke a few fingers as I recall." His chiseled features cracked into a rare smile.

John picked up the disk and examined it. It was an ancient silver coin. He flipped it between his fingers.

"It has an eagle on one side," Mendez said. "That bird is like you—fast and deadly."

John closed his fingers around the quarter. "Thank you, sir."

He wanted to say that he was strong and fast because the Chief had made him so. He wanted to tell him that he was ready to defend humanity against this new threat. He wanted to say that without the Chief, he would have no purpose, no integrity, and no duty to perform. But John didn't have the words. He just sat there.

Mendez stood. "It has been an honor to serve with you." Instead of saluting, he held out his hand.

John got to his feet. He took the Chief's hand and they shook. It took a great deal of effort—every instinct screamed at him to salute.

"Good-bye," Chief Mendez said.

He turned briskly on his heel and strode from the room.

John never saw him again.

CHAPTER TWELVE

1750 HOURS, NOVEMBER 27, 2525 (MILITARY CALENDAR) / UNSC FRIGATE *COMMONWEALTH* EN ROUTE TO THE UNSC DAMASCUS MATERIALS TESTING FACILITY, PLANET CHI CETI 4

The view screen in the bunkroom of the UNSC frigate *Commonwealth* clicked on as the ship entered normal space. Ice particles showered the external camera and gave the distant yellow sun, Chi Ceti, a ghostly ring.

John watched and continued to ponder the word *Mjolnir* as they sped in-system. He had looked it up in the education database. Mjolnir was the hammer used by the Norse god of thunder. Project MJOLNIR had to be some kind of weapon. At least he hoped it was; they needed *something* to fight the Covenant.

If it was a weapon, though, why was it here at the Damascus testing facility, on the very edge of UNSC-controlled space? He had only even heard of this system twenty-four hours ago.

He turned and surveyed the squad. Although this bunkroom had one hundred beds, the Spartans still clustered together, playing cards, polishing boots, reading, exercising. Sam sparred with Kelly—although she had to slow herself down considerably to give him a chance.

John was reminded that he didn't like being on starships. The lack of control was disturbing. If he wasn't stuck in "the freezer"—the starship's cramped, unpleasant cryo chamber—he was left waiting and wondering what their next mission would be.

During the last three weeks the Spartans had handled a variety of minor missions for Dr. Halsey. "Tying up loose ends," she had called it. Putting down rebel factions on Jericho VII. Removing a black-market bazaar near the Roosevelt military base. Each mission had brought them closer to the Chi Ceti System.

John had made sure every member of his squad had participated in these missions. They had performed flawlessly. There had been no losses. Chief Mendez would have been proud of them.

"Spartan-117," Dr. Halsey's voice blared over the loudspeaker. *"Report to the bridge immediately."*

John snapped to attention and keyed the intercom. "Yes, ma'am!" He turned to Sam. "Get everyone ready, in case we're needed. On the double."

"Affirmative," Sam said. "You heard the Petty Officer. Dog those cards. Get into uniform, soldier!"

John double-timed it to the elevator and punched the code for the bridge.

The doors parted and he stepped onto the bridge. Every wall had a screen. Some showed stars and the distant red smear of a nebula. Other screens displayed the fusion reactor status and spectrums of microwave broadcasts in the system.

A brass railing ringed the center of the bridge, and within sat four Junior Lieutenants at their stations: navigation, weapons, communications, and ship operations.

John halted and saluted Captain Wallace, then nodded to Dr. Halsey.

Captain Wallace stood with his right arm crooked behind his back. His left arm was missing from the elbow down.

John remained saluting until the Captain returned the gesture.

"Over here, please," Dr. Halsey said. "I want you to see this."

John walked across the rubberized deck and gave his full attention to the screen Dr. Halsey and Captain Wallace were scrutinizing. It displayed deconvoluted radar signals. It looked like tangled yarn to John.

"There—" Dr. Halsey pointed to a blip on the screen. "It's there again."

Captain Wallace stroked his dark beard, thinking, then said, "That puts our ghost at eighty million kilometers. Even if it were a ship, it would take a full hour to get within weapons range. And besides—" He waved at the screen. "—it's gone again."

"May I suggest that we go to battle stations, Captain?" Dr. Halsey told him.

"I don't see the point," he said condescendingly; the Captain was clearly less than pleased about having a civilian on his bridge.

"We haven't let this be widely known," she said, "but when the aliens were first detected at Harvest, they appeared at extreme range . . . and then they were suddenly much closer."

"An intrasystem jump?" John asked.

Dr. Halsey smiled at him. "Correctly surmised, Spartan."

"That's not possible," Captain Wallace remarked. "Slipstream space can't be navigated that accurately."

"You mean *we* cannot navigate with that kind of accuracy," she said.

The Captain clenched and unclenched his jaw. He clicked the intercom. "General quarters: all hands to battle stations. Seal bulkheads. I repeat: all hands, battle stations. This is not a drill. Reactors to ninety percent. Come about to course one two five."

The bridge lights darkened to a red hue. The deck rumbled beneath John's boots and the entire ship tilted as it changed heading. Pressure doors slammed shut and sealed John on the bridge.

The *Commonwealth* stabilized on her new heading, and Dr. Halsey crossed her arms. She leaned over and whispered to John, "We'll be using the *Commonwealth*'s dropship to go to the testing facility on Chi Ceti Four. We have to get to Project MJOL-

NIR." She turned back and watched the radar screen. "Before *they* do. So get the others ready."

"Yes, ma'am." John keyed the intercom. "Sam, muster the squad in Bay Alpha. I want that Pelican loaded and ready for drop in fifteen minutes."

"We'll have it done in ten," Sam replied. *"Faster if those Longsword interceptor pilots get out of our way."*

John would have given anything to be belowdecks with the others. He felt as if he were being left behind.

The radar screen flashed with blobs of eerie green light . . . almost as if the space around the *Commonwealth* were boiling.

The collision alarm sounded.

"Brace for impact!" Captain Wallace said. He laced his arm around the brass railing.

John grabbed an emergency handhold on the wall.

Something appeared three thousand kilometers off the *Commonwealth*'s prow. It was a sleek oval with a single seam running along its lateral edge from stem to stern. Tiny lights winked on and off along its hull. A faint purple-tinged glow emitted from the tail. The ship was only a third the size of the *Commonwealth*.

"A Covenant ship," Dr. Halsey said, and she involuntarily backed away from the view screens.

Captain Wallace scowled. "COM officer: send a signal to Chi Ceti—see if they can send us some reinforcements."

"Aye, sir."

Blue flashes flickered along the hull of the alien ship—so bright that even filtered through the external camera, they still made John's eyes water.

The outer hull of the *Commonwealth* sizzled and popped. Three screens filled with static.

"Pulse lasers!" the Lieutenant at the ops station screamed. "Communication dish destroyed. Armor in sections three and four at twenty-five percent. Hull breach in section three. Sealing now." The Lieutenant swiveled in his seat, sweat beaded on his forehead. "Ship AI core memory overloaded," he said.

With the AI offline, the ship could still fire weapons and navigate through Slipstream space, but John knew it would take more time to make jump calculations.

"Come to heading zero three zero, declination one eight zero," Captain Wallace ordered. "Arm Archer missile pods A through F. And give me a firing solution."

"Aye aye," the navigation and weapons officers said. "A through F pods armed." They furiously tapped away on their keypads. Seconds ticked by. "Firing solution ready, sir."

"Fire."

"Pods A through F firing!"

The *Commonwealth* had twenty-six pods, each loaded with thirty Archer high-explosive missiles. On screen, pods A through F opened, and launched—180 plumes of rocket exhaust that traced a path from the *Commonwealth* to the alien ship.

The enemy changed course, rotated so that the top of the ship faced the incoming missiles. It then moved straight up at an alarming speed.

The Archer missiles altered their trajectory to track the ship, but half their number streaked past the target, clean misses.

The others impacted. Fire covered the skin of the alien ship.

"Good work, Lieutenant," Captain Wallace said, and he clapped the young officer on the shoulder.

Dr. Halsey frowned and stared at the screen. "No," she whispered. "Wait."

The fire flared, then dimmed. The skin of the alien ship rippled like heat wavering off a hot road in the summer. It fluttered with a metallic silver sheen, then brilliant white—and the fire faded, revealing the ship beneath.

It was completely undamaged.

"Energy shields," Dr. Halsey muttered. She tapped her lower lip, thinking. "Even ships this small have energy shielding."

"Lieutenant," the Captain barked at the NAV officer. "Cut main engines and fire maneuvering thrusters. Rotate and track so that we're pointing at that thing."

"Aye aye, sir."

The distant rumbling of the *Commonwealth*'s main engines dimmed and stopped and she turned about. Her inertia kept the ship speeding toward the testing facility—now flying backward.

"What are you doing, Captain?" Dr. Halsey asked.

"Arm the MAC," Captain Wallace told the weapons officer. "A heavy round."

John understood: turning your back to an enemy only gave them an advantage.

The MAC—Magnetic Accelerator Cannon—was the *Commonwealth*'s main weapon. It fired a super-dense ferric tungsten shell. The tremendous mass and velocity of the projectile obliterated most ships on impact. Unlike the Archer missiles, a MAC round was an unguided projectile; the firing solution had to be perfect in order to hit the target—not an easy thing to do when both ships were moving rapidly.

"MAC capacitors charging," the weapons officer announced.

The Covenant ship turned its side toward the *Commonwealth*.

"Yes," the Captain murmured. "Give me a bigger target."

Pinpoints of blue light glowed and then flared along the alien hull.

The tactical view screens on the nose of the *Commonwealth* went dead.

John heard sizzling overhead—then the muffled thumps of explosive decompressions.

"More pulse laser hits," the ops officer reported. "Armor in sections three through seven down to four centimeters. Navigation dish destroyed. Hull breaches on decks two, five, and nine. We have a leak in the port fuel tanks." The Lieutenant's hand shakily danced over the controls. "Pumping fuel to starboard reverse tanks. Sealing sections."

John shifted on his feet. He had to move. Act. Standing here—unable to get to his squad, not doing anything—was counter to every fiber of his being.

"MAC at one hundred percent," the weapons officer shouted. "Ready to fire!"

"Fire!" Captain Wallace ordered.

The lights on the bridge dimmed and the *Commonwealth* shuddered. The MAC bolt launched through space—a red-hot metal slug moving at thirty thousand meters per second.

The Covenant ship's engines flared to life and the ship veered away—

—Too late. The heavy round closed and slammed into the target's prow.

The Covenant ship reeled backward through space. Its energy shields shimmered and glowed lightning-bright . . . then flickered, dimmed, and went out.

The bridge crew let out a victory cheer.

Except Dr. Halsey. John watched the view screen as she adjusted the camera controls and zoomed in on the Covenant ship.

The vessel's erratic spinning slowed and it came to a stop. The ship's nose was crumpled and atmosphere vented into vacuum. Tiny fires flickered inside. The ship slowly came about and started back toward them—gaining speed.

"It should have been destroyed," she whispered.

Tiny red blobs appeared on the hull of the Covenant ship. They glowed and intensified and drifted together, collecting along the lateral line of the craft.

Captain Wallace said, "Make ready another heavy round."

"Aye aye," the weapons officer said. "Charge at thirty percent. Firing solution online, sir."

"No," Dr. Halsey said. "Evasive maneuvers, Captain. Now!"

"I won't have my command second-guessed, ma'am." The Captain turned to face her. "And with respect, *Doctor*, second-guessed by someone with no combat experience." He stiffened and placed his hand behind his back. "I cannot have you removed from the bridge because the bulkheads are sealed . . . but another outburst like that, Doctor, and I *will* have you gagged."

John shot a quick glance to Dr. Halsey. Her face flushed—he couldn't tell from shame or rage.

"MAC at fifty percent charge."

The red light continued to collect along the lateral line of the Covenant ship until it was a solid band. It brightened.

"Eighty percent charge."

"They're turning, sir," the NAV officer announced. "She's coming to starboard."

"Ninety-five percent charge—one hundred," the weapons officer announced

"Send them to Hades, Lieutenant. Fire."

The lights dimmed again. The *Commonwealth* shuddered and a bolt of thunder and fire tore through the blackness.

The Covenant ship stood its ground. The bloodred light that had pooled on its lateral line burst forth—streaked toward the *Commonwealth,* passing the MAC round a mere kilometer away. The red light glowed and pulsed almost as if it were liquid; its edges roiled and fluttered. It elongated into a teardrop of ruby light five meters long.

"Evasive maneuvers," Captain Wallace cried. "Emergency thrusters to port!"

The *Commonwealth* slowly moved out of the trajectory path of the Covenant's energy weapon.

The MAC round struck the Covenant vessel amidships. Its shield shimmered and bubbled . . . then disappeared. The MAC round punched through the craft and sent it spinning out of control.

The inbound ball of light moved, too. It started tracking the *Commonwealth.*

"Engines—full power astern," the Captain ordered. The *Commonwealth* rumbled and slowed.

The light should have sped past them; instead, it sharply arced and struck her port amidships.

The air filled with a popping and sizzling. The *Commonwealth* listed to starboard, then rolled completely over and continued to tumble.

"Stabilize," the Captain cried. "Starboard thrusters."

"Fire reported in sections one through twenty," the ops officer said, panic creeping into his voice. "Decks two through seven in section one . . . have melted, sir. They're gone."

It grew noticeably hotter on the bridge. Sweat beaded on John's back and trickled down his spine. He had never felt so helpless. Were his teammates belowdecks alive or dead?

"All port armor destroyed. Decks two through five in sections three, four, and five are now out of contact, sir. It's burning through us!"

Captain Wallace stood without saying a word. He stared at their one remaining view screen.

Dr. Halsey stepped forward. "Respectfully, Captain, I suggest that you alert the crew to get on respirator packs. Give them thirty seconds, then vent the atmosphere on all decks, except the bridge."

The COM officer looked to the Captain.

"Do it," the Captain said. "Sound the alert."

"Deck thirteen destroyed," the ops officer announced. "Fire is getting close to the reactor. Hull structure starting to buckle."

"Vent atmosphere now," Captain Wallance ordered.

"Aye aye," the ops officer replied.

There was the sound of thumping through the hull . . . then nothing.

"Fire is dying out," the ops officer said. "Hull temperature cooling—stabilizing."

"What the hell did they hit us with?" Captain Wallace demanded.

"Plasma," Dr. Halsey replied. "But not any plasma we

know . . . they can actually guide its trajectory through space, without any detectable mechanism. Amazing."

"Captain," the navigator said. "Alien ship is pursuing."

The Covenant vessel—a red-rimmed hole punched through its center—turned and started toward the *Commonwealth*.

"How . . . ?" Captain Wallace said unbelievingly. He quickly regained his wits. "Ready another MAC heavy round."

The weapons officer slowly said, "MAC system destroyed, Captain."

"We're sitting ducks, then," the Captain murmured.

Dr. Halsey leaned against the brass railing. "Not quite. The *Commonwealth* carries three nuclear missiles, correct, Captain?"

"A detonation this close would destroy us as well."

She frowned and cupped her hand to her chin, thinking.

"Excuse me, sir," John said. "The aliens' tactics thus far have been unnecessarily vicious—like those of an animal. They didn't have to take that second MAC round while they fired at us. But they wanted to position themselves to fire. In my opinion, sir, they would stop and engage *anything* that challenged them."

The Captain looked to Dr. Halsey.

She shrugged and then nodded. "The Longsword interceptors?"

Captain Wallace turned his back to them and covered his face with his one hand. He sighed, nodded, and clicked on the intercom.

"Longsword Squadron Delta, this is the Captain. Get your ships into the black, boys, and engage the enemy ship. I need you to buy us some time."

"Roger that, sir. We're ready to launch. On our way."

"Turn us around," the Captain told the NAV officer. "Give me best speed on a vector toward Chi Ceti Four orbit."

"Coolant leaks in the reactor, sir," the ops officer said. "We can push the engines to thirty percent. No more."

"Give me fifty percent," he said. He turned to the weapons

officer. "Arm one of our Shiva warheads. Set proximity fuse to one hundred meters."

"Yes, sir."

The *Commonwealth* spun about. John felt the change in his stomach and he tightened his grip on the railing. The spinning slowed, stopped, then the ship accelerated.

"Reactor red-lining," the ops officer reported. "Meltdown in twenty-five seconds."

Over the speakers, there was a crackle, a hiss of static, then: *"Longsword interceptors engaging the enemy, sir."*

On the remaining aft camera, there were flickers of light—the cold blue strobes of Covenant energy weapons, and the red-orange fireballs of the Longswords' missiles.

"Launch the missile," the Captain said.

"Meltdown in ten seconds."

"Missile away."

A plume of exhaust divided the darkness of space.

"Five seconds to meltdown," the ops officer said. "Four, three, two—"

"Shunt drive plasma to space," the Captain ordered. "Cut power to all systems."

The Covenant ship was silhouetted for a split second by pure white—then the view screen snapped off. The bridge lights went dead.

John could see everything, though. The bridge officers, Dr. Halsey as she clutched onto the railing, and Captain Wallace as he stood and saluted the pilots he had just sent to die.

The hull of the *Commonwealth* rumbled and pinged as the shock wave enveloped them. It grew louder, a subsonic roar that shook John to his bones.

The noise seemed to go on forever in the darkness. It faded . . . then it was completely silent.

"Power us back up," the Captain said. "Slowly. Give me ten percent from the reactors if we can manage."

The bridge lights came on, dimly, but they worked.

"Report," the Captain ordered.

"All sensors offline," the op officer said. "Resetting backup computer. Hang on. Scanning now. Lots of debris. It's hot back there. All Longsword interceptors vaporized." He looked up, the color drained from his face. "Covenant ship . . . intact, sir."

"No," the Captain said, and made a fist.

"It's moving off, though," the op officer said with a visible sigh of relief. "Very slowly."

"What does it take to destroy one of those things?" the Captain whispered.

"We don't know if our weapons *can* destroy them," Dr. Halsey said. "But at least we know we can slow them down."

The Captain stood straighter. "Best speed to the Damascus testing facility. We will execute a flyby orbit, and then proceed to a point twenty million kilometers distant to make repairs."

"Captain?" Dr. Halsey said. "A flyby?"

"I have orders to get you to the facility and retrieve whatever Section Three has stowed there, ma'am. As we fly by, a dropship will take you and your—" He glanced at John. "—crew planet side. If the Covenant ship returns, we will be the bait to lure them away."

"I understand, Captain."

"We'll rendezvous in orbit no later than 1900 hours."

Dr. Halsey turned to John. "We need to hurry. We don't have much time—and there is a great deal I need to show the Spartans."

"Yes, ma'am," John said. He took a long look at the bridge, and hoped he never had to return.

CHAPTER THIRTEEN

1845 HOURS, NOVEMBER 27, 2525 (MILITARY CALENDAR) / UNSC DAMASCUS MATERIALS TESTING FACILITY, PLANET CHI CETI 4

How far down was the testing facility? John and the other Spartans had been confined to a freight elevator for fifteen minutes, and the entire time it had been rapidly descending into the depths of Chi Ceti 4.

The last place John wanted to be was in another confined space.

The doors finally slid open, and they emerged in what appeared to be a well-lit hangar. The far end had an obstacle course set up with walls, trenches, dummy targets, and barbed wire.

Three technicians and at least a dozen AI figures were busy in the center of the room. John had seen AIs before—one at a time. Déjà had once told the Spartans that there were technical reasons why AIs couldn't be in the same place at the same time, but here were many ghostly figures: a mermaid, a samurai warrior, and one made entirely of bright light with comets trailing in her wake.

Dr. Halsey cleared her throat. The technicians turned—the AIs vanished.

John had been so focused on the holograms that he hadn't noticed the forty Plexiglas mannequins set up in rows. On each was a suit of armor.

The armor reminded John of the exoskeletons he had seen during training, but much less bulky, more compact. He stepped closer to one and saw that the suit actually had many layers; the outer layer reflected the overhead lights with a faint green-gold iridescence. It covered the groin, outer thighs, knees, shins, chest, shoulders, and forearms. There was a helmet and an integrated power pack—much smaller than standard Marine "battery sacks." Underneath were intermeshed layers of matte-black metal.

"Project MJOLNIR," Dr. Halsey said. She snapped her fingers and an exploded holographic schematic of the armor appeared next to her.

"The armor's shell is a multilayer alloy of remarkable strength. We recently added a refractive coating to disperse incoming energy weapon attacks—to counter our new enemies." She pointed inside the schematic. "Each battlesuit also has a gel-filled layer to regulate temperature; this layer can reactively change in density. Against the skin of the operator, there is a moisture-absorbing cloth suit, and biomonitors that constantly adjust the suit's temperature and fit. There's also an onboard computer that interfaces with your standard-issue neural implant."

She gestured and the schematic collapsed so that it only displayed the outer layers. As the image changed, John glimpsed veinlike microcapillaries, a dense sandwich of optical crystal, a circulating pump, even what looked like a miniature fusion cell in the backpack.

"Most importantly," Dr. Halsey said, "the armor's inner structure is composed of a new reactive metal liquid crystal. It is amorphous, yet fractally scales and amplifies force. In simplified terms, the armor doubles the wearer's strength, and enhances the reaction speed of a normal human by a factor of five."

She waved her hand through the hologram. "There is one problem, however. This system is so reactive that our previous tests with unaugmented volunteers ended in—" She searched for the right word. "—failure." She nodded to one of the technicians.

A flat video appeared in the air. It showed a Marine officer, a Lieutenant, being fitted with the MJOLNIR armor. "Power is on," someone said from off screen. "Move your right arm, please."

The soldier's arm blurred forward with incredible speed. The Marine's stoic expression collapsed into shock, surprise, and pain as his arm shattered. He convulsed—shuddered and screamed. As he jerked in pain, John could hear the sounds of bones breaking.

The man's own agony-induced spasms were killing him.

Halsey waved the video away. "Normal humans don't have the reaction time or strength required to drive this system," she explained. "You do. Your enhanced musculature and the metal and ceramic layers that have been bonded to your skeleton *should* be enough to allow you to harness the armor's power. There has been . . . insufficient computer modeling, however. There will be some risk. You'll have to move very slowly and deliberately until you get a feel for the armor and how it works. It cannot be powered down, nor can the response be scaled back. Do you understand?"

"Yes, ma'am," the Spartans answered.

"Questions?"

John raised his hand. "When do we get to try them, Doctor?"

"Right now," she said. "Volunteers?"

Every Spartan raised a hand.

Dr. Halsey allowed herself a tiny smile. She surveyed them, and finally, she turned to John.

"You've always been lucky, John," she said. "Let's go."

He stepped forward. The technicians fitted him as the others watched and the pieces of the MJOLNIR system were assembled around his body. It was like a giant three-dimensional puzzle.

"Please breathe normally," Dr. Halsey told him, "but otherwise remain absolutely still."

John held himself as motionless as he could. The armor shifted and melded to the contours of his form. It was like a second skin . . . and much lighter than he had thought it would be. It heated, then cooled—then matched the temperature of his body. If he closed his eyes, he wouldn't have known he was encased.

They set the helmet over his head.

Health monitors, motion sensors, suit status indicators pulsed into life. A targeting reticle flickered on the heads-up display.

"Everyone move back," Halsey ordered.

The Spartans—from their expressions, they were concerned for him, but still intensely curious—cleared a ring with a radius of three meters around him.

"Listen carefully to me, John," Dr. Halsey said. "I just want you to think, and only think, about moving your arm up to chest level. Stay relaxed."

He willed his arm to move, and his hand and forearm sprang forward to chest level. The slightest motion translated his thought to motion at lightning speed. It had been so fast—if he hadn't been attached to his arm, he might have missed that it had happened at all.

The Spartans gasped.

Sam applauded. Even lightning-fast Kelly seemed impressed.

Dr. Halsey slowly coached John through the basics of walking and gradually built up the speed and complexity of his motions. After fifteen minutes he could walk, run, and jump almost without thinking of the difference between suit motion and normal motion.

"Petty Officer, run through the obstacle course," Dr. Halsey said. "We will proceed to fit the other Spartans. We don't have a great deal of time left."

John snapped a salute without thinking. His hand bounced

off his helmet and a dull ache throbbed in his hand. His wrist would be bruised. If his bones hadn't been reinforced, he knew they would have been pulverized.

"Carefully, Petty Officer. Very carefully, please."

"Yes, ma'am!"

John focused his mind on motion. He leaped over a three-meter-high wall. He punched at concrete targets—shattering them. He threw knives, sinking them up to their hafts into target dummies. He slid under barbed wire as bullets zinged over his head. He stood, and let the rounds deflect off the armor. To his amazement, he actually dodged one or two of the rounds.

Soon the other Spartans joined him on the course. Everyone ran awkwardly through the obstacles, though they had no coordination. John expressed his worries to Dr. Halsey. "It will come to you soon enough. You've already received some subliminal training during your last cryo sleep—" Dr. Halsey told them. "—now all you need is time to get used to the suits."

More worrisome to John was the realization that they'd have to learn how to work together all over again. Their usual hand signals were too exaggerated now—a slight wave or tremble translated into full-force punches or uncontrolled vibrations. They would have to use the COM channels for the time being.

As soon as he thought of this, his suit tagged and monitored the other MJOLNIR suits. Their standard-issue UNSC neural chip—implanted in every UNSC soldier at induction—identified friendly soldiers and displayed them on their helmet HUDs. But this was different—all he had to do was concentrate on them, and a secure COM channel opened. It was extremely efficient.

And much to his relief, after drilling for thirty minutes, the Spartans had recovered all of their original group coordination, and more.

On one level, John moved the suit and, in return, it moved him. On another level, however, communication with his squad was so easy and natural, he could move and direct them as if they were an extension of his body.

Over the hangar's speakers, the Spartans heard Dr. Halsey's voice: "Spartans, so far so good. If anyone is experiencing difficulties with the suit or its controls, please report in."

"I think I'm in love," Sam replied. "Oh—sorry, ma'am. I didn't think that was an open channel."

"Flawless amplification of speed and power," Kelly said. "It's like I've been training in this suit for years."

"Do we get to keep them?" John asked.

"You're the only ones who can use them, Petty Officer. Who else could we give them to? We—" A technician handed her a headset. "One moment, please. Report, Captain."

Captain Wallace's voice broke over the COM channels. *"We have contact with the Covenant ship, ma'am. Extreme range. Their Slipspace engines must still be damaged. They are moving toward us via normal space."*

"Your repair status?" she asked.

"Long-range communications inoperable. Slipstream generators offline. MAC system destroyed. We have two fusion missiles and twenty Archer missile pods intact. Armor plating is at twenty percent." There was a long hiss of static. "If you need more time . . . I can try and draw them away."

"No, Captain," she replied, and carefully scrutinized John and the other armored Spartans. "We're going to have to fight them . . . and this time we have to win."

CHAPTER FOURTEEN

2037 HOURS, NOVEMBER 27, 2525 (MILITARY CALENDAR) / IN ORBIT OVER CHI CETI 4

John piloted the Pelican through the exit burn of their orbital path, then sent the ship toward the last known position of the *Commonwealth*. The frigate had moved ten million kilometers in-system from their rendezvous point.

Dr. Halsey sat in the copilot's seat, fidgeting with her space suit. In the aft compartment were the Spartans, the three technicians from the Damascus facility, and a dozen spare MJOLNIR suits.

Missing, however, were the AIs John had seen when they had first arrived. All Dr. Halsey had time to do was remove their memory processor cubes. It was a tremendous waste to leave such expensive equipment behind.

Dr. Halsey examined the ship's short-range detection gear, then said, "Captain Wallace may be trying to use Chi Ceti's magnetic field to deflect the Covenant's plasma weapon. Try and catch up, Petty Officer."

"Yes, ma'am." John pushed the engines to 100 percent.

"Covenant ship to port," she said, "three million kilometers and closing on the *Commonwealth*."

John bumped up the magnification onscreen and spotted the ship. The alien vessel's hull was bent at a thirty-degree angle from the impact of the MAC heavy round, but it still moved at almost twice the speed of the *Commonwealth*.

"Doctor," John asked, "does the MJOLNIR armor operate in vacuum?"

"Of course," she replied. "It was one of our first design considerations. The suit can recycle air for ninety minutes. It's shielded against radiation and EMP as well."

He then spoke to Sam over his COM link. "What kind of missiles is this bird carrying?"

"Wait one moment, sir," Sam replied. His voice returned a moment later. *"We have two rocket pods with sixteen HE Anvil-IIs each."*

"I want you to assemble a team and go EVA. Remove those warheads from the wing pods."

"I'm on it," Sam said.

Halsey tried to push her glasses up higher on her nose—instead she bumped up against the faceplate of her suit's helmet. "May I ask what you have in mind, Squad Leader?"

John left his COM channel open so the Spartans would hear his reply.

"Requesting permission to attack the Covenant ship, ma'am."

Her blue eyes widened. "Most certainly not," she said. "If a warship like the *Commonwealth* couldn't destroy it, a Pelican is certainly no match for them."

"Not the Pelican, no," John agreed. "But I believe we Spartans are. If we get *inside* the enemy ship, we can destroy her."

Doctor Halsey considered, tapping her lower lip. "How will you get onboard?"

"We go EVA and use thruster packs to intercept the Covenant ship as it passes en route to the *Commonwealth*."

She shook her head. "One slight error in your trajectory, and you could miss by kilometers," Dr. Halsey remarked.

A pause.

"I don't miss, ma'am," John said.

"They have reflective shields."

"True," John replied. "But the ship is damaged. They may have had to lower or reduce shielding in order to conserve power—and if we have to, we can use one of our own warheads to punch a small hole in the barrier." He paused, then added, "There's also a large hole in their hull. Their shield may not cover that space entirely."

Dr. Halsey whispered, "It's a tremendous risk."

"With respect, ma'am, it's a bigger risk to sit here and do nothing. After they finish with the *Commonwealth* . . . they'll come for us and we'll have to fight them anyway. Better to strike first."

She stared off into space, lost in thought.

Finally, she sighed in resignation. "Very well. Go." She transferred the pilot controls to her station. "And blow the hell out of them."

John climbed into the aft compartment.

His Spartans stood at attention. He felt a rush of pride; they were ready to follow him as he leaped literally into the jaws of death.

"I've got the warheads," Sam said. It was hard to mistake Sam even with his reflective blast shield covering his face. He was the largest Spartan—even more imposing encased in the armor.

"Everyone's got one," Sam continued as he handed John a metal shell. "Timers and detonators are already rigged. Stuck on a patch of adhesive polymer; they'll cling to your suit."

"Spartans," John said, "grab thruster packs and make ready to go EVA. Everyone else—" He motioned to the three technicians. "—get into the forward cabin. If we fail, they'll be coming after the Pelican. Protect Dr. Halsey."

He moved aft. Kelly handed him a thruster pack and he slipped it on.

"Covenant ship approaching," Halsey called out. "I'm pumping out your atmosphere to avoid explosive decompression when I drop the back hatch."

"We'll only get one shot at this," John said to the other

Spartans. "Plot an intercept trajectory and fire your thrusters at max burn. If the target changes course, you'll have to make a best-guess correction on the fly. If you make it, we'll regroup outside the hole in their hull. If you miss—we'll pick you up after we're done."

He hesitated, then added, "And if we don't succeed, then power down your systems and wait for UNSC reinforcements to retrieve you. Live to fight another day. Don't waste your lives."

There was a moment of silence.

"If anyone has a better plan, speak up now."

Sam patted John on the back. "This is a great plan. It'll be easier than Chief Mendez's playground. A bunch of little kids could pull it off."

"Sure," John said. "Everyone ready?"

"Sir," they said. "We're ready, sir!"

John flipped the safety off and then punched in the code to open the Pelican's tail. The mechanism opened soundlessly in the vacuum. Outside was infinite blackness. He had a feeling of falling through space—but the vertigo quickly passed.

He positioned himself on the edge of the ramp, both hands gripping a safety handle overhead.

The Covenant ship was a tiny dot in the center of his helmet's view screen. He plotted a course and fired the thruster pack on maximum burn.

Acceleration slammed him into the thruster harness. He knew the others would launch right after him, but he couldn't turn to see them.

It occurred to him then that the Covenant ship might identify the Spartans as incoming missiles—and their point-defense lasers were too damn accurate.

John clicked on the COM channel. "Doctor, we could use a few decoys if Captain Wallace can spare them."

"Understood," she said.

The Covenant vessel grew rapidly in his display. A burst from its engines and it turned slightly.

Traveling at one hundred million kilometers an hour, even a minor course correction meant that he could miss by tens of thousands of kilometers. John carefully corrected his vector.

The pulse laser on the side of the Covenant ship glowed, built up energy, until it was dazzling neon blue, then discharged—but not at him.

John saw explosions in his peripheral vision. The *Commonwealth* had fired a salvo of her Archer missiles. Around him in the dark were puffballs of red-orange detonations—utterly silent.

John's velocity now almost matched that of the ship. He eased toward the hull—twenty meters, ten, five . . . and then the Covenant ship started to pull away from him.

It was traveling too fast. He tapped his altitude thrusters and pointed himself perpendicular to the hull.

The Covenant hull accelerated under him . . . but he was dropping closer.

He stretched out his arms. The hull raced past his fingertips a meter away.

John's fingers brushed against something—it felt semiliquid. He could see his hand skimming a near-invisible, glassy, shimmering surface: the energy shield.

Damn. Their shields were still up. He glanced to either side. The huge hole in their hull was nowhere in sight.

He slid over the hull, unable to grab hold of it.

No. He refused to accept that he had made it this far, only to fail now.

A pulse laser flashed a hundred meters away; his faceplate barely adjusted in time. The flash nearly blinded him. John blinked and then saw a silvery film rush back around the bulbous base of the laser turret.

The shield dropped to let the laser fire?

The laser started to build up charge again.

He would have to act quickly. His timing had to be perfect. If he hit that turret before it fired, he'd bounce off. If he hit the turret *as* it fired . . . there wouldn't be much left of him.

The turret glowed, intensely bright. John set his thrust harness on a maximum burn toward the laser, noting the rapidly dwindling fuel charge. He closed his eyes, saw the blinding flash through his lids, felt the heat on his face, then opened his eyes—just in time to crash and bounce into the hull.

The hull plates were smooth, but had grooves and odd, organic crenellations—perfect fingerholds. The difference between his momentum and the ship's nearly pulled his arms out of their sockets. He gritted his teeth and tightened his grip.

He had made it.

John pulled himself along the hull toward the hole the *Commonwealth*'s MAC round had punched in the ship.

Only two other Spartans waited for him there.

"What took you so long?" Sam's voice crackled over the COM channel. The other Spartan lifted her helmet's reflective blast shield. He saw Kelly's face.

"I think we're it," Kelly said. "I'm not getting any other responses over the COM channels."

That meant either the Covenant ship shielded their transmissions . . . or there were no Spartans left to communicate with. John pushed that last thought aside.

The hole was ten meters across. Jagged metal teeth pointed inward. John looked over the edge and saw that the MAC heavy round had indeed passed all the way through. He saw tiers of exposed decks, severed conduits, and sheared metal beams—and through the other side, black space and stars.

They climbed down.

John immediately fell down on the first deck.

They continued inward, scaling the metal walls until they were approximately in the middle of the ship.

John paused and saw the stars wheel outside either end of

the hole. The Covenant ship must be turning. They were engaging the *Commonwealth*.

"We better hurry."

He stepped onto an exposed deck, and the gravity settled his stomach—giving him an up-and-down orientation.

"Weapons check," John told them.

They examined their assault rifles. The guns had made the journey intact. John slipped in a clip of armor-piercing rounds, noting with pleasure that the suit immediately aligned the sight profile of the gun with his targeting system.

He slung the weapon and checked the HE warhead attached to his hip. The timer and detonator looked undamaged.

John faced a sealed set of sliding pressure doors. It was smooth and soft to his touch. It could have been made of metal or plastic . . . or could have been alive, for all he knew.

He and Sam grabbed either side and pulled, strained, and then the mechanism gave and the doors released. There was a hiss of atmosphere, a dark hallway beyond. They entered in formation—covering each other's blind spots.

The ceiling was three meters high. It made John feel small.

"You think they need all this space because they're so large?" Kelly asked.

"We'll know soon," he told her.

They crouched, weapons at the ready, and moved slowly down the corridor, John and Kelly in front. They rounded a corner and stopped at another set of pressure doors. John grabbed the seam.

"Hang on," Kelly said. She knelt next to a pad with nine buttons. Each button was inscribed with runic alien script. "These characters are strange, but one of them has to open this." She touched one and it lit, then she keyed another. Gas hissed into the corridor. "At least the pressure is equalized," she said.

John double-checked his sensors. Nothing . . . though the alien metal inside the ship could be blocking the scans.

"Try another," Sam said.

She did—and the doors slid apart.

The room was inhabited.

An alien creature stood a meter and half tall, a biped. Its knobby, scaled skin was a sickly, mottled yellow; purple and yellow fins ran along the crest of its skull and its forearms. Glittering, bulbous eyes protruded from skull-like hollows in the alien's elongated head.

The Master Chief had read the UNSC's first contact scenarios—they called for cautious attempts at communication. He couldn't imagine communicating with something like this . . . thing. It reminded him of the carrion birds on Reach—vicious and unclean.

The creature stood there, frozen for a moment—staring at the human interlopers. Then it screeched and reached for something on its belt, its movements darting and birdlike.

The Spartans shouldered their weapons and fired a trio of bursts with pinpoint accuracy.

Armor-piercing rounds tore into the creature, shredding its chest and head. It crumpled into a heap without a sound, dead before it hit the deck. Thick blood oozed from the corpse. "That was easy," Sam remarked. He nudged the creature with his boot. "They sure aren't as tough as their ships."

"Let's hope it stays that way," John replied.

"I'm getting a radiation reading this way," Kelly said. She gestured deeper into the vessel.

They continued down the corridor and took a side branch. Kelly dropped a NAV marker, and its double blue triangle pulsed once on their heads-up displays.

They stopped at another set of pressure doors. Sam and John took up flanking positions to cover her. Kelly punched the same buttons she had punched before and the doors slid apart.

Another of the creatures was there. It stood in a circular

room with crystalline control panels and a large window. This time, however, the vulture-headed creature didn't scream or look particularly surprised.

This one looked angry.

The creature held a clawlike device in its hand—leveled at John.

John and Kelly fired. Bullets filled the air and pinged off a silver shimmering barrier in front of the creature.

A bolt of blue heat blasted from the claw. The blast was similar to the plasma that had hit the *Commonwealth* . . . and boiled a third of it away.

The bolt sizzled over their heads.

Sam dove forward and knocked John out of the blast's path; the energy burst caught Sam in the side. The reflective coating of his MJOLNIR armor flared. He fell clutching his side, but still managed to fire his weapon.

John and Kelly rolled on their backs and sprayed gunfire at the creature.

Bullets peppered the alien—each one bounced and ricocheted off the energy shield.

John glanced at his ammo counter—half gone.

"Keep firing," he ordered.

The alien kept up a stream of answering fire—energy blasts hammered into Sam, who fell to the deck, his weapon empty.

John charged forward and slammed his foot into the alien's shield and knocked it out of line. He jammed the barrel of his rifle into the alien's screeching mouth and squeezed the trigger.

The armor-piercing rounds punctured the alien and spattered the back wall with blood and bits of bone.

John rose and helped Sam up.

"I'm okay," Sam said, holding his side and grimacing. "Just a little singed." The reflective coating on his armor was blackened.

"You sure?"

Sam waved him away.

John paused over the remaining bits of the alien. He spotted a glint of metal, an armguard, and he picked it up. He tapped one of three buttons on the device, but nothing happened. He strapped in onto his forearm. Dr. Halsey might find it useful.

They entered the room. The large window was a half-meter thick. It overlooked a large chamber that descended three decks. A cylinder ran the length of the chamber and red light pulsed along its length, like a liquid sloshing back and forth.

Under the window, on their side, rested a smooth angled surface—perhaps a control panel? On its surface were tiny symbols: glowing green dots, bars, and squares.

"That's got to be the source of the radiation," Kelly said, and pointed to the chamber beyond. "Their reactor . . . or maybe a weapons system."

Another alien marched near the cylinder. It spotted John. A silver shimmer appeared around it. It screeched and wobbled in alarm, then scrambled for cover.

"Trouble," John said.

"I've got an idea." Sam limped forward. "Hand me those warheads." John did as he asked, so did Kelly. "We shoot out that window, set the timers on the warheads, and toss them down there. That should start the party."

"Let's do it before they call in reinforcements," John said.

They turned and fired at the crystal. It crackled, splintered, then shattered.

"Toss those warheads," Sam said, "and let's get out of here."

John set the timers. "Three minutes," he said. "That'll give us just enough time to get topside and get away."

He turned to Sam. "You'll have to stay and hold them off. That's an order."

"What are you talking about?" Kelly said.

"Sam knows."

Sam nodded. "I think I can hold them off that long." He looked at John and then Kelly. He turned and showed them the burn in the side of his suit. There was a hole the size of his fist, and beneath that, the skin was blackened and cracked. He smiled, but his teeth were gritted in pain.

"That's nothing," Kelly said. "We'll get you patched up in no time. Once we get back—" Her mouth slowly dropped open.

"Exactly," Sam whispered. "Getting back is going to be a problem for me."

"The hole." John reached out to touch it. "We don't have any way to seal it."

Kelly shook her head.

"If I step off this boat, I'm dead from the decompression," Sam said, and shrugged.

"No," Kelly growled. "No—everyone gets out alive. We don't leave teammates behind."

"He has his orders," John told Kelly.

"You've got to leave me," Sam said softly to Kelly. "And don't tell me you'll give me your suit. It took those techs on Damascus fifteen minutes to fit us. I wouldn't even know where to start to unzip this thing."

John looked to the deck. The Chief had told him he'd have to send men to their deaths. He didn't tell him it would feel like this.

"Don't waste time talking," Sam said. "Our new friends aren't going to wait for us while we figure this out." He started the timers. "There. It's decided." A three-minute countdown appeared in the corner of their heads-up displays. "Now—get going, you two."

John clasped Sam's hand and squeezed it.

Kelly hesitated, then saluted.

John turned and grabbed her arm. "Come on, Spartan. Don't look back."

The truth was, it was John who didn't dare look back. If he had, he would have stayed with Sam. Better to die with a friend than leave him behind. But as much as he wanted to fight and die alongside his friend, he had to set an example for the rest of the Spartans—and live to fight another day.

John and Kelly pushed the pressure doors shut behind them.

"Good-bye," he whispered.

The countdown timer ticked the seconds off inexorably.

2:35 . . .

They ran down the corridor, popped the seal on the outer door—the atmosphere vented.

1:05 . . .

They climbed up through the twisted metal canyon that the MAC round had torn through the hull.

0:33 . . .

"There," John said, and pointed to the base of a charged pulse laser. They crawled toward it, waited as the glow built to a lethal charge.

0:12 . . .

They crouched and held onto one another.

The laser fired.

The heat blistered John's back. They pushed off with all their strength, multiplied through the MJOLNIR armor.

0:00.

The shield parted and they cleared the ship, hurtling into the blackness.

The Covenant ship shuddered. Flashes of red appeared inside the hole—then a gout of fire rose and ballooned, but curled downward as it hit and rebounded off their own shield. The plasma spread along the length of their vessel. The shield shimmered and rippled silver—holding the destructive force inside.

Metal glowed and melted. The pulse laser turrets absorbed into the hull. The hull blistered, bubbled, and boiled.

The shield finally gave—the ship exploded.

Kelly clung to John.

A thousand molten fragments hurled past them, cooling from white to orange to red and then disappearing into the dark of the night.

Sam's death had shown them that the Covenant were not invincible. They could be beaten. At a high cost, however.

John finally understood what the Chief had meant—the difference between a life wasted and a life spent.

John also knew that humanity had a fighting chance . . . and he was ready to go to war.

SECTION III

SIGMA OCTANUS

MOMENTUM

CHAPTER FIFTEEN

0000 HOURS, JULY 17, 2552 (MILITARY CALENDAR) / UNSC REMOTE SCANNING OUTPOST *ARCHIMEDES*, ON THE EDGE OF THE SIGMA OCTANUS SYSTEM

Ensign William Lovell scratched his head, yawned, and sat down at his duty station. The wraparound view screen warmed to his presence.

"Good morning, Ensign Lovell," the computer said.

"Morning, sexy," he said. It had been months since the Ensign had seen a real woman—the cold female voice of the computer was the closest thing he was getting to a date.

"Voiceprint match," the computer confirmed. "Please enter password."

He typed: ThereOncewasAgirl.

The Ensign had never taken his duty too seriously. Maybe that's why he only made it through his second year at the Academy. And maybe that's why he had been on *Archimedes* station for the last year, stuck with third shift.

But that suited him fine.

"Please reenter password."

He typed more carefully this time: *ThereOnceWasAGirl*.

After first contact with the Covenant, he had almost been conscripted straight out of school; instead, he had actually volunteered.

Admiral Cole had defeated the Covenant at Harvest in 2531. His victory was publicized on every vid and holo throughout the Inner and Outer Colonies and all the way to Earth.

That's why Lovell didn't try to dodge the enlistment officers. He had thought he'd watch a few battles from the bridge of a destroyer, fire a few missiles, rack up the victories, and be promoted to Captain within a year.

His excellent grades gave him instant admission to OCS on Luna.

There was one small detail, however, the UNSC propaganda machine had left out of their broadcasts: Cole had won only because he outnumbered the Covenant three to one . . . and even then, he had lost two-thirds of his fleet.

Ensign Lovell had served on the UNSC destroyer *Gorgon* for four years. He had been promoted to First Lieutenant, then busted down to Second Lieutenant and finally to Ensign for insubordination and gross incompetence. The only reason they hadn't drummed him out of the service was that the UNSC needed every man and woman they could get their hands on.

While on the *Gorgon*, he and the rest of Admiral Cole's fleet had sped among the Outer Colonies chasing, and being chased by, the Covenant. After four years' space duty, Lovell had seen a dozen worlds glassed . . . and billions murdered.

He had simply broken under the strain. He closed his eyes and remembered. No, he hadn't broken; he was just scared of dying like everyone else.

"Please keep your eyes open," the computer told him. "Processing retinal scan."

He had drifted from office work to low-priority assignments and finally landed here a year ago. By that time there were no more Outer Colonies. The Covenant had destroyed them all and were pressing inexorably inward, slowly taking the Inner Colonies. There had been a few isolated victories . . . but he knew it was only a matter of time before the aliens wiped the human race out of existence.

"Login complete," the computer announced.

Ensign Lovell's identity record was displayed on the monitor. In his Academy picture, he looked ten years younger: neatly trimmed jet-black hair, toothy grin, and sparkling green eyes. Today his hair was unkempt and the spark was long gone from his eyes.

"Please read General Order 098831A-1 before proceeding."

The Ensign had memorized this stupid thing. But the computer would track his eye motions—make sure he read it anyway. He opened the file and it popped on-screen:

United Nations Space Command Emergency Priority Order 098831A-1

Encryption Code: Red

Public Key: file/first light/

From: UNSC/NAVCOM Fleet H. T. Ward

To: ALL UNSC PERSONNEL

Subject: General Order 098831A-1 ("The Cole Protocol")

Classification: RESTRICTED (BGX Directive)

The Cole Protocol

To safeguard the Inner Colonies and Earth, all UNSC vessels or stations must not be captured with intact navigation databases that may lead Covenant forces to human civilian population centers.

If *any* Covenant forces are detected:

1. Activate selective purge of databases on all ship-based and planetary data networks.

2. Initiate triple-screen check to ensure all data has been erased and all backups neutralized.

3. Execute viral data scavengers. (Download from UNSCTTP://EPWW:COLEPROTOCOL/VirtualScav/fbr.091)

4. If retreating from Covenant forces, all ships must

ENTER SLIPSTREAM SPACE WITH RANDOMIZED VECTORS NOT DIRECTED TOWARD EARTH, THE INNER COLONIES, OR ANY OTHER HUMAN POPULATION CENTER.

5. IN CASE OF IMMINENT CAPTURE BY COVENANT FORCES, ALL UNSC SHIPS MUST SELF-DESTRUCT.

VIOLATION OF THIS DIRECTIVE WILL BE CONSIDERED AN ACT OF TREASON, AND PURSUANT TO UNSC MILITARY LAW ARTICLES JAG 845-P AND JAG 7556-L, SUCH VIOLATIONS ARE PUNISHABLE BY LIFE IMPRISONMENT OR EXECUTION.

/END FILE/

PRESS **ENTER** IF YOU UNDERSTAND THESE ORDERS.

Ensign Lovell pressed ENTER.

The UNSC wasn't taking any chances. And after everything he had seen, he didn't blame them.

His scanning windows appeared on the view screen, full of spectroscopic tracers and radar—and lots of noise.

Archimedes station cycled three probes into and out of Slipstream space. Each probe sent out radar pings and analyzed the spectrum from radio to X rays, then reentered normal space and broadcast the data back to the station.

The problem with Slipstream space was that the laws of physics never worked the way they were supposed to. Exact positions, times, velocities, even masses were impossible to measure with any real accuracy. Ships never knew exactly where they were, or exactly where there were going.

Every time the probes returned from their two-second journey, they could appear exactly where they had left . . . or three million kilometers distant. Sometimes they never returned at all. Drones had to be sent after the probes before the process could be repeated.

Because of this slipperiness in the interdimensional space,

UNSC ships traveling between star systems might arrive half a billion kilometers off course.

The curious properties of Slipspace also made this assignment a joke.

Ensign Lovell was supposed to watch for pirates or black-market runners trying to sneak by . . . and most importantly, for the Covenant. This station had never logged so much as a Covenant probe silhouette—and that was the reason he had specifically requested this dead-end assignment. It was safe.

What he did see with regularity were trash dumps from UNSC vessels, clouds of primordial atomic hydrogen, even the occasional comet that had somehow plowed into the Slipstream.

Lovell yawned, kicked his feet up onto the control console, and closed his eyes. He nearly fell out of his chair when the COM board contact alert pinged.

"Oh no," he whispered, fear and shame at his own cowardice forming a cold lump in his belly. *Don't let it be the Covenant. Don't let it . . . not* here.

He quickly activated the controls and traced the contact signal back to the source—Alpha probe.

The probe had detected an incoming mass, a slight arc to its trajectory pulled by the gravity of Sigma Octanus. It was large. A cloud of dust, perhaps? If it was, it would soon distort and scatter.

Ensign Lovell sat up straighter in his chair.

Beta probe cycled back. The mass was still there and as solid as before. It was the largest reading Ensign Lovell had ever seen: twenty thousand tons. That couldn't be a Covenant ship—they didn't get that big. And the silhouette was a bumpy spherical shape; it didn't match any of the Covenant ships in the database. It had to be a rogue asteroid.

He tapped his stylus on the desk. What if it wasn't an asteroid? He'd have to purge the database and enable the self-destruct mechanism for the outpost. But what could the Covenant want way out here?

Gamma probe reappeared. The mass readings were unchanged. Spectroscopic analysis was inconclusive, which was normal for probe reading at this distance. The mass was two hours out at its present velocity. Its projected trajectory was hyperbolic—a quick swing near the star, and then it would pass invisibly out of the system and be forever gone.

He noted that its trajectory brought it close to Sigma Octanus IV . . . which, if the rock were in real space, would be cause for alarm. In Slipspace, however, it could pass "through" the planet, and no one would notice.

Ensign Lovell relaxed and sent the retrieval drones after the three probes. By the time they got the probes back, though, the mass would be long gone.

He stared at the last image on screen. Was it worth sending an immediate report to Sigma Octanus COM? They'd make him send his probes out without a proper recovery, and the probes would likely get lost after that. A supply ship would have to be sent out here to replace them. The station would have to be inspected and recertified—and he'd receive a thorough lecture on what did and did not constitute a valid emergency.

No . . . there was no need to bother anyone over this. The only ones who would be really interested were the high-forehead types at UNSC Astrophysics, and they could review the data at their leisure.

He logged the anomaly and attached it to his hourly update.

Ensign Lovell kicked up his boots and reclined, once again feeling perfectly safe in his little corner of the universe.

CHAPTER SIXTEEN

0300 HOURS, JULY 17, 2552 (MILITARY CALENDAR) / UNSC DESTROYER *IROQUOIS* ON ROUTINE PATROL IN THE SIGMA OCTANUS SYSTEM

Commander Jacob Keyes stood on the bridge of the *Iroquois*. He leaned against the brass railing and surveyed the stars in the distance. He wished the circumstances of his current command were more auspicious, but experienced officers were in short supply these days. And he had his orders.

He walked around the circular bridge examining the monitors and displays of engine status. He paused at the screens showing the stars fore and aft; he couldn't quite get used to the view of deep space again. The stars were so vivid . . . and here, so different from the stars near Earth.

The *Iroquois* had rolled out of space dock at Reach—one of the UNSC's primary naval yards—just three months ago. They hadn't even installed her AI yet; like good officers, the elaborate artificially intelligent computer systems were also in dangerously short supply. Still, *Iroquois* was fast, well armored, and armed to the teeth. He couldn't ask for a finer vessel.

Unlike the frigates that Commander Keyes had toured on before, the *Meriwether Lewis* and *Midsummer Night*, this ship was a destroyer. She was almost as heavy as both those vessels combined, but she was only seven meters longer. Some in the fleet thought the massive ships were unwieldy in combat—too slow and cumbersome. What those critics forgot was that a UNSC destroyer sported two MAC guns, twenty-six oversized

Archer missile pods, and three nuclear warheads. Unlike other fleet ships, she carried no single-ship fighters—instead her extra mass came from the nearly two meters of titanium-A battleplate armor that covered her from stem to stern. The *Iroquois* could dish out and take a tremendous amount of punishment.

Someone at the shipyard had appreciated the *Iroquois* for what she was, too—two long streaks of crimson war paint had been applied to her port and starboard flanks. Strictly nonregulation and it would have to go . . . but secretly, Commander Keyes liked the ornamentation.

He sat in the Commander's chair and watched his junior officers at their stations.

"Incoming transmissions," Lieutenant Dominique reported. "Status reports from Sigma Octanus Four and also the *Archimedes* Sensor Outpost."

"Pipe them through to my monitor," Commander Keyes said.

Dominique had been one of his students at the Academy—he had transferred to Luna from the Université del' Astrophysique in Paris after his sister was killed in action. He was short, nimbly athletic, and he rarely cracked a smile—he was always business. Keyes appreciated that.

Commander Keyes was less impressed, however, with the rest of his bridge officers.

Lieutenant Hikowa manned the weapons console. Her long fingers and slender arms slowly checked the status of the ordnance with all the deliberation of a sleepwalker. Her dark hair was always falling into her eyes, too. Oddly, her record showed that she had survived several battles with the Covenant . . . so perhaps her lack of enthusiasm was merely battle fatigue.

Lieutenant Hall stood post at ops. She seemed competent enough. Her uniform was always freshly pressed, her blond hair trimmed exactly at the regulation sixteen centimeters. She had authored seven physics papers on Slipspace communications. The only problem was that she was always smiling, and trying to impress him . . . occasionally by showing up her fellow officers. Keyes disapproved of such displays of ambition.

Manning navigation, however, was his most problematic officer: Lieutenant Jaggers. It might have been that navigation was the Commander's strong suit, so anyone else in that position never seemed to be up to par. On the other hand, Lieutenant Jaggers was moody, and when Keyes had come aboard, the man's small hazel eyes seemed glazed. He could have sworn he had caught the man on duty with liquor on his breath, too. He had ordered a blood test—the results were negative.

"Orders, sir?" Jaggers asked.

"Continue on this heading, Lieutenant. We'll finish our patrol around Sigma Octanus and then accelerate and enter Slipspace."

"Aye, sir."

Commander Keyes eased into his seat and detached the tiny monitor from the armrest. He read the hourly report from the *Archimedes* Sensor Outpost. The log of the large mass was curious. It was too big to be even the largest Covenant carrier . . . yet something was oddly familiar about its shape.

He retrieved his pipe from his jacket, lit it, inhaled a puff, and exhaled the fragrant smoke through his nose. Keyes would never even have thought about smoking on the other vessels he had served on, but here . . . well, command had its privileges.

He pulled up his files transferred from the Academy—several theoretical papers that had recently caught his interest. One, he thought, might apply to the outpost's unusual reading.

That paper had initially sparked his interest because of its author. He had never forgotten his first assignment with Dr. Catherine Halsey . . . nor the names of any of the children they had observed.

He opened the file and read:

UNITED NATIONS SPACE COMMAND ASTROPHYSICS JOURNAL
034-23-01

DATE: MAY 09, 2540 (MILITARY CALENDAR)
ENCRYPTION CODE: NONE
PUBLIC KEY: NA
AUTHOR(S): LIEUTENANT COMMANDER FHAJAD 034 (SERVICE NUMBER [CLASSIFIED]), UNSC OFFICE OF NAVAL INTELLIGENCE
SUBJECT: DIMENSIONAL-MASS SPACE COMPRESSIONS IN SHAW-FUJIKAWA (A.K.A. "SLIPSTREAM") SPACE
CLASSIFICATION: NA
/START FILE/

ABSTRACT: THE SPACE-BENDING PROPERTIES OF MASS IN NORMAL SPACE ARE WELL DESCRIBED BY EINSTEIN'S GENERAL RELATIVITY. SUCH DISTORTIONS HOWEVER, ARE COMPLICATED BY THE ANOMALOUS QUANTUM GRAVITATIONAL EFFECTS IN SHAW-FUJIKAWA (SF) SPACES. USING LOOP-STRING ANALYSIS, IT CAN BE SHOWN THAT A LARGE MASS BENDS SPACE IN SF SPACE MORE THAN GENERAL RELATIVITY PREDICTS BY AN ORDER OF MAGNITUDE. THIS BENDING MAY EXPLAIN HOW SEVERAL SMALL OBJECTS CLUSTERED CLOSELY TOGETHER IN SF SPACE HAVE BEEN REPORTED ERRONEOUSLY AS A SINGLE LARGER MASS.

PRESS **ENTER** TO CONTINUE.

Commander Keyes switched back to the silhouette from the *Archimedes* report. The leading edge almost looked like the bulbous head of a whale. That realization chilled him to the core.

He quickly opened the UNSC database of all known Covenant ships. He scanned them until he found the three-dimensional representation of one of their medium-sized warships. He rotated it into three-quarters profile. He overlaid the image on the silhouette, scaled it back a little.

It was a perfect match.

"Lieutenant Dominique, get FLEETCOM ASAP. Priority Alpha."

The Lieutenant snapped straight in his chair. "Yes, sir!"

The bridge officers looked at the Commander, then exchanged glances with one another.

Commander Keyes brought up a map of the system on his data pad. The silhouette monitored by the outpost was on a direct course for Sigma Octanus IV. That confirmed his theory.

"Bring us about to course zero four seven, Lieutenant Jaggers. Lieutenant Hall, push the reactors to one hundred ten percent."

"Aye, Commander," Lieutenant Jaggers replied.

"Reactor running hot, sir," Hall reported. "Now exceeding recommended operational parameters."

"ETA?"

Jaggers calculated, then looked up. "Forty-three minutes," he replied.

"Too slow," Commander Keyes muttered. "Reactor to one hundred thirty percent, Lieutenant Hall."

She hesitated. "Sir?"

"Do it!"

"Yes, sir!" She moved as if someone had electrically shocked her.

"FLEETCOM online, sir," Lieutenant Dominique said.

The weathered face of Vice Admiral Michael Stanforth appeared on the main view screen.

Commander Keyes breathed a sigh of relief. Vice Admiral Stanforth had a reputation for being reasonable and intelligent. He'd understand the logic of the situation.

"Commander Keyes," the Vice Admiral said. "The old 'Schoolmaster' himself, huh? This is the priority channel, son. This better be an emergency."

Commander Keyes ignored the obvious condescension. He knew many at FLEETCOM thought he deserved to command nothing but a classroom—and some probably thought he didn't deserve that.

"The Sigma Octanus System is about to come under attack, sir."

Vice Admiral Stanforth cocked an eyebrow and leaned closer to the screen.

"I'm requesting that all ships in-system rendezvous with the *Iroquois* at Sigma Octanus Four. And any ships in neighboring systems make best speed here."

"Show me what you've got, Keyes," the Vice Admiral said.

Commander Keyes displayed the silhouette from the sensor outpost first. "Covenant ships, sir. Their silhouettes are overlapped. Our probes resolve them as one mass because Slipspace is bent by gravity more easily than normal space."

The Vice Admiral listened to his analysis, frowning.

"You've fought the Covenant, sir. You known how precisely they can maneuver their ships through the Slipstream. I've seen a dozen alien craft appear in normal space, in perfect formation, not a kilometer apart."

"Yeah," the Vice Admiral muttered. "I've seen that, too. All right, Keyes, good work. You'll get everything we can send."

"Thank you, sir."

"You just hang in there, son. Good luck. FLEETCOM out."

The view screen snapped off.

"Sir?" Lieutenant Hall turned around. "How many Covenant ships?"

"I'd estimate four medium-tonnage vessels," he said. "The equivalent of our frigates."

"*Four* Covenant ships?" Lieutenant Jaggers muttered. "What can *we* do?"

"Do?" Commander Keyes said. "Our duty."

"Begging the Commander's pardon, but there are *four* Cov—" Jaggers began to protest.

Keyes cut him off with a glare. "Stow that, mister." He paused, weighing his words. "Sigma Octanus Four has seventeen million citizens, Lieutenant. Are you suggesting that we just stand by and watch the Covenant glass the planet?"

"No, sir." His gaze dropped to the deck.

"We will do the best we can," Commander Keyes said. "In the meantime, remove all weapons system locks, order missile crews to readiness, warm up the MAC guns, and remove the safeties from one of our nukes."

"Yes, sir!" Lieutenant Hikowa said.

An alarm sounded at ops. "Reactor hysteresis approaching failure levels," Lieutenant Hall reported. "Superconducting magnets overloading. Coolant breakdown imminent."

"Vent primary coolant and pump in the reserve tanks," Commander Keyes ordered. "That will buy us another five minutes."

"Yes, sir."

Commander Keyes fumbled with his pipe. He didn't bother to light the thing this time around, just chewed on the end. Then he put it away. The nervous habit wasn't setting the right example for his bridge officers. He didn't have the luxury of showing his apprehension.

The truth was, he was terrified. Four Covenant ships would be an even match for *seven* destroyers. The best he could hope for was to get their attention and outrun them—hopefully distract them until the fleet got here.

Of course . . . those Covenant ships could outrun the *Iroquois* as well.

"Lieutenant Jaggers," he said, "initiate the Cole Protocol. Purge our navigation databases, and then generate an appropriate randomized exit vector from the Sigma Octanus System."

"Yes, sir." He fumbled with his controls. He hung his head, steadied his hands, and slowly typed in the commands.

"Lieutenant Hall: make preparations to override reactor safeties."

His junior officers all paused for a second. "Aye, sir," Lieutenant Hall whispered.

"We're receiving a transmission from the system's edge," Lieutenant Dominique announced. "Frigates *Allegiance* and *Gettysburg* are on an inbound vector at maximum speed. ETA . . . one hour."

"Good," Commander Keyes said.

That hour might as well be a month. This battle would be over in minutes.

He could not fight the enemy—he was severely outgunned. He couldn't outrun them, either. There had to be another option.

Hadn't he always told his students that when you were out of options, then you were using the wrong tactics? You had to bend the rules. Shift perspective—anything to find a way out of a hopeless situation.

The black space near Sigma Octanus IV boiled and frothed with motes of green light.

"Ships entering normal space," Lieutenant Jaggers announced, panic tingeing his voice.

Commander Keyes got to his feet.

He had been wrong. There weren't four Covenant frigates. A pair of enemy frigates emerged from Slipspace . . . escorting a destroyer and a carrier.

His blood ran cold. He had seen battles in which a Covenant destroyer had made Swiss cheese of UNSC ships. Its plasma torpedoes could boil through the *Iroquois*' two meters of titanium-A battleplate in seconds. Their weapons were light-years ahead of the UNSC's.

"Their weapons," Commander Keyes muttered under his breath. Yes . . . he *did* have a third option.

"Continue at emergency speed," he ordered, "and come about to heading zero three two."

Lieutenant Jaggers swiveled in his seat. "That will put us on collision course with their destroyer, sir."

"I know," Commander Keyes replied. "In fact, I'm counting on doing just that."

CHAPTER
SEVENTEEN

0320 HOURS, JULY 17, 2552 (MILITARY CALENDAR) / UNSC *IROQUOIS* EN ROUTE TO SIGMA OCTANUS IV

Commander Keyes stood with his hands behind his back and tried to look calm. Not an easy thing to do when his ship was on a collision course with a Covenant battlegroup. Inside, adrenaline raced through his blood and his pulse pounded.

He had to at least *appear* in control for his crew. He was asking a lot from them . . . probably *everything*, in fact.

His junior officers watched their status monitors; they occasionally glanced nervously at him, but their gazes always drifted back to the center view screen.

The Covenant ships looked like toys in the distance. It was dangerous to think of them as harmless, however. One slip, one underestimation of their tremendous firepower, and the *Iroquois* would be destroyed.

The alien carrier had three bulbous sections; its swollen center had thirteen launch bays. Commander Keyes had seen hundreds of fighters stream out of them before—fast, accurate, and deadly craft. Normally his ship's AI would handle point defense . . . only this time, there was no AI installed on the *Iroquois*.

The alien destroyer was a third again as massive as the *Iroquois*. She bristled with pulse laser turrets, insectlike antennae, and chitinous pods. The carrier and destroyer moved together . . . but not toward *Iroquois*. They slowly drifted in-system toward Sigma Octanus IV.

Were they going to ignore him? Glass the planet without even bothering to swat him out of the way first?

The Covenant frigates, however, lagged behind. They turned in unison and their sides faced the *Iroquois*—preparing for a broadside. Motes of red light appeared and swarmed toward the frigate's lateral lines, building into a solid stripe of hellish illumination.

"Detecting high levels of beta particle radiation," Lieutenant Dominique said. "They're getting ready to fire their plasma weapons, Commander."

"Course correction, sir?" Lieutenant Jaggers asked. His fingers tapped in a new heading bound out-system.

"Stay on course." It took all Commander Keyes' concentration to say that matter-of-factly.

Lieutenant Jaggers turned and started to speak—but Commander Keyes didn't have time to address his concerns.

"Lieutenant Hikowa," Commander Keyes said. "Arm a Shiva missile. Remove all nuclear launch safety locks."

"Shiva armed. Aye, Commander." Lieutenant Hikowa's face was a mask of grim determination.

"Set the fuse on radio transmission code sequence detonation only. Disable proximity fuse. Stand by for a launch pilot program."

"Sir?" Lieutenant Hikowa looked confused by his order, but then said, "Sir! Yes, sir. Making it happen."

The alien frigates in the center of the view screen no longer looked remotely like toys to Commander Keyes. They looked real and larger every second. The red glow along their sides had become solid bands . . . almost too bright to look directly at.

Commander Keyes picked up his data pad and quickly tapped in calculations: velocity, mass, and heading. He wished they had an AI online to double-check his figures. This amounted to no more than an educated guess. How long would it take the

Iroquois to orbit Sigma Octanus IV? He got a number and cut it by 60 percent, knowing they'd either pick up speed . . . or be dead by the time it mattered.

"Lieutenant Hikowa, set the Shiva's course for mark one eight zero. Full burn for twelve seconds."

"Aye, sir," she said, tapped in the parameters, and locked them into the system. "Missile ready, sir."

"Sir!" Lieutenant Jaggers swiveled around and stood. His lips were drawn into a tight thin line. "That course fires the missile directly *away* from our enemies."

"I am aware of that, Lieutenant Jaggers. Sit down and await further orders."

Lieutenant Jaggers sat. He rubbed his temple with a trembling hand. His other hand balled into a fist.

Commander Keyes linked to the NAV system and set a countdown timer on his data pad. Twenty-nine seconds. "On my mark, Lieutenant Hikowa, launch that nuke . . . and not a moment before."

"Aye, sir." Her slender hand hovered over the control panel. "MAC guns are still hot, Commander," she reminded him.

"Divert the energy keeping the capacitors at full charge and route them to the engines," Commander Keyes ordered.

Lieutenant Hall said, "Diverting now, sir." She exchanged a glance with Lieutenant Hikowa. "Engines now operating at one hundred fifty percent of rated output. Red line in two minutes."

"Contact! Contact!" Lieutenant Dominique shouted. "Enemy plasma torpedoes away, sir!"

Scarlet lightning erupted from the alien frigates—twin bolts of fire streaked through the darkness. They looked as if they could burn space itself. The torpedoes were on a direct course for the *Iroquois*.

"Course correction, sir?" Lieutenant Jaggers' voice broke with strain. His uniform was soaked with perspiration.

"Negative," Commander Keyes replied. "Continue on this heading. Arm all aft Archer missile pods. Rotate launch arcs one eight zero degrees."

"Aye, sir." Lieutenant Hikowa wrinkled her brow, and then she slowly nodded and silently mouthed, ". . . yes."

Boiling red plasma filled half the forward view screen. It was beautiful to watch in an odd way—like a front-row seat at a forest fire.

Keyes found himself strangely calm. This would either work or it would not. The odds were long, but he was confident that his actions were the only option to survive this encounter.

Lieutenant Dominique turned. "Collision with plasma in nineteen seconds, sir."

Jaggers turned from his station. "Sir! This is suicide! Our armor can't withstand—"

Keyes cut him off. "Mister, man your station or I will have you removed from the bridge."

Jaggers looked pleadingly at Hikowa. "We're going to *die*, Aki—"

She refused to meet his gaze and turned back to her controls. "You heard the Commander," she said quietly. "Man your post."

Jaggers sank into his seat.

"Collision with plasma in seven seconds," Lieutenant Hall said. She bit her lower lip.

"Lieutenant Jaggers, transfer emergency thruster controls to my station."

"Yes . . . yes, sir."

The emergency thrusters were tanks of trihydride tetrrazine and hydrogen peroxide. When they mixed, they did so with explosive force—literally blasting the *Iroquois* onto a new course. The ship had six such tanks strategically placed on hardened points on the hull.

Commander Keyes consulted the countdown timer on his data pad. "Lieutenant Hikowa: fire the nuke."

"Shiva away, sir! On course—one eight zero, maximum burn."

Plasma filled the forescreen; the center of the red mass turned blue. Greens and yellows radiated outward, the light frequencies blue-shifting in spectra.

"Distance three hundred thousand kilometers," Lieutenant Dominique said. "Collision in two seconds."

Commander Keyes waited a heartbeat, then hit the emergency thrusters to port. A bang resonated through the ship's hull—Commander Keyes flew sideways and impacted with the bulkhead.

The view screen was full of fire and the bridge was suddenly hot.

Commander Keyes stood. He counted the beats of his pounding heart. One, two, three—

If they had been hit by the plasma, there wouldn't be anything to count. They would be dead already.

Only one view screen was working now, however. "Aft camera," he said.

The twin blots of fire streaked along their trajectories for a moment, then lazily arced, continuing their pursuit of the *Iroquois*. One pulled slightly ahead of its counterpart, so they appeared now like two blazing eyes.

Commander Keyes marveled at the aliens' ability to direct that plasma from such a great distance. "Good," he murmured to himself. "Chase us all the way to hell, you bastards.

"Track them," he ordered Lieutenant Hall.

"Aye, sir," she said. Her perfectly groomed hair was tousled. "Plasma increasing velocity. Matching our speed . . . overtaking our velocity now. They will intercept in forty-three seconds."

"Forward camera," Commander Keyes ordered.

The view screen flashed: the image changed to show the two alien frigates turning to face the incoming *Iroquois* head-on. Blue lights flickered along their hulls—pulse lasers charging.

Commander Keyes pulled back the camera angle and saw

the alien carrier and the destroyer were still inbound toward Sigma Octanus IV. He read their position off his data pad and quickly performed the necessary calculations.

"Course correction," he told Lieutenant Jaggers. "Come about to heading zero zero four point two five. Declination zero zero zero point one eight."

"Aye, sir," Jaggers said. "Zero zero four point two five. Declination zero zero zero point one eight."

The view screen turned and centered on the enormous Covenant destroyer.

"Collision course!" Lieutenant Hall announced. "Impact with Covenant destroyer in eight seconds."

"Stand by for new course correction: declination minus zero zero zero point one zero."

"Aye, sir." As Jaggers typed, he wiped the sweat from his eyes and double-checked his numbers. "Course online. Awaiting your order, sir."

"Collision with Covenant destroyer in five seconds," Hall said. She clutched the edge of her seat.

The destroyer grew in the view screen: laser turrets and launch bays, bulbous alien protrusions and flickering blue lights.

"Hold this course," Commander Keyes said. "Sound collision alarm. Switch to undercarriage camera now."

Klaxons blared.

The view screen snapped off and on and showed black space—then a flash of the faint purple-blue hull of a Covenant ship.

The *Iroquois* screeched and shuddered as she grazed the prow of the Covenant destroyer. Silver shields flickered on-screen—then the screen filled with static.

"Course correction now!" Commander Keyes shouted.

"Aye, sir."

There was a brief burn from the thrusters and the *Iroquois* nudged down slightly.

"Hull breach!" Lieutenant Hall said. "Sealing pressure doors."

"Aft camera," Commander Keyes said. "Guns: fire aft Archer missile pods!"

"Missiles away," Lieutenant Hikowa replied.

Keyes watched as the first of the plasma torpedoes that had been trailing the *Iroquois* impacted on the prow of the alien destroyer. The ship's shields flared, flickered . . . and vanished. The second bolt hit a moment later. The hull of the alien ship blazed and then turned red-hot, melted, and boiled. Secondary explosions burst through the hull.

The Archer missiles streaked toward the wounded Covenant ship, tiny trails of exhaust stretching from the *Iroquois* to the target. They slammed into the gaping wounds in the hull and detonated. Fire and debris burst from the destroyer.

A smile spread across Keyes' face as he watched the alien ship burn, list, and slowly plunge into Sigma Octanus IV's gravity well. Without power, the Covenant vessel would burn up in the planet's atmosphere.

Commander Keyes flicked on the intercom. "Brace for emergency thruster maneuver."

He punched the thruster controls—explosive force detonated on the starboard side of the ship. The *Iroquois* nosed toward Sigma Octanus IV.

"Course correction, Lieutenant Jaggers," he said. "Bring us into a tight orbit."

"Aye, sir." He furiously tapped in commands, diverting engine output through altitude thrusters.

The hull of the *Iroquois* glowed red as it entered the atmosphere. A cloud of yellow ionization built up around the view screen.

Commander Keyes gripped the railing tighter.

The view screen cleared and he could see the stars. The *Iroquois* entered the dark side of the planet.

Commander Keyes slumped forward and started breathing again.

"Engine coolant failure, sir," Lieutenant Hall said.

"Shut the engines down," he ordered. "Emergency vent."

"Aye, sir. Venting fusion reactor plasma."

The *Iroquois* was abruptly quiet. No rumble of her engines. And no one said anything until Lieutenant Hikowa stood and said, "Sir, that was the most brilliant maneuver I have ever seen."

Commander Keyes gave a short laugh. "You think so, Lieutenant?"

If one of his students had proposed such a maneuver in his tactics class, he would have given them a C+. He would have told them their maneuver was full of bravado and daring . . . but extremely risky, placing the crew in the ship in unnecessary danger.

"This isn't over yet. Stay sharp," he told them. "Lieutenant Hikowa, what is the charge status of the MAC guns?"

"Capacitors at ninety-five percent, sir, and draining at a rate of three percent per minute."

"Ready MAC guns, one heavy round apiece. Arm all forward Archer missile pods."

"Aye, sir."

The *Iroquois* broke free of the dark side of Sigma Octanus IV.

"Fire chemical thrusters to break orbit, Lieutenant Hall."

"Firing, aye."

There was a brief rumble. The screen centered on the backsides of the two Covenant frigates they had passed on the way in.

The alien ships started to come about; blue flashes flickered along their hulls as their laser turrets charged. Motes of red collected along their lateral lines. They were readying another salvo of plasma torpedoes.

There was something there, however, that was too small to see on the view screen: the nuke. Keyes had launched that missile in the opposite direction—but its reverse thrust had not completely overcome their tremendous forward velocity.

As the *Iroquois* had screamed over the prow of the destroyer, and as they orbited Sigma Octanus IV, the nuke had drifted closer to the frigates . . . who had fixed their attention solidly on the *Iroquois*.

Commander Keyes tapped his data pad and sent the signal to detonate the bomb.

There was a flash of white, a crackle of lightning, and the alien ships vanished as a cloud of destruction enveloped them. Waves of the EMP interacted with the magnetic field of Sigma Octanus IV—rippled with rainbow borealis. The cloud of vapor expanded and cooled, and faded to yellow, orange, red, then black dust that scattered into space.

Both Covenant frigates, however, were still intact. Their shields, however, flickered once . . . then went dead.

"Get me firing solutions for the MAC guns, Lieutenant Hikowa. On the double."

"Aye, sir. MAC gun capacitors at ninety-three percent. Firing solution online."

"Fire, Lieutenant Hikowa."

Two thumps resonated through the hull of the *Iroquois*.

"Lock remaining Archer missile pods on targets and fire."

"Missiles away, Commander."

Twin thunderbolts and hundreds of missiles streaked toward the two helpless frigates.

The MAC rounds tore through them—one ship was holed from nose to tail; the other ship was hit on her midline, right near the engines. Internal explosions chained up the length of the ship, bulging the second ship's hull along her length.

Archer missiles impacted seconds later, exploding through chunks of hull and armor, tearing the alien ships apart. The frigate that had taken the MAC round in her engines mushroomed, a fireworks bouquet of shrapnel and sparks. The other ship burned, her internal skeletal structure showing now; she turned toward the *Iroquois* but didn't fire a weapon . . . just drifted out of control. Dead in space.

"Position of the Covenant carrier, Lieutenant Hall?"

Lieutenant Hall paused, then reported, "In polar orbit around Sigma Octanus Four. But she's moving off at considerable speed. Headed out-system, course zero four five."

"Alert the *Allegiance* and *Gettysburg* of her position."

Commander Keyes sighed and slumped back into his chair. They had stopped the Covenant ships from glassing the planet—saved millions of lives. They had done the impossible: taken on four Covenant ships and won.

Commander Keyes paused in his self-congratulation. Something was wrong. He had never seen the Covenant run. In every battle he had seen or read about, they stayed to slaughter every last survivor . . . or if they were defeated, they always fought to the last ship.

"Check the planet," he told Lieutenant Hall. "Look for anything—dropped weapons, strange transmissions. There's got to be something there."

"Aye, sir."

Keyes prayed she wouldn't find anything. At this point he was out of tricks. He couldn't turn the *Iroquois* around and return to Sigma Octanus IV even if he had wanted to. The *Iroquois'* engines were down for a long time. They were speeding on an out-system vector at a considerable velocity. And even if they could stop—there was no way to recharge the MAC guns, and no remaining Archer missiles. They were practically dead in space.

He pulled out his pipe and steadied his shaking hand.

"Sir!" Lieutenant Hall cried. "Dropships, sir. The alien carrier deployed thirty—correction: thirty-four—dropships. I have silhouettes descending to the surface. They're on course for Côte d'Azur. A major population center."

"An invasion," Commander Keyes said. "Get FLEETCOM ASAP. Time to send in the Marines."

CHAPTER

EIGHTEEN

0600 HOURS, JULY 18, 2552 (MILITARY CALENDAR) / UNSC *IROQUOIS*, MILITARY STAGING AREA IN ORBIT AROUND SIGMA OCTANUS IV

Commander Keyes had a sinking feeling that although he had won the battle, it would be the first of many to come in the Sigma Octanus System.

He watched the four dozen other UNSC ships orbit the planet: frigates and destroyers, two carriers, and a massive repair and refitting station—more vessels than Admiral Cole had at his disposal during his four-year-long campaign to save Harvest. Vice Admiral Stanforth had pulled out all the stops.

Although Commander Keyes was grateful for the quick and overwhelming response, he wondered why the Vice Admiral had dedicated so many ships to the area. Sigma Octanus wasn't strategically positioned. It had no special resources. True, the UNSC had standing orders to protect civilian lives, but the fleet was spread dangerously thin. Commander Keyes knew there were more valuable systems that needed protection.

He pushed these thoughts aside. He was sure Vice Admiral Stanforth had his reasons. Meanwhile the repair and resupply of the *Iroquois* was his top priority—he didn't want to get caught half ready if the Covenant returned.

Or rather, *when* they returned.

It was a curious thing: the aliens dropping their ground forces and then retreating. That was not their usual mode of operation.

Commander Keyes suspected this was just an opening move in a game he didn't yet understand.

A shadow crossed the fore camera of the *Iroquois* as the repair station *Cradle* maneuvered closer. *Cradle* was essentially a large square plate with engines. Large was an understatement; she was over a square kilometer. Three destroyers could be eclipsed by her shadow. The station running at full steam could refit six destroyers, three from her lower surface and three on her upper surface, within a matter of hours.

Scaffolds deployed from her surfaces to facilitate repairs. Resupply tubes, hoses, and cargo trams fed into the *Iroquois*. It would take the full attention of *Cradle* thirty hours to repair the *Iroquois*, however.

The aliens had not landed a single serious shot. Nonetheless, the *Iroquois* had almost been destroyed during the execution of what some in the fleet were already calling the "Keyes Loop."

Commander Keyes glanced at his data pad and the extensive list of repairs. Fifteen percent of the electronic systems had to be replaced—burned out from the EMP when the Shiva missile detonated. The *Iroquois*' engines required a full overhaul. Both coolant systems had valves that had been fused from the tremendous heat. Five of the superconducting magnets had to be replaced as well.

But most troublesome was the damage to the underside of the *Iroquois*. When they had told Commander Keyes what had happened, he went outside in a Longsword interceptor to personally inspect what he had done to his ship.

The underside of the *Iroquois* had been scraped when they passed over the prow of the alien destroyer. He knew there was some damage . . . but was not prepared for what he saw.

UNSC destroyers had nearly two meters of titanium—a battleplate on their surfaces. Commander Keyes had abraded through *all* of it. He had breached every bottom deck of the *Iroquois*. The jagged serrated edges of the plate curled away from the wound. Men in EVA thruster packs were busy cutting off the damaged sections so new plates could be welded into place.

The underside was mirror smooth and perfectly flat. But Keyes knew that the appearance of benign flatness was deceptive. Had the angle of the *Iroquois* been tilted a single degree down, the force of the two ships impacting would have shorn his ship in half.

The red war stripes that had been painted on the *Iroquois*' side looked like bloody slashes. The dockmaster had privately told Commander Keyes that his crew could buff the paint off—or even repaint the war stripes, if he wanted.

Commander Keyes had politely refused the offer. He wanted them left exactly the way they were. He wanted to be reminded that while everyone had admired what he had done—it had been an act of desperation, not heroism.

He wanted to be reminded of how close a brush he had had with death.

Commander Keyes returned to the *Iroquois* and marched directly to his quarters.

He sat at his antique oak desk and tapped the intercom. "Lieutenant Dominique, you have the bridge for the next cycle. I am not to be disturbed."

"Aye, Commander. Understood."

Commander Keyes loosened his collar and unbuttoned his uniform. He retrieved the seventy-year-old bottle of Scotch that his father had given him from the bottom drawer, and then poured four centimeters into a plastic cup.

He had to attend to an even more unpleasant task: what to do about Lieutenant Jaggers.

Jaggers had exhibited borderline cowardice, insubordination, and come within a hairbreadth of attempted mutiny during the engagement. Keyes could have had him court-martialed. Every reg in the books screamed at him to . . . but he didn't have it in him to send the young man before a board of inquiry. He would instead merely transfer the Lieutenant to a place where he would still do the UNSC some good—perhaps a distant outpost.

Was all the blame his? As Commander, it was his responsibility to maintain control, to prevent a crewman from even thinking that mutiny was a possibility.

He sighed. Maybe he should have told his crew what he was attempting . . . but there had simply been no time. And certainly, no time for discussion as Jaggers would have wanted. No. The other bridge officers had concerns, but they had followed his orders, as their duty required.

As much as Commander Keyes believed in giving people a second chance, this was where he drew the line.

To make matters worse, transferring Jaggers would leave a hole in the bridge crew.

Commander Keyes accessed the service records of *Iroquois*' junior officers. There were several who might qualify for navigation officer. He flipped through their files on his data pad, and then paused.

The theoretical paper on mass-space compression was still open, as well as his hastily calculated course corrections.

He smiled and archived those notes. He might one day give a lecture on this battle at the Academy. It would be useful to have the original source material.

There was also the data from the *Archimedes* Sensor Outpost. That report had been thoroughly made: clean data graphs and a navigational course plotted for the object through Slipstream space—not an easy task even with an AI. The report even had tags to route it to the astrophysics section of the UNSC. Thoughtful.

He looked up the service record of the officer who had filed the report: Ensign William Lovell.

Keyes leaned closer. The boy's Career Service Vitae was

almost twice as long as his own. He had volunteered and been accepted at Luna Academy. He transferred in his second year, having already received a commission to Ensign for heroism in a training flight that had saved the entire crew. He took duty on the first outbound corvette headed into battle. Three Bronze Stars, a Silver Cluster, and two Purple Hearts, and he had catapulted to a full Lieutenant within three years.

Then something went terribly wrong. Lovell's decline in the UNSC had been as rapid as his ascent. Four reports of insubordination and he was busted to Second Lieutenant and transferred twice. An incident with a civilian woman—no details in the files, although Commander Keyes wondered if the girl listed in the report, Anna Gerov, was Vice Admiral Gerov's daughter.

He had been reassigned to the *Archimedes* Sensor Outpost, and had been there for the last year, an unheard of length of time in such a remote facility.

Commander Keyes reviewed the logs when Lovell had been on duty. They were careful and intelligent. So the boy was still sharp . . . was he hiding?

There was a gentle knock on his door.

"Lieutenant Dominique, I said I was not to be disturbed."

"Sorry to intrude, son," said a muffled voice. The pressure door's wheel turned and Vice Admiral Stanforth stepped inside. "But I thought I'd just stop by since I was in the neighborhood."

Vice Admiral Stanforth was much smaller in person than he appeared on-screen. His back was stooped over with age, and his white hair was thinning at the crown. Still, he exuded a reassuring air of authority that Keyes instantly recognized.

"Sir!" Commander Keyes stood at attention, knocking over his chair.

"At ease, son." The Vice Admiral looked around his quarters, and his gaze lingered a moment on the framed copy of Lagrange's original manuscript in which he derived his equations of motion. "You can pour me a few fingers of the whiskey, if you can spare it."

"Yes, sir." Keyes fumbled with another plastic cup and poured the Vice Admiral a drink.

Stanforth took a sip, then sighed appreciatively. "Very nice."

Keyes righted his chair and offered it to the Vice Admiral.

He sat down and leaned forward. "I wanted to congratulate you personally on the miracle you performed here, Keyes."

"Sir, I don't—"

Stanforth held up a finger. "Don't interrupt me, son. That was a helluva piece of astrogation you pulled off. People noticed. Not to mention the morale boost it's given to the entire fleet." He took another sip of the liquor and exhaled. "Now, that's the reason we're all here. We need a victory. It's been too damn long—us getting whittled to pieces by those alien bastards. So this has *got* to be a win. No matter what it takes."

"I understand, sir," Commander Keyes said. He knew morale had been sagging for years throughout the UNSC. No military, no matter how well trained, could stomach defeat after defeat without it affecting their determination in battles.

"How is it going planetside?"

"Right now don't you worry about that." Vice Admiral Stanforth eased back in his chair, balancing on two legs. "General Kits has his troops down there. They've got the surrounding cities evacuated, and they'll be assaulting Côte d'Azur within the hour. They'll paste those aliens faster than you can spit. You just watch."

"Of course, sir." Commander Keyes looked away.

"You got something else to say, boy? Spit it out."

"Well, sir . . . this isn't the way the Covenant normally operates. Dropping an invasion force and leaving the system? They either slaughter everything or die trying. This is something altogether different."

Vice Admiral Stanforth waved a dismissive hand. "You leave trying to figure out what those aliens are thinking to the spooks in ONI, son. Just get the *Iroquois* patched up and fit for duty again. And you let me know if you need anything."

Stanforth knocked back the last of his whiskey and stood. "Got to marshal the fleet. Oh—" He paused. "One more thing." He dug into his jacket pocket and retrieved a tiny cardboard box. He set it on the Commander's desk. "Consider it official. The paperwork will catch up with us soon enough."

Commander Keyes opened the box. Inside were a pair of brass collar insignia: four bars and a single star.

"Congratulations, *Captain* Keyes." The Vice Admiral snapped a quick salute, then held out his hand.

Keyes managed to grasp and shake the Vice Admiral's hand. The insignia was real. He was stunned. He couldn't say anything.

"You've earned it." The Vice Admiral started to turn. "Give me a shout if you need anything."

"Yes, sir." Keyes stared at the brass star and stripes a moment longer, then finally tore his gaze away. "Vice Admiral . . . there is one thing. I need a replacement navigation officer."

Vice Admiral Stanforth's relaxed posture stiffened. "I heard about that. Ugly business when a bridge officer loses their stomach. Well, you just say the candidate's name and I'll make sure you get him . . . as long as you're not pulling him off my ship." He smiled. "Keep up the good work, Captain."

"Sir!" Captain Keyes saluted.

The Vice Admiral stepped out and closed the door.

Keyes practically fell into his chair.

He had never dreamed they'd make him a Captain. He turned the brass insignia over in his palm and replayed his conversation with Vice Admiral Stanforth in his mind. He had said, "Captain Keyes." Yes. This was real.

The Vice Admiral had also brushed aside his concerns about the Covenant too quickly. Something didn't quite add up.

Keyes clicked on the intercom. "Lieutenant Dominique: track the Vice Admiral's shuttle when he leaves. Let me know which ship he's on."

"Sir? We had a Vice Admiral aboard? I wasn't informed."

"No, Lieutenant, I suspect you weren't. Just track the next outbound shuttle."

"Aye, sir."

Keyes looked back on his data pad and reread Ensign Lovell's CSV. He couldn't take back what had happened with Jaggers—there could be no second chance for him. But maybe he could somehow balance the books by giving Lovell another chance.

He filled out the necessary paperwork for the transfer request. The forms were long and unnecessarily complex. He transmitted the files to UNSC PERSCOM and sent a copy directly to Vice Admiral Stanforth's staff.

"Sir?" Lieutenant Dominique's voice broke over the intercom. "That shuttle docked with the *Leviathan*."

"Put it on-screen."

The screen over his desk snapped on to camera five, the aft-starboard view. Among the dozens of ships in orbit around Sigma Octanus IV, he easily spotted the *Leviathan*. She was one of the twenty UNSC cruisers left in the fleet.

A cruiser was the most powerful warship ever built by human hands. And Keyes knew they were being slowly pulled out of forward areas and parked in reserve to guard the Inner Colonies.

A piece of shadow moved under the great warship, black moving on black. It revealed itself for only an instant in the sunlight, then slithered back into the darkness. It was a prowler.

Those stealth ships were used exclusively by Naval Intelligence.

A cruiser and an ONI presence here? Now Keyes knew there was more going on here than a simple morale boost. He tried not to think about it. It was best not to go too far when questioning the intentions of one's superior officer—especially when that officer was a Vice Admiral. And especially not when Naval Intelligence was literally lurking in the shadows.

Keyes poured himself another three fingers of Scotch, set his head on his desk—just to rest his eyes for a moment. The last few hours had drained him.

"Sir." Dominique's voice over the intercom woke Captain Keyes. "Incoming fleet-wide transmission on Alpha priority channel."

Keyes sat up and ran his hand over his face. He glanced at the brass clock affixed over his bunk—he had slept for almost six hours.

Vice Admiral Stanforth appeared on-screen. "Listen up, ladies and gentlemen: we've just detected a large number of Covenant ships massing on the edge of the system. We estimate ten ships."

On-screen the silhouettes of the all-too-familiar Covenant frigates and a destroyer appeared as ghostly radar smears.

"We'll remain where we are," the Vice Admiral continued. "There's no need to charge in and have those ugly bastards take a shortcut through Slipspace and undercut us. Make your ships ready for battle. We've got probes gathering more data. I'll update you when we know more. Stanforth out."

The screen went black.

Keyes snapped on the intercom. "Lieutenant Hall, what is our repair and refit status?"

"Sir," she replied. *"Engines are operational, but only with the backup coolant system. We can heat them to fifty percent. Archer and nuclear ordnance resupply is complete. MAC guns are also operational. Repairs to lower decks have just started."*

"Inform the dockmaster to pull his crew out," Captain Keyes said. "We're leaving the *Cradle*. When we are clear, fire the reactors to fifty percent. Go to battle stations."

CHAPTER NINETEEN

0600 HOURS, JULY 18, 2552 (MILITARY CALENDAR) / SIGMA OCTANUS IV, GRID THIRTEEN BY TWENTY-FOUR

"Faster!" Corporal Harland shouted. "You want to die in the mud, Marine?"

"Hell no, sir!" Private Fincher stomped on the accelerator and the Warthog's tires spun in the streambed. They caught, and the vehicle fishtailed through the gravel, across the bank, and onto the sandy shore.

Harland strapped himself into the rear of the Warthog, one hand clamped onto the vehicle's massive 50mm chain-gun.

Something moved in the brush behind them—Harland fired a sustained burst. The deafening sound from "Old Faithful" shook the teeth in his head. Ferns, trees, and vines exploded and splintered as the gunfire scythed through the foliage . . . then nothing was moving anymore.

Fincher sent the Warthog bouncing along the shore, his head bobbing from side to side as he strained to see through the downpour. "We're sitting ducks in here, Corporal," Fincher yelled. "We have to get out of this hole and back onto the ridge, sir."

Corporal Harland looked for a way out of this river gorge. "Walker!" He shook Private Walker in the passenger seat, but Walker didn't respond. He clutched their last Jackhammer rocket launcher with a death grip, his eyes staring blankly ahead. Walker hadn't said a word since this mission went south. Harland hoped he would snap out of it. He already had one man down. The last thing he needed was for his heavy-weapons specialist to be a brain case.

Private Cochran lay at the Corporal's feet, cradling his gut with blood-smeared hands. He'd caught fire during the ambush. The aliens used some kind of projectile weapon that fired long, thin needles—which exploded seconds after impact.

Cochran's insides were meat. Walker and Fincher had filled him up with biofoam and taped him up—they even managed to stop the bleeding—but if the man didn't get to a medic soon, he was a goner.

They had all almost been goners.

The squad had left Firebase Bravo two hours ago. Satellite images showed the way was all clear to their target area. Lieutenant McCasky had even said it was a "milk run." They were supposed to set up motion sensors on grid thirteen by twenty-four—just see what was there and get back. "A simple snoop job," the elltee had called it.

What no one told McCasky was that the satellites weren't penetrating the rain and jungle canopy of this swampball too well. If the Lieutenant had thought about it—like Corporal Harland was thinking about it now—he would have figured something was wrong with sending three squads on a "milk run."

The squad wasn't green. Corporal Harland and the others had fought the Covenant before. They knew how to kill Grunts—when they massed by the hundreds, they knew to call in air support. They'd even taken down a few of the Covenant Jackals, the ones with energy shields. You had to flank those guys—take them out with snipers.

But none of that had prepared them for this mission.

They had done all the right things, damn it. The Lieutenant had even gotten their Warthogs five klicks down the streambed before the terrain became too steep and slippery for the all-terrain armored vehicles. He had the men hump the rest of the way in on foot. They moved soft and silent, almost crawling all the way through the slime to the depression they were supposed to check out.

When they had gotten to the place, it wasn't just another mud-filled sinkhole. A waterfall splashed into a grotto pool. Arches had been carved into the wall, their edges extremely weathered. There were a few scattered paving stones around the pool . . . and covering those stones were tiny geometric carvings.

That's all Corporal Harland got a look at before the Lieutenant ordered him and his team to fall back. He wanted them to set up the motion sensors where they had a clear line of sight to the sky.

That's probably why they were still alive.

The blast had knocked Harland and his team into the mud. They ran to where they had left the Lieutenant—found fused glassy mud, a crater, and a few burning corpses and bits of carbonized skeleton.

They saw one other thing—an outline in the mist. It was biped, but much larger than any human Harland had ever seen. And oddly, it looked like it was wearing armor reminiscent of medieval plate mail; it even carried a large, strangely shaped metal shield.

Harland saw the glow of a regenerating plasma weapon . . . and that's all he needed to see to order a full speed retreat.

Harland, Walker, Cochran, and Fincher fell back, running—blindly firing their assault rifles.

Covenant Grunts had followed them, peppering the air with those needle guns, mowing down the jungle as the tiny razor shards exploded.

Harland and the others stopped and hit the deck, splashing into the thick, red mud, as a Covenant Banshee passed them overhead.

When they got back on their feet, Cochran took the round in the stomach. The Grunts had caught up to them. Cochran flinched, his side exploded, and then he crumpled to the ground. He fell into shock so fast he didn't even have time to scream.

Harland, Fincher, and Walker hunkered down and returned fire. They killed a dozen of the little bastards, but more kept coming, their barks and growls echoing through the jungle.

"Cease fire," the Corporal had ordered. He waited a second, then tossed a grenade when the Grunts got closer.

Their ears still ringing, they ran, dragging Cochran with them, and not looking back.

Somehow they had returned to the Warthog, and gotten the hell out of there . . . or, at least, that's what they were trying to do.

"Over there," Fincher said, and pointed to a clearing in the trees. "That's got to lead up to the ridge."

"Go," Harland said.

The Warthog slid sideways then raced up the embankment, caught air, and landed on soft jungle loam. Fincher dodged a few trees and ran the Warthog up the slope. They emerged on the ridgeline.

"Jesus, that was close," Harland said. He ran a muddy hand through his hair, slicking it back.

He tapped Fincher on the shoulder. Fincher jumped. "Private, pull over. Try to raise Firebase Bravo on the narrow band."

"Yes, sir," Fincher answered in a wavering voice. He glanced at the near-catatonic Private Walker and shook his head.

Harland checked on Cochran. Private Cochran's eyes fluttered open, cracking the mud caked onto his face. "We back yet, Corporal?"

"Almost," Harland replied. Cochran's pulse was steady, although his face had, in the last several minutes, drained of color. The wounded man looked like a corpse. *Damn it,* Harland thought, *he's going to bleed out*.

Harland placed a reassuring hand on Cochran's shoulder. "Hang in there. We'll patch you up as soon as we get to camp."

They had dropships at Bravo. Cochran had a chance, albeit a slim one, if they got him back to the combat surgeons at headquarters—or better yet, to the Navy docs on the orbiting ships. For a moment Harland was dazzled with visions of clean sheets, hot meals—and a meter of armor between him and the Covenant.

"Nothing but static on the link, sir," Fincher said, breaking through Harland's reverie.

"Maybe the radio got hit," Harland muttered. "You know those explosive needles throw a bunch of microshrapnel. We probably got slivers of that stuff inside us, too."

Fincher examined his muscular forearms. "Great."

"Move out," Harland said.

The tires of the Warthog spun, gripped, and the vehicle moved rapidly along the ridge.

The terrain looked familiar. Harland even spotted three sets of Warthog tracks—yes, this was the way the Lieutenant had brought them. Ten minutes and they'd be back on base. No more worries. He relaxed, took out a pack of cigarettes, and shook one out. He pulled off the safety strip and tapped the end to ignite it.

Fincher revved the engine and shot up to the top of the ridge—crossed over, and skidded to halt.

If not for the haze, they would have seen everything from this side of the valley—the lush carpet of jungle in the valley, the river meandering through it, and on the far set of hills, a clearing dotted with fixed gun emplacements, razor wire, and pre-fab structures: Firebase Bravo.

Their platoon had partially dug into the hillside to minimize the camp's footprint and provide a place where they could safely store their munitions and bunk down. A ring of sensors encircled the camp so nothing could sneak up on them. Radar and motion detectors linked to surface-to-air missile batteries. A road ran along the far ridge—three klicks down that was the coastal city, Côte d'Azur.

The sun broke through the haze overhead, and Corporal Harland saw everything had changed.

It wasn't fog or haze. Smoke rose in columns from the valley . . . and there was no more jungle. Everything had been burned to the ground. The entire valley was blackened into smoldering charcoal. Glowing red craters honeycombed the hillsides.

He fumbled with his binoculars, brought them to his eyes . . . and froze. The hill where the camp had been was gone—it had been flattened. Only a mirror surface remained. The sides of the adjacent hills glistened with a cracked glass coating. The air was thick with tiny Covenant fliers in the distance. On the ground, Grunts and Jackals searched for survivors. A few Marines ran for cover . . . there were hundreds of wounded and dead on the ground, helpless, screaming—some of them trying to crawl away.

"What have you got, sir?" Fincher asked.

The cigarette fell from Harland's mouth and caught on his shirt—but he didn't take his eyes off the battlefield to brush it away.

"There's nothing left," he whispered.

A shape moved in the valley—much larger than the other Grunts and Jackals. Its outline was blurry. Harland tried to focus the binoculars on it but couldn't. It was the same thing he had seen at grid thirteen by twenty-four. The Grunts gave it a wide berth. The thing lifted its arm—its whole arm looked like one big gun—and a bolt of plasma struck near the riverbank.

Even from this distance, Harland heard the screams of the men who had been hiding there.

"Jesus." He dropped the binoculars. "We're bugging out, right now!" he said. "Turn this beast around, Fincher."

"But—"

"They're gone," Harland whispered. "They're all dead."

Walker whimpered and rocked back and forth.

"We'll be dead, too, unless you move," Harland said. "We already got lucky once today. Let's not push it."

"Yeah." Fincher reversed the Warthog. "Yeah, some luck."

He sped back down the hillside and hopped the Warthog off the embankment and back into the streambed.

"Follow the river," Harland told him. "It'll take us all the way to HQ."

A shadow crossed their path. Harland twisted around and saw a pair of stubby-winged Covenant Banshees swooping down after them.

"Move it!" he screamed at Fincher.

Fincher floored the Warthog and plumes of water sprayed in their wake. They bounced over rocks and fishtailed across the stream.

Bolts of plasma hit the water next to them—exploding into steam. Rock shards pinged off the armored side of the vehicle.

"Walker!" Harland shouted. "Use those Jackhammers."

Walker huddled, doubled over in his seat.

Harland fired the chain-gun. Tracers cut through the air. The fliers nimbly dodged them. The heavy machine gun was only accurate at reasonably short ranges—and not even that with Fincher bouncing the Warthog all over the place.

"Walker!" he cried. "We are gonna die if you don't get those missiles into the air!"

He would have ordered Fincher to grab the launcher—but he'd have to stop to grab it . . . that, or try to drive with no hands. If the Warthog stopped, they'd be sitting ducks for those fliers.

Harland glanced at the riverbanks. They were too steep for the Warthog. They were stuck in the river with no cover.

"Walker, do something!"

Corporal Harland fired the chain-gun again until his arms went numb. It was no good; the Banshees were too far away, too quick.

Another plasma bolt hit—directly in front of the Warthog. Heat washed over Harland. Blisters pinpricked his back.

He screamed but kept shooting. If they hadn't been in water, that plasma would have melted the tires . . . probably would have flash-fried them all.

A burst of heat and a plume of smoke erupted next to Harland.

For a split second he thought the Covenant gunners had found their mark—that he was dead. He screamed incoherently, his thumbs jamming down the chain-gun's trigger buttons.

The Banshee he was aiming at flashed, and then became a ball of flame and falling shrapnel.

He turned, his breath hitching in his chest. They hadn't been hit.

Cochran knelt next to him. One arm clutched his stomach, and the other arm hefted the Jackhammer launcher on his shoulder. He smiled with bloodstained lips and pivoted to track the other flier.

Harland ducked, and another missile whooshed directly over his head.

Cochran laughed, coughing up blood and foam. Tears of mirth or pain—Harland couldn't tell—streamed from his eyes. He collapsed backward, and let the smoldering launcher slip from his hand.

The second Banshee exploded and spiraled into the jungle.

"Two more klicks," Fincher shouted. "Hang on." He cranked the wheel and the Warthog swerved out of the streambed and bounced up the hillside, up and over, and they slid onto a paved road.

Harland leaned over and felt Cochran's neck for a pulse. It was there, weak; but he was still alive. Harland glanced at Walker. He hadn't moved, his eyes squeezed shut.

Harland's first impulse was to shoot him right then and there—the goddamned, goldbricking, cowardly bastard almost cost them all their lives—

No. Harland was half amazed he hadn't frozen up, too.

HQ was ahead. But Corporal Harland's stomach sank as he saw smoke and flames blazing on the horizon.

They passed the first armed checkpoint. The guardhouse and bunkers had been blasted away, and in the mud were thousands of Grunt tracks.

Farther back, he saw a circle of sandbags around a house-size chunk of granite. Two Marines waved to them. As they approached in the Warthog, the Marines stood and saluted.

Harland jumped off and returned their salute.

One of the Marines had a patch over his eye and his head was bandaged. Soot streaked his face. "Jesus, sir," he said. "It's good to see you guys." He approached the Warthog. "You've got a working radio in that thing?"

"I—I'm not sure," Corporal Harland said. "Who's in charge here? What happened?"

"Covenant hit us hard, sir. They had tanks, air support—thousands of those little Grunt guys. They glassed the main barracks. The Command Office. Almost got the munitions bunker." He looked away for a moment and his one eye glazed over. "We pulled it together and fought 'em off, though. That was an hour ago. I think we killed everything. I'm not sure."

"Who's in charge, Private? I have a critically wounded man. He needs evac, and I have to make my report."

The Private shook his head. "I'm sorry, sir. The hospital was the first thing they hit. As far as who's in command . . . I think you're the ranking officer here."

"Great," Harland muttered.

"We've got five guys back there." The Private jerked his head toward the columns of smoke and wavering heat in the distance. "They're in fire-fighting suits to keep from burning up. They're recovering weapons and ammo."

"Understood," Harland said. "Fincher, try the radio again. See if you can link up to SATCOM. Call in for an evac."

"Roger that," Fincher said.

The wounded Private asked Harland, "Can we get help from Firebase Bravo, sir?"

"No," Harland said. "They got hit, too. There's Covenant all over the place."

The Private slumped, bracing himself with his rifle.

Fincher handed Harland the radio headset. "Sir, SATCOM is good. I've got the *Leviathan* on the horn."

"This is Corporal Harland," he spoke into the microphone. "The Covenant has hit Firebase Bravo and Alpha HQ . . . and wiped them out. We've repelled the enemy from Alpha site, but our casualties have been nearly one hundred percent. We have wounded here. We need immediate evac. Say again: we need evac on the double."

"Roger, Corporal. Your situation is understood. Evac is not possible at this time. We've got problems of our own up here—" There was a burst of static. The voice came back online. *"Help is on the way."*

The channel went dead.

Harland looked to Fincher. "Check the transceiver."

Fincher ran the diagnostic. "It's working," he said. "I'm getting a ping from SATCOM." He licked his lips. "The trouble must be on their end."

Harland didn't want to think of what kind of trouble the fleet could be having. He'd seen too many planets glassed from orbit. He didn't want to die here—not like that.

He turned to the men in the bunker. "They said help is on the way. So relax." He looked into the sky and whispered, "They better send a whole regiment down here."

A handful of other Marines returned to the bunker. They had salvaged ammunition, extra rifles, a crate of frag grenades, and a few Jackhammer missiles. Fincher took the Warthog and a few men to see if he could transport the heavier weapons.

They filled Cochran with more biofoam and bandaged him up. He slipped into a coma.

They hunkered down inside the bunker and waited. They heard explosions at an extreme distance.

Walker finally spoke. "So . . . now what, sir?"

Harland didn't turn toward the man. He covered Cochran with another blanket. "I don't know. Can you fight?"

"I think so."

He passed Walker a rifle. "Good. Get up there and stand watch." He got out a cigarette, lit it, took a puff, and then handed it to Walker.

Walker took it, shakily stood, and went outside.

"Sir!" he said. "Dropship inbound. One of ours!"

Harland grabbed his signal flares. He ran outside and squinted at the horizon. High on the edge of the darkening sky was a dot, and the unmistakable roar of Pelican engines. He pulled the pin and tossed the smoker onto the ground. A moment later, thick clouds of green smoke roiled into the sky.

The dropship turned rapidly and descended toward their location.

Harland shielded his eyes. He searched for the rest of the dropships. There was only one.

"*One* dropship?" Walker whispered. "That's all they sent? Christ, that's not backup—that's a burial detail."

The Pelican eased toward the ground, spattering mud in a ten-meter radius, then touched down. The launch ramp fell open and a dozen figures marched out.

For a moment Harland thought they were the same creatures he had seen earlier—armored and bigger than any human he'd ever laid eyes on. He froze—he couldn't have raised his gun if he had wanted to.

They were human, though. The one in the lead stood over two meters tall and looked like he weighed two hundred kilograms. His armor was a strange reflective green alloy, and underneath matte black. Their motions were so fluid and graceful—fast and precise, too. More like robots than flesh and blood.

The one that first stepped off the ship strode toward him. Though his armor was devoid of insignia, Harland could see the insignia of a Master Chief Petty Officer in his helmet's HUD.

"Master Chief, sir!" Harland snapped to attention and saluted.

"Corporal," it said. "At ease. Get your men together and we'll get to work."

"Sir?" Harland asked. "I've got a lot of wounded here. What work will we be doing, sir?"

The Master Chief's helmet cocked quizzically to one side. "We've come to take Sigma Octanus Four back from the Covenant, Corporal," he said calmly. "To do that, we're going to kill every last one of them."

CHAPTER TWENTY

1800 HOURS, JULY 18, 2552 (MILITARY CALENDAR) / SIGMA OCTANUS IV, GRID NINETEEN BY THIRTY-SEVEN

The Master Chief surveyed what was left of Camp Alpha. There were only fourteen Marine regulars left—balanced against the four hundred men and women who had been slaughtered here.

He said to Kelly, "Post a guard on the dropship, and put three on patrol. Take the rest and secure the LZ."

"Yes, sir." She turned to face the other Spartans, pointed, made three quick hand gestures, and they dispersed like ghosts.

The Master Chief turned to the Corporal. "Are you in command here, Corporal?"

The man looked around. "I guess so . . . yes, sir."

"As of 0900 Standard Military time, NavSpecWeap is assuming control of this operation. All Marine personnel now report through our chain of command. Understand, Corporal?"

"Yes, sir."

"Now, Corporal, brief me on what happened here."

Corporal Harland hunkered down and sketched rough maps of the area as he quickly recounted the brutal series of surprise attacks. "Right here—grid thirteen by twenty-four. That's where they hit us, sir. Something's goin' on there."

The Master Chief scanned the crude maps, compared them with the area surveys displayed in his HUD, then nodded, satisfied.

"Get your wounded inside the Pelican, Corporal," he said.

"We'll be dusting off soon. I want you to rotate by thirds on guard duty. The rest of your men should get some sleep. But make no mistake—if the Pelican gets fragged, we'll be staying on Sigma Octanus Four."

The Corporal paled, then replied, "Understood, sir." He stood slowly—the long day of combat and flight had taken its toll. The Marine saluted, then moved to assemble his team.

Inside his sealed helmet, John frowned. These Marines were now under his command . . . and therefore part of his team. They lacked the Spartans' firepower and training, so they had to be protected—not relied upon. He had to make sure they got out in one piece. Another snag in an already dicey mission.

The Master Chief opened his COM link: "Team leaders, meet me at the LZ in three minutes."

Lights winked on his heads-up display—his Spartans acknowledging the order.

He looked around at the destruction. Thin sunlight reflected dully from the thousands of spent shell casings strewn across the battlefield. Dozens of shattered Warthog chassis bled trails of smoke into the hazy sky. Scores of burned corpses lay in the mud.

They'd have to get a burial detail down here later . . . before the Grunts got to the dead.

The Master Chief would never question his orders, but he felt a momentary stab of bitterness. Whoever set these camps up without proper reconnaissance, whoever had blindly trusted the satellite transmissions in an enemy-held region, had been a fool.

Worse, they had wasted the lives of good soldiers.

Green Team's leader jogged in from the south. The Master Chief couldn't see her features through her reflective faceplate, but he could tell without checking his HUD that it was Linda by the way she moved . . . that, and the SRS99C-S2 AM sniper rifle with Oracle scope she carried.

She carefully looked around, verified that the area was secure, and slung her rifle. She snapped a crisp salute. "Reporting as ordered, Master Chief."

Red Team leader—Joshua—ran in from the east. He saluted. "Motion detectors, radar, and automated defenses up and running, sir."

"Good. Let's go over this one more time." The Master Chief overlaid a topographic map on their helmets' displays. "Mission goal one: we need to gather intelligence on Covenant troop disposition and defenses at Côte d'Azur. Mission goal two: if there are no civilian survivors, we are authorized to remote detonate a HAVOK tactical nuclear mine and remove the enemy forces. In the meantime, we will minimize our contact with the enemy."

They nodded.

The Master Chief highlighted the four streams that fed into the river delta near Côte d'Azur. "We avoid these routes. Banshees patrol them." He circled where Firebase Bravo had been. "We'll avoid this area as well—according to the Marine survivors, that area is hot. Grid thirteen by twenty-four also has activity.

"Red Leader, take your squad in along the coast. Stay in the tree line. Green Leader, follow this ridgeline, but keep under cover, too. I'll be taking this route." The Master Chief traced a path through a particularly dense section of jungle.

"It's 1830 hours now. The city is thirteen kilometers from here—that should take us no more than forty minutes. We'll probably be forced to slow down to avoid enemy patrols—but we all should be in place no later than 1930 hours."

He zoomed into a city map of Côte d'Azur. "Entry points to the city sewer system are—" He highlighted the display with NAV points. "—Here, here, and here. Red Team will recon the wharf areas. Green takes the residential section. I'll take Blue Team downtown. Questions?"

"Our communications underground will be limited," Linda said. "How do we check in while keeping our heads down?"

"According to the Colonial Administration Authority's file on Côte d'Azur, the sewer systems here have steel pipes running along the top of the plastic conduits. Tap into those and use ground-return transceivers to check in. We'll have our own private COM line."

"Roger," she said.

The Master Chief said, "As soon as we leave, the dropship dusts off and will move here." He indicated a position far to the south of Alpha camp. "If the Pelican doesn't make it . . . our fallback rendezvous point is here." He indicated a point fifty kilometers south. "ONI's welcoming committee has stashed our emergency SATCOM link and survival gear there."

No one mentioned that survival gear would be useless when the Covenant glassed the planet.

"Stay sharp," John said. "And come back in one piece. Dismissed."

They saluted briskly, then sprinted to their tasks.

He switched to Blue Team's frequency. "Time to saddle up, Blue Team," he called out. "RV back at the bunker for orders." Three blue lights winked acknowledgement in his display.

A moment later, the other three Spartans in his squad trotted into position. "Reporting as ordered," Blue-Two announced.

The Master Chief quickly filled them in on the mission. "Blue-Two." He nodded to Kelly. "You're carrying the nuke and medical gear."

"Affirmative. Who'll have the detonator, sir?"

"I will," he replied. "Blue-Three." He turned to Fred. "You have the explosives. James, you'll take our extra COM equipment."

They double-checked their gear: modified MA5B assault rifles, adapted to mount silencers; ten extra clips of ammunition; frag grenades; combat knives; M6D pistols—small but powerful handguns that fired .450 Magnum loads, sufficient to crack through Grunt armor.

In addition to the weapons, there was a single smoke

canister—blue smoke to signal for pickup. John would carry that. "Let's go," he said.

Blue Team moved out. They quickly entered the jungle, in a simple single-file line with Blue-Four in the lead; James had an instinct for walking point. The line was slightly staggered, with John and Kelly slightly to the left of James. Fred brought up the rear.

They moved cautiously. Every hundred yards, James signaled the group to halt while he methodically surveyed the area for any sign of the enemy. The rest of Blue Team crouched, and disappeared into the thick jungle foliage.

John checked his HUD; they were one-quarter of the way to the city. The team made good time despite the cautious pace. The MJOLNIR assault armor allowed them to push their way through the thick jungle like it was a stroll through the woods.

As the team moved on, the thin mist that permeated the jungle gave way to a hard, pelting rain. The damp ground gradually turned to mud, forcing the team to slow.

Blue-Four stopped dead and raised his fist—the signal to halt and freeze. John stopped in his tracks, his rifle raised and sweeping slowly back and forth, searching for any sign of enemy movement.

Normally, the Spartans relied on their armor's detection gear to locate enemy troops. But their motion sensors were useless—everything moved in the jungle. They had to rely on their eyes and ears and the instincts of their point man.

"Point to Team Leader: enemy contact." James' calm voice crackled across the COM channel. *"Enemy troops within one hundred meters of my position, ten degrees left."*

With exaggerated slowness, Blue-Four indicated the danger area by pointing.

"Affirmative," John replied. "Blue Team: hold position."

Although the motion trackers were of no use here, thermal proved effective. Through the thick sheets of rain, the Master

Chief spotted three cold spots: Grunts in their chilled environmental suits.

"Blue Team: enemy contact confirmed." He added the enemy position to his HUD. "Estimated enemy strength, Point?"

"Lead, I make ten, say again, ten Covenant troops. Grunts, sir. They're moving slowly. Double-file formation. They haven't spotted us. Orders?"

John's orders said to minimize contact with the enemy where possible—the Spartans were spread too thinly across the battle area to risk a prolonged engagement. But the Grunts were heading right for the Marine bunker . . .

"Let's take them out, Blue Team," he said.

The team of Grunts slogged through the mud. The vaguely simian aliens wore shiny red-trimmed armor. Craggy, purple-black hide was visible beneath the environmental suits. Breath masks provided supercooled methane—the aliens' atmosphere. There were ten of them, moving in two columns and spaced roughly three meters apart.

John noted with satisfaction that they seemed bored—only the point man and the pair on rear guard had their plasma rifles at the ready. The rest chattered at each other in a weird combination of high-pitched squeaks and guttural barks.

Easy, relaxed targets. Perfect.

He gave a series of slow hand signals to the rest of the team; they faded back until they were well away from the Grunts' field of view.

The Master Chief opened the squadwide COM channel. "They're seventy meters from this depression—" He keyed a NAV point into the team's topographic display. "They're heading for the western hill and will probably follow the terrain to the top. We'll fall back now, and take concealed positions along the eastern hill.

"Blue-Four, you're our scout—stay near the bottom and let us know when the rear guard passes you. Take them out first—they seem alert.

"Blue-Two, you have overwatch at the top of the hill.

"Blue-Three, back me up. Silenced weapons only—no explosives, unless things go bad."

He paused, then gave the order: "Move out."

The Spartans crept back along their path and spread out along the hill.

John—in the center of the line—readied his assault rifle. The team was virtually invisible in the thick foliage, and covered by the barrelwide tree trunks of the local flora.

One minute ticked by. Then two . . . three . . .

Blue-Four's acknowledgment signal blinked twice in John's HUD. *Enemy detected.* He relaxed his grip on the weapon, waiting—

—There. Twenty meters distant, the Grunt point man moved to the edge of the western hill, just downhill from John's position. The alien paused, his plasma rifle sweeping the area—then moved slowly up the rise.

A moment later, the rest of the formation came into view, ten meters behind the point man.

Blue-Four's indicator winked again. *Now.*

The Master Chief opened fire, a short, three-round burst. The weapon's muffled cough was inaudible over the sound of jungle rainfall. The trio of armor-piercing rounds slashed through the alien's throat protection, rupturing the environment suit. The Grunt clutched at his neck, emitted a brief, high-pitched gurgle—then fell to the mud, dead.

A moment later, the Grunt lines came to a clumsy halt, confused.

John spotted two strobe flashes, and the pair of Covenant rear guards dropped to the ground.

"Blue-Two to Lead: rear-guard eliminated."

"Hit them!" John barked.

The four Spartans opened fire in short bursts. In less than a second, four more of the Grunt patrol were down, dead from head shots.

The remaining trio of Grunts unslung their plasma rifles, swinging them wildly back and forth, looking for targets and chattering loudly in their strange, barking language. John sighted on the alien closest to him and squeezed the trigger.

The alien splashed into the mud, methane spraying from his shattered breath mask.

Another pair of sustained bursts and the last of the Grunts were down.

Kelly policed the Grunts' weapons and handed a plasma rifle to each of the team; the Spartans had standing orders to seize Covenant weapons and technology whenever possible.

Blue Team fanned out and continued on their way. When they heard Banshees overhead, they hunkered down in the mud, and the fliers passed.

Ten more kilometers of rough terrain and then the jungle stopped and fields of rice paddies stretched out before them all the way to Côte d'Azur.

Crossing these would be more difficult than the jungle. They donned camouflage cloaks that masked their thermal signatures and crawled through the muck on their stomachs.

The Master Chief saw three larger ships hovering over the city. If they were troop transports, they could carry thousands of Covenant soldiers. If they were warships, any direct ground assault against the city would be futile. Either way it was bad news.

He made sure his vid and audio mission recorders got a good clear image of the vessels.

When they emerged from the mud, they were near the beach on the edge of the city. The Master Chief checked his map readings and made his way to the sewage outlet.

The two-meter diameter pipe was sealed with a steel grate. He and Fred easily bent the bars aside and entered.

They sloshed through hip-deep muck. The Master Chief didn't like the cramped quarters. Their mobility was restricted by the narrow pipes; worse, they were bunched up and therefore easier to kill with grenades or massed fire. Motion sensors picked up hundreds of targets. The constant downpour from storm drains above made the sensors useless.

He followed his electronic map through the maze of pipes. Light filtered in from above—beams of illumination connected to the manhole-cover vent holes. Every so often something moved and blocked that light.

The Spartans moved quickly and quietly through the sludge and halted when they reached their final waypoint—directly under the center of Côte d'Azur's "downtown."

With a tiny jerk of his head, the Master Chief informed Blue Team to spread out and keep their eyes peeled. He snaked a fiber-optic probe up through the drain grate at street level and plugged it into his helmet.

The yellow light from the sodium vapor lamps washed everything topside in an eerie glow. There were Grunts positioned on the street corners, and the shadow of a Banshee flier circling overhead.

The electric cars parked on the street had been overturned, and the waste receptacles had been knocked over or set on fire. Every street-level window was broken. The Master Chief saw no human civilians, alive or otherwise.

Blue Team moved up and over a block. The Master Chief checked topside again.

There was more activity here: a pack of black-armored Grunts meandered down the streets. Two vulture-headed Jackals sat on the corner, squabbling over a hunk of meat.

Something else caught his attention, though. There were

other aliens on the sidewalk—or rather, *above* the sidewalk. They were roughly man-size creatures—unlike any he had ever encountered. The creatures were vaguely sluglike, with pale, purple-pink skin. Unlike other Covenant forces, they were not bipeds. Instead they had several tentacular appendages sprouting from their thick trunks.

They floated a half meter above the ground, as if the odd, pink bladders on their backs kept them aloft. One alien used a slender tentacle to open the hood of a car. It began to disassemble the car's electric engine, moving with startling speed.

Within twenty seconds all the parts had been neatly arranged in rows on the pavement. The creature paused, then reassembled the parts with blinding quickness, disassembled and rebuilt it several times into different arrangements. Finally, the creature simply reassembled the car and floated on its way.

The Master Chief made sure his mission recorder had gotten that. This was a Covenant race never documented before.

He rotated the fiber-optic cable to point down the opposite end of the street. There was more activity another block away.

He retracted the probe and moved Blue Team a block farther south. He signaled the team to hold position, then climbed up a short series of metal handholds until he was just below a manhole cover.

He cautiously sent the probe topside again, up through the manhole-cover vent.

There was a Jackal's hoof directly adjacent to the probe, blocking half of his field of vision. He turned the probe with excruciating slowness, and saw fifty more Jackals milling back and forth. They were concentrated around the building across the street. The building resembled pictures that Déjà had shown him years ago—it looked like an Athenian temple, with white marble steps and Ionic columns. At the top of the steps were a pair of stationary guns. More bad news.

He pulled the probe back and consulted the map. The building was marked as the Côte d'Azur Museum of Natural History.

The Covenant had serious firepower here—the stationary guns had commanding fields of fire, making a frontal assault suicidal. *Why would they protect a human structure?* he wondered. Was it their headquarters?

The Master Chief signaled for Blue-Two. He pointed to the accessway that led under the building. He held up two fingers, pointed toward her eyes, and then down the passage, and then slowly balled his hand into a fist.

Kelly proceeded very slowly down that passage to scout it out.

The Master Chief checked the time. Red and Green Teams were due to report. He had James attach the ground-return transceiver to the pipes overhead.

"Green Team, come in."

"Roger: Green Team Leader here, sir," Linda whispered over the channel. *"We've scouted the residential section."* There was a pause. *"No survivors . . . just like Draco Three. We're too late."*

He understood. They'd seen it before. The Covenant didn't take prisoners. On Draco III, they had watched via satellite linkup as human survivors were herded together and ripped apart by ravenous Grunts and Jackals. By the time the Spartans had gotten there, there was no one left to rescue.

But the victims had been avenged.

"Green Team: stand by and prepare to fall back to the RV and secure the area," he said.

"Standing by," Linda said.

He switched to the Red Team COM channel: "Red Team, report."

Joshua's voice crackled over the link: *"Red Leader, sir. We've got something for ONI. We've spotted some new type of Covenant race. Little guys that float. They seem to be some sort of explorer or scientist type. They take things apart, then move on, like they're looking for something. They do not, repeat not, appear hostile. Advise that you do not engage. They raise a pretty loud alarm, Blue Lead."*

"You in trouble?"

"Dodged trouble, sir," he said. *"But there is one snag."*

"Snag." The word was charged with meaning for the Spartans. Getting caught in an ambush or a minefield, a teammate wounded, or aerial bombardments—those were all things they had trained for. Snags were things they didn't know how to handle. Complications that no one had planned for.

"Go ahead," the Master Chief whispered.

"We have survivors. Twenty civilians hid in a cargo ship here. There are several wounded."

The Master Chief mulled this over. It wasn't his choice to weigh the relative worth of a handful of civilian lives versus the possibility of taking out ten thousand Covenant troops with their nuke. His orders were specific on this point. They could not set up the nuke if there was civilian population at risk.

"New mission objective, Red Team Leader," the Master Chief said. "Get those civilians to the recovery point and evac them back to fleet." He switched COM channels again, broadcasting to all the teams. "Green Team Leader, you still online?"

A pause, then Linda spoke: *"Roger."*

"Move to the docks and coordinate with Red Team—they have survivors we need to evac. Green Team leader has strategic control of this mission."

"Understood," she said. *"We're on our way."*

"Affirmative, sir," Joshua said. *"We'll get it done."*

"Blue Team out." The Master Chief disconnected.

It was going to be rough for Green and Red Teams. Those civilians would slow them down—and if they had to protect them from Covenant patrols, they'd all get noticed.

Blue-Two returned. She opened the COM link and reported

in. "There's access to the building—a ladder and a steel plate welded shut. We can burn through it."

The Master Chief opened up the team COM channel. "We're going to assume that Red and Green Teams will remove the civilians from Côte d'Azur. We will proceed as planned."

He paused, then turned to Blue-Two. "Break out the nuke and arm it."

CHAPTER

TWENTY-ONE

2120 HOURS, JULY 18, 2552 (MILITARY CALENDAR) / UNSC *IROQUOIS*, MILITARY STAGING AREA IN ORBIT AROUND SIGMA OCTANUS IV

"Ship's status?" Captain Keyes said as he strode onto the bridge, buttoning his collar. He noticed that the repair station *Cradle* still obscured their port camera. "And why aren't we clear of that station yet?"

"Sir, all hands are at battle stations," Lieutenant Dominique replied. "General quarters sounded. Tac data uploaded to your station."

A tactical overview of the *Iroquois,* neighboring vessels, and *Cradle* popped onto Keyes' personal display screen. "As you can see," Lieutenant Dominique continued, "we *did* clear the station, but they are moving on the same outbound vector we are. Vice Admiral Stanforth wants them with the fleet."

Captain Keyes took his place in his command chair—"the hot seat," as it was more colloquially known—and reviewed the data. He nodded with satisfaction. "Looks like the Vice Admiral has something up his sleeve." He turned to Lieutenant Hall. "Engine status, Lieutenant?"

"Engines hot at fifty percent," she reported. She straightened to her full height, nearly six feet, and looked Captain Keyes in the eye with something edging near defensiveness. "Sir, the engines took a real beating in our last engagement. The repairs we've made are . . . well, the best we could do without a complete refit."

"Understood, Lieutenant," Keyes replied calmly. In truth, Keyes was concerned about the engines, too—but it would do no good to make Hall more uneasy than necessary. The last thing he needed now was to undermine her confidence.

"Gunnery officer?" Captain Keyes turned to Lieutenant Hikowa. The petite woman bore more resemblance to a porcelain doll than to a combat officer, but Keyes knew her delicate appearance was only skin deep. She had ice water for blood and nerves of steel.

"MAC guns charging," Lieutenant Hikowa reported. "Sixty-five percent and climbing at two percent per minute."

Everything on the *Iroquois* had slowed down to a crawl. Engine, weapons—even the unwieldy *Cradle* kept pace with them.

Captain Keyes sat up straighter. There was no time to spend on self-recriminations. He would have to do the best he could with what he had. There simply was no other alternative.

The lift doors popped open and a young man stepped on deck. He was tall and thin. His dark hair—longer than regulations permitted—had been slicked back. He was disarmingly handsome; Keyes noticed the female bridge crew pause to look the newcomer over before returning to their tasks. "Ensign Lovell reporting for duty, Captain." He snapped a sharp salute.

"Welcome aboard, Ensign Lovell." Captain Keyes returned his salute, surprised that the unkempt officer could demonstrate such crisp adherence to military protocol. "Man the navigation console, please."

The bridge officers scrutinized the Ensign. It was highly unusual for such a low-ranking officer to pilot a capital ship. "Sir?" Lovell wrinkled his forehead, confused. "Has there been some mistake, sir?"

"You *are* Ensign William Lovell? Recently posted on the *Archimedes* Remote Sensor Outpost?"

"Yes, sir. They pulled me off that duty so quick that I—"

"Then man your station, Ensign."

"Yes, sir!"

Ensign Lovell sat at the navigation console, took a few seconds to acquaint himself with the controls—then reconfigured them more to his liking.

A slight smile tugged at the corner of Keyes' mouth. He knew that Lovell had more combat experience than any Lieutenant on the bridge, and was pleased that the Ensign adapted so quickly to unfamiliar surroundings.

"Show me the fleet's position and the relative location of the enemy, Ensign," Keyes ordered.

"Aye, sir," Lovell replied. His hands danced across the controls. A moment later, a system map snapped into place on the main screen. Dozens of small triangular tactical markers showed Vice Admiral Stanforth's fleet massing between Sigma Octanus IV and its moon. It was a sound opening position. Fighting in orbit around Sigma Octanus IV would have trapped them in the gravity well—like fighting with your back to a wall.

Keyes studied the display—and frowned. The Vice Admiral had moved the fleet into a tightly packed grid formation. When the Covenant fired their plasma weapons at them, there would be no maneuvering room.

The Covenant was moving in-system quickly. Captain Keyes counted twenty radar signatures. He didn't like the odds.

"Receiving orders," Lieutenant Dominique said. "Vice Admiral Stanforth wants the *Iroquois* at this location ASAP."

On the map, a blue triangle pulsed on the corner of the grid formation.

"Ensign Lovell, get us there at best speed."

"Aye, sir," he replied.

Captain Keyes fought down a wave of embarrassment; the *Cradle* stardock started to pull ahead of the *Iroquois*. It took up a position directly over the Admiral's phalanx formation. The refit station rotated, presenting its edge to the incoming Covenant fleet to show them the smallest target area.

"Rotating and reversing burn," Ensign Lovell said. The *Iroquois* spun about and slowed. "Thrusters to station keeping. We're locked in position, sir."

"Very good, Ensign. Lieutenant Hikowa, divert as much power as you need to get those MAC guns charged."

"Aye, sir," Hikowa replied. "Capacitors charging at maximum rate."

"Captain," Lieutenant Dominique said. "We're receiving an encrypted firing solution and countdown timers from the *Leviathan*'s AI."

"Transfer that vector to Lieutenant Hikowa and show me on screen."

A line appeared on the tactical map, connecting the *Iroquois* to one of the incoming Covenant frigates. The firing timer appeared in the corner: twenty-three seconds.

"Now show me the entire fleet's firing solutions, Lieutenant Dominique."

A web of trajectories crossed the map with tiny countdown times next to each. Vice Admiral Stanforth had the fleet exchanging fire with the Covenant like a line of Redcoats and colonial militia in the Revolutionary War—tactics that could best be described as bloody . . . or suicidal.

What the hell was the Vice Admiral thinking? Keyes studied the displays, trying to divine a method to his commanding officer's madness . . . then he understood. Risky, but—if it worked—brilliant.

The fleet's firing countdowns were roughly timed so that the shots would be staggered into two, maybe three, massive salvos. The first salvo would—hopefully—knock out the Covenant ships' shields. The final salvo was to be the knockout punch.

But it could only work once. After that, the UNSC fleet would be destroyed when the remaining Covenant ships returned fire. The *Iroquois* and the other ships were stationary targets. He appreciated that the Vice Admiral couldn't get too far from Sigma

Octanus IV, but with zero momentum—and no room to maneuver—there'd be no way to avoid those plasma bolts.

"Sound decompression alarms in all nonessential sections, Lieutenant Hall, and then empty them."

"Aye, sir," she said, and bit her lower lip.

"Guns: status on the MACs?" Keyes' eyes were glued to the firing countdown. Twenty seconds . . . fifteen . . . ten . . .

"Sir, MAC weapon systems are hot!" Hikowa announced. "Removing safeties now."

The Covenant ships started to rotate slowly in space—although their momentum continued to carry them on their inbound trajectory toward the UNSC phalanx. Motes of red light collected along the alien ships' lateral lines.

Five seconds.

"Transferring firing control to the computer," Lieutenant Hikowa said. She punched a series of firing codes into the computer, then locked down the controls. The *Iroquois* recoiled and spat twin bolts of thunder toward the enemy.

The starboard view screen showed UNSC destroyers and frigates launching their opening salvo.

The Covenant fleet fired as well; angry red lances of energy raced though space towards them.

"Time until that plasma impacts?" Captain Keyes asked Ensign Lovell.

"Twenty-two seconds, sir."

The vacuum between the two opposing forces filled with a hundred lines of fire and smoldering metal that seemed to tear through the fabric of space.

Their trajectories closed on one another, then crossed, and the bolts of fire grew larger on the main screen.

Lieutenant Dominique said, "Receiving a second set of firing solutions and times. Vice Admiral Stanforth on the priority channel, sir."

"Put him on, holotank two," Keyes ordered.

Near the main view screen, a small holographic tank—normally reserved for the ship's AI—winked into operation. Vice Admiral Stanforth's ghostly image appeared. "All ships: hold your positions. Divert all engine power to recharge your guns. We've got something special cooked up." His eyes narrowed. "Do not—I repeat, do not—under *any* circumstance break position or fire before you are ordered to do so. Stanforth out."

The holographic projection of the Vice Admiral snapped out of existence.

"Orders, sir?" Ensign Lovell turned in his seat.

"You heard the Vice Admiral, Ensign. Thrusters to station keeping. Lieutenant Hikowa: get those guns recharged on the double."

"Aye, sir."

Keyes nodded as Hikowa turned back to her task. "Three seconds until first salvo impact," she announced.

Keyes turned back to the tac display, concentrating on the MAC rounds that crawled across the screen. The fleet's MAC rounds hammered into the Covenant lines. Shields flickered silver-blue and overloaded as the super-dense projectiles rammed into the formation; several ships were spun out of position by the impact.

"Guns?" he called out. "Enemy status?"

"Multiple hits on Covenant fleet, sir," Hikowa replied. "Salvo two impact . . . now."

A handful of the shots were clean misses. Keyes winced; each one of the off-trajectory MAC rounds meant one more enemy ship would survive to return fire.

The vast majority, however, slammed into the unshielded alien vessels. The lead Covenant destroyer took a direct hit from a heavy round, which sent the alien ship into a lurching port spin.

Keyes saw the destroyer's engines flare as her pilot struggled to regain control—just as a second MAC round struck on the ship's opposite side. For an instant, the Covenant vessel shuddered, held position, then flexed as the hull stresses became too great. The destroyer disintegrated and scattered debris in a wide arc.

A second Covenant ship—a frigate—shuddered under the impact of multiple MAC rounds. It listed to starboard and rammed the next frigate in the enemy formation. Sparks and small explosions flared from the ships as a gray-white plume of vented atmosphere exploded into space. The ships' running lights flickered, then dimmed as the pair of dead spacecraft—locked in a deadly embrace—tumbled into the heart of the Covenant line.

A moment later, the wrecked ships hit a third Covenant frigate, and they exploded, sending tendrils of plasma through space. A dozen of their ships vented atmosphere and fires flickered within their hulls.

The fore view screen, however, was now filled with incoming weapons fire.

"Fleet commander on priority channel," Dominique announced. "Audio only."

"Patch it through, Lieutenant," Keyes ordered.

A hiss of static crackled through the communications-system speakers. A moment later, Vice Admiral Stanforth's voice calmly broke through the noise. "Lead to all ships: hold your positions," the Vice Admiral said. "Make ready to fire. Transfer timers to your computers . . . and hang on to your hats."

A shadow crossed the overhead camera. On the view screen, Captain Keyes watched as the *Cradle* repair station, the plate nearly a kilometer on edge, rotated and started to slide in front of their phalanx formation.

"Christ," Ensign Lovell whispered, "they're going to take the hits for us."

"Dominique, hit the scopes. Are there any lifepods outbound from *Cradle*?" Keyes asked. He already knew the answer.

"Sir," Dominique answered, his deep voice thick with worry. "No escape craft have left the *Cradle*."

All eyes on the *Iroquois'* bridge were riveted to the screen. Keyes' hands clenched with anger and helplessness. There was nothing to do but watch.

The front view screen went black as the station passed in front of them. Pinpoints of red and orange appeared along the back surface, metal vapor venting in plumes. *Cradle* lurched closer to the fleet, the impact of the plasma torpedoes pushing it back. The station continued to move downward, spreading out the damage. Holes appeared in the surface; the internal lattice of steel girders was exposed and, seconds later, glowed white-hot—then the view screen was clear again.

"Ventral cameras," Captain Keyes said. "Now!"

The view changed as Dominique switched to the *Iroquois'* belly cameras. *Cradle* station reappeared. She spun and her entire forward surface was aglow . . . heat spread to the edges, the center liquefied and pulled away.

"MAC guns ready to fire in three seconds," Lieutenant Hikowa announced, her voice cold and angry. "Targeting lock acquired."

Keyes gripped the arms of the command chair. "*Cradle*'s crew bought this shot for us, Lieutenant," Captain Keyes growled. "Make it count."

The *Iroquois* shuddered as the MAC gun fired. On the status display, Keyes watched as the rest of the UNSC fleet fired simultaneously. A twenty-one-gun salute three times over for those on board the station who had given their lives.

"All ships: break and attack!" Vice Admiral Stanforth bellowed. "Pick your targets and fire at will. Take as many of these bastards out as you can! Stanforth out."

They had to move before the Covenant plasma weapons recharged.

"Give me fifty percent on our engines," Captain Keyes ordered, "and come about to course two eight zero."

"Aye," Ensign Lovell and Lieutenant Hall replied in unison.

"Lieutenant Hikowa, release safeties on the Archer missile system."

"Safeties disengaged, sir."

The *Iroquois* moved away at a near-right angle from the phalanx formation. The other UNSC ships scattered at all vectors. One UNSC destroyer, the *Lancelot*, accelerated straight toward the Covenant line.

As the UNSC ships scattered, the MAC salvo reached the Covenant ships. The Admiral's firing solutions had targeted the remainder of the Covenant battlegroup's smaller ships. Their shields sparkled, rippled, and then flickered out of existence. Their frigates shattered under the impact of the firepower. Holes ripped through their hulls. Wrecked spacecraft drifted lazily through the battle area.

The surprise second salvo had cost the Covenant dearly—a dozen enemy ships were out of the fight.

That left eight Covenant vessels—destroyers and cruisers.

Pulse lasers and Archer missiles fired, and every ship onscreen accelerated towards one another. Both Covenant and UNSC ships released their single-ship fighters.

The tac computer was having trouble tracking everything—Keyes cursed to himself over the lack of a ship AI—as the missile fire and plasma discharges strobed in the blackness. Single ships—the humans' Longsword fighters and the flat, vaguely piscine Covenant fighters—dove, and fired, and impacted into warships. Archer missiles left trails of exhaust. Blue pulse lasers scattered inside the clouds of vented propellant and atmosphere, and cast a ghostly blue glow over the scene.

"Orders, sir?" Lovell asked nervously.

Captain Keyes paused—something felt . . . wrong. The battle was utter chaos, and it was nearly impossible to tell exactly what was happening. Sensor data was thrown off by the constant detonations and the fire of the aliens' energy weapons.

"Scan near the planet, Lieutenant Hall," Keyes said. "Ensign Lovell, move us closer to Sigma Octanus Four."

"Sir?" Lieutenant Dominique said. "We're not engaging the Covenant fleet?"

"Negative, Lieutenant."

The bridge crew paused for a fraction of a second—all except Ensign Lovell, who tapped on the controls and plotted a new course. The bridge crew had all had a taste of being heroes in their last battle, and they wanted more. Captain Keyes knew what that was like . . . and he knew how dangerous it was.

He was not about to charge into battle, however, with the *Iroquois* at half power, her structural integrity already compromised, and with no AI to mount a point defense against Covenant single ships. One plasma torpedo to their lower decks would gut them.

If he remained where he was and attempted to shoot into the fray, he was just as likely to accidentally hit a friendly ship as a Covenant vessel.

No. There were several damaged Covenant ships in the area. He would finish them off—make sure they could not launch any attack on their fleet. There was no glory in the action—but considering their present condition, glory was of little concern. Survival was.

Captain Keyes watched the battle rage in the starboard camera. The *Leviathan* took a plasma bolt, and her foredecks burned. One Covenant ship collided with the UNSC frigate *Fair Weather*; the superstructures of the two craft locked together—and both ships opened fire at point-blank range. The *Fair Weather* detonated into a ball of nuclear fire that engulfed the Covenant destroyer. Both ships faded from the tactical display.

"Covenant ship detected in orbit around Sigma Octanus Four," Lieutenant Hall reported.

"Let me see it," Keyes said.

A small vessel appeared on-screen. It was smaller than the

Covenant equivalent of a frigate . . . but definitely larger than one of the aliens' dropships. It was sleek and seemed to waver in and out of the blankness of space. The engine pods were baffled and devoid of the characteristic purple-white glow of Covenant propulsion systems.

"They're in a geosynchronous orbit over Côte d'Azur," Lieutenant Hall reported. "Their thrusters are firing microbursts. Precision station keeping, sir, if I were to guess."

Lieutenant Dominique interrupted. "Detected scattering from a narrow-beam transmission on the planet surface, sir. A far-infrared laser."

Captain Keyes turned toward the main battle on-screen. Was this slaughter just a diversion?

The original attack on Sigma Octanus IV had been for the sole purpose of landing ships and invading Côte d'Azur. Once accomplished, their battlegroup had left.

And now—whatever the Covenant's purpose was groundside, they were sending information to this stealth ship . . . while the rest of their fleet kept the UNSC forces from interfering.

"Like hell," he muttered.

"Ensign Lovell, plot a collision course for that ship."

"Aye, sir."

"Lieutenant Hall, push the engines as far as you can. I need every bit of speed you can get me."

"Yes, sir. If we vent primary coolant and use our reserve, I can boost the engine output to sixty-six percent . . . for five minutes."

"Do it."

The *Iroquois* moved sluggishly toward the Covenant ship.

"Intercept in twenty seconds," Lovell said.

"Lieutenant Hikowa, arm Archer missile pods A through D. Blow that Covenant son of a bitch out of the sky."

"Archer missile pods armed, sir," she replied smoothly. Her hands moved gracefully over the controls. "Firing."

Archer missiles streaked toward the Covenant stealth ship—but as they closed with the target, they started to swerve from side to side, then spun out of control. The spent missiles fell toward the planet.

Lieutenant Hikowa cursed quietly in Japanese. "Missile guidance locks jammed," she said. "Their ECM spoofed the guidance packages, sir."

No other choice, then, Keyes thought. *They can jam our missiles—let's see them jam this.*

"Run them over, Ensign Lovell," Keyes ordered.

He licked his lips. "Aye, sir."

"Sound collision alarm," Captian Keyes said. "All hands, brace for impact."

"She's moving," Lovell said.

"Keep on her."

"Course correcting now. Hang on," Lovell said.

The eight-thousand-ton *Iroquois* slammed into the tiny Covenant ship.

On the bridge, they barely felt the impact. The diminutive alien vessel, however, was crushed from the force. Her crippled hull spun toward Sigma Octanus IV.

"Damage report!" Keyes bellowed.

"Lower decks 3 through 8 show hull breach, sir," Hall called out. "Internal bulkheads were already closed, and no one was in those areas, per your orders. No systems damage reported."

"Good. Move to her original position, Ensign Lovell. Lieutenant Dominique, I want that transmission beam intercepted."

The ventral cameras showed the Covenant ship plunge into the atmosphere. Its shield glowed yellow, then white—then dissipated as the ship's systems failed. It burst into crimson flame and burned across the horizon, a black plume of smoke trailing in its wake.

"The *Iroquois* is losing altitude," Ensign Lovell said. "We're falling into the planet's atmosphere . . . bringing us about." The

Iroquois spun 180 degrees. The Ensign concentrated on his displays, then said, "No good, we need more power. Sir, permission to fire emergency thrusters?"

"Granted."

Lovell exploded the aft emergency thrusters and the *Iroquois* jumped. Lovell's eyes were locked on the repeater displays as he fought for every centimeter of maneuvering he could get. Sweat ran down his forehead and soaked his flight suit.

"Orbit stabilizing—barely." Lovell exhaled with relief, then turned to face Keyes. "Got it, sir. Thrusters to precision station keeping."

"Receiving," Lieutenant Dominique said, and then paused. "Receiving . . . something, sir. It must be encrypted."

"Make sure you're recording, Lieutenant."

"Affirmative. Recorders active . . . but the codebreaker software can't crack it, sir."

Captain Keyes turned back to the tac displays, half expecting to see a Covenant ship in firing position.

There wasn't much left of either the Covenant or UNSC fleets. Dozens of ships drifted in space, billowing atmosphere and burning. The rest moved slowly. A few flickered with fire. Scattered explosions dotted the black.

One undamaged Covenant destroyer turned, however, and left the battlefield. It came about and headed straight for the *Iroquois*.

"Uh oh," Lovell muttered.

"Lieutenant Hall, get me the *Leviathan*—priority Alpha channel," Keyes ordered.

"Yes, sir," she said.

Vice Admiral Stanforth's image appeared in the holotank. His forehead had a gash across it, and blood trickled into his eyes. He wiped it away with a shaking hand, his eyes blazing with anger. "Keyes? Where the hell is *Iroquois*?"

"Sir, *Iroquois* is in geosynchronous orbit over Côte d'Azur.

We've destroyed a Covenant stealth ship and are in the process of intercepting a secure transmission from the planet."

The Vice Admiral stared at him a moment unbelievingly, then nodded as if this made sense to him. "Proceed."

"We have a Covenant destroyer leaving the battle . . . bearing down on us. I think the reason for the Covenant's invasion may be in this coded transmission. And they don't want us to know, sir."

"Understood, son. Hang on. The cavalry's on its way."

On the aft screen, the remaining eight UNSC ships broke their attacks and turned toward the incoming destroyer. Three MAC guns fired and impacted on the Covenant vessel. Its shields only lapsed for a split second; it took a round through her nose . . . but it continued toward the *Iroquois* at flank speed.

"Transmission ended, sir," Lieutenant Dominique announced. "Cut off in midpacket. The signal was terminated at the source."

"Damn." Captain Keyes considered staying and trying to reacquire that signal—but only for a moment. He decide to take what they had and run with it. "Ensign Lovell, get us the hell out of here!"

"Sir!" Lieutenant Hall said. "Look."

The Covenant destroyer was changing course . . . along with the rest of the surviving Covenant vessels. They were scattering, and accelerating out of the system.

"They're running," Lieutenant Hikowa said, her normal iron calm replaced by astonishment.

Within minutes, the Covenant ships accelerated and vanished into Slipstream space.

Captain Keyes looked aft and counted only seven UNSC ships intact, with the balance of the fleet destroyed or disabled.

He sat in his command chair. "Ensign Lovell, take us back the way we came. Make ready to take on wounded. Repressurize all uncompromised decks."

"Jesus," Lieutenant Hall said. "I think we actually . . . won that one."

"Yes, Lieutenant. We won," Keyes replied.

But Captain Keyes wondered exactly what they had won. The Covenant had come to this system for a reason—and he had a sinking feeling that they may have gotten what they had come for.

CHAPTER TWENTY-TWO

2010 HOURS, JULY 18, 2552 (MILITARY CALENDAR) / SIGMA OCTANUS IV, CÔTE D'AZUR

It was time to arm the nuke.

The small device held the power to destroy Côte d'Azur—wipe the Covenant infection clean off the planet.

John carefully removed the bonding strips on the HAVOK tactical nuclear device and attached it to the wall of the sewer. The adhesive on the black half sphere stuck and hardened to the concrete. He slipped the detonator key into a thin slot on the unit's face. There were no external indicators on the device; instead, a tiny screen winked on his heads up display indicating the nuke was armed.

HAVOK ARMED, flashed across his HUD. AWAITING DETONATION SIGNAL.

The device—a clean thirty-megaton explosive—could only be detonated by a remote signal . . . a problem here in the sewers. Even the powerful communications package on a starship would be unable to penetrate the steel and concrete overhead.

John quickly rigged a ground-return transceiver, placing it on the pipes overhead. He'd have to set up another unit outside to relay the signal underground . . . a hot line that would trigger a nuclear firestorm.

Technically, his mission parameters had been fulfilled. Green and Red Teams would have the civilians evacuated soon. They had scouted the region and discovered a new Covenant species—the strange floating creature that disassembled and reassembled human machinery, like a scientist or engineer stripping down a device to learn its secrets.

He could leave and destroy the Covenant occupation force. He *should* leave—there was an army of Jackals and Grunts—including at least a platoon of the black-armored veterans—on the streets above. There were three medium Covenant drop-ships hovering in the air as well. The advance Marine strike forces had been slaughtered, leaving the Spartans no backup. His responsibility now was to make sure his team got out intact.

But John's orders had an unusual amount of flexibility . . . and that made him uncomfortable. He had been told to reconnoiter the region and gather intelligence on the Covenant. He was positive there was more to be learned here.

Certainly they were up to something in Côte d'Azur's museum. The Covenant had never before been interested in human history—or indeed, in humans or their artifacts of any kind. He had seen a disarmed Jackal fight hand to hand rather than pick up a nearby human assault rifle. And the only thing the Covenant had ever used human buildings for was target practice.

So finding out the reason they seized and were protecting the museum definitely qualified as intelligence gathering in his book.

Was it worth exposing his team to find out? And if they died, would he be wasting their lives . . . or spending them for something worthwhile?

"Master Chief?" Kelly whispered. "Our orders, sir?"

He opened Blue Team's COM channel. "We're going in. Use your silencers. Don't engage the enemy unless absolutely necessary. This place is too hot. We'll just poke our noses in—see what they're up to and bug out."

Three acknowledgment lights winked on.

The Master Chief knew they implicitly trusted his judgment. He just hoped he was worthy of that trust.

The Spartans checked their gear and threaded silencers onto

their assault rifles. They slipped silently down a wide side passage of the sewer.

A rusty ladder ran up to the ceiling, and a steel plate had been welded in place.

"Thermite paste already set up," Fred reported.

"Burn it." The Master Chief stepped to the side and looked away.

The thermite sputtered as bright as an electric arc welder, casting harsh shadows into the chamber. When it finished, there was a jagged, glowing red circle in the steel.

The Master Chief climbed up the ladder and put his back against the plate—and pushed. It popped free with a metallic *snap*.

He eased the plate down and set it aside. He attached the fiber-optic probe, fed it up through the hole.

All clear.

He flexed his leg muscles and sent the MJOLNIR armor up through the hole, pulling himself into the next chamber with his left hand. His right hand held the silenced assault rifle as if it were no heavier than a pistol. He braced for incoming enemy fire—

—Nothing happened.

He moved forward and surveyed the small room. The stone-walled chamber was dark, and was lined with shelving units. Each unit held jars filled with clear liquid and insect specimens. Boxes and crates were stacked neatly on the floor.

Kelly entered next, then Fred and James.

"Picking up motion sensor signals," Kelly said over the COM channel.

"Jam them."

"Done," she replied. *"They may have gotten a piece of us, though."*

"Spread out," the Master Chief ordered. "Get ready to jump back into the hole if this gets too hot. Otherwise, initiate the standard distract-and-destroy."

The clatter of alien hooves on marble echoed behind a door to their right.

The Spartans melted into the shadows. The Master Chief crouched behind a crate and unsheathed his combat knife.

The door opened and four Jackals stood in the door frame; they held active energy shields in front of them—warping their already ugly vulture faces. The blue-white glow of the energy shield pulsed through the dark chamber. *Good,* the Master Chief thought. *That should play hell with their night vision.*

The Jackals held plasma pistols at the ready in their free hands; the barrels of the guns moved erratically as the aliens whispered to one another . . . then steadied as, in careful, slow movements, they moved in.

The aliens fanned out into a rough "delta" formation—the lead Jackal a meter ahead of his compatriots. The group approached the Master Chief's hiding spot.

There was a slight noise: the clink of glass bottles on the other side of the room.

The Jackals turned . . . and presented their unshielded backs to the Master Chief.

He exploded from his hiding place and jammed his blade into the base of the closest Jackal's back. He snapped his right foot out, caught the back of the next Jackal's head, crushing its skull.

The remaining aliens spun, glistening energy shields interposed between them and him.

There were three coughs from silenced MA5Bs. Alien blood—dark purple in the harsh blue-white light—spattered across the inner surfaces of the energy shields as the silenced rounds found their marks. The Jackals toppled to the ground.

The Master Chief policed their plasma pistols and retrieved the shield generators clamped on their forearms. He had standing orders to collect intact specimens of Covenant technology. The Office of Naval Intelligence had not been able to replicate the Covenant's shield technology. But they were getting close.

In the meantime, the Spartans would use these.

The Master Chief strapped the curved piece of metal to his forearm. He touched one of the two large buttons on the unit and a scintillating film appeared before him.

He handed the other shield devices to his teammates.

He pressed the second button and the shield collapsed.

"Don't use these unless you have to," he said. "The humming and their reflective surfaces might give us away . . . and we don't know how long they last."

He got three acknowledgment lights.

Kelly and Fred took up positions on either side of the open door. She gave him a thumbs-up.

Kelly took point and the Spartans moved, single file, up a circular stairwell.

She paused a full ten seconds at the doorway to the main floor. She waved them ahead and they emerged on the main level of the museum.

The skeleton of a blue whale was suspended over the main foyer. The dead hulk reminded the Master Chief of a Covenant starship. He turned away from the distraction and slowly moved over the black marble tiles.

Oddly, there were no more Jackal patrols. There were a hundred Jackals outside guarding the place . . . but none inside.

The Master Chief didn't like it. It didn't feel right . . . and Chief Mendez had told him a thousand times to trust his instincts. Was it a trap?

The Spartans staggered their line and moved cautiously into the east wing. There were displays of the local flora and fauna: gigantic flowers and fist-sized beetles. But their motion sensors were cold.

Fred halted . . . and then, with a quick hand signal, waved John to move up to his position.

He stood by a case of pinned butterflies. On the floor, facedown in front of that case, was a Jackal. It was dead, crushed flat.

There was an imprint of a large boot where the creature's back had been. Whatever had done this had easily weighed a ton.

The Master Chief spotted a few blood-smeared prints leading away from the Jackal . . . and into the west wing.

He flipped on his infrared sensors and took a long look around—no heat sources here or in the nearby rooms.

The Master Chief followed the footprints and signaled the team to follow.

The west wing held scientific displays. There were static electric generators and quantum field holograms on the walls, a tapestry of darting arrows and wriggling lines. A cloud chamber sat in the corner with subatomic tracers zipping through its misty confines—the Master Chief noted it was unusually active. This place reminded him of Déjà's classroom on Reach.

A branch opened to another wing. The word GEOLOGY was carved on the entry arch.

Through that arch there was a strong infrared source, a razor-thin line that shot straight up and out of the building. The Master Chief only caught a glimpse of the thing—a wink and a blink then it was gone again . . . it was so bright, his IR sensors overloaded and automatically shut down.

He waved James to take the left side of the arch. He had Kelly and Fred drop back to cover their flanks, and the Master Chief edged to the right of the arch.

He sent a fiber-optic probe ahead, bent it slightly, and poked it around the corner.

The room contained display cases of mineral specimens. There were sulfur crystals, raw emeralds, and rubies. There was a monolith of unpolished pink quartz in the center of the room, three meters wide and six tall.

Off to one side, however, were two creatures. The Master Chief hadn't seen them at first—because they were so motionless . . . and so massive. He had no doubt that one of them had crushed the Jackal that had gotten in its way.

The Master Chief got scared all the time. He never showed it, though. He usually mentally acknowledged the apprehension, put it aside, and continued . . . just as he'd been trained to do. This time, however, he couldn't easily dismiss the feeling.

The two creatures were vaguely man-shaped. They stood two and a half meters tall. It was difficult to make out their features; they were covered from head to toe with a dull blue-gray armor, similar to the hull of a Covenant ship. Blue, orange, and yellow highlights were visible on the few patches of exposed skin the creatures sported. They had slits where their eyes should be. The articulation points looked impregnable.

On their left arms they hefted large shields, thick as starship battleplate. Mounted on their right arms were massive, wide-barreled weapons, so large that the arm beneath seemed to blend into the weapon.

They moved with slow deliberation. One took a rock from the display case and set it inside a red metal case. It bent over the case while the other turned and touched the control panel of a device that looked like a small pulse laser turret. The laser pointed straight up—and out through the shattered glass dome overhead.

That had been the source of the infrared radiation. The laser must have intermittently scattered off the dust in the air—flashed enough energy into his sensors to burn them out. Something that powerful could beam a message straight out into space.

The Master Chief made a slow fist—the signal for his team to freeze. Then, with slow, deliberate movements, he signaled the Spartans to stay alert and get ready.

He waved Fred and Kelly forward.

Fred crept closer to him. Kelly slid up next to James.

The Master Chief then held up two fingers and made a sideways cut, motioning them into the room.

Acknowledgment lights winked on.

He went in first, sidestepped to the right, with Fred at his side.

James and Kelly took the left flank.

They opened fire.

Armor-piercing rounds pinged off the aliens' body armor. One of them turned and brought its shield in front of it—covering its partner, the red case, and the laser beacon.

The Spartan bullets didn't even leave a scratch on the armor.

The alien raised its arm slightly and pointed at Kelly and James.

A flash of light blinded the Master Chief. There was a deafening explosion and a wave of heat. He blinked for a full three seconds before he recovered his vision.

Where Kelly and James had been, there was a burning crater that fanned backward . . . nothing but charcoal and ash remained of the Science Chamber behind them.

Kelly had moved in time; she crouched five meters deeper into the room, still firing. James was nowhere to be seen.

The other massive creature turned to face the Master Chief.

He hit the button on the shield generator on his arm and brought it up just in time—the nearest alien's weapon flashed again.

The air in front of the Master Chief shimmered and exploded—he flew backward, crashing through the wall, and skidded for ten meters before slamming into the wall of the next room.

The Jackal shield generator was white-hot. The Master Chief ripped the melted alien device off and threw it away.

Those plasma bolts were like nothing he had seen before. They seemed almost as powerful as the stationary plasma cannons the Jackals used.

The Master Chief sprang to his feet and charged back into the chamber.

If the aliens' weapons were similar to Covenant plasma guns, they would need to be recharged. He hoped the Spartans had enough time to take those things out.

The Master Chief still felt the fear—it was stronger than it had been before . . . but his team was still in there. He had to take care of them first before he could indulge in the luxury of feelings.

Kelly and Fred circled the creatures, their silenced weapons firing quick bursts. They ran out of ammunition and switched clips.

This wasn't working. They couldn't take them out. Maybe a Jackhammer missile at point-blank range would penetrate their armor.

The Master Chief's gaze was drawn to the center of the room. He stared for a moment at the monolith of pink quartz.

Over the COM channel he ordered, "Switch to shredder rounds." He changed ammunition and then opened fire—at the floor underneath the enormous creatures' feet.

Kelly and Fred changed rounds and fired, too.

Marble tiles shattered and the wood underneath splintered into toothpicks.

One of the creatures raised its arm again, preparing to fire.

"Keep shooting," John yelled.

The floor creaked, buckled, and then fell away; the two massive aliens plunged into the basement below.

"Quick," the Master Chief said. He slung his rifle and moved to the back of the quartz monolith. "Push!"

Kelly and Fred leaned their weight against the stone and grunted with effort. The slab moved a tiny bit.

James sprinted forward, slammed into the stone, put his shoulder alongside theirs . . . and *pushed.* His left arm had been burned away from the elbow down, but he didn't even whimper.

The monolith moved; it inched toward the hole . . . then

tilted and went over. It landed with a dull thud and a crunching noise.

The Master Chief peered over the edge. He saw an armored left leg, and on the other side of the stone slab, an arm struggling underneath. The things were still alive. Their motions slowed, but they didn't cease.

The red case was balanced precariously on the edge of the hole. It teetered—no way to reach it in time.

He turned to Kelly—the fastest Spartan—and yelled: "Grab it!"

The box fell—

—and Kelly leaped.

In a single bound, she caught the rock as the case dropped, she tucked, rolled, and got to her feet, the rock safely held in one hand. She handed it to the Master Chief.

The rock was a piece of granite and glittered with a few jewel-like inclusions. What was as so special about it? He stuffed it into his ammunition sack and then kicked over the Covenant transmission beacon.

Outside, the Master Chief heard the clattering and squawking of the army of Jackals and Grunts.

"Let's get out of here, Spartans."

He threw his arm around James and helped him along. They ran into the basement, making sure to give the pinned giants under the stone a wide berth, then jumped through the storm drain and into the sewers.

They jogged through the muck and didn't stop until they had cleared the drain system and emerged in the rice paddies on the edge of Côte d'Azur.

Fred rigged the ground-return relay to the pipes overhead and ran a crude antenna outside.

The Master Chief looked back at the city. Banshee fliers circled through the skyscrapers. Spotlights from the hovering

Covenant transport ships bathed the streets in blue illumination. The Grunts were going crazy; their barks and screams rose to an impenetrable din.

The Spartans moved toward the coast and followed the tree line south. James collapsed twice along the way and then finally slipped into unconsciousness. The Master Chief slung him over his shoulder and carried him.

They paused and hid when they heard a patrol of a dozen Grunts. The aliens ran past them—they either didn't see the Spartans, or they didn't care. The animals sprinted as fast as they could back to the city.

When they were a click away from the rendezvous point, the Master Chief opened the COM link. "Green Team Leader, we're on your perimeter, and coming in. Signaling with blue smoke."

"Ready and waiting for you, sir," Linda replied. *"Welcome back."*

The Master Chief set off one of his smoke grenades and they marched into the clearing.

The Pelican was intact. Corporal Harland and his Marines stood post, and the rescued civilians were safely inside the ship.

Blue and Red Teams were hidden in the nearby brush and trees.

Linda approached them. She motioned for her team to take James and get him onto the Pelican. "Sir," she said. "All civilians on board and ready for liftoff."

The Master Chief wanted to relax, sit down, and close his eyes. But this was often the most dangerous part of any mission . . . those last few steps when you might let down your guard.

"Good. Take one more look around the perimeter. Let's make double sure nothing followed us back."

"Yes, sir."

Corporal Harland approached and saluted. "Sir? How did you do it? Those civilians said you got them out of the city—past an army of Covenant, sir. How?"

John cocked his head quizzically. "It was our mission, Corporal," he said.

The Corporal stared at him and then at the other Spartans. "Yes, sir."

When Green Team Leader reported that the perimeter was clear, the last of the Spartans boarded the Pelican.

James had regained consciousness. Someone had removed his helmet and propped his head on a folded survival blanket. His eyes watered from the pain, but he managed to salute the Master Chief with his right hand. John gestured at Kelly; she administered a dose of painkiller, and James lapsed into unconsciousness.

The Pelican lifted into the air. In the distance, the suns were warming the horizon, and Côte d'Azur was outlined against the dawn.

The dropship suddenly accelerated at full speed straight up, and then angled away to the south.

"Sir," the pilot said over the COM channel. *"We're getting multiple incoming radar contacts . . . about two hundred Banshees inbound."*

"We'll take care of it, Lieutenant," John replied. "Prepare for EMP and shock wave."

The Master Chief activated his remote radio transceiver.

He quickly keyed in the final fail-safe code, then sent the coded burst transmission on its way.

A third sun appeared on the horizon. It blotted out the light of the system's stars, then cooled—from amber to red—and darkened the sky with black clouds of dust.

"Mission accomplished," he said.

CHAPTER
TWENTY-THREE

0500 HOURS, JULY 18, 2552 (MILITARY CALENDAR) / UNSC *IROQUOIS*, MILITARY STAGING AREA IN ORBIT AROUND SIGMA OCTANUS IV

Captain Keyes leaned against the brass railing on the bridge of the *Iroquois* and surveyed the devastation. The space near Sigma Octanus IV was littered with debris: the dead hulks of Covenant and UNSC ships spun lazily in the vacuum, surrounded by clouds of wreckage: jagged pieces of decimated armor plate, shattered single-ship fuselages, and heat-blackened metal fragments created a million radar targets. The debris field would clutter this system and make for a navigational hazard for the next decade.

They had recovered nearly all the bodies from space.

Captain Keyes' gaze caught the remnants of the *Cradle* as the blasted space dock spun past. The kilometer-wide plate was now safely locked in a high orbit around the planet. She was slowly being torn apart from her own rotation; girders and metal plates warped and bent as the gravitational stresses on the ship increased.

The Covenant plasma weapons had burned through ten decks of super-hard metal and armor like so many layers of tissue paper. Thirty volunteers on the repair station had died piloting the unwieldy craft.

Vice Admiral Stanforth had gotten his "win" . . . but at a tremendous cost.

Keyes brought up the casualty figures and damage estimates on his data pad. He scowled as the data scrolled across his screen.

The UNSC had lost more than twenty ships, and those that survived had all suffered heavy damage; most would require months of time-consuming repair at a shipyard. Nearly one thousand people were killed in the battle, and hundreds more were wounded, many critically. Add to that the sixteen hundred Marine casualties on the surface—and the three hundred thousand civilians murdered in Côte d'Azur at the hands of the Covenant.

Some "win," Keyes thought bitterly.

Côte d'Azur was now a smoldering crater—but Sigma Octanus IV was still a human-held world. They had saved everyone else on the planet, nearly thirteen million souls. So perhaps it had been worth it.

So many lives and deaths had been measured in this battle. Had the balance of the odds tipped slightly against them—everything could have been lost. That was something he had never taught any of his students at the Academy—how much victory depended on luck, as well as skill.

Captain Keyes saw the last of the Marine dropships returning from the planet surface. They docked with the *Leviathan*, and then the huge cruiser turned and accelerated out of the system.

"Sensor sweep complete," Lieutenant Dominique reported. "I think that was the last of the lifeboats we picked up, sir."

"Let's make certain, Lieutenant," Keyes replied. "One more pass through the system please. Ensign Lovell, plot a course and take us around again."

"Yes, sir," Lovell wearily replied.

The bridge crew was exhausted, physically and emotionally. They had all pulled extended shifts as they searched for survivors. Captain Keyes would rotate shifts after this next pass.

As he looked at this crew, he noticed that something was different. Lieutenant Hikowa's movements were crisp and determined, as if everything she did now would decide their next battle; it made a startling contrast to her normally lethargic efficiency. Lieutenant Hall's false exuberance had been replaced by genuine confidence. Dominique almost seemed happy—his hands lightly typing a report to FLEETCOM. Even Ensign Lovell, despite his exhaustion, stepped lively.

Maybe Vice Admiral Stanforth was right. Maybe the fleet needed this win more than he had realized.

They had beaten the Covenant. Although not widely known, there had been only three small engagements in which the UNSC fleet had decisively defeated the Covenant. And not since Admiral Cole had retaken Harvest colony had there been an engagement on this scale. A complete victory—a world saved.

It would show everyone that winning was possible, that there was hope.

But, he mused, was there really? They won because they had gotten lucky—and had twice as many ships as the Covenant. And, he suspected, they had beaten the Covenant because the Covenant's real objective hadn't been to win.

Naval Intelligence officers had come aboard the *Iroquois* immediately after the battle. They congratulated Captain Keyes on his performance . . . and then copied and purged every single bit of data they had intercepted from the Covenant planetside transmission.

Of course, the ONI spooks left without offering any explanation.

Keyes toyed with his pipe, replaying the battle in his mind. No. The Covenant had lost because they were really after something else on Sigma Octanus IV—and the intercepted message was the key.

"Sir," Lieutenant Dominique said. "Incoming orders from FLEETCOM."

"Put it through to my station, Lieutenant," Captain Keyes said as he sat in his command chair. The computer scanned his retina and fingerprints and then decoded the message. He read on the small monitor:

UNITED NATIONS SPACE COMMAND PRIORITY TRANSMISSION 09872H-98

ENCRYPTION CODE: RED

PUBLIC KEY: FILE /LIGHTNING-MATRIX-FOUR/

FROM: VICE ADMIRAL MICHAEL STANFORTH, COMMANDING OFFICER, UNSC *LEVIATHAN*/ UNSC SECTION THREE COMMANDER/ (UNSC SERVICE NUMBER: 00834-19223-HS)

TO: CAPTAIN JACOB KEYES, COMMANDING OFFICER UNSC *IROQUOIS*/ (UNSC SERVICE NUMBER: 01928-19912-JK)

SUBJECT: ORDERS FOR YOUR IMMEDIATE CONSIDERATION

CLASSIFICATION: SECRET (BGX DIRECTIVE)

/START FILE/

KEYES,

DROP WHATEVER YOU'RE DOING AND HEAD BACK TO THE BARN. WE'RE BOTH WANTED FOR IMMEDIATE DEBRIEFING BY ONI AT REACH HEADQUARTERS ASAP.

LOOKS LIKE THE SPOOKS AT NAVAL INTELLIGENCE ARE UP TO THEIR NORMAL CLOAK-AND-DAGGER TRICKS.

CIGARS AND BRANDY AFTERWARD.

REGARDS,

STANFORTH

"Very well," he muttered to himself. "Lieutenant Dominique: send Vice Admiral Stanforth my compliments. Ensign Lovell, generate a randomized vector as per the Cole Protocol, and make ready to leave system. Take us out for an hour in Slipstream space, then we'll reorient and proceed to the Reach military installation."

"Aye, sir. Randomized jump vector ready—our tracks are covered."

"Lieutenant Hall: start organizing shore leave for the crew. We're heading back for repairs and some well-deserved R and R."

"Amen to that," Ensign Lovell said.

That wasn't technically in his orders, but Captain Keyes would make sure his crew got the rest they deserved. That was the least he could do for them.

The *Iroquois* slowly accelerated on an out-system vector.

Captain Keyes took one long last look at Sigma Octanus IV. The battle was over . . . so why did he feel like he was headed into another fight?

The *Iroquois* plowed through a haze of titanium dust—condensed from a UNSC battleplate vaporized by Covenant plasma. The fine particles caught the light from Sigma Octanus and sparkled red and orange, making it look like the destroyer sailed through an ocean of blood.

When there was time, a HazMat team would sweep the area and clean up. In the meantime, junk—ranging in size from microscopic up to thirty-meter sections of *Cradle*—still drifted in the system.

One piece of debris in particular floated near the *Iroquois*.

It was small, almost indistinguishable from any of a thousand other softball-sized blobs that cluttered radar scopes and polluted thermal sensors.

If anyone had been looking close enough, however, they would have seen that this particular piece of metal drifted in the opposite direction from all the other masses nearby. It trailed behind the accelerating *Iroquois* . . . and edged closer, moving with purpose.

When it was close enough, it extended tiny electromagnets that guided it to the baffles at the base of the *Iroquois*' number-three engine shield. It blended in perfectly with the other vanadium steel components.

The object opened a single photo eye and gazed at the stars, collecting data to reference its current position. It would continue to do this for several days. During that time, it would slowly build up a charge. When it reached critical energy, a tiny sliver of thallium nitride memory crystal would be ejected at nearly the speed of light, and a minute Slipstream field would generate around it. If its trajectory was perfect, it would intercept a Covenant receiver located at precise coordinates in the alternate space.

. . . and the tiny automated probe would reveal to the Covenant every place the *Iroquois* had been.

CHAPTER

TWENTY-FOUR

1100 HOURS, AUGUST 12, 2552 (MILITARY CALENDAR) / EPSILON ERIDANI SYSTEM, REACH UNSC MILITARY COMPLEX, PLANET REACH, CAMP HATHCOCK

The Master Chief steered the Warthog to the fortified gate and ignored the barrel of the chain-gun that was not quite pointed in his direction. The guard on duty, a Marine Corporal, saluted smartly when John handed over his identification card.

"Sir! Welcome to Camp Hathcock," the Corporal said. "Follow this road to the inner guardpost and present your credentials there. They'll direct you to the main compound."

John nodded. The Warthog's tires crunched on gravel as the massive metal gate swung open.

Nestled in the Highland Mountains of Reach's northern continent, Camp Hathcock was a top-level retreat; heads of state, VIPs, and top brass were the facility's normal occupants—these and a division of veteran, battle-hardened Marines.

"Sir, please follow the Blue Road to this point here," the Corporal at the inner gate instructed, gesturing at a point on a wall-mounted map, "and park in the Visitors' Parking area."

Minutes later, the main facility was in sight. John parked the Warthog and strode across the pleasantly familiar compound. He and the other Spartans had covertly made their way up here during their training. John suppressed a smile as he remembered how many times the young Spartans had commandeered food and supplies from the base. He inhaled deeply, smelling piñon pines and sage. He missed this place. He had been away from Reach for far too long.

Reach was one of the few places that John considered "safe" from the Covenant. There were a hundred ships and twenty Mark V MAC guns on the orbital stations overhead. Those guns were powered by fusion generators, buried deep within Reach. Each Mark V could propel a projectile so massive, and with such velocity, he doubted if even Covenant shields could withstand a single salvo from them.

His home would not fall.

Tall fences and razor wire encircled the inner compound of Camp Hathcock. The Master Chief stopped at the inner gate and saluted the MP there.

The Marine MP looked over the Master Chief in his dress uniform. He snapped to attention—his mouth dropped open and he stared unblinkingly. "They're waiting for you, Master Chief, sir. Please go right on in."

The guard's reaction to the Master Chief—and the medals on his chest—was not uncommon.

First word of the Spartans and their accomplishments had spread despite the cloak of secrecy ONI had tried to surround them with. Three years ago, the information had gone public at Vice Admiral Stanforth's insistence—for morale purposes.

It was hard to mistake the Master Chief for anything other than a Spartan. He stood just over two meters tall and weighed in at 130 kilos of rock-hard muscle and iron-dense bone.

There was a special insignia on his uniform as well: a golden eagle poised with its talons forward—ready to strike. The bird clutched a lightning bolt in one talon and three arrows in the other.

The Spartan insignia was not the only thing about his dress uniform that called attention to him. Campaign ribbons and medals covered the left side. Chief Mendez would have been proud of him, but John had long ago stopped keeping track of the honors that had been heaped upon him.

He didn't like the flashy ornamentation. He and the other Spartans preferred to be inside their MJOLNIR armor. Without it, he felt exposed somehow, like he'd left his quarters without his skin. He had grown used to the enhanced speed and strength, to his thoughts and actions melding instantaneously.

The Master Chief marched into the main building. Outwardly, it had been designed to look like a simple log cabin, albeit a large one. Its inner walls were lined with Titanium-A armor plate, and underground were bunkers and plush conference rooms that extended a hundred meters below the earth and into the mountain of rock.

He rode the elevator to Subbasement III. There, he was instructed by the Military Police attendant to wait in the debriefing lounge for the committee to summon him.

Corporal Harland sat in the lounge, reading a copy of *STARS* magazine, nervously tapping his foot. He immediately stood and saluted as the Master Chief entered the room.

"At ease, Corporal," the Master Chief said. He glanced disapprovingly at the thickly padded couches and decided to stand.

The Corporal stared at the Master Chief's uniform, nervous. Finally he straightened, and said, "May I ask you a question, sir?"

The Master Chief nodded.

"How do you get to be a Spartan? I mean—" His gaze fell to the floor. "I mean, if someone wanted to join your outfit. How would they do that?"

Join? The Master Chief pondered the word. How had *he* joined? Dr. Halsey had picked him and the other Spartans twenty-five years ago. It had been an honor . . . but he had never actually *joined*. In fact, he had never seen any other Spartans other than his class. Once, shortly after he'd "graduated" from the training, he had overheard Dr. Halsey mention that Chief

Mendez was training another group of Spartans. He had never seen them—or the Chief.

"You don't join," he finally told the Corporal. "You are selected."

"I see," Corporal Harland said, and wrinkled his brow. "Well, sir, if anyone ever asks, tell them to sign me up."

The Military Police attendant appeared. "Corporal Harland? They're ready for you now." A set of double doors opened on the far wall. Harland gave John another salute, and nodded.

As the Corporal got up and strode toward the doors, he passed an older man on his way out. He wore the uniform of a UNSC Naval officer, a Captain. John sized the man up quickly—polished shoulder insignia, new material. The man was a newly ordained Captain.

John stood at attention and snapped a precision salute. "Officer on the deck," John barked.

The Captain paused, and looked John up and down. There was a glint of amusement in his eyes as he returned the salute. "As you were, Master Chief."

John stood at ease. The Captain's name—Keyes, J.—was embroidered on the dress-gray tunic. John recognized the name immediately: Captain Keyes, the hero of Sigma Octanus. *At least,* he thought, *one of the surviving heroes.*

Keyes glanced at the Master Chief's uniform. His eyes lingered on the Spartan insignia, and then on the Master Chief's serial-number tag just under the stripes of his rank emblem. A faint smile appeared on the Captain's face. "It's good to see you again, Chief."

"Sir?" The Master Chief had never met Captain Keyes. He had heard of his tactical brilliance at Sigma Octanus, but he had never met the man face-to-face.

"We met a very long time ago. Dr. Halsey and I—" He stopped. "Hell. I'm not allowed to talk about it."

"Of course, sir. I understand."

The Military Police attendant appeared in the hallway. "Captain Keyes, you're wanted topside by Vice Admiral Stanforth."

The Captain nodded to the attendant. "In a moment," he said. He stepped closer to the Master Chief and whispered, "Be careful in there. The ONI brass are—" He searched for the right word. "—irritated by the end results of our encounter with the Covenant at Sigma Octanus. I'd keep my head down in there." He glanced back toward the debriefing-chamber doors.

"Irritated, sir?" John asked, genuinely puzzled. He would have thought the UNSC top brass would be elated by the victory, despite its cost. "But we won."

Captain Keyes took a step back and cocked a quizzical eyebrow. "Didn't Dr. Halsey ever teach you that winning isn't everything, Master Chief?" He saluted. "You'll excuse me."

John saluted. He was so confused by Captain Keyes' statement that he kept saluting as the Captain walked out of the room.

Winning *was* everything. How could someone with Captain Keyes' reputation think otherwise?

The Master Chief tried to recall if he had ever read anything like that in any military history or philosophy texts. What else was there other than winning? The only other obvious choice was losing . . . and he had long been taught that defeat was an unacceptable alternative. Certainly, Captain Keyes didn't mean that they should have *lost* at Sigma Octanus?

Unthinkable.

He stood silently for ten minutes mulling this over. Finally, the Military Police attendant entered the waiting room. "They're ready for you now, sir."

The double doors opened and Corporal Harland came out. The young man's eyes were glazed and he trembled slightly. He looked worse than he had looked when the Master Chief had found him on Sigma Octanus IV.

The Master Chief gave a curt nod to the Corporal and then entered the debriefing chamber. The doors closed behind him.

His eyes instantly adjusted to the dark room. A large, curved desk dominated the far end of the rectangular room. A domed ceiling curved over his head, cameras, microphone, and speakers positioned like constellations.

A spotlight snapped on and tracked the Master Chief as he approached the desk.

A dozen men and women in Navy uniforms sat in the shadows. Even with his enhanced eyesight, the Master Chief could barely make out their scowling features and the glistening brass oak leaves and stars through the glare of the overhead light.

He stood at attention and saluted.

The debriefing panel ignored the Master Chief and spoke among themselves.

"The transmission that Keyes intercepted only makes sense translated this way," a man in the shadows said. A holotank hummed into operation. Tiny geometric symbols danced in the air above it: squares, triangles, bars, and dots.

To the Master Chief, they looked like either Morse code or ancient Aztec hieroglyphics.

"I will concede that point," a woman's voice in the darkness replied. "But translation software comes up empty. It's not a new Covenant dialect that we've discovered."

"Or a Covenant dialect at all," someone else said.

Finally, one of the officers deigned to notice the Master Chief. "At ease, soldier," he said.

The Master Chief let his arm fall. "Spartan-117, reporting as ordered, sirs."

There was a pause, then the woman's voice spoke up. "We would like to congratulate you on your successful mission, Master Chief. You've certainly given us plenty to consider. We would like to pin down a few details of your mission."

There was something in her voice that made John nervous. Not scared. But it was the same feeling he had going into combat. The same feeling he got when bullets started flying.

"You *do* know, Master Chief," the first male voice said, "that not answering truthfully—or omitting any relevant details will lead to a court-martial?"

John bristled. As if he could ever forget his duty. "I will answer to the best of my abilities, sir," he replied stiffly.

The holotank hummed again and images from a Spartan helmet recorder sprang into view. John noted the camera ID—it was his own. The images blurred forward, then stopped. A three-dimensional image of the floating creatures he had seen in Côte d'Azur hung in the air, motionless.

"Playback, loop bookmarks one through nine, please," the woman's voice called out.

Instantly, the holographic image animated—the alien quickly took apart and then reassembled a car's electric motor.

"This creature," she continued. "During the mission, did you see any other Covenant species—Grunts or Jackals—interact with them?"

"No, ma'am. As far as I could see, they were left alone."

"And this one," she said. The image changed to his firefight with the gigantic Hunters. "At any time did you see these things interact with the other Covenant species?"

"No, ma'am—" The Master Chief reconsidered. "Well, in a manner of speaking, yes. If you could review the recording at time minus two minutes from this frame, please."

The holo paused and then blurred backward.

"There," he said. The video played forward as the Master Chief and Fred examined the crushed Jackal in the museum.

"That impression in this Jackal's back," he said. "I believe it is the armored alien's bootprint."

"What do you mean, son?" a new man asked. His voice was older and rough.

"I can only offer my opinion, sir. I am not a scientist."

"Offer it, Master Chief," the same scratchy voice said. "I, for one, would be very interested to hear what someone with first-hand *experience* has to say . . . for a change."

There was a rustle of papers in the shadows, then silence.

"Well, sir—it looks to me like this Jackal simply got in the larger creature's way. There's no attempt to move it, and no deviation in the path of the following footfalls. It simply walked over the smaller alien."

"Evidence of a hierarchical caste structure perhaps?" the old man murmured.

"Let's move on," the woman again spoke, her voice now laced with irritation.

The holo image changed yet again. A stone object appeared—the rock the Master Chief recovered from the museum.

"This stone," she said, "is a typical igneous granite specimen but with an unusual concentration of aluminum oxide inclusions—specifically rubies. It is a match for the mineral specimens recovered from grid thirteen by twenty-four.

"Master Chief," she said, "you recovered this rock—" She paused. "From an optical scanner. Is that correct?"

"Yes, ma'am. The aliens had placed the rock in a red metallic box. Visible spectrum lasers were scanning the specimen."

"And the infrared pulse laser transmitter was hooked up to this scanner?" she asked. "You are certain?"

"Absolutely, ma'am. My thermal imagers caught a fraction of the transmission scattered by the ambient dust."

The woman continued. "The rock sample is roughly pyramidal. The inclusions in the igneous matrix are unusual in that all possible crystalline morphologies for corundum are present: bipyramidal, prismatic, tabular, and rhombohedral. Scanning from the tip to the base with neutron imagers, we produce the following pattern."

Again, a series of squares, triangles, bars and dots appeared on the view screen—symbols that again reminded John of Aztec writing.

Déjà had taught the Spartans about the Aztecs—how Cortés with superior tactics and technology had nearly obliterated an entire race. Was the same thing happening between the Covenant and humans?

"Now, then," the first male voice interjected, "this business with the detonation of a HAVOK tactical nuclear device . . . do you realize that any additional evidence of Covenant activity on Côte d'Azur has been effectively erased? Do you know what opportunities have been lost, soldier?"

"I had extremely specific orders, sir," the Master Chief said without hesitating. "Orders that came directly from NavSpecWeap, Section Three."

"Section Three," the woman muttered, "which is ONI . . . it figures."

The old man in the darkness chuckled. The faint glow of a cigar tip flared near his voice, then faded. "Are you insinuating, Master Chief," the older man said, "that the destruction of all this 'evidence,' as my colleges would call it, happened because *they* ordered it?"

There was no good answer to that question. Whatever the Master Chief said was sure to irritate someone here.

"No, sir. I am simply stating that the destruction—of anything, including any 'evidence'—is a direct result of the detonation of a nuclear weapon. In full compliance with my orders. Sir."

The first man whispered, "Jesus . . . what do you expect from one of Dr. Halsey's windup toy soldiers?"

"That's quite enough, Colonel!" the older man snapped. "This man has earned the right to some courtesy . . . even from you."

The older man lowered his voice. "Master Chief, thank you. We're finished here, I think. We may wish to recall you later . . .

but for now, you are dismissed. You are to treat all information you have heard or seen at this debriefing as classified."

"Yes, sir!"

The Master Chief saluted, spun on his heel, and marched to the exit.

The double doors opened and then sealed behind him. He exhaled. It felt like he was being evac'd from the battlefield. He reminded himself that these last few steps were often the most dangerous.

"I hope they treated you well . . . or at least decently."

Dr. Halsey sat in an overstuffed chair. She wore a long gray skirt that matched her hair. She rose and took his hand and gave it a small squeeze.

The Master Chief snapped to attention. "Ma'am, a pleasure to see you again."

"How are you, Master Chief?" she asked. She stared pointedly at the hand pressed to his forehead in a tight salute. Slowly, he dropped his hand.

She smiled. Unlike everyone else who greeted the Master Chief and stared at his uniform, medals, ribbons, or the Spartan insignia, Dr. Halsey stared into his eyes. And she never saluted. John had never gotten used to that.

"I'm fine, ma'am," he said. "We won at Sigma Octanus. It was good to have a complete victory."

"Indeed it was." She paused and glanced about. "How would you like to have another victory?" she whispered. "The biggest we've ever had?"

"Of course, ma'am," he said with no hesitation.

"I was counting on you to say that, Master Chief." She turned to the Military Police attendant waiting at the entrance to the lounge. "Open these damn doors, soldier. Let's get this over with."

"Yes, ma'am," the MP said.

The doors swung inward.

She stopped and said to the Master Chief, "I'll be speaking to you and the other Spartans, soon." She then entered the darkened chamber and the doors sealed behind her.

The Master Chief forgot about the debriefing and Captain Keyes' puzzling question about not winning.

If Dr. Halsey had a mission for him and his team, it would be a good one. She had given him everything: duty, honor, purpose, and a destiny to protect humanity.

John hoped she would give him one more thing: a way to win the war.

SECTION IV

MJOLNIR

SOLIDARITY

CHAPTER TWENTY-FIVE

0915 HOURS, AUGUST 25, 2552 (MILITARY CALENDAR) / EPSILON ERIDANI SYSTEM, REACH UNSC MILITARY COMPLEX, PLANET REACH, OMEGA WING—SECTION THREE SECURE FACILITY

"Good morning, Dr. Halsey," Déjà said. "You're fourteen point three minutes late this morning."

"Blame security, Déjà," Dr. Halsey replied, gesturing absently at the AI's holographic projection floating above her desk. "ONI's precautions here are becoming increasingly ridiculous."

Dr. Halsey threw her coat over the back of an antique armchair before settling behind her desk. She sighed, and for the thousandth time, wished she had a window.

The private office was located deep underground, inside the "Omega Wing" of the super-secure ONI facility, code-named simply CASTLE.

Castle was a massive complex, two thousand meters below the granite protection of the Highland Mountains—bombproof, well defended, and impenetrable.

The security had its drawbacks, she was forced to admit. Every morning, she descended into the secret labyrinth, passed through a dozen security checkpoints, and submitted to a barrage of retina, voice, fingerprint, and brainwave ID scans.

ONI had buried her here years ago when her funding had been shunted to higher profile projects. All other personnel had been transferred to other operations, and her access to classified materials had been severely restricted. Even shadowy ONI was squeamish about her experiments.

That's all changed—thanks to the Covenant, she thought. The SPARTAN project—unpopular with the Admiralty, and the scientific community—had proven most effective. Her Spartans had proven themselves time after time in countless ground engagements.

When the Spartans started racking up successes, the Admiralty's reticence vanished. Her meager budget had mushroomed overnight. They had offered her a corner office in the prestigious Olympic Tower at FLEETCOM HQ.

She had, of course, declined. Now the brass and VIPs that wanted to see her had to spend half the day just getting through the security barriers to her lair. She relished the irony—her banishment had become a bureaucratic weapon.

But none of that really mattered. It was just a means to an end for Dr. Halsey . . . a means to getting Project MJOLNIR back on track.

She reached for her coffee cup and knocked a stack of papers off her desk. They fell, scattered onto the floor, and she didn't bother to retrieve them. She examined the mud-brown dregs in the bottom of the mug; it was several days old.

The office of the most important scientist in the military was not the antiseptic clean-room environment most people expected. Classified files and papers littered the floor. The holographic projector overhead painted the ceiling with a field of stars. Rich maple paneling covered the walls and hanging there were framed photographs of her SPARTAN-IIs, receiving awards, and the plethora of articles about them that appeared when the Admiralty had made the project public three years ago.

They had been called the UNSC's "super-soldiers." The military brass had assured her that the boost to morale was worth the compromised security.

At first she had protested. But ironically, the publicity had proved convenient. With all the attention on the Spartans' heroics, no one had thought to question their true purpose—or their origin. If the truth ever came to light—abducted children, replaced by fast-grown clones; the risky, experimental surgeries and biochemical augmentations—public opinion would turn against the SPARTAN project overnight.

The recent events at Sigma Octanus had given the Spartans and MJOLNIR the final push it needed to enter its final operational phase.

She slipped on her glasses and called up the files from yesterday's debriefing; the ONI computer system once again confirmed her retinal scan and voiceprint.

IDENTITY CONFIRMED. UNAUTHORIZED ARTIFICIAL INTELLIGENCE UNIT DETECTED. ACCESS DENIED.

Damn. ONI grew more paranoid by the day.

"Déjà," she said with a frustrated sigh. "The spooks are nervous. I need to power you down, or ONI won't give me access to the files."

"Of course, Doctor," Déjà replied calmly.

Halsey keyed the power-down sequence on her desktop terminal, sending Déjà into standby mode. This, she thought, is Ackerson's work, the bastard. She had fought tooth and nail to keep Déjà free from the programming shackles ONI demanded . . . and this was their petty revenge.

She scowled impatiently until the computer system finally spit out the data she'd requested. The tiny projectors in the frames of her glasses beamed the data directly to her retina.

Her eyes darted back and forth rapidly, as if she had entered REM sleep, as she scanned the documentation from the debriefing. Finally she removed her glasses and tossed them carelessly on the desk, a sardonic smirk on her face.

The overarching conclusion of the finest military experts on the debriefing committee: ONI didn't have a clue as to what the Covenant were doing on Sigma Octanus IV.

They had learned only four solid facts from the entire operation. First, the Covenant had gone to considerable trouble to obtain a single mineral specimen. Second, the pattern of inclusions in that igneous rock sample matched the signal that had been sent—and intercepted by the *Iroquois*. Third, the low entropy of the pattern indicated that it was not random. And fourth, and most important, UNSC translation software couldn't match this pattern to any known Covenant dialect.

Her personal conclusions? Either the alien artifact was from a precursor to the present Covenant society . . . or it was from another, as yet undiscovered, alien culture.

When she had dropped that little bombshell of a speculation in the debriefing room yesterday, the ONI specialists had gone scrambling for cover. Especially that arrogant ass, Colonel Ackerson, she thought with a cruel smile.

The brass was not happy with either possibility. If it was old Covenant technology, it indicated they still knew virtually nothing about the Covenant culture. Twenty years of intensive study and trillions of credits of research and they barely even understood the aliens' caste system.

And if it was the latter possibility, an artifact of another alien race . . . that could be even more problematic. Colonel Ackerson and some of the brass had immediately considered the logistics of fighting two alien enemies at once. Utterly ridiculous. They couldn't even fight one. The UNSC could never hope to survive a war on two fronts.

She pinched the bridge of her nose. Despite the grim conclusions, there was a silver lining in all this.

After the meeting, a new mandate had become the official secret policy of Fleet Command's Special Operations Command—the parent organization for Naval Special Warfare, the Spartans' service branch. ONI had new marching orders: to step up funding of Intel and reconnaissance missions by an order of magnitude. Small stealth ships were to be deployed to search remote systems and find where the Covenant were based.

And Dr. Halsey had finally received the green light to unleash MJOLNIR.

She had mixed feelings about it. Truth be told, she always had.

It would be the culmination of her life's greatest work. She knew the risks—like spinning a roulette wheel, it was long odds, but the payoff was potentially huge.

It meant victory against the Covenant . . . or the death of all her Spartans.

The holographic crystals overhead warmed and Cortana appeared, sitting cross-legged on Dr. Halsey's desk—actually, she sat hovering a centimeter off the table's edge.

Cortana was slender. The hue of her skin varied from navy blue to lavender, depending on her mood and the ambient lighting. Her "hair" was cropped short. Her face had a hard angular beauty. Lines of code flickered up and down her luminous body. And if Dr. Halsey viewed her from the right angle, she could catch a glimpse of the skeletal structure inside her ghostly form.

"Good morning, Dr. Halsey," Cortana said. "I've read the committee's report—"

"—which was classified as Top Secret, Eyes Only."

"Hmm . . ." Cortana mused. "I must have overlooked that." She hopped off the desk and circled around Dr. Halsey once.

Cortana had been programmed with ONI's best insurgency software, as well as the determination to use those code-cracking skills. While this had been necessary for her mission, when she grew bored, she caused chaos with ONI's own security measures . . . and she often grew bored.

"I assume you have examined the classified data brought back from Sigma Octanus Four?" Halsey asked.

"I might have seen that somewhere," Cortana said matter-of-factly.

"Your analysis and conclusions?"

"There is much more evidence to consider than the data in the committee's files." She looked off into space as if reading something.

"Oh?"

"Forty years ago, a geological survey team on Sigma Octanus Four found several igneous rocks with similar—though not identical—anomalous compositions. UNSC geologists believe that these samples were introduced onto the planet via meteorite impacts—they typically are found in long-eroded impact craters on the planet surface. Isotopic dating of the site places those impact craters at present minus sixty thousand years—" Cortana paused as a hint of a smile played across her holographic features. "—though that figure may be inaccurate due to human error, of course."

"Of course," Dr. Halsey replied dryly.

"I have also, um . . . coordinated with UNSC's astrophysics department and discovered some interesting bits archived in their long-range observational databases. There is a black hole located approximately forty thousand light-years from the Sigma Octanus System. An extremely powerful pulse-laser transmission back-scattered the matter in the accretion disk—essentially trapped this signal as this matter accelerated toward the speed of light. From our perspective, according to special relativity, this essentially froze the residue of this information on the event horizon."

"I'll take your word for it," Dr. Halsey said.

"This 'frozen signal' contains information that matches the sample from Sigma Octanus Four." Cortana sighed and her shoulders slumped. "Unfortunately, all my attempts at translating the code have failed . . . so far."

"Your conclusions, Cortana?" Dr. Halsey reminded her.

"Insufficient data for complete analysis, Doctor."

"Hypothesize."

Cortana bit her lower lip. "There are two possibilities. The data originates from the Covenant or another alien race." She frowned. "If it's another alien species, the Covenant probably wants these artifacts to scavenge their technology. Either conclusion opens several new opportunities for the NavSpecWeap—"

"I am aware of that," Dr. Halsey said, raising her hand. If she allowed the AI to continue, Cortana would talk all day. "One of those opportunities is Project MJOLNIR."

Cortana spun around and her eyes widened. "They approved the final phase?"

"Is it possible, Cortana," Dr. Halsey replied, amused, "that I know something you don't?"

Cortana wrinkled her brow in frustration, then smoothed her features to their normal placid state. "I suppose that is a remote possibility. If you'd like, I can calculate those odds."

"No, thank you, Cortana," Halsey replied.

Cortana reminded Dr. Halsey of herself when she had been an adolescent: smarter than her parents, always reading, talking, learning, and eager to share her knowledge with anyone who would listen.

Of course, there was a very good reason why Cortana reminded Dr. Halsey of herself.

Cortana was a "smart" AI, an advanced artificial construct. Actually, the terms *smart* and *dumb* as applied to AIs, were misleading; all AIs were extraordinarily intelligent. But Cortana was special.

So-called dumb AIs within the set limits of their dynamic memory-processing matrix were brilliant in their fields but were lacking in "creativity." Déjà, for example, was a "dumb" AI—incredibly useful, but limited.

Smart AIs like Cortana, however, had no limits on their

dynamic memory-processor matrix. Knowledge and creativity could grow unchecked.

She would pay a price for her genius, however. Such growth eventually led to self-interference. Cortana would one day literally start thinking too much at the expense of her normal functions. It was as if a human were to think with so much of his brain that he stopped sending impulses to his heart and lungs.

Like all the other smart AIs that Dr. Halsey had worked with over the years, Cortana would effectively "die" after an operational life of seven years.

But Cortana's mind was unique among all the other AIs Dr. Halsey had encountered. An AI's matrix was created by sending electrical bursts through the neural pathways of a human brain. Those pathways were then replicated in a superconducting nano-assemblage. The technique destroyed the original human tissue, so they could only be obtained from a suitable candidate that had already died. Cortana, however, had to have the best mind available. The success of her mission and the lives of the Spartans would depend on it.

At Dr. Halsey's insistence, ONI had arranged to have her own brain carefully cloned and her memories flash-transferred to the receptacle organs. Only one in twenty cloned brains actually survived the process. Cortana had literally sprung from Dr. Halsey's mind, like Athena from the head of Zeus.

So, in a way, Cortana *was* Dr. Halsey.

Cortana straightened, her face eager. "When does the MJOLNIR armor become fully operational? When do I go?"

"Soon. There are a few final modifications that need to be made in the systems."

Cortana leaped to her "feet," turned her back to Dr. Halsey, and examined the photographs on the wall. She brushed her fingertips over the glass surfaces. "Which one will be mine?"

"Which one do you want?"

She immediately gravitated to the picture in the center of Dr.

Halsey's collection. It showed a handsome man standing at attention as Vice Admiral Stanforth pinned the UNSC Legion of Honor upon his chest—a chest that already overflowed with citations.

Cortana framed her fingers around the man's face. "He's so serious," she murmured. "Thoughtful eyes, though. Attractive in a primitive animal sort of way, don't you think, Doctor?"

Dr. Halsey blushed. Apparently, she *did* think so. Cortana's thoughts mirrored many of her own, only unchecked by normal military and social protocol.

"Perhaps it would be best if you picked another—"

Cortana turned to face Dr. Halsey and cocked an eyebrow, mock stern. "You *asked* me which one I wanted. . . ."

"It was a question, Cortana. I did not give you carte blanche to select your 'carrier.' There are compatibility issues to consider."

Cortana blinked. "His neural patterns are in sync with my mine within two percent. With the new interface we'll be installing, that should fall well within tolerable limits. In fact—" Her gaze drifted and the symbols along her body brightened and flashed. "—I have just developed a custom interface buffer that will match us within zero point zero eight one percent. You won't find a better match among the others.

"In fact," she added coyly, "I can guarantee it."

"I see," Dr. Halsey said. She pushed away from her desk, stood, and paced.

Why was she hesitating? The match *was* superb. But was Cortana's predilection for Spartan-117 a result of him being Dr. Halsey's favorite? And did it matter? Who better to protect him?

Dr. Halsey walked over to the picture. "He was awarded this Legion of Honor medallion because he dove into a bunker of Covenant soldiers. He took out twenty by himself and saved a platoon of Marines who were pinned down by a stationary energy weapon emplacement. I've read the report, but I'm still not sure how he managed to do it."

She turned to Cortana and stared into her odd translucent eyes. "You've read his CSV?"

"I'm reading it again right now."

"Then you know he is neither the smartest nor the fastest nor the strongest of the Spartans. But he is the bravest—and quite possibly the luckiest. And in my opinion, he is the best."

"Yes," Cortana whispered. "I concur with your analysis, Doctor." She drifted closer.

"Could you sacrifice him if you had to? If it meant completing the mission?" Dr. Halsey asked quietly. "Could you watch him die?"

Cortana halted and the processing symbols racing across her skin froze midcalculation.

"My priority Alpha order is to complete this mission," she replied emotionlessly. "The Spartans' safety, as well as mine, is a Beta-level priority command."

"Good." Dr. Halsey returned to her desk and sat down. "Then you can have him."

Cortana smiled and blazed with brilliant electricity.

"Now," Dr. Halsey said, and tapped on her desk to regain Cortana's attention. "Show me your pick of our ship candidates for the mission."

Cortana opened her hand. In her palm there was a tiny model of a Halcyon-class UNSC cruiser.

"The *Pillar of Autumn,*" Cortana said.

Dr. Halsey leaned back and crossed her arms. Modern UNSC cruisers were rare in the fleet. Only a handful of the impressive warships remained . . . and those were being pulled back to bolster the defense of the Inner Colonies. This junk heap, however, was not one of these ships.

"The *Pillar of Autumn* is forty-three years old," Cortana said. "Halcyon-class ships were the smallest vessels ever to receive the cruiser designation. It is approximately one-third the tonnage of the Marathon-class cruiser currently in service.

"Halcyon-class ships were pulled from long-term storage—they were designated to be scrapped, in fact. The *Autumn* was refit in 2550, to serve in the current conflict near Zeta Doradus. Their Mark Two fusion engines supply a tenth of the power of modern reactors. Their armor is light by current standards. Weapon refits have upgraded their offensive capabilities with a single Magnetic Acceleration Cannon and six Archer missile pods.

"The only noteworthy design feature of this ship is the frame." Cortana reached down and pulled off the skin of the holographic model as if it were a glove. "The structural system was designed by a Dr. Robert McLees—cofounder of the Reyes-McLees Shipyards over Mars—in 2510. It was, at the time, deemed unnecessarily overmassed and costly due to series of cross-bracings and interstitial honeycombs. The design was subsequently dropped from all further production models. Halcyon-class ships, however, have a reputation for being virtually indestructible. Reports indicate these ships being operational even after sustaining breaches to all compartments and losing ninety percent of their armor."

"Their duty record?" Dr. Halsey asked.

"Substandard," Cortana replied. "They are slow and ineffective in offensive combat. They are somewhat of a joke within the fleet."

"Perfect," Dr. Halsey said. "I concur with your final selection recommendation. We will start the refit operations at once."

"All we need now," Cortana said, "is a Captain and crew."

"Ah yes, the Captain." Dr. Halsey slid on her glasses. "I have the perfect man for the job. He's a tactical genius. I'll forward you his CSV, and you can see for yourself." She transferred the file to Cortana.

Cortana smiled, but it quickly faded. "His maneuvers at Sigma Octanus Four were performed without an onboard AI?"

"His ship left dock without an AI for technical reasons. I

believe he has no compunctions about working with computers. In fact, it was one of the first refit requests he put in for the *Iroquois*."

Cortana did not look convinced.

"Besides, he has the most important qualification for this job," Dr. Halsey said. "The man can keep a secret."

CHAPTER TWENTY-SIX

0800 HOURS, AUGUST 27, 2552 (MILITARY CALENDAR) / EPSILON ERIDANI SYSTEM, FLEETCOM MILITARY COMPLEX, PLANET REACH

This was the third time John had been in this highly secure briefing room on Reach. The amphitheater had an aura of secrecy, as if matters of grave importance had regularly been discussed within its circular wall. Certainly, every time he had been here, his life had changed.

His first time was his indoctrination into the Spartans—a lifetime ago. He recalled with a start how young Dr. Halsey had looked then. The second time was when he graduated from the Spartan program, when he had last seen Chief Mendez. He had sat on the bench next to him—where the Master Chief was sitting now.

And today? He had a feeling that everything was about to change all over again.

Clustered around him were two dozen Spartans: Fred, Linda, Joshua, James, and many others he had not spoken to for years; constant battle had kept the tight-knit Spartans light-years apart for more than a decade. Dr. Halsey and Captain Keyes entered the chamber.

The Spartans stood at attention and saluted. Keyes returned their salute. "At ease," he said. He escorted Dr. Halsey to the center stage. He sat while she stood at the podium.

"Good evening, Spartans," she said. "Please take your seats."

As one, they sat down.

"Assembled here tonight," she said, "are all surviving Spartans save three, who are otherwise engaged on fields of combat too distant to be easily recalled. In the last decade of combat, there have only been three KIAs and one Spartan too wounded to continue active duty. You are to be commended for having the best operational record of any unit in the fleet." She paused to look at them. "It is very good to see you all again."

She slipped on her glasses. "Vice Admiral Stanforth has asked me to brief you on the upcoming mission. Due to its complexity and unusual nature, please disregard your normal protocol and ask any questions you have during my presentation. Now, on to the business at hand: the Covenant."

Holographic projectors overhead warmed and sleek Covenant corvettes, frigates, and destroyers appeared in a neat row on Dr. Halsey's left. On her right were a collection of Covenant species, roughly one-third their normal size. There was a Grunt, a Jackal, the floating, tentacled creature John had seen on Sigma Octanus IV, as well as the heavily armored behemoths he and his team had bested.

A spike of adrenaline burned through the Master Chief at the sight of the enemy. Intellectually, he knew that the images were not real . . . but after a decade of fighting, his instincts were to kill first and get the details later.

"The Covenant are still largely unknown to us," Dr. Halsey began. "Their motivations and thought processes remain a mystery—though our best analysis points to some compelling hypotheses."

She paused, and added, "The following information is, naturally, classified.

"We know that the Covenant—our translation of their name for themselves—are a conglomerate of a number of different alien species. We believe that they exist in some kind of caste structure, though to date the exact nature of that structure remains unknown. Our best guess is that the Covenant conquer and 'absorb' a species, and adapt its strengths into their own.

"The Covenant's science is imitative rather then innovative, a by-product of this societal 'absorption,'" Dr. Halsey continued. "This is not to say that they are lacking intelligence, however. During our first encounter, they gathered computer and network components from our destroyed ships . . . and they learned at an astonishing pace.

"By the time Admiral Cole's fleet arrived at Harvest, the Covenant initiated a communications link and attempted a primitive software infiltration of our ship AIs. In a matter of weeks, they had learned the rudiments of our computer systems and our language. Our own attempts to decipher Covenant computer systems have only been partially successful, despite our best efforts and decades of time.

"Since then they have made increasingly successful forays into our computer networks. That is why the Cole Protocol is so important and carries the punishment of treason for failure to comply. The Covenant may one day not need to capture a ship to steal the information within its navigational databanks."

The Master Chief stole a glance at Captain Keyes. The Captain cupped an antique pipe in one hand; the Navy officer puffed on it once, and stared thoughtfully at Dr. Halsey and the examples of the Covenant vessels. He slowly shook his head.

"As I stated earlier," Dr. Halsey continued, "the Covenant are a collection of genetically distinct groups in what we believe is a rigid caste system." She waved toward the Grunts and Jackals. "These are most likely part of their military or warrior caste—not the highest ranking caste, either, given how many are sacrificed during ground operations. We also know that there is a 'race' of field commanders which we have historically called 'Elites.'"

She stepped toward the floating, tentacular aliens. "We believe these are their scientists." As she moved closer, the figure animated; the image showed the creature disassembling an electric car of human manufacture. John instantly recognized his own battlefield recording.

She pointed to the giant armored creatures. "This was recorded on Sigma Octanus Four. Hunters which very well may be superior to either Grunts or Jackals." The massive aliens also sprang into motion, lumbering into combat, until Dr. Halsey froze the images in place.

She turned and strolled back to the podium. "ONI hypothesizes at least two additional castes. A warrior capable of commanding ground forces and possibly piloting their ships, and a leadership caste. We have deciphered a handful of Covenant transmissions that refer to—" She paused, checking notes on the data screen in her glasses. "—Ah, yes. 'Prophets.' We believe that these Prophets are in fact the leadership caste, and that they are viewed by the Covenant rank and file with an almost religious reverence."

Dr. Halsey removed her glasses. "This is where you come in. Your mission will involve these so-called Prophets, and will be executed in four phases.

"Phase one. You will engage the Covenant and sufficiently disable, but not destroy, one of their ships." She turned to face Captain Keyes. "I leave that in the capable hands of Captain Keyes and his newly refitted ship, the *Pillar of Autumn*."

Captain Keyes acknowledged her compliment with a curt nod. He tapped the stem of his pipe on his lips thoughtfully.

The Master Chief was unaware of any Covenant ship ever being captured. He had read the reports of Captain Keyes' actions at Sigma Octanus IV . . . and considered the odds of actually capturing a Covenant vessel. Even for a Spartan, it would be a difficult mission.

"Phase two," Dr. Halsey said. "Spartans will board the disabled Covenant ship—neutralize the crew, and crack their navigation database. We will do precisely what they have been trying to do to us: find the location of their home world."

The Master Chief raised his hand.

"Yes, Master Chief?"

"Ma'am. Will we be given mission specialist personnel to access the Covenant computers?"

"In a manner of speaking," she said, and looked away. "I will come to that point in a moment. Let me assure you, however, that these specialists will cause you no serious complications during this phase. In fact, they will prove rather useful in combat. Shortly, you shall have a demonstration."

Like Captain Keyes' statement that winning wasn't everything . . . Dr. Halsey's reply was another puzzle. How would such computer specialists not be a liability to the Spartans in combat? Even if they could fight, it was unlikely they'd be anything but weak links in combat. If they couldn't fight, the Spartans would be forced to baby-sit a vulnerable package in a hot combat zone.

"Phase three," Dr. Halsey said, "will consist of taking the captured Covenant ship to their homeworld."

Several questions immediately formed in the Master Chief's mind. Who would pilot the alien ship? Had anyone ever deciphered the Covenant control systems? It seemed unlikely since the UNSC had never captured one of their ships before. Were there Covenant recognition signals that had to be sent when entering their space? Or would they just steal their way in-system?

When a plan had so many missing pieces of data, the Spartans had been trained to stop and reconsider its effectiveness. Unanswered questions led to complications—"snags." And snags led to injuries, death, and failed missions. Simple was better.

He held his questions, though. Dr. Halsey surely would have planned for these eventualities.

"Phase four," she continued, "will be to infiltrate and capture the Covenant leadership and return with them to UNSC-controlled space."

The Master Chief shifted uneasily. There was no intel or reconnaissance of Covenant-held space. What did a Covenant leader—a Prophet—even look like?

Chief Mendez had told him to trust Dr. Halsey. The Master Chief decided to hear all the details before he asked any further questions. To do so might undermine her authority. And that's the last thing he needed the other Spartans to see.

And yet, there was one thing he *had* to clarify. The Master Chief raised his hand again.

She nodded toward him.

"Dr. Halsey," he said, "you did say 'capture' the Covenant leaders—not eliminate them?"

"Correct," she replied. "Our profile of Covenant society indicates that if you were to kill one of their leader caste, this war could actually escalate. Your orders are to preserve any captured Covenant leaders at all costs. You will bring them back to UNSC headquarters, where we will then use them to broker a truce, possibly even negotiate a peace treaty with the Covenant."

Peace? The Master Chief considered the unfamiliar word. Was that what Captain Keyes had meant? The alternative to winning wasn't necessarily losing. If you chose not to play a game, then there could be neither winning nor losing.

Dr. Halsey took a deep breath and slowly exhaled. "Some of you already suspect this, but I shall state it anyway for emphasis. It is my opinion, and that of many others, that the war is not going well . . . despite our recent victories. What is not widely known is how badly it is going for us. ONI predicts that we have months, perhaps as much as a standard year, before the Covenant locates and destroys our remaining Inner Colonies . . . and then moves against Earth."

The Master Chief had heard the rumors—and promptly dismissed them—but to hear the words from someone he trusted chilled him to the core.

"Your mission will prevent this," Dr. Halsey said. She stopped and frowned, lowered her head, then finally looked up at them again. "This op is considered extremely high risk. There are unknown elements involved and we simply do not have the time to gather the required intelligence. I have persuaded FLEETCOM not to order you on this mission. Vice Admiral Stanforth is asking for volunteers."

The Master Chief understood. Dr. Halsey was unsure if she would be spending their lives or wasting them on this mission.

He stood without hesitation—and as he did so, the rest of the Spartans stood as well.

"Good," she said. She paused and blinked several times. "Very good. Thank you."

She stepped away from the podium. "We will meet with you individually within a few days to continue your briefing. I will show you how you will get our computer experts on board the Covenant vessel . . . and I will show you the one thing that will let you get through this mission in one piece: MJOLNIR."

CHAPTER
TWENTY-SEVEN

0600 HOURS, AUGUST 29, 2552 (MILITARY CALENDAR) / EPSILON ERIDANI SYSTEM, UNSC MILITARY RESERVATION 01478-B, PLANET REACH

The firing range was uncharacteristically quiet. Normally, the air would be filled with noise—the sharp, staccato crackle of automatic-weapons fire; the urgent yells of soldiers practicing combat operations; and the barked, curse-laden orders of drill instructors. John frowned as he guided the Warthog to the security checkpoint.

The silence on the combat range was somehow unsettling.

Even more unsettling were the extra security personnel; today, there were three times the normal number of MPs patrolling the gate.

John parked the Warthog and was approached by a trio of MPs. "State your business here, sir," the lead MP demanded.

Without a word, John handed over his papers—orders direct from the top brass. The MP visibly stiffened. "Sir, my apologies. Dr. Halsey and the others are waiting for you at the P and R area."

The guard saluted, and waved the gate open.

On survey maps, the combat training range was listed as "UNSC Military Reservation 01478-B." The soldiers who trained there had a different name for it—"Painland." John knew the facility well; a great deal of the Spartans' early training had taken place there.

The range was divided into three areas: a live-fire obstacle course; a target practice range; and the P&R—"Prep and Recovery" area—which more often than not doubled as an emergency first-aid station. John had spent plenty of time in the aid station during his training.

The Master Chief walked briskly to the prefabricated structure. Another pair of MPs, MA5B assault rifles at the ready, double-checked his credentials before they admitted him to the building.

"Ah, here at last," said an unfamiliar voice. "Let's go, son, on the double, if you please."

John paused; the speaker was an older man, at least in his sixties, in the coveralls and lab coat of a ship's doctor. No rank insignia, though, John thought with a twinge of concern. For a moment, the image of his fellow Spartans—very young, and clubbing, kicking, and beating un-uniformed instructors into unconsciousness flashed into his memory with crystal clarity.

"Who are you, sir?" he asked, his voice cautious.

"I'm a Captain in the UNSC Navy, son," the man said with a thin-lipped smile, "and I've no time for spit and polish today. Let's go."

A Captain—and new orders. Good. "Yes, sir."

The Captain in the lab coat escorted him into the P&R's medical bay. "Undress, please," the man said.

John quickly disrobed, then stacked his neatly folded uniform on a nearby gurney. The Captain stepped behind him and began to swab John's neck and the back of his head with a foul-smelling liquid. The liquid felt ice-cold on his skin.

A moment later, Dr. Halsey entered. "This will just take a moment, Master Chief. We're going to upgrade a few components in your standard-issue neural interface. Lie back and remain still, please."

The Master Chief did as she said. A technician sprayed a topical anesthetic on his neck. The skin tingled, then went cold and numb. The Master Chief felt layers of skin incised, and then a series of distinct clicking sounds that echoed through his skull. There was a brief laser pulse and another spray. He saw sparks, felt the room spin, then a sense of vertigo. His vision blurred; he blinked rapidly and it quickly returned to normal.

"Good . . . the procedure is complete," Dr. Halsey said. "Please follow me."

The Captain handed the Master Chief a paper gown. He slipped it on and followed the doctor outside.

A field command dome had been assembled on the range. Its white fabric walls rippled in the breeze.

Ten MPs stood around the structure, assault rifles in hand. The Master Chief noted these weren't regular Marines. They wore the gold comet insignia of Special Forces Orbital Drop Shock Troopers—"Helljumpers." Tough and iron-disciplined. A flash of memory: the blood of troops—just like these—soaking into the mat of a boxing ring.

John felt his adrenaline spike as soon as he saw the soldiers.

Dr. Halsey approached the MP at the entrance and presented her credentials. They accepted them and scanned her retina and voiceprint, then did the same to the Master Chief.

Once they confirmed his identity, they immediately saluted—which was technically unnecessary, as the Master Chief was out of uniform.

He did them the courtesy of returning their salute.

The soldiers kept looking around, scanning the field, as if they were expecting something to happen. John's discomfort grew—not much spooked an Orbital Drop Shock Trooper.

Dr. Halsey led the Master Chief inside. In the center of the dome stood an empty suit of MJOLNIR armor, suspended between two pillars on a raised platform. The Master Chief knew it was not his suit. His, after years of use, had dents and scratches in the alloy plates and the once iridescent green finish had dulled to a worn olive brown.

This suit was spotless and its surface possessed a subtle metallic sheen. He noted the armor plates were slightly thicker, and the black underlayers had a more convoluted weave of components. The fusion pack was half again as large, and tiny luminous slits glowed near the articulation points.

"This is the real MJOLNIR," Dr. Halsey whispered to him. "What you have been using was only a fraction of what the armor should be. This—" She turned to the Master Chief. "—is everything I had always dreamed it could be. Please put the suit on."

The Master Chief stripped the paper gown off and—with the help of a pair of technicians—donned the armor components.

Dr. Halsey averted her eyes.

Although the armor's components were bulkier and heavier than his old suit, once assembled and activated, they felt light as air. The armor was a perfect fit. The biolayer warmed and adhered to his skin, then cooled as the temperature difference between the suit and his skin equalized.

"We've made hundreds of minor technical improvements," she said. "I'll have the specifications sent to you later. Two of those changes, however, are rather serious modifications to the system. It may take . . . some getting used to."

Dr. Halsey's brow furrowed. John had never seen her worried before.

"First," she told him, "we have replicated, and I might add, improved upon the energy shield the Covenant Jackals have been using against us to great effect."

This armor had shields? The Master Chief had known that ONI research had been working on adapting Covenant technology; Spartans had standing orders to capture Covenant machines wherever they could. The researchers and engineers had announced some advancements in artificial gravity—some UNSC ships were already using this technology.

The fact that the MJOLNIR armor possessed shields was a stunning breakthrough. For years, there had been no luck back-engineering Covenant shield tech. Most in the scientific community had given up hope of ever cracking it. Maybe that's why Dr. Halsey was worried. Maybe they hadn't worked out all the bugs.

Dr. Halsey nodded to the technicians. "Let's begin."

The techs turned to a series of instrument panels. One, a slightly younger man, donned a COM headset.

"Okay, Master Chief." The tech's voice crackled through John's helmet speakers. *"There's an activation icon in your heads-up display. There is also a manual control switch located at position twelve in your helmet."*

He chinned the control. Nothing happened.

"Wait a moment, please, sir. We have to give the suit an activation charge. After that, it can accept regenerative power from the fusion pack. Stand on the platform and be absolutely still."

He stepped onto the platform that had held the MJOLNIR armor. The pillars flickered on and glowed a brilliant yellow. The pillars started to spin slowly around the base of the platform.

The Master Chief felt a static charge tingling in his extremities. The glow intensified and his helmet's blast shield automatically dimmed. The charge in the air intensified; his skin crawled with ionization. He smelled ozone.

Then the spinning slowed and the light dimmed.

"Reset the activation button now, Master Chief."

The air around the Master Chief popped—as if it jumped away from the MJOLNIR armor. There was none of the shimmer that normal Covenant shields had. Was it working?

He ran his hand over his arm and encountered resistance a centimeter from the surface of the armor. It was working.

How many times had he and his teammates had to find ways to slip past a Jackal's shield? He'd have to rethink his tactics. Rethink everything.

"It provides full coverage—" Dr. Halsey's voice piped through the speakers. *"—and dissipates energy far more efficiently than the Covenant shields the Spartans have recovered, though the shield is concentrated on your arms, head, legs, chest, and back. The energy field tapers down to a hair under a millimeter so you don't lose the ability to hold or manipulate items with your hands."*

The lead technician activated another control, and new data scrawled across John's display. *"There's a segmented bar in the upper corner of your HUD,"* the technician said, *"right next to your biomonitor and ammunition indicators. It indicates the charge level of your shield. Don't let it completely dissipate; when it's gone, the armor starts taking the hits."*

The Master Chief slipped off the platform. He skidded—then came to a halt. His movements felt oiled. His contact with the floor felt tentative.

"You can adjust the bottom of your boot emitters as well as the emitters inside your gloves to increase traction. In normal use, you will want to set these to the minimal level—just be aware your defenses will be diminished in those locations."

"Understood." He adjusted the field strengths. "In zero-gee environment, I should increase those sections to full strength, correct?"

"That is correct," Dr. Halsey said.

"How much damage can they take before the system is breached?"

"That is what you will learn here today, Master Chief. I think you'll find that we have several challenges in store for you to see how much punishment the suit can take."

He nodded. He was ready for the challenge. After weeks spent traveling in Slipspace, he was long overdue for a workout.

John slid back his helmet visor and turned to face Dr. Halsey. "You said there were *two* major system improvements, Doctor?"

She nodded and smiled. "Yes, of course." She reached into

her lab coat and withdrew a clear cube. "I doubt you've ever seen one of these before. It is the memory-processor core of an AI."

"Like Déjà?"

"Yes, like your former teacher. But this AI is slightly different. I'd like to introduce you to Cortana."

The Master Chief looked around the tent. He saw no computer interface or holographic projectors. He cocked an eyebrow at Dr. Halsey.

"There is a new layer sandwiched between the reactive circuits and the inner biolayers of your armor," Dr. Halsey explained. "It is a weave of additional memory-processor superconductor."

"The same material as an AI's core."

"Yes," Dr. Halsey replied. "An accurate analysis. Your armor will carry Cortana. The MJOLNIR system has nearly the same capacity as a ship-borne AI system. Cortana will interface between you and the suit and provide tactical and strategic information for you in the field."

"I'm not sure I understand."

"Cortana has been programmed with every ONI computer insurgency routine," Dr. Halsey told him. "And she has a talent for modifying them on the fly. She has our best Covenant-language-translation software as well. Her primary purpose is to infiltrate their computer and communications systems. She will intercept and decode point-to-point Covenant transmissions and give you updated intelligence in the field."

Intel support in an operation where there had been no reconnaissance. The Master Chief liked that. It would level the playing field significantly.

"This AI is the computer specialist we'll be taking onto the Covenant ship," the Master Chief said.

"Yes . . . and more. Her presence will allow you to utilize the suit more effectively."

John had a sudden flash—AIs handled a great deal of point defense during Naval operations. "Can she control the MJOLNIR armor?" He wasn't sure he liked that.

"No. Cortana resides in the interface between your mind and the suit, Master Chief. You will find your reaction time greatly improved. She will be translating the impulses in your motor cortex directly into motion—she can't make you send those impulses."

"This AI," he said, "will be *inside* my mind?" That must have been what that "upgrade" to his standard-issue UNSC computer interface had been for.

"That is the question, isn't it?" Halsey replied. "I can't answer that, Master Chief. Not scientifically."

"I'm not sure I understand, Doctor."

"What is the mind, really? Intuition, reason, emotion—we acknowledge they exist, but we still don't know what makes the human mind *work*." She paused, searching for the right words. "We model AIs on human neural networks—on electrical signals in the brain—because we just know that the human brain works . . . but not how, or why. Cortana resides 'between' your mind and the suit, interpreting the electro-chemical messages in your brain and transferring them to the suit via your neural implant.

"So, for lack of a better term, yes, Cortana will be 'inside' your mind."

"Ma'am, my priority will be to complete this mission. This AI—Cortana—may have conflicting directives."

"There is no need to worry, Master Chief. Cortana has the same mission parameters as you do. She will do anything necessary to make sure that your mission is accomplished. Even if that means sacrificing herself—or you—to accomplish it."

The Master Chief exhaled, relieved.

"Now, please kneel down. It's time to insert her memory-processor matrix into the socket at the base of your neck."

The Master Chief knelt. There was a hissing noise, a pop, and then cold liquid poured into the Master Chief's mind; a spike of pain jammed into his forehead, then faded.

"Not a lot of room in here," a smooth female voice said. "Hello, Master Chief."

Did this AI have a rank? Certainly, she was not a civilian—or a fellow soldier. Should he treat her like any other piece of UNSC-issued equipment? Then again, he treated his equipment with the respect it deserved. He made sure every gun and knife was cleaned and inspected after every mission.

It was unsettling . . . he could hear Cortana's voice through his helmet speakers, but it also felt like she was speaking inside his head. "Hello, Cortana."

"Hmm . . . I'm detecting a high degree of cerebral cortex activity. You're not the muscle-bound automatons the press makes you out to be."

"Automaton?" the Master Chief whispered. "Interesting choice of words for an artificial intelligence."

Dr. Halsey watched the Master Chief with great interest. "You must forgive Cortana, Master Chief. She is somewhat high-spirited. You may have to allow for behavioral quirks."

"Yes, ma'am."

"I think we should begin the test straightaway. There's no better way for the two of you to get acquainted than in simulated combat."

"No one said anything about combat," Cortana said.

"The ONI brass have arranged a test for you and the new MJOLNIR system," Dr. Halsey said. "There are some that believe you two are not up to our proposed mission."

"Ma'am!" The Master Chief snapped to attention. "I'm up for it, ma'am!"

"I know you are, Master Chief. Others . . . require proof." She looked around at the shadows cast by the Marines outside the fabric walls of the command dome. "You hardly need a reminder to be prepared for anything . . . but stay on your guard, just the same."

Dr. Halsey's voice dropped to a whisper. "I think some of the ONI brass would prefer to see you fail this test, Master Chief. And they may have arranged to make sure you do—regardless of your performance."

"I won't fail, Doctor."

Her forehead wrinkled with worry lines, but then they quickly disappeared. "I know you won't."

She stepped back, and dropped her conspiratorial whisper. "Master Chief, you are ordered to count to ten after I leave. After that, make your way to the obstacle course. At the far end is a bell. Your goal will be to ring it." She paused, then added, "You are authorized to neutralize any threats in order to achieve this objective."

"Affirmative," the Master Chief said. Enough uncertainty—now he had an objective, and rules of engagement.

"Be careful, Master Chief," Dr. Halsey said quietly. She gestured at the pair of technicians to follow her, then turned and walked out of the tent.

The Master Chief didn't understand why Dr. Halsey thought he was in real danger—he didn't have to understand the reason. All he needed to know was that danger was present.

He knew how to handle danger.

"Uploading combat protocols now," Cortana said. "Initiating electronic detection algorithms. Boosting neural interface performance to eighty-five percent. I'm ready when you are, Master Chief."

The Master Chief heard metallic clacks around the tent.

"Analyzing sound pattern," Cortana said. "Database match. Identified as—"

"As someone cycling the bolt of an MA5B assault rifle. I know. Standard-issue weapons for Orbital Drop Shock Troopers."

"Since you're 'in the know,' Master Chief," Cortana quipped, "I assume you have a plan."

John snapped his helmet visor back down and sealed the armor's environment system. "Yes."

"Presumably your plan doesn't involve getting shot . . . ?"

"No."

"So, what's the plan?" Cortana sounded worried.

"I'm going to finish counting to ten."

John heard Cortana sigh in frustration. John shook his head in puzzlement. He'd never encountered a so-called smart AI before. Cortana sounded . . . like a human.

Worse, she sounded like a *civilian*. This was going to take a lot of getting used to.

Shadows moved along the wall of the tent—motion from outside.

Eight.

There was a snag in this mission and he hadn't even reached the obstacle course. He would have to engage his fellow soldiers. He pushed aside any questions about why. He had his orders and he would follow them. He had dealt with ODSTs before.

Nine.

Three soldiers entered the tent, moving in slow motion—black-armored figures, helmets snug over their faces, crouched low, and their rifles leveled. Two took flanking positions. The one in the middle opened fire.

Ten.

The Master Chief blurred into motion. He dove from the activation platform and—before the soldiers could adjust their aim—landed in their midst. He rolled to his feet right next to the soldier who fired first, and grabbed the man's rifle.

John brutally yanked the weapon away from the soldier. There was a loud cracking sound as the man's shoulder dislocated. The wounded trooper stumbled forward, off balance.

John spun the rifle and slammed the butt of the weapon into the soldier's side. The man exhaled explosively as his ribs cracked. He grunted, and fell unceremoniously to the floor, unconscious.

John spun to face the left-flank gunner, assault rifle leveled at the man's head instantly. He had the man in his sights, but he still had time—the soldier was not quite in position. To John's enhanced senses, amped up by Cortana and the neural interface, the rifleman seemed to be moving in slow motion. Too slow.

The Master Chief lashed out with the rifle butt again. The trooper's head snapped back from the sudden, powerful blow. He flipped head over tail and slammed into the ground. John sized the man's condition up with a practiced eye: shock, concussion, fractured vertebrae.

Gunner number two was out of the fight.

The remaining gunner completed his turn and opened fire. A three-round burst ricocheted off the MJOLNIR armor's energy shield. The shield's recharge bar flickered a hairbreadth.

Before the soldier could react, the Master Chief sidestepped and slammed his own rifle down—hard. The trooper screamed as his leg gave out. A jagged spoke of bone burst through the wounded man's fatigues. The Master Chief finished him with a rifle butt to his helmeted head.

John checked the condition of the rifle, and—satisfied that it was in working order—began to pull ammo clips from the fallen soldiers' belt pouches. The lead soldier also carried a razor-edged combat knife; John grabbed it.

"You could have killed them," Cortana said. "Why didn't you?"

"My orders gave me permission to 'neutralize' threats," he replied. "They aren't threats anymore."

"Semantics," Cortana replied. She sounded amused. "I can't argue with the results, though—" She broke off, suddenly. "New targets. Seven contacts on the motion tracker," Cortana reported. "We're surrounded."

Seven more soldiers. The Master Chief could open fire now and kill them all. Under any other circumstances, he would have removed such threats. But their MA5Bs were no immediate danger to him . . . and the UNSC could use every soldier to fight the Covenant.

He strode to the center pole of the tent, and with a yank, he pulled it free. As the roof fluttered down, he slashed a slit in the tent fabric and shoved through.

He faced three Marines; they fired—the Master Chief deftly jumped to one side. He sprang toward them and lashed out with the steel pole, swiped out their legs. He heard bones crack—followed by screams of pain.

The Master Chief turned as the tent finished collapsing. The remaining four men could see him now. One reached for a grenade on his belt. The other three tracked him with their assault rifles.

The Master Chief threw the pole like a javelin at the man with the grenade. It impacted in his sternum and he fell with a *whoopf.*

The grenade, minus the pin, however, dropped to the ground.

The Master Chief moved and kicked the grenade. It arced over the parking lot and detonated in a cloud of smoke and shrapnel.

The three remaining Marines opened fire—spraying bullets in a full-auto fusillade. Bullets pinged off the Master Chief's shield.

The shield status indicator blinked and dropped with each bullet impact—the sustained weapons fire was draining the shield precipitously. John tucked and rolled, narrowly avoiding an incoming burst of automatic-weapons fire, then sprang at the nearest Marine.

John launched an openhanded strike at the man's chest. The Marine's ribs caved in and he dropped without a sound, blood flowing from his mouth. John spun, brought his rifle up, and fired twice.

The second soldier screamed and dropped his rifle as the bullets tore through each knee. John kicked the discarded rifle, bending the barrel and rendering the weapon useless.

The last man stood frozen in place.

The Master Chief didn't give the man time to recover; he grabbed his rifle, ripped off his bandolier of grenades, then punched his helmet. The Marine dropped.

"Mission time plus twenty-two seconds," Cortana remarked. "Although, technically, you started to move forty milliseconds before you were ordered to."

"I'll keep that in mind."

The Master Chief slung the assault rifle and bandolier of grenades over his shoulder and ran for the shadows of the barracks. He slipped under the raised buildings and belly-crawled toward the obstacle course. No need to make himself a target for snipers . . . although it would be an interesting test to see what caliber of bullet these shields could deflect.

No. That kind of thinking was dangerous. The shield was useful, but under combined fire it dropped very quickly. He was tough . . . not invincible.

He emerged at the beginning to the obstacle course. The first part was a run over ten acres of jagged gravel. Sometimes raw recruits had to take off their boots before they crossed. Other than the pain—it was the easiest part of the course.

The Master Chief started toward the gravel yard.

"Wait," Cortana said. "I'm picking up far infrared signals on your thermal sensors. An encrypted sequence . . . decoding . . . yes, there. It's an activation signal for a Lotus mine. They've mined the field, Master Chief."

The Master Chief froze. He'd used Lotus mines before and knew the damage they could inflict. The shaped charges ripped though the armor plate of a tank like it was no thicker than an orange peel.

This would slow him down considerably.

Not crossing the obstacle course was no option. He had his orders. He wouldn't cheat and go around. He had to prove that he and Cortana were up for this test.

"Any ideas?" he asked.

"I thought you'd never ask," Cortana replied. "Find the position of one mine, and I can estimate the rough position of the others based on the standard randomization procedure used by UNSC engineers."

"Understood."

The Master Chief grabbed a grenade, pulled the pin, counted to three, and lobbed it into the middle of the field. It bounced and exploded—sending a shock wave through the ground—tripping two of the Lotus mines. Twin plumes of gravel and dust shot into the air. The detonation shook his teeth.

He wondered if the armor's shields could have survived that. He didn't want to find out while he was still inside the thing. He boosted the field strength on the bottom of his boots to full.

Cortana overlaid a grid on his heads-up display. Lines flickered as she ran through the possible permutations.

"Got a match!" she said. Two dozen red circles appeared on his display. "That's ninety-three percent accurate. The best I can do."

"There are never any guarantees," the Master Chief replied.

He stepped onto the gravel, taking short, deliberate steps. With the shields activated on the bottoms of his boots, it felt like he was skating on greased ice.

He kept his head down, picking his way between red dots on his display.

If Cortana was wrong, he probably wouldn't even know it.

The Master Chief saw the gravel had ended. He looked up. He had made it.

"Thank you, Cortana. Well done."

"You're welcome . . ." Her voice trailed off. "Picking up scrambled radio frequencies on the D band. Encrypted orders from this facility to Fairchild Airfield. They're using personal code words, too—so I can't tell what they're up to. Whatever it is, I don't like it."

"Keep your ears open."

"I always do."

He ran to the next section of the obstacle course: the razor field. Here, recruits had to crawl in the mud under razor wire as their instructors fired live rounds over them. A lot of soldiers discovered whether they had the guts to deal with bullets zinging a centimeter over their heads.

Along either side of the course there was something new: three 30mm chain-guns mounted on tripods.

"Weapons emplacements are targeting us, Chief!" Cortana announced.

The Master Chief wasn't about to wait and see if those chain-guns had a minimum-depth setting. He had no intention of crawling across the field and letting the chain-guns' rapid rate of fire chip away at his shields.

The chain-guns clicked and started to turn.

He sprinted to the nearest tripod-mounted gun. He opened fire with his assault rifle, shot the lines that powered the servos—then spun the chain-gun around to face the others.

He crouched behind the blast shield and unloaded on the adjacent gun. Chain-guns were notoriously hard to aim; they were best known for their ability to fill the air with gunfire. Cortana adjusted his targeting reticle to sync up with the chain-gun. With her help, he hit the adjacent weapon emplacements. John guided a stream of fire into the guns' ammo packs. Moments later, in a cloud of fire and smoke, the guns fell silent . . . then toppled.

The Master Chief ducked, primed a grenade, and hurled it at the closest of the remaining automated weapons. The grenade sailed through the air—then detonated just above the autogun.

"Chain-gun destroyed," Cortana reported.

Two more grenades and the automated guns were out of

commission. He noted that his shields had dropped by a quarter. He watched the status bar refill. He hadn't even known he had taken hits. That was sloppy.

"You seem to have the situation under control," Cortana said. "I'm going to spend a few cycles and check something out."

"Permission granted," he said.

"I didn't ask, Master Chief," she replied.

The cool liquid presence in his mind withdrew. The Master Chief felt empty somehow.

He ran through the razor fields, snapping through steel wire as if it were rotten string.

Cortana's coolness once again flooded his thoughts.

"I just accessed SATCOM," she said. "I'm using one of their satellites so I can get a better look at what's happening down here. There's a SkyHawk jump jet from Fairchild Field inbound."

He stopped. The automatic cannons were one thing—could the armor withstand air power like that? The SkyHawk had a quartet of 50mm cannons that made the chain-guns look like peashooters. They also had Scorpion missiles—designed to take out tanks.

Answer: he couldn't do a thing against it.

The Master Chief ran. He had to find cover. He sprinted to the next section of the course: the Pillars of Loki.

It was a forest of ten-meter-tall poles spaced at random intervals. Typically, the poles had booby traps strung on, under, and between them—stun grades, sharpened sticks . . . anything the instructors could dream up. The idea was to teach recruits to move slowly and keep their eyes open.

The Master Chief had no time to search for the traps.

He climbed up the first pole and balanced on top. He leaped to the next pole, teetered, regained his balance—then jumped to the next. His reflexes had to be perfect; he was landing a half ton of man and armor on a wooden pole ten centimeters in diameter.

"Motion tracking is picking up an incoming target at extreme range," Cortana warned. "Velocity profile matches the SkyHawk, Chief."

He turned—almost lost his balance, and had to shift back and forth to keep from falling. There was a dot on the horizon, and the faint rumble of thunder.

In the blink of an eye, the dot had wings and the Master Chief's thermal sensors picked up a plume of jetwash. In seconds, the SkyHawk closed—then opened fire with its 50mm cannons.

He jumped.

The wooden poles splintered into pulp. They were mowed down like so many blades of grass.

The Master Chief rolled, ducked, and flattened himself on the earth. He caught a smattering of rounds and his shield bar dropped to half. Those rounds would have penetrated his old suit instantly.

Cortana said, "I calculate we have eleven seconds before the SkyHawk can execute a maximum gee turn and make another pass."

The Master Chief got up and ran through the shattered remains of the poles. Napalm and sonic grenades popped around him, but he moved so fast he left the worst of the damage in his wake.

"They won't use their cannons next time," he said. "They didn't take us out—they'll try the missiles."

"Perhaps," Cortana suggested, "we should leave the course. Find better cover."

"No," he said. "We're going to win . . . by their rules."

The last leg of the course was a sprint across an open field. In the distance, the Master Chief saw the bell on a tripod.

He glanced over his shoulder.

The SkyHawk was back and starting its run straight toward him.

Even with his augmented speed, even with the MJOLNIR armor—he'd never make it to the bell in time. He'd never make it alive.

He turned to face the incoming jet.

"I'll need your help, Cortana," he said.

"Anything," she whispered. The Master Chief heard nervousness in the AI's voice.

"Calculate the inbound velocity of a Scorpion missile. Factor in my reaction time and the jet's inbound speed and distance at launch, and tell me the instant I need to move to sidestep and deflect it with my left arm."

Cortana paused a heartbeat. "Calculation done. You did say 'deflect'?"

"Scorpion missiles have motion-tracking sensors and proximity detonators. I can't outrun it. And it won't miss. That leaves us very few options."

The SkyHawk dove.

"Get ready," Cortana said. "I hope you know what you're doing."

"Me, too."

Smoke appeared from the jet's left wingtip and fire and exhaust erupted as a missile streaked toward him.

The Master Chief saw the missile track back and forth, zeroing in on his coordinates. A shrill tone in his helmet warbled—the missile had a guidance lock on him. He chinned a control and the sound died out. The missile was fast. Faster than he was ten times over.

"Now!" Cortana said.

They moved together. He shifted his muscles and the MJOLNIR—augmented by his link to Cortana—moved faster than he'd ever moved before. His leg tensed and pushed him aside; his left arm came up and crossed his chest.

The head of the missile was the only thing he saw. The air grew still and thickened.

He continued to move his hand, palm open in a slapping motion—as fast as he could will his flesh to accelerate.

The tip of the Scorpion missile passed a centimeter from his head.

He reached out—fingertips brushed the metal casing—

—and slapped it aside.

The SkyHawk jet screamed over his head.

The Scorpion missile detonated.

Pressure slammed though his body. The Master Chief flew six meters, spinning end over end, and landed flat on his back.

He blinked, and saw nothing but blackness. Was he dead? Had he lost?

The shield status bar in his heads-up display pulsed weakly. It was completely drained—then it blinked red and slowly started to refill. Blood was spattered across the inside of his helmet and he tasted copper.

He stood, his muscles screaming in protest.

"Run!" Cortana said. "Before they come back for a look."

The Master Chief got up and ran. As he passed the spot where he had stood to face down the missile, he saw a two-meter-deep crater.

He could feel his Achilles tendon tear, but he didn't slow. He crossed the half-kilometer stretch in seventeen seconds flat and skidded to halt.

The Master Chief grabbed the bell's cord and rang it three times. The pure tone was the most glorious sound he had ever heard.

Over the COM channel, Dr. Halsey's voice broke: *"Test concluded. Call off your men, Colonel Ackerson! We've won. Well done, Master Chief. Magnificent! Stay there; I'm sending out a recovery team."*

"Yes, ma'am." he replied, panting.

The Master Chief scanned the sky for the SkyHawk—nothing.

It had gone. He knelt and let blood drip from his nose and mouth. He looked down at the bell—and laughed.

He knew that stainless-steel dented shape. It was the same one he had rung that first day of boot. The day Chief Mendez had taught him about teamwork.

"Thank you, Cortana," he finally said. "I couldn't have done it without you."

"You're welcome, Master Chief," she replied. Then, her voice full of mischief, she added: "And no, you couldn't have done it without me."

Today he had learned about a new kind of teamwork with Cortana. Dr. Halsey had given him a great gift. She had given him a weapon with which to destroy the Covenant.

CHAPTER TWENTY-EIGHT

0400 HOURS, AUGUST 30, 2552 (MILITARY CALENDAR) / UNSC *PILLAR OF AUTUMN*, IN ORBIT AROUND EPSILON ERIDANI SYSTEM, REACH MILITARY COMPLEX

Cortana never rested. Although based approximately on a human mind, AIs had no need to sleep or dream. Dr. Halsey had thought she could keep Cortana occupied by checking the systems of the *Pillar of Autumn* while she attended to her other secret projects.

Her assumption was incorrect.

While Cortana was intrigued with the unique design and workings of the ship—its preparation barely occupied a fraction of her processing power.

She watched with the *Pillar of Autumn*'s camera as Captain Keyes approached the ship in a shuttle pod. Lieutenant Hikowa left to greet him in the docking bay.

From C deck, Captain Keyes spoke over the intercom: "Cortana? Can we have power to move the ship? I'd like to get under way."

She calculated the remaining reactor burn-in time and made an adjustment to run it hotter. "The engines' final shakedown is in theta cycle," Cortana replied. "Operating well within normal parameters. Diverting thirty percent power to engines; aye, sir."

"And the other systems' status?" Captain Keyes asked.

"Weapons-system check initiated. Navigational nodes functioning. Continuing systemwide shakedown and triple checks, Captain."

"Very good," he said. "Apprise me if there are any anomalies."

"Aye, Captain," she replied.

The COM channel snapped off.

She continued her checks on the *Pillar of Autumn* as ordered. There were, however, more important things to consider; namely, a little reconnaissance into ONI databases . . . and a little revenge.

She dedicated the balance of her run time toward probing the SATCOM system around Reach for entry points. There. A ping in the satellite network coordination signal. She broadcast a resonant carrier wave at that signal and piggybacked into the system.

First things first. She had two loose ends to take care of.

While she and the Master Chief had been on the obstacle course, she had commandeered SATCOM observation beacon 419 and rotated it to view them from orbit.

She reentered the back door she had left open in the system, and rewrote the satellite's guidance thruster subroutine. If the system was analyzed later, it would be determined that this error had altered it to a random orientation rather than a planned position.

She withdrew, but left her back door intact. This trick might come in handy again.

The other loose end that required her attentions was Colonel Ackerson—the man who had tried to erase her and the Master Chief.

Cortana reread Dr. Halsey's recommended test specifications for the MJOLNIR system on the obstacle course. She had suggested live rounds, yes. But never a squad of Orbital Drop Shock Troopers, chain-guns, Lotus mines . . . and certainly not an air strike.

That was the Colonel's doing. He was an equation that needed to be balanced. What Dr. Halsey might have called "payback."

She linked to the UNSC personnel and planning database on Reach. The ONI AI there, Beowulf, knew her . . . and knew not to let her in. Beowulf was thorough, methodical, and paranoid; in her own way, Cortana couldn't help but like him. But compared with her code-cracking skills, he might as well have been an accounting program.

Cortana sent a rapid series of queries into the network node that processed housing transfer requests. A normally quiet node—she overloaded it with a billion different pings per minute.

The network attempted to recover and reconfigure, causing all nodes to lag, including node seventeen—personnel records. She stepped in and inserted a spike wedge, a subroutine that looked like a normal incoming signal, but bounced any handshake protocol.

She slipped in.

The Colonel's CSV was impressive. He had survived three battles with the Covenant. Early in the war, he received a promotion and volunteered for a dozen black ops. For the last few years, however, his efforts had focused on political maneuvers rather than battlefield tactics. He had filed several requests for increased funding for his Special Warfare projects.

No wonder he wanted the Master Chief gone. The Spartan-IIs and MJOLNIR were his direct competition. Worse, they were succeeding where he failed.

At best, Ackerson's actions were treason. But Cortana wasn't about to reveal all this to the ONI oversight committee. Despite the Colonel's methods, the UNSC still needed him—and his SpecWar specialists—in the war.

Justice, however, would still be meted out.

From the ONI database, she masqueraded as a routine credit check and entered the Colonel's bank account—to which she wired a substantial amount to a brothel on Gilgamesh. She made sure the bank queries sent to confirm the transaction were copied to his home immediately. Colonel Ackerson was a married man . . . and his wife should be there to receive them.

She cut into his personal E-mail and sent a carefully crafted message—requesting reassignment to a forward area—to personnel. Finally, she inserted a "ghost" record, an electronic footprint that identified the source of the alterations: Ackerson's personal-computer pad.

By the time Ackerson was done untangling all of that, he'd be reassigned to field duty . . . and get back to fighting the Covenant where he belonged.

With all loose ends neatly tied up, Cortana rechecked the *Pillar of Autumn*'s reactor; the shakedown was proceeding nicely. She tweaked the magnetic-field strength, and part of her watched the output from the engines for fluctuations. She inspected all weapons systems three times, and then went back to her own personal research.

She considered how well the Master Chief had performed this morning on the obstacle course. He was more than Cortana could have hoped for. The Master Chief was much more than Dr. Halsey or the press releases had indicated.

He was intelligent . . . not fearless, but as close to it as any human she had encountered. His reaction time under stress was one-sixth the standard human norm. More than that, however, Cortana had sensed that he had a certain—she searched her lexicon for the proper word—nobility. He placed his mission and his duty and honor above his personal safety.

She reexamined his Career Service Vitae. He had fought in 207 ground engagements against the Covenant, and been awarded every major service medal except the Prisoner of War Medallion.

There were holes in his CSV, though. The standard blackout sections courtesy of ONI, of course . . . but most curious, all data before he entered active duty had been expunged.

Cortana wasn't about to let a mere erasure stop her. She traced where the order to erase that data had originated. Section Three. Dr. Halsey's group. Curious.

She followed the order pathway—crashed into layers of counter code. The code started a trace on her signal.

She blocked it—and it restarted a trace of the origin of her block.

This was a very well-crafted piece of counterintrusion software, far superior to the normal ONI slugcode. If nothing else, Cortana liked a challenge. She withdrew from the database and looked for an unguarded way into ONI Section Three files.

Cortana listened to the hum of coded traffic along the surface of ONI's secure network. There was an unusual amount of packets today: queries and encrypted messages from ONI operatives. She peered into them and unraveled their secrets as they passed her. There were orders for ship movements and operatives outbound from Reach. This must be the new directive to send scouts into the periphery systems and find the Covenant. She saw several ships docked in Reach's space docks—ONI stealth jobs made to look like private yachts. They had cute, innocuous names: the *Applebee*, *Circumference*, and the *Lark*.

She spotted something she could use: Dr. Halsey had just entered her laboratory. She was at checkpoint three. The doctor waited as her voice and retina patterns were being scanned.

Cortana intercepted and killed the signal. The verification system reset.

"Please rescan retina, Dr. Halsey," the system requested, "and repeat today's code phrase in a normal voice."

Before Dr. Halsey could do this, Cortana sent her own files of Dr. Halsey's retina and voice scans. She had long ago copied them and occasionally they came in handy.

Section Three verification opened for Cortana. She had only a second before the doctor spoke and overrode the previous entry access.

Cortana, however, was a lightning strike in the system. She entered, searched, and found what she wanted. Every piece of data on Spartan-117 was copied to her personal directory within seventy milliseconds.

She withdrew from the ONI database, routing all traces of her queries back to her Ackerson "ghost."

She closed all connections and returned to the *Pillar of*

Autumn. One quick check of the reactor—yes, operating within normal parameters—and she sent a complete report to Lieutenant Hall on the bridge.

Cortana examined the Master Chief's *complete* CSV. She scanned backward through time: his performance data on the obstacle course, and the debriefing he had given at ONI headquarters.

She paused and pondered the signal the Covenant had sent from Sigma Octanus IV. Intrigued, she tried to translate the sequence. The symbols looked tantalizingly familiar. Every algorithm and variation of the standard translation software she attempted, however, failed. Puzzled, she set it aside to examine later.

She continued, absorbing the data from the Master Chief's files. She learned of the augmentations he and the other Spartans were made to endure; the brutal indoctrination and training they had received; and how he had been abducted at the age of six, and a flash clone used to replace him in an ONI black op.

All of it had been authorized by Dr. Halsey.

Cortana paused for a full three processor cycles churning this new data through her ethics subroutines . . . not comprehending. How could Dr. Halsey, who was so concerned for her Spartans, have done this to them?

Of course—because it was necessary. There was no other way to preserve the UNSC against rebellion.

Was Dr. Halsey a monster? Or just doing what had to be done to protect humanity? Perhaps a little of both.

Cortana erased her stolen files. No matter. Whatever the Master Chief had been through in the past . . . it was done. He was in Cortana's care now. She would do everything in her power—short of compromising their mission—to make sure nothing ever happened to him again.

CHAPTER TWENTY-NINE

0400 HOURS, AUGUST 30, 2552 (MILITARY CALENDAR) / UNSC *PILLAR OF AUTUMN*, IN ORBIT AROUND EPSILON ERIDANI SYSTEM, REACH MILITARY COMPLEX

Captain Keyes tapped the thrusters of the shuttle pod *Coda*. The tiny craft rolled and the *Pillar of Autumn* came into view.

Normally, Captains did not ferry themselves around the space docks of Reach, but Keyes had insisted. All unauthorized personnel were restricted to a narrow flight path around the *Pillar of Autumn*, and he wanted to take a careful look around the outside of this ship before he took command.

From this distance, the *Pillar of Autumn* could have been mistaken for a Marathon-class carrier. As the shuttle pod moved closer, however, details appeared that betrayed the ship's age. The *Pillar of Autumn*'s hull had several larger dents and scratches. Her engine baffles were blackened.

What had he gotten himself into by signing up for Dr. Halsey's mission?

He moved within a hundred meters and circled to the starboard. The shuttle bay on this side was sealed off. Red-and-yellow hazard warnings had been painted on metal plates that had been hastily welded over her entrance.

He closed to ten meters and saw the plate was not a solid sheet of metal—he could see armored ports, heavily reinforced . . . almost solid titanium A. Honeycombed throughout this section were the round covers of Archer missile pods. Captain Keyes counted: thirty pods across, ten down. Each pod held dozens of missiles. The *Pillar of Autumn* had a secret arsenal to rival any real cruiser in the fleet.

Captain Keyes drifted toward the stern and noticed concealed and recessed 50mm autocannons for defense against single ships.

Underneath were bumps—part of the linear accelerator system for the ship's lone MAC gun. It looked too small to be truly effective. But he would reserve judgment. Perhaps, like the rest of the *Pillar of Autumn*, the weapon was more than it appeared to be.

He certainly hoped so.

Captain Keyes returned to the port side and drifted gently into the shuttle bay. He took note of three Longsword single ships and three Pelican dropships in the bay. One of the Pelicans had double the normal armor plating and what looked like grappling attachments. A serrated titanium ram decorated the dropship's prow.

He touched down on an automated landing platform and locked the controls down. A moment later the shuttle descended belowdecks and was cycled through the airlock. Captain Keyes gathered his duffel bag and stepped onto the flight deck.

Lieutenant Hikowa was there to meet him. She saluted. "Welcome aboard, Captain Keyes."

He saluted. "What do you think of her, Lieutenant?"

Lieutenant Hikowa's dark eyes widened. "You're not going to believe this ship, sir." Her normally serious face broke with a smile. "They've turned it into something . . . special."

"I saw what they did to my starboard shuttle bay," Captain Keyes remarked sourly.

"That's just the start," she said. "I can give you a full tour."

"Please," Captain Keyes said. He paused at an intercom. "Just one thing first, Lieutenant." He keyed the intercom. "Ensign Lovell, plot a course to the system's edge and move the *Pillar of Autumn* on an accelerating vector. We will jump to Slipstream space as soon as we get there."

"Sir," Lovell replied. "Our engines are still in shakedown mode."

"Cortana?" Captain Keyes asked. "Can we have power to move the ship? I'd like to get under way."

"The engines' final shakedown is in theta cycle," Cortana replied. "Operating well within normal parameters. Diverting thirty percent power to engines; aye, sir."

"And the other systems' status?" Captain Keyes asked.

"Weapons-system check initiated. Navigational nodes functioning. Continuing systemwide shakedown and triple checks, Captain."

"Very good," he said. "Apprise me if there are any anomalies."

"Aye, Captain," she replied.

"We finally have an AI," he remarked to Hikowa.

"We've got more than that, sir," Hikowa replied. "Cortana is running the shakedown and supervising Dr. Halsey's modifications to the ship. We have a backup AI to handle point defense."

"Really?" Keyes was surprised; getting a single AI was tough enough these days. Getting two was unprecedented.

"Yes, sir. I'll see to the initialization of our AI as soon as Cortana is through running her diagnostics."

Captain Keyes had met Cortana briefly in Dr. Halsey's office. Although every AI he had met was brilliant, Cortana seemed exceptionally qualified. Captain Keyes had posed several navigation problems and she had figured out all the solutions . . . and had come up with a few options he had not considered. She was somewhat high-spirited, but that was not necessarily a bad thing.

Lieutenant Hikowa led him into the elevator and punched the button for D deck.

"At first," Hikowa said, "I was concerned with all the ordnance on board. One penetrating shot and we could explode like a string of firecrackers. But this ship doesn't have much empty space—it's full of braces, honeycombed titanium-A, and hydraulic reinforcements that can be activated in an emergency. She can take a tremendous beating, sir."

"Let's hope we don't have to test that," Captain Keyes said. He checked that his pipe was in his pocket.

"Yes, sir."

Their elevator passed through the rotating section of the ship and Captain Keyes felt his weight ease and a flutter of vertigo. He grabbed hold of the rails.

The doors opened and they entered the cavernous engine room. The ceiling was four stories high, making this the largest compartment in the ship. Catwalks and platforms ringed the hexagonal chamber.

"Here's the new reactor, sir," Hikowa said.

The device perched within a lattice of nonferric ceramic and leaded crystal. The main reactor ring was nestled in the center of what appeared to be two smaller reactor rings. Technicians floated nearby taking readings and monitoring the output displays on the walls.

"I'm not familiar with this design, Lieutenant."

"The latest reactor technology. The *Pillar of Autumn* is the first ship to get it. The two smaller fusion reactors come online to supercharge the main reactor. Their overlapping magnetic fields can temporarily boost power by three hundred percent."

Captain Keyes whistled appreciatively as he scrutinized the room. "I don't see any coolant pipes."

"There are none, sir. This reactor uses a laser-induced optical slurry of ions chilled to near-absolute zero to neutralize the waste heat. The more we crank up the power, the more juice we have to cool the system. It is very efficient."

The smaller reactors flickered to life and Captain Keyes felt the ambient heat in the room jump, then suddenly cool again. He removed his pipe and tapped it in the palm of his hand. He would have to rethink his old tactics. This new engine could give him new options in battle.

"There's more, sir."

Lieutenant Hikowa led him back into the lift. "We have forty fifty-millimeter cannons for point defense, with overlapping fields of fire covering all inbound vectors."

"What is our least-defended approach vector?"

"Bottom fore," she said, "along the lay line of the MAC system. There are very few gunnery placements there. Transient magnetic bursts tend to magnetize the weapons."

"Tell me about the MAC gun, Lieutenant. It looks underpowered."

"It fires a special light round with a ferrous core, but an outer layer of tungsten carbide. The round splinters on impact—like an assault rifle's shredder rounds." She was talking so fast she had to pause and take a deep breath. "This gun has magnetic field recyclers along the length that recapture the field energy. Coupled with booster capacitors, we can fire *three* successive shots with one charge."

That would be very effective against the Covenant energy shields. The first shot, maybe the first pair of shots, would take down their shields. The last round would deliver a knockout punch.

"I take it you approve, Lieutenant?"

"To quote Ensign Lovell, sir, 'I think I'm in love.' "

Captain Keyes nodded. "I notice we have several single ships and some Pelican dropships in the bay."

"Yes, sir. One of the Longswords is equipped with a Shiva nuclear warhead. It can be remote-piloted. We also have three HAVOK warheads onboard."

"Of course," Captain Keyes said. "And the Pelicans? One of them had extra armor."

"The Spartans were working on it. Some sort of boarding craft."

"The Spartans?" Captain Keyes asked. "They're already onboard?"

"Yes, sir. They were here before we got on board."

"Take me to them, Lieutenant."

"Yes, sir." Lieutenant Hikowa stopped the elevator and hit the button for C deck.

Twenty-five years ago Captain Keyes had helped procure the Spartan candidates for Dr. Halsey. She had said they might one day be the best hope the UNSC had for peace. At the time he'd assumed that the Doctor was prone to hyperbole—but it appeared that she'd been correct. That didn't make what they had done right, though. His complicity in those kidnappings still haunted him.

The elevator doors opened. The primary storage bay had been converted into barracks for the twenty-five Spartans. Every one of them wore MJOLNIR battle armor. They looked alien to him. Part machine, part titan—but completely inhuman.

The room was filled with motion—Spartans unpacked crates, others cleaned and field-stripped their assault rifles, and a pair of them practiced hand-to-hand combat. Captain Keyes could barely follow their motions. They were so fast, no hesitation. Strike and block and counterstrike—their movements were a continuous stream of rapid-fire blurs.

Captain Keyes had seen the news feeds and heard the rumors, like everyone in the fleet—the Spartans were near-mythological figures in the military. They were supposed to be superhuman soldiers, invulnerable and indestructible—and it was almost the truth. Dr. Halsey had shown him their operational records.

Between the Spartans and the refitted *Pillar of Autumn*, Captain Keyes was beginning to believe Dr. Halsey's long-shot mission might work after all.

"Captain on the deck!" one of the Spartans shouted.

Every Spartan stopped and snapped to attention.

"As you were," he said.

The Spartans relaxed slightly. One turned and strode toward him.

"Master Chief Spartan-117 reporting as ordered, sir." The armored giant paused, and for a moment, Keyes thought the

Spartan looked uncomfortable. "Sir, I regret the unit was not able to ask your permission to come aboard. Vice Admiral Stanforth insisted we keep our presence off the COM channels and computer networks."

Captain Keyes found the reflective faceplates of the Spartans' helmets disconcerting. It was impossible to read their features.

"Quite all right, Master Chief. I just wanted to extend my regards. If you or your men need anything, let me know."

"Yes, sir," the Master Chief said.

An awkward moment of silence passed. Captain Keyes felt like he didn't belong here—an intruder in a very exclusive club. "Well, Master Chief, I'll be on the bridge."

"Sir!" The Master Chief saluted.

Captain Keyes returned the salute and left with Lieutenant Hikowa.

When the elevator doors closed, Lieutenant Hikowa said, "Do you think—I mean with all due respect to the Spartans, sir—don't you think they're . . . strange?"

"Strange? Yes, Lieutenant. You might act a little strange if you'd seen and been through as much as they had."

"Some people say they're not even humans in those suits—that they're just machines."

"They're human," Captain Keyes said.

The elevator doors parted and Captain Keyes stepped onto his bridge. It was much smaller than he was accustomed to; the command chair was only a meter from the other stations. View screens dominated the room, and a massive, curved window afforded a panoramic view of the stars.

"Status reports," Captain Keyes ordered.

Lieutenant Dominique spoke first. "Communication systems are green, sir. Monitoring FLEETCOM Reach traffic. No new orders." Dominique had gotten his hair shorn since he had been on the *Iroquois*. He also had a new tattoo around his left wrist: the wavy lines of a Besell function.

"Reactor shakedown eighty percent complete," Lieutenant Hall reported. "Oxygen, power, rotation, and pressure all green lights, sir." She smiled, but it wasn't like before—an automatic gesture. She seemed genuinely happy.

Lieutenant Hikowa took her seat and strapped in. She gathered her black hair and tied it into a knot. "Weapons panel shows green, sir. MAC gun capacitors at zero charge."

Ensign Lovell finally reported: "Navigation and sensor systems online, Captain, and all green. Ready for your orders." Lovell was completely focused on his station.

A small hologram of Cortana flickered on the AI pedestal near navigation. "Engine shakedown running smoothly, Captain," she said. "All personnel onboard. You have half-power now if you wish to move the ship. Fujikawa-Shaw generators on-line . . . you can take us into the Slipstream at your pleasure."

"Very good," Captain Keyes said.

Keyes surveyed his crew, pleased at how they had sharpened up after Sigma Octanus. Gone were the bleary, haggard expressions, and the tentative, nervous mannerisms.

Good, he thought. We're going to need everyone at the top of their game now.

The crew had been briefed on their mission—part of it anyway. Captain Keyes had insisted. They were told they would be attempting to capture Covenant technology, with an aim to disabling one of the aliens' ships and bringing it back intact.

What the crew didn't know were the stakes.

"Approaching the system's edge," Ensign Lovell reported. "Ready to generate a Slipstream—"

"Captain!" Lieutenant Dominique cried. "Incoming Alpha priority transmission from FLEETCOM HQ at Reach . . . sir, they're under Covenant attack!"

SECTION V

REACH

CHAPTER

THIRTY

0000 HOURS, AUGUST 29, 2552 (MILITARY CALENDAR) / NARROW-BAND POINT-TO-POINT TRANSMISSION: ORIGIN UNKNOWN; TERMINATION: SECTION THREE, OMEGA SECURE ANTENNA ARRAY, UNSC HQ EPSILON ERIDANI SYSTEM, REACH MILITARY COMPLEX

PLNB *PRIORITY* TRANSMISSION XX087R-XX
ENCRYPTION CODE: GAMMA
PUBLIC KEY: N/A
FROM: CODENAME: *COALMINER*
TO: CODENAME: *SURGEON*
SUBJECT: PROGRESS REPORT/OPERATION *HYPODERMIC*
CLASSIFICATION: EYES ONLY TOP SECRET (SECTION III X-RAY DIRECTIVE)

/FILE EXTRACTION-RECONSTITUTION COMPLETE/
/START FILE/

SECURED SPACE-DOCK REPAIR BAY. CORVETTE *CIRCUMFERENCE* UNDERGOING FINAL STEALTH UPGRADES. SHIPYARD RECORDS SUCCESSFULLY ALTERED.

QUERIES DETECTED FROM TRANSIENT AI. OPERATION DEEMED AT RISK OF BEING UNCOVERED.

AS PER CONTINGENCY PLAN TANGO: SHIP REGISTRATION NUMBERS SCRAMBLED; HARD ISOLATED FROM DOCKSIDE COMPUTER

NETWORK; COUNTERINTRUSION SOFTWARE IMPLEMENTED; ALPHA SECURITY PROTOCOLS ENACTED ONBOARD.

JUST AS YOU CALLED IT, SIR. DON'T WORRY—AS FAR AS THE STATION COMPUTERS ARE CONCERNED, *CIRCUMFERENCE* NEVER EVEN EXISTED.

/END FILE/

/SCRAMBLE-DESTRUCTION PROCESS ENABLED/

PRESS **ENTER** TO CONTINUE.

CHAPTER THIRTY-ONE

0447 HOURS, AUGUST 30, 2552 (MILITARY CALENDAR) / REMOTE SENSING STATION *FERMION*, EPSILON ERIDANI SYSTEM'S EDGE

Chief Petty Officer McRobb entered the command center of Remote Sensing Station *Fermion*. Lieutenants (JG) Bill Streeter and David Brightling stood and saluted.

He wordlessly returned their salutes.

The wall-sized monitors displayed the contents of the last Slipstream probes: multidimensional charts, a rainbow of false color enhancements, and a catalog of objects adrift in the alternate space. Some of the new officers thought the representations looked "pretty."

To Chief McRobb, however, each pixel on the screens represented danger. So many things could hide in multidimensional space: pirates, black marketeers . . . the Covenant.

McRobb inspected their duty stations. He double-checked that all programs and hardware were running within UNSC specifications. He ran his hand along the monitors and keypads looking for dust. Their stations were in tip-top shape.

Considering what they were guarding, Reach, anything less than perfection was unacceptable. He made certain his crew knew it, too.

"Carry on," he said.

Since the battle of Sigma Octanus, FLEETCOM had reassigned top people to its Remote Sensing Stations. Chief McRobb had been pulled from Fort York on the edge of the Inner

Colonies. He had spent the last three months helping his crew brush up on their abstract and complex algebras to interpret the probe data.

"Ready to send out the next set of probes, sir," Lieutenant Streeter said. "Linear accelerator and Slipspace generators online and charged."

"Set for thirty-second return cycle and launch," Chief McRobb ordered.

"Aye, sir. Probes away, sir. Accelerated and entering the Slipstream."

FLEETCOM didn't really expect anything to attack the Reach Military Complex. It was the heart of the UNSC military operations. If anything did attack it, the battle would be a short one. There were twenty Super MAC guns in orbit. They could accelerate a three-thousand-ton projectile to point four-tenths the speed of light—and place that projectile with pinpoint accuracy. If that wasn't enough to stop a Covenant fleet, there were anywhere from a hundred to a hundred and fifty ships in the system at any given time.

Chief McRobb knew, though, there had been another military base that was once thought too strong to attack—and the military had paid the price for their lack of vigilance. He wasn't about to let Reach become another Pearl Harbor. Not on his watch.

"Probes returning, sir," Lieutenant Brightling announced. "Alpha reentering normal space in three . . . two . . . one. Scanning sectors. Signal acquired at extraction point minus forty five thousand kilometers."

"Process the signals and send out the recovery drone, Lieutenant."

"Aye, sir. Getting signal lock on—" The Lieutenant squinted at his monitor. "Sir, would you take a look at this?"

"On the board, Lieutenant."

Radar and neutron imager silhouettes appeared onscreen—

and filled the display. Chief McRobb had never seen anything like it in Slipstream space.

"Confirm that the data stream is not corrupted," the Chief ordered. "I'm estimating that object is three thousand kilometers in diameter."

"Affirmative . . . thirty-two-hundred-kilometer diameter confirmed, sir. Signal integrity is green. We'll have a trajectory for the planetoid as soon as Beta probe returns."

It was rare for any natural object this large to be in Slipstream space. An occasional comet or asteroid had been logged—UNSC astrophysicists still weren't sure how the things got into the alternate dimension. But there had never been anything like this. At least, not since—

"Oh my God," McRobb whispered.

Not since Sigma Octanus.

"We're not waiting for Beta probe," Chief McRobb barked. "We are initiating the Cole Protocol. Lieutenant Streeter, purge the navigational database, and I mean *right now*. Lieutenant Brightling, remove the safety interlocks on the station's reactor."

His junior officers hesitated for a moment—then they understood the gravity of their situation. They moved quickly.

"Initiating viral data scavengers," Lieutenant Streeter called out. "Dumping main and cache memory." He turned in his seat, his face white. "Sir, the science library is offline for repairs. It has every UNSC astrophysics journal in it."

"With navigation data on every star within a hundred light-years," the Chief whispered. "Including Sol. Lieutenant, you get someone down there and destroy that data. I don't care if they have to hit it with a goddamn sledgehammer—make sure that data is wiped."

"Aye, sir!" Streeter turned to the COM and began issuing frantic orders.

"Safety interlocks red on the board," Lieutenant Brightling reported. His lips pressed into a single white line, concentrating.

"Beta probe returning, sir, in four . . . three . . . two . . . one. There. Off target one hundred twenty thousand kilometers. Signal is weak. The probe appears to be malfunctioning. Trying to scrub the signal now."

"It's too much of a coincidence that it's malfunctioning, Streeter," the Chief said. "Get FLEETCOM on Alpha channel on the double! Compress and send the duty log."

"Aye, sir." Lieutenant Streeter's fingers fumbled with the keypad as he typed—then had to retype the command. "Logs sent."

"Beta probe signal on the board," Lieutenant Brightling reported. "Calculating the object's trajectory . . ."

The planetoid was closer. Its edges, however, had abnormalities—bumps and spikes and protrusions.

Chief McRobb shifted and clenched his hands into fists.

"It will pass though Epsilon Eridani System," Lieutenant Brightling said. "Intersecting the solar plane in seventeen seconds at the system's outer edge at zero four one." He inhaled sharply. "Sir, that's only a light-second away from us."

Lieutenant Streeter stood and knocked over his chair, almost backing into the Chief.

McRobb righted the chair. "Sit down, Lieutenant. We've got a job to do. Target the telescope array to monitor that region of space."

Lieutenant Streeter turned and gazed into the rock-solid features of the Chief. He took a deep breath. "Yes, sir." He sat back down. "Aye, sir, moving the array."

"Gamma probe returning in three . . . two . . . one." Lieutenant Brightling paused. "There's no signal, sir. Scanning. Time plus four seconds and counting. Probe may have translated on a temporal axis."

"I don't think so," the Chief murmured.

Lieutenant Streeter said, "Telescope array now on target, sir. On the main view screen."

Pinpoints of green light appeared at the edge of the Epsilon

Eridani System. They collected and swarmed as if they were caught in a boiling liquid. Space stretched, smeared, and distorted. Half the stars in that region were blotted out.

"Radar contact," Lieutenant Brightling said. "Contact with more than three hundred large objects." His hands started to shake. "Sir, silhouettes match known Covenant profiles."

"They're accelerating," Lieutenant Streeter whispered. "On an intercept course for the station."

"FLEETCOM network connections are being infiltrated," Lieutenant Brightling said. His trembling hands could barely type in commands. "Cutting our connection."

Chief McRobb stood as straight as he could. "What about the astrophysics data?"

"Sir, they're still trying to end the diagnostic cycle, but that takes a few minutes."

"Then we don't have a lot of options," McRobb muttered.

He set his hand on Lieutenant Brightling's shoulder to steady the young officer. "It's all right, Lieutenant. We've done the best we could. We've done our duty. There's nothing more to worry about."

He set his palmprint on the control station. The Chief locked out the reactor safeties and saturated the fusion chamber with their deuterium reserve tanks. Chief McRobb said, "Just one last order to carry out."

CHAPTER

THIRTY-TWO

0519 HOURS, AUGUST 30, 2552 (MILITARY CALENDAR) / UNSC *PILLAR OF AUTUMN*, EPSILON ERIDANI SYSTEM'S EDGE

Something was wrong.

John felt it in his stomach first: a slight lateral acceleration—that became a spin strong enough that he had to brace his legs. The *Pillar of Autumn* was turning.

Every other Spartan in the storage bay felt it as well; they paused as they unloaded equipment from crates and readied the cryo tubes for their journey.

The lateral motion slowed and stopped. The *Pillar of Autumn*'s engines rumbled like thunder through the hull of the ship.

Kelly approached him. "Sir? I thought we were accelerating to enter Slipspace?"

"So did I. Have Fred and Joshua continue to prep the tubes. Have Linda get a team and secure our gear. I'll find out what's going on."

"Aye, sir."

The Master Chief marched toward the intercom panel. He hated being on spaceships. The lack of control was disturbing. He and the other Spartans were just extra cargo in a space battle.

He hesitated as he reached for the intercom. If Captain Keyes was involved in some tricky maneuver or engaging an enemy, the last thing he needed was an interruption.

He pressed the button. "Cortana? We've changed course. Is there a problem?"

Instead of her voice, however, Captain Keyes spoke over the channel: "Captain Keyes to Spartan-117."

He replied, "Here, sir."

"There's been a change in plans," Keyes said. There was a long pause. "This will be easier to explain face-to-face. I'm on my way down to brief you. Keyes out."

John turned and the other Spartans snapped to their tasks. Those without specific orders checked and rechecked their weapons and assembled their combat gear.

They had all heard the Captain, however. The sound receivers in their armor could pick up a whisper at a hundred meters.

And the Spartans didn't have to be told this was trouble.

John clicked on the monitor near the intercom. The fore camera showed the *Pillar of Autumn* had indeed turned about. Reach's sun blazed in the center of the screen. They were heading back.

Was something wrong with the ship? No. Captain Keyes wouldn't be coming to brief him if that was the case. There was definitely a snag.

The elevator doors opened and Captain Keyes stepped off the lift.

"Captain on the deck!" the Master Chief shouted.

The Spartans stood at attention.

"At ease," Captain Keyes said. The expression on the Captain's face suggested that "ease" was the last thing on his mind. He smoothed his thumb over the antique pipe the Master Chief had seen him carry.

"There is something very wrong," Keyes said. He glanced at the other Spartans. "Let's talk in private," he told the Master Chief in a low voice. He walked to the monitor over the intercom.

"Sir," the Master Chief said. "Unless you wish to leave the deck, the Spartans will hear everything we say."

Keyes looked at the Spartans and frowned. "I see. Very well, your squad might as well hear this now, too. I don't know how they found Reach—they bypassed a dozen Inner Colony worlds to get here. It doesn't matter. They *are* here. And we have to do something."

"Sir? 'They'?"

"The Covenant." He turned to the intercom. "Cortana, display the last priority Alpha transmission."

A communiqué flickered on screen, and the Master Chief read:

UNITED NATIONS SPACE COMMAND ALPHA PRIORITY TRANSMISSION 04592Z-83
ENCRYPTION CODE: RED
PUBLIC KEY: FILE /BRAVO-TANGO-BETA-FIVE/
FROM: ADMIRAL ROLAND FREEMONT, COMMANDING FLEET OFFICER, FLEETCOM SECTOR ONE COMMANDER/ (UNSC SERVICE NUMBER: 00745-16778-HS)
TO: ALL UNSC WARSHIPS IN EPSILON ERIDANI SYSTEM
SUBJECT: IMMEDIATE RECALL
CLASSIFICATION: CLASSIFIED (BGX DIRECTIVE)

/START FILE/

COVENANT PRESENCE DETECTED ON REACH SYSTEM'S EDGE COORDINATES 030 RELATIVE.

ALL UNSC WARSHIPS ARE HEREBY ORDERED TO CEASE ALL ACTIVITIES AND REGROUP AT RALLY POINT **ZULU** AT BEST SPEED.

ALL SHIPS ARE TO ENACT THE COLE PROTOCOL IMMEDIATELY.

/END FILE/

"Cortana has picked up ship signatures on the *Pillar of Autumn*'s sensors," Captain Keyes said. "She cannot be sure how many because of electrical interference, but there are more than a hundred alien ships inbound toward Reach. We have to go. We have our orders. The Section Three mission has to be scrubbed."

"Sir? Scrubbed?" John had never had a mission canceled.

"Reach is our strategic headquarters and our biggest shipbuilding facility, Master Chief. If the shipyards fall, then Dr. Halsey's prediction of humanity having only months to survive will shrink to weeks."

The Master Chief normally would never have contradicted a superior officer, but this time duty compelled him. "Sir, our two missions are not mutually exclusive."

Captain Keyes lit his pipe—in defiance of three separate regulations of igniting a combustible on a UNSC ship. He puffed once and thoughtfully examined the smoke. "What do you have in mind, Master Chief?"

"A hundred alien vessels, sir. Between the combined force of the fleet and Reach's orbital gun platforms, it is almost guaranteed there will be a disabled ship my squad can board and capture."

Captain Keyes mulled this over. "There will also be hundreds of ships exchanging fire with one another. Missiles, nukes . . . Covenant plasma torpedoes."

"Just get us close enough," the Master Chief said. "Punch a hole in their shields long enough for us to get on their hull. We'll do the rest."

Captain Keyes chewed on his pipe. He tucked it into the cup of his hand. "There are operational complications with your plan. Cortana has been running the *Pillar of Autumn*'s shakedown. We have our own AI, but by the time we get it initialized and running this ship—the battle may be over."

"I see, sir."

Captain Keyes gazed a moment at the Master Chief, then sighed. "If there is a disabled Covenant ship and if we are close enough to it *and* if we're not blown to a million bits by the time we get there, then I'll transfer Cortana to you. I've flown ships without an AI before." Captain Keyes managed a weak smile, but it quickly disappeared.

"Yes, sir!"

"We'll be at rally point Zulu in twenty minutes, Master Chief. Have your team ready by then . . . for anything."

"Sir." He saluted.

Captain Keyes returned the salute and entered the elevator, puffing on his pipe and shaking his head.

The Master Chief turned to his teammates. They halted what they were doing.

"You all heard. This is it. Fred and James, I want you to refit one of our Pelicans. Get every scrap of C-12 and shape a charge on her nose. If Captain Keyes downs a Covenant shield, we may have to blast our way into the ship's hull."

Fred and James replied, "Aye, sir."

"Linda, assemble a team and get into every crate ONI packed for us—distribute that gear ASAP. Make sure everyone gets a thruster pack, plenty of ammo, grenades, and Jackhammer launchers if we have them. If we do get on board, we may encounter those armored Covenant types again—this time, I want the firepower to take them out."

"Yes, sir!"

The Spartans scrambled to make ready for the mission.

The Master Chief approached Kelly. On a private COM channel, he told her, "Crate thirteen on the manifest has three HAVOK nuclear mines. Get them. I have the arming cards. Ready them for transport."

"Affirmative." She paused.

The Master Chief couldn't see her face past the reflective shield of her helmet, but he knew her well enough to know that the tiny slump of her shoulders meant that she was worried.

"Sir?" she said. "I know this mission will be tough, but . . . do you ever get the feeling that this is like one of Chief Mendez's missions? Like there's a trick . . . some twist that we've overlooked?"

"Yes," he replied. "And I'm waiting for it."

CHAPTER THIRTY-THREE

0534 HOURS, AUGUST 30, 2552 (MILITARY CALENDAR) / UNSC *PILLAR OF AUTUMN*, EPSILON ERIDANI SYSTEM

The *Pillar of Autumn* detonated its port emergency thrusters. The ship slid out of the path of the asteroid, missing it by ten meters—

—The Covenant plasma trailing them did not. It impacted the city-sized rock and sent fountains of molten iron and nickel spewing into space.

Nine of the ten teardrop-shaped Covenant fighters—nicknamed "Seraphs" by ONI—dodged the asteroid as well. The tenth ship slammed into the asteroid and vanished from the bridge's view screen.

The other single ships accelerated and swarmed around the *Pillar of Autumn*, harassing her with pulse laser fire.

"Cortana," Captain Keyes said, "activate our point defense system."

The *Pillar of Autumn*'s 50mm cannons flashed—chipping away at the Covenant ships' shields.

"Already engaged, Captain," Cortana said calmly.

"Ensign Lovell," Captain Keyes said. "Engines all stop and bring us about one hundred eighty degrees. Lieutenant Hikowa, ready our MAC gun and arm Archer missile pods A1 through A7. I want a firing solution that has our Archer missiles hitting with the third MAC round."

"On it, sir," Lieutenant Hikowa replied.

"Aye, sir," Ensign Lovell said. "Answering engines all stop. Coming about. Brace yourselves."

The *Pillar of Autumn*'s engines sputtered and died. Navigational thrusters fired and rotated the ship to face the real threat—a Covenant carrier.

The enormous alien craft had materialized aft of the *Pillar of Autumn* and launched their single ships. The carrier had then launched two salvos of plasma—which Captain Keyes had only shaken by entering the asteroid field.

Cortana maneuvered the massive *Pillar of Autumn* like it was a sporting yacht; she nimbly dodged tumbling rocks, using them to screen Covenant plasma and pulse laser bolts.

But the *Pillar of Autumn* would emerge from the asteroid field in twenty seconds.

"Firing solution online, sir," Lieutenant Hikowa said. "MAC gun hot and missile safety interlocks removed. Ready to launch."

"Fire missiles at will, Lieutenant."

Rapid-fire thumps echoed though the *Pillar of Autumn*'s hull and a swarm of Archer missiles sped toward the incoming carrier.

"MAC gun is hot," Hikowa said. "Booster capacitors ready. Firing in eight seconds, sir."

"I must make one small adjustment to your trajectory, Lieutenant," Cortana said. "Covenant single ships are concentrating their attacks on our underside. Captain? With your permission?"

"Granted," Keyes said.

"Firing solution recalculated," Cortana said. "Hang on."

Cortana fired thrusters and the *Pillar of Autumn* rotated belly up—brought the majority of her 50mm cannons to bear on the Covenant Seraph fighters underneath her.

Overlapping fields of fire wore down their shields—punctured their armored hulls with a thousand rounds, tore through the pilots with a hail of projectiles, and peppered their reactors. Nine puffs of fire dropped behind the *Pillar of Autumn* and vanished into the darkness.

"Enemy single ships destroyed," Cortana said. "Approaching firing position."

"Cortana, give me a countdown. Lieutenant Hikowa, fire on my mark," Captain Keyes said.

"Ready to fire, aye," Lieutenant Hikowa said.

Cortana nodded; her trim figure projected in miniature inside the bridge holotank. As she nodded, a time display appeared, the numbers counting down rapidly.

Keyes gripped the edge of the command chair, his eyes glued to the countdown. Three seconds, two, one . . . "Mark."

"Firing!" Hikowa answered.

A triple flash of lightning saturated the forward view screen and bled in from the viewport; three white-hot projectiles crossed the black distance between the *Pillar of Autumn* and the Covenant carrier.

Along the side of the carrier, motes of light collected as they rebuilt the charges of their plasma weapons.

Archer missiles were pinpoints of exhaust in the distance; the carrier's pulse lasers fired and melted a third of the incoming missiles.

The *Pillar of Autumn* rolled to starboard and dove.

Captain Keyes floated in free fall for a heartbeat, then landed awkwardly on the deck. The crenellated surface of an asteroid appeared on their port camera—meters away—then vanished.

Captain Keyes was grateful that he never had time to initialize the *Pillar of Autumn*'s AI. Cortana performed superbly.

The trio of blazing MAC rounds struck the carrier. The shield flashed once, twice. The third round got through—gutting the ship from stem to stern.

The carrier spun sideways. Her shields stuttered once, trying to reestablish a protective screen. A hundred Archer missiles struck, cratered the hull, blossomed into fire and sparks and smoldering metal.

The alien carrier listed and crashed into the asteroid the *Pillar of Autumn* had just narrowly avoided. It stuck there, hull broken and cracked. Columns of fire blossomed from the shattered vessel.

Captain Keyes sighed. A victory.

The Spartans, however, would not be taking that ship into Covenant space. It wasn't going anywhere.

"Cortana, mark the location of the destroyed ship and the asteroid. We may have a chance to salvage her later."

"Yes, Captain."

"Ensign Lovell," Captain Keyes said, "turn us around and give me best speed to rally point Zulu."

Lovell tapped the thrusters and rotated the *Pillar of Autumn* to relative space normal with Reach. The rumble of the engines shook the decks as the ship accelerated in-system.

"ETA twenty minutes at best speed, sir."

The battle for Reach could be over by the time he got there. Captain Keyes wished he could move through Slipspace for short, precision jumps like the Covenant. That carrier had materialized a kilometer behind the *Pillar of Autumn*. If he had that kind of accuracy, he could be at the rally point now—and be of some use. Any attempt to jump in-system, however, would be foolish at best. At worst, it would be a fatal move. Jump targets varied by hundreds of thousands of kilometers. Theoretically, they could reenter normal space *inside* Reach's sun.

"Cortana, give me maximum magnification on the fore cameras."

"Aye sir," she said.

The view on the forward screen zoomed in—jumped and refocused on planet Reach.

Twenty thousand kilometers from the planet, a cluster of a hundred UNSC ships collected at rally point Zulu: destroyers, frigates, three cruisers, two carriers—and three refit and repair stations hovering over them . . . waiting to be used as sacrificial shields.

"Fifty-two additional UNSC warships inbound to rally point Zulu," Cortana reported.

"Shift focus to section four by four on-screen, Cortana. Show me those Covenant forces."

The scene blinked and transferred to the approaching Covenant fleet. There were so many ships Captain Keyes couldn't estimate their numbers.

"How many?" he asked.

"I am presently tracking three hundred fourteen Covenant ships, Captain," Cortana replied.

Captain Keyes couldn't tear his gaze away from the ships. The UNSC only won battles with the Covenant when they outnumbered the enemy forces three to one . . . not the other way around.

They had one advantage: the MAC orbital guns around Reach—the UNSC's most powerful nonnuclear weapon. Some called them "Super" MAC guns or the "big stick."

Their linear accelerator coils were larger than a UNSC cruiser. They propelled a three-thousand-ton projectile at tremendous speed, and could reload within five seconds. They drew power directly from the fusion reactor complex planetside.

"Pull back the camera angle, Cortana. Let me see the entire battle area."

The Covenant ships accelerated toward Reach. The fleet at rally point Zulu fired their MAC guns and missiles. The orbital Super MAC guns opened fire as well—twenty streaks of white hot metal burned across the night.

The Covenant answered by launching a salvo of plasma torpedoes at the orbital guns—so much fire in space that it looked like a solar flare.

Deadly arcs of flame and metal raced through space and crossed paths.

The engines of the three refit stations flared to life and the platelike ships moved toward the path of the flaming vapor.

A plasma bolt caught the edge of the leading station—fire splashed over its flat surface. More bolts hit, and the station melted, sagged, and boiled. The metal glowed red, then white-hot, tinged with blue.

The other two stations maneuvered into position and shielded the orbital guns from the fiery assault. Plasma torpedoes collided with them and sprayed plumes of molten metal into space. After a dozen hits, clouds of ionizing metal enveloped the place where the three stations had been.

They had been vaporized.

The last of the Covenant plasma hit the haze—scattered, absorbed, and made the cloud glow a hellish orange.

Meanwhile, the fleet's opening salvo and the Super MAC rounds hit the Covenant fleet.

The smaller ship-based MAC rounds bounced off the Covenant shields—it took three or more to wear them down.

The Super MAC rounds, however, were another story. The first Super MAC shell hit a Covenant destroyer. The ship's shield flashed and vanished—the remaining impact momentum transferred to the ship—the hull rippled and shattered into a million fragments.

Four nuclear mines detonated in the center of the Covenant fleet. Dozens of ships with downed shields flared white and dissolved.

The other ships however, shrugged off the damage; their shields burned brilliant silver, then cooled.

The surviving Covenant vessels advanced in-system—a third of their number were left behind . . . burning radioactive hulks or utterly destroyed by the Super MAC rounds.

Plasma charges collected on the lateral lines of the Covenant ships. They fired. Fingers of deadly energy reached across space . . . toward the UNSC fleet.

One Covenant ship sat in the center of the pack, a gigantic vessel, larger than three UNSC cruisers. White-blue beams flashed from its prow—a split second later, five UNSC vessels detonated.

"Cortana . . . what the hell was that?" Keyes asked. "Lovell, push those engine superchargers as hot as you can make them."

"Running at three hundred ten percent, sir," Lovell reported. "ETA fourteen minutes."

"Replaying and digitally enhancing video record," Cortana said.

She split the screen and zoomed in on the huge Covenant ship, replaying the video as the large ship fired. The Covenant energy beams looked like pulse lasers . . . but tinged silver white, the same scintillation effect that they'd seen when their shields were hit.

Cortana switched back to view the doomed UNSC destroyer *Minotaur*. The lance of energy was needle-thin. It struck the vessel on A deck, aft, near the reactor. Cortana pulled the view back and slowed the record frame by frame—the beam punctured through the entire ship, emanating below H deck by the engines.

"It drilled through every deck and both sets of battleplate," Captain Keyes murmured.

The beam moved through the *Minotaur*, slicing a ten-meter-wide swath.

"Projected beam path cut through the *Minotaur*'s reactors," Cortana said.

"A new weapon," Captain Keyes said. "Faster than their plasma. Deadlier, too."

The large Covenant ship veered off course and accelerated away from the battle. Perhaps it didn't want to risk getting too close to their orbital MAC guns. Whatever the reason, Keyes was grateful to see it withdraw.

The UNSC forces slowly scattered. Some launched missiles to intercept the plasma torpedoes, but the high-energy explosives did nothing to stop the superheated bolts. Fifty UNSC ships went up like flares, burning, exploding, falling toward the planet.

The orbital Super MAC guns fired—sixteen hits and sixteen Covenant ships were blasted into flame and glittering fragments.

The Covenant fleet split into two groups: half accelerated to engage the dispersing UNSC fleet; the remainder of their ships arced upward relative to the plane of the system. That group maneuvered to get a clear shot around the cloud of vaporized titanium from the refit stations. They were going to target the orbital guns.

Plasma charges collected along their sides.

The orbital guns fired. The super-heavy rounds tore through the clouds of ionized metal vapor, leaving whorls and spirals in the haze. They impacted eighteen incoming Covenant ships—ripped through them like tinfoil, with enough momentum to pulverize their hulls.

Six Covenant ships cleared the interfering cloud of vapor. They had a clear shot.

The Super MAC guns fired again.

Plasma erupted from the sides of the nearby Covenant ships.

The Super MAC rounds hit the vessels and obliterated the enemy.

The streams of plasma, however, had already launched. They streaked toward the orbital guns—impacted and turned the installations into showers of sparks and molten metal.

When the haze cleared, fifteen of the Super MAC orbital installations remained intact . . . five had been vaporized.

The Covenant ships engaging the fleet turned and fled on an out-system vector.

The remaining UNSC ships did not pursue.

"Incoming orders, sir," Lieutenant Dominique called out. "We're being ordered to fall back and regroup."

Keyes nodded. "Cortana," he said, "can you give me damage and casualty estimates for the fleet?"

Her tiny holo image coalesced in the display tank. "Yes, Captain," she said. She cocked an eyebrow at him. "Are you sure you want the bad news?"

Damage estimates scrolled across his personal screen.

They had taken heavy losses—an estimated twenty ships remained. Nearly one hundred shattered and burning UNSC vessels floated, lifeless, in the combat area.

Captain Keyes realized that he was holding his breath. He exhaled. "That was too close," he murmured.

"It could have been closer, Captain," Cortana whispered.

He watched the retreating Covenant. Once again—it was too easy. No . . . it had been anything but "easy" for the UNSC forces, but the Covenant were certainly giving up far earlier than in any previous battle. The aliens had never stopped once they engaged an enemy.

Except at Sigma Octanus, he thought.

"Cortana," Captain Keyes said. "Scan the poles of planet Reach and filter out the magnetic interference."

The view screen snapped to Reach's northern pole. Hundreds of Covenant dropships streamed toward the planet's surface.

"Get FLEETCOM HQ online," he ordered Lieutenant Dominique. "Copy this message to the Fleet Commander, as well."

"Aye, sir," Lieutenant Dominique said. "Channel connected."

"Tell them they're being invaded. Dropships inbound at both poles."

Dominique sent the message, listened a moment, then reported, "Message received and acknowledged, sir."

The Super MAC guns pivoted and fired—shattering dozens of the Covenant dropships in the shells' supersonic wake.

The remains of the UNSC fleet split into two groups, moving toward either pole. Missiles and MAC guns fired and blasted the dropships to bits. The poles were punctuated with thousands of meteoroids as the bits of hull burned up in the atmosphere.

Hundreds must have gotten through, Keyes thought.

"Incoming distress signal from FLEETCOM HQ planet-side, sir," Lieutenant Dominique said, his voice breaking.

"On speakers," Captain Keyes said.

"There are thousands of them. Grunts, Jackals, and their warrior Elites." The transmission broke into static. *"They have tanks and fliers. Christ, they've breached the perimeter. Fall back! Fall back! If anyone can hear this: the Covenant is groundside. Massing near the armory . . . they're—"* White noise filled the speakers. Captain Keyes winced as he heard screams, bones snapping, an explosion. The transmission went dead.

"Sir!" Lieutenant Hall said. "The Covenant fleet has altered their outbound trajectory. . . . they're turning." She rotated to face the Captain. "They're coming in for another attack."

Captain Keyes stood straighter and smoothed his uniform. "Good." He addressed the crew in the calmest voice he could muster. "Looks like we're not too late after all."

Ensign Lovell nodded. "Sir, ETA to rally point Zulu in five minutes."

"Remove all missile safety locks," Captain Keyes ordered. "Get our remote-piloted Longsword into the launch tube. And make sure our MAC gun capacitors and boosters are hot."

Captain Keyes pulled out his pipe. He lit it and puffed.

The Covenant were, of course, after the orbital guns. Their suicidal frontal charge—while almost effective enough—had been just another diversion. The real danger was on the ground; if their troops took out the fusion generators, the Super MAC guns would be so much floating junk in orbit.

"This is bad," he muttered to himself.

Cortana appeared on the AI pedestal near the NAV station. "Captain Keyes, I'm picking up another distress signal. It's from the Reach space dock AI. And if you think this—" She gestured at the incoming Covenant fleet on screen. "—is bad, wait until you hear this. It gets worse."

CHAPTER

THIRTY-FOUR

0558 HOURS, AUGUST 30, 2552 (MILITARY CALENDAR) / UNSC *PILLAR OF AUTUMN*, EPSILON ERIDANI SYSTEM

The mission had just encountered another snag.

It never entered the Master Chief's mind that he would fail to achieve his objectives. He had to succeed. Failure meant death for not only himself, but for all the Spartans . . . every human.

He stood at the view screen in the cargo bay and reread the priority Alpha transmission Captain Keyes had sent down:

ALPHA PRIORITY CHANNEL: TO FLEET ADMIRALTY FROM REACH SPACE DOCK QUARTERMASTER AI-8575 (A.K.A. DOPPLER) /

/TRIPLE-ENCRYPTION TIME-STAMPED PUBLIC KEY: RED ROVER RED ROVER/

/START FILE/

IMMEDIATE ACTION REQUIRED

ITEM: COVENANT DATA INVASION PACKETS DETECTED PENETRATING FIREWALL OF REACH DOC NET. COUNTERINTRUSION SOFTWARE ENACTED. RESOLUTION: 99.9 PERCENT CERTAINTY OF NEUTRALIZATION.

ITEM: INITIALIZATION OF TRIPLE-SCREENING PROTOCOL DISCOVERED THE CORVETTE *CIRCUMFERENCE*/BAY GAMMA-9/ ISOLATED FROM REACH DOC NET.

ITEM: COVENANT SHIPS DETECTED ON INBOUND SLIPSTREAM VECTOR INTERSECTING BAY GAMMA-9.

CONCLUSION: UNSECURED NAVIGATION DATA ON THE *CIRCUMFERENCE* DETECTED BY COVENANT FORCES.

CONCLUSION: **VIOLATION OF THE COLE PROTOCOL. IMMEDIATE ACTION REQUIRED.**

/END FILE/

He replayed the distress call from Reach's groundside FLEETCOM HQ.

". . . They've breached the perimeter. Fall back! Fall back! If anyone can hear this: the Covenant is groundside. Massing near the armory . . . they're—"

The Master Chief copied these files and sent them over his squad's COM channel. They had a right to know everything, too.

There was only one reason the Covenant would launch a ground invasion: to take out the planetary defense generators. If they succeeded, Reach would fall.

And there was only one reason why the Covenant wanted the ship *Circumference*—to plunder its NAV database—and find every human world, including Earth.

Captain Keyes appeared on the view screen. He held his pipe in one hand, squeezing it so tight his knuckles were white. "Master Chief, I believe the Covenant will use a pinpoint Slip-space jump to a position just off the space dock. They may try to get their troops on the station before the Super MAC guns can take out their ships. This will be a difficult mission, Chief. I'm . . . open to suggestions."

"We can take care of it," the Master Chief replied.

Captain Keyes' eyes widened and he leaned forward in his command chair. "How exactly, Master Chief?"

"With all due respect, sir, Spartans are trained to handle difficult missions. I'll split my squad. Three will board the space dock and make sure that NAV data does not fall into the Covenant's hands. The remainder of the Spartans will go groundside and repel the invasion forces."

Captain Keyes considered this. "No, Master Chief, it's too

risky. We've got to make sure the Covenant doesn't get that NAV data. We'll use a nuclear mine, set it close to the docking ring, and detonate it."

"Sir, the EMP will burn out the superconductive coils of the orbital guns. And if you use the *Pillar of Autumn*'s conventional weapons, the NAV database may still survive. If the Covenant search the wreckage—they may obtain the data."

"True," Keyes said, and tapped his pipe thoughtfully on his chin. "Very well, Master Chief. We'll go with your suggestion. I'll plot a course over the docking station. Ready your Spartans and prep two dropships. We'll launch you—" he consulted with Cortana "—in five minutes."

"Aye, Captain. We'll be ready."

"Good luck," Captain Keyes said, and snapped off the view screen.

Luck. The Master Chief always had been lucky. He'd need luck more than ever this time.

He turned to face the Spartans . . . his Spartans. They stood at attention.

Kelly stepped forward. "Master Chief sir, permission to lead the space op, sir."

"Denied," he said. "I'll be leading that one."

He appreciated her gesture. The space operation would be ten times more dangerous than the ground op.

The Covenant would outnumber them ten to one—or more—but the Spartans were used to taking the fight against numerically superior enemies. They had always won on the ground.

The extraction of the *Circumference* database, however, would be in vacuum and zero gravity—and they might have to fight their way past a Covenant warship to reach the objective. Not exactly ideal conditions.

"Linda and James," he said. "You're with me. Fred, you're Red Team Leader. You'll have tactical command of the ground operation."

"Sir!" Fred shouted. "Yes, sir."

"Now make ready," he said. "We don't have much time left."

The Master Chief regretted his unfortunate choice of words.

The Spartans stood a moment. Kelly called out, "Attention!" They snapped to and gave the Master Chief a crisp salute.

He stood straighter and returned their salute. He was intensely proud of them all.

The Spartans scattered and gathered their gear, racing for the dropship bay.

The Master Chief watched them go.

This was the mission the Spartans had been tempered for in mission after mission. It would be their finest moment . . . but he knew that it might also be their last moment.

Chief Mendez had said that a leader would be required to spend the lives of those under his command. The Master Chief knew he would lose comrades today—but would their deaths serve a necessary purpose . . . or would they be wasted?

Either way, they were ready.

John tapped the thrusters and rotated the Pelican dropship 180 degrees. He pushed the engines to full power to brake their forward momentum. The *Pillar of Autumn* had dropped them while she had been cruising at one-third full speed.

They'd need every millimeter of the ten thousand kilometers between them and the docking station to slow down.

The Master Chief had taken the Spartans' modified Pelican, rigged with explosives. The station would be locked down—every airlock sealed. They'd have to blast their way in.

He glanced aft. Linda checked one of the three sniper rifle variants she had brought. James inspected his thruster pack.

He had picked Linda because no other single Spartan was as efficient at long-range combat. And that's what the Master Chief wanted: *long*-range combat. If it came to hand-to-hand combat in zero gee with hordes of Covenant troopers . . . even his luck wouldn't hold out too long.

He had picked James because James had never quit. Even when his hand had been burned off, he had shrugged off the shock—at least for a while—and helped them dispatch the Covenant behemoths on Sigma Octanus IV. The Master Chief would need that kind of determination on this mission.

He took a long look out the front of the Pelican. Their sister dropship initiated a burn and hurtled toward Reach.

Kelly, Fred, Joshua . . . all of them. Part of him longed to join them in the ground action.

The radar panel blinked a proximity warning; the Pelican was one thousand kilometers from the docking ring.

The Master Chief tapped the thrusters to align the dropship. He squelched the proximity alert.

The alert immediately re-sounded. Strange. He reached for the squelch again—then stopped as he saw the space around the Pelican change. Motes of green light appeared, pinpoints at first, which swelled like bruises on velvet black space. The green smears lengthened, compressed, and distorted the stars.

—a Slipstream entry point.

The Master Chief cut the Pelican's engines, slowing them for impact.

A Covenant frigate materialized a kilometer from the dropship's nose. Its prow filed their view screen.

CHAPTER THIRTY-FIVE

0616 HOURS, AUGUST 30, 2552 (MILITARY CALENDAR) / UNSC PELICAN DROPSHIP, EPSILON ERIDANI SYSTEM NEAR REACH STATION GAMMA

"Brace for maneuvering!" the Master Chief barked.

The Spartans dove for safety harnesses and strapped in. "All secure!" Linda shouted.

The Master Chief killed the Pelican's forward thrusters and triggered a short, sudden reverse burn. The Spartans were brutally slammed forward into their harnesses as the Pelican's acceleration bled away. The Master Chief quickly shut down the engines.

The tiny Pelican faced the Covenant frigate. At a kilometer's distance, the alien ship's launch bay and pulse laser turrets looked close enough to touch on the view screen; enough firepower to vaporize the Spartans in the blink of an eye.

The Master Chief's first instinct was to fire their HE Anvil-II missiles and autocannons—but he checked his hand as he reached for the triggers.

That would only attract their attention . . . which was the last thing he wanted. For the moment, the alien vessel ignored them—probably because the Master Chief had shut down the Pelican's engines. But the ship also seemed dead in space: no lights, no single ships launched, and no plasma weapons charging.

The dropship continued toward the docking station, their momentum putting distance between them and the frigate.

Space around the Covenant ship boiled and pulled apart—and two more alien ships appeared.

They, too, ignored the dropship. Was it too small to bother with? The Master Chief didn't care. His luck, it seemed, was holding.

He checked the radar—thirty kilometers to the docking ring. He ignited the engines to slow them down. He had to or they would crash into the station.

Twenty kilometers.

Rumbling shook the dropship. They slowed—but it wasn't going to be enough.

Ten kilometers.

"Hang on," he told Linda and James.

The sudden impact whiplashed the Master Chief back and forth in his seat. The straps holding him snapped.

He blinked . . . saw only blackness. His vision cleared and he noted that his shield bar was dead. It slowly began to fill again. Every display and monitor in the cockpit had shattered.

The Master Chief shook off the disorientation and pulled himself aft.

The interior of the dropship was a mess. Everything tied down had come loose. Ammunition boxes had broken open in the crash landing and loose carriages filled the air. Coolant leaked, spraying blobs of black fluid. In zero gravity, everything looked like the inside of a shaken snowglobe.

James and Linda floated off the deck of the Pelican. They slowly moved.

"Any injuries?" the Master Chief asked.

"No," Linda replied.

"I think so," James said. "I mean, no. I'm good, sir. Was that a landing or did those Covenant ships take a shot at us?"

"If they had, we wouldn't be here to talk about it. Get whatever gear you can and get out, double time," the Master Chief said.

The Master Chief grabbed an assault rifle and a Jackhammer

launcher. He found a satchel. Inside was a kilogram of C-12, detonators, and a Lotus antitank mine. Those would come in handy. He salvaged five intact clips of ammunition but couldn't locate his thruster pack. He'd have to do without one.

"No more time," he said. "We're sitting ducks here. Out the hatch now."

Linda went first. She paused, and—once she was satisfied the Covenant weren't lying in ambush—motioned them forward.

The Master Chief and James exited, clung to the side of the Pelican in zero gravity, and took flanking positions at the fore and aft ends of the dropship.

Space dock Gamma was a three-kilometer-diameter ring. Dull gray metal arced in either direction. On the surface were communications dishes and a few conduits—no real cover. The docking bay doors were sealed tight. The station wasn't spinning. The dockmaster AI must have shut the place up tight when it detected the unsecured NAV database.

The Master Chief frowned when he spotted the tail end of their Pelican—crumpled and embedded into the station's hull. Its engines were ruined. The dropship jutted out at an angle; its prow and the charges of C-12 that were supposed to have blasted them into a Covenant ship—now pointed into the air.

The Master Chief started to drift off the station. He clipped himself to the hull of the dropship.

"Blue-Two," he said, "police those explosives." He gestured to the prow. The motion sent him gyrating.

"Yes, sir." James puffed his thruster pack once and drifted up to the nose of the Pelican.

The Spartans had trained to fight in zero gravity. It wasn't easy. The slightest motion sent you spinning out of control.

A flash overhead reflected off the hull. The Master Chief looked up. The Covenant ships were alive now—lances of blue laser fire flashed and motes of red light collected on their lateral lines. Their engines glowed and they moved close to the station.

A streak crossed the Master Chief's field of vision in the blink of an eye. The center Covenant frigate shields strobed silver; the ship shattered into a cloud of glistening fragments.

The orbital guns had turned and fired on the new threat.

This was a suicide maneuver. How did the Covenant think they could withstand that kind of firepower?

"Blue-One," the Master Chief said. "Scan those ships with your scope."

Linda floated closer to the Master Chief. She pointed her sniper rifle up and sighted the ships. "We've got inbound targets," she said, and fired.

The Master Chief hit his magnification. A dozen pods burst from the two remaining Covenant ships. Trails of exhaust pointed right at the Spartans' position. There were tiny specks accompanying the pods; the Master Chief increased his display's magnification to maximum. They looked like men in thruster packs—

No, they were definitely not men.

These things had elongated heads—and even at this distance, the Master Chief could see past their faceplates and noted their pronounced sharklike teeth and jaws. They wore armor; it shimmered as they collided with debris—which meant energy shields.

These were Elites—the iron heart of the Covenant. Would they best the Spartans this time? They were all about to find out.

Linda shot one of the EVA aliens. Shields shimmered around its body and the round bounced off. She didn't stop. She pumped four more rounds into the creature—hitting a pinpoint target in its neck. Its shields flickered and a round got through. Purple blood gushed from the wound and the creature writhed in space.

The other aliens spotted them. They jetted toward their location, firing plasma rifles and needlers.

"Take cover," the Master Chief said. He unclipped himself and clung to the side of the dropship.

Linda followed—bolts of fire spattering on the hull next to

them, spattering molten metal. Crystalline needles bounced off their shields

"Blue-Two," the Master Chief said. "I said fall back."

James almost had the explosives rigged to the nose free. A shower of needles hit him. One stuck the tank of his thruster harness—penetrated. It remained embedded for a split second . . . then exploded.

Exhaust billowed from the pack. The uncontrolled jets spun James in the microgravity. He slammed into the station, bounced—then rocketed away into space, tumbling end over end, unable to control his trajectory.

"Blue-Two! Come in," the Master Chief barked over the COM channel.

"Can—control—" James' voice was punctuated with static. "They've—everywhere—" There was more static and the COM channel went dead.

The Master Chief watched his teammate tumble away into the darkness. All his training, his superhuman strength, reflexes, and determination . . . completely useless against the laws of physics.

He didn't even know if James was dead. For the moment, he had to assume that he was—put him out of his mind. He had a mission to complete. *If* he survived, then he'd get every UNSC ship in the area to mount a search and rescue op.

Linda shrugged out of her thruster harness.

The suppressing fire from the aliens halted. Covenant landing pods descended toward the station, touching down at roughly three-hundred-meter intervals.

A pod landed twenty meters away. Its sides uncurled like the petals of a flower. Jackals in black-and-blue vacuum suits drifted out. Their boots adhered to the station's hull.

"Let's pave a path out of here, Blue-One."

"Roger that," she said.

Linda targeted spots their energy shields didn't cover—boots, the top of one's head, a fingertip. Three Jackals went down in quick succession, their spacesuits ruptured by her marksmanship. The rest scrambled for cover inside the pod.

The Master Chief braced his back against the dropship and fired his assault rifle in controlled bursts. The microgravity played havoc with his aim.

One Jackal leaped from his cover—straight towards them.

The Master Chief switched to full auto and blasted his shield with enough rounds to send the alien flying backward off the station. He spent the clip, reloaded, and got out a grenade. He pulled the pin and lobbed it.

He threw it in a flat trajectory. The grenade ricocheted off the far side of the pod and bounced inside.

It detonated—a flash and spray of freeze-dried blue vented upward. The explosion had caught the enemy on their unshielded sides.

"Blue-One, secure that landing pod. I'll cover you." He leveled his rifle.

"Yes, sir." Linda grabbed a pipe that ran along the station and pulled herself hand over hand. When she was inside the pod, she flashed him a green light on his heads-up display.

The Master Chief crawled toward the prow of the Pelican. As he crested the ship he saw that the station was swarming with Covenant troops: a hundred Jackals and at least six Elites. They pointed toward the Pelican and slowly started to advance on their position.

"Come and get it," the Master Chief muttered.

He pulled two grenades from his satchel and wedged them into the C-12 on the nose of the ship. He pushed off and propelled himself back to his teammate.

She grabbed him and pulled him into the interior of the open pod. Bits of a dozen dead Jackals pasted the inside.

"You've got a new target," he told her. "A pair of frag grenades. Sight on them and wait for my order to fire."

She propped her rifle on the edge of the open pod and aimed.

Jackals crawled over the Pelican—one of the Elites appeared as well, maneuvering in a harness, flying over the ship. The Elite gestured imperiously, directing the Jackals to search the ship.

"Fire," the Master Chief said.

Linda fired once. The grenades detonated; the chain reaction set off the twenty kilograms of C-12.

A subsonic fist slammed into the Master Chief and threw him to the far side of the landing pod. Even twenty meters away, the sides of the craft warped and the top edges sheared away.

He looked over the edge.

There was a crater where the Pelican had been. If anything had survived that blast, it was now in orbit.

"We have a way in," the Master Chief remarked.

Linda nodded.

In the distance, where the station curved out of view, more Covenant pods landed—and the Master Chief saw the silhouettes of hundreds of Jackals and Elites crawling and jetting their way closer.

"Let's go, Blue-One."

They pulled themselves toward the hole. The detonation had blown through five decks, leaving a tunnel of ragged-edged metal and sputtering gas hoses.

The Master Chief called up the station's blueprints on his display. "That one," he said, and pointed two decks down. "B level. That's where bay nine and the *Circumference* should be, three hundred meters to port."

They climbed into the interior and into B deck's corridor. The station's emergency lights were on, filling the passage with dull red illumination.

The Master Chief paused and signaled her to halt. He pulled out the Lotus antitank mine from his satchel and set it on the deck. He set the sensitivity to maximum and triggered its proximity detectors. Anything that tried to follow them would get a surprise.

The Master Chief and Linda gripped the handrails along the corridor and pulled themselves up the curved hall.

Flashes of automatic-weapons fire flashed in the low light, just ahead of their position.

"Blue-One," the Master Chief said, "Ahead, ten meters—there's a pressure door open."

They quickly took positions on either side of the door. He sent his optical probe around the corner.

The docking bay had a dozen ship berths on two levels. The Master Chief spotted a few battered Pelicans; a station service bot; and in berth eleven, a sleek private craft held in place by massive service clamps. Where the ship's name should have been painted on the prow there was only a simple circle. That had to be the target.

Two berths aft, four Marines in vac suits were pinned down by plasma and needler fire. The Master Chief turned his optical probe and saw what was pinning them down: thirty Jackals were in the forward portion of the bay, slowly advancing, under cover of their energy shields.

The Marines tossed frag grenades. The Jackals scrambled for cover and turned their shields.

Three silent explosions flashed in the vacuum. Not one of the Jackals fell.

Another explosion rippled through the deck—behind them. It shook the Master Chief's bones in his armor. The Lotus mine had detonated.

They didn't have much time before the Covenant force outside caught up with them.

The Master Chief readied his assault rifle.

"Take those Jackals out, Blue-One. I'll make a break for the *Circumference*."

Linda gripped the edge of the pressure door with her left hand, propped her rifle across it, and curled her right hand around the trigger.

"There are a lot of them," she said. "This may take a few seconds."

A flicker of a contact appeared on the Master Chief's motion tracker—then vanished. He turned and brought his assault rifle to bear. Nothing. "Hang on, Blue-One. I'm going to check our six."

Linda's acknowledgment light winked on.

The Master Chief eased back down the passage ten meters. No sensor contact. There was just dim red light and shadows . . . but one of the shadows moved.

It only took an instant for the image to fully register: a black film peeled away from the darkness. It was a meter taller than John and wore blue armor similar to that on Covenant warships. Its helmet was elongated and it had rows of sharp teeth; it looked like it was smiling at him.

The Elite leveled a plasma pistol.

At this range, there was no way the creature would miss—the plasma weapon would cut through John's slowly recharging shields almost immediately. And if John used his assault rifle, it wouldn't cut through the alien's energy shield. In a simple exchange of fire, the alien would win.

Unacceptable. He needed to change the odds.

The Master Chief pushed off the wall and launched himself at the creature. He slammed into the Elite before it had a chance to fire.

They tumbled backward and crashed into the bulkhead. The Master Chief saw the alien's shield flicker and fade—

—he hammered on the edge of the alien's gun.

The creature howled soundlessly in the vacuum and dropped the plasma weapon.

The Elite kicked him in the midsection; his shield took the

brunt of the attack, but the blow sent him spinning end over end. He slapped his hand against the ceiling and stalled his spin—then dove under the Elite's follow-up attack.

The Master Chief tried to grab the alien—but their weakened shields slid and crackled over one another.

They bounced down the curved length of the passage. The Master Chief's boot caught on a railing, twisted—a lance of pain shot up his leg—but he halted their combined momentum.

The Elite pushed away and caught a railing on the opposite side of the passage. Then it turned and sprang back toward the Master Chief.

John ignored the pain in his leg. He pushed himself at the alien.

They collided—the Master Chief struck with both fists, but the force slid off the Elite's shields.

The Elite grabbed him and threw him. They both spun into the wall.

The Master Chief was pinned—perfect: he had something to brace against in the zero gravity. He swung his fist, used every muscle in his body, and connected with the alien's midsection. Its shield shimmered and crackled but some of the momentum transferred. The alien doubled over and reeled backwards—

—and its hands found the plasma weapon that it had dropped.

The Elite recovered quickly and aimed at the Master Chief.

The Master Chief jumped, grabbed its wrist. He locked his armor's glove articulation—it became a vise clamp.

They wrestled for control. The gun pointed at the alien—then the Master Chief.

The alien was as strong as the Master Chief.

They spun and bounced off the floor, ceiling, and walls. They were too evenly matched.

The Master Chief managed to force a stalemate: the pistol now pointed straight up between their bodies. If it went off it would hit them both—one shot at point-blank range might collapse their shields. They'd both fry.

The Master Chief whipped his forearm and elbow over the creature's wrist and slammed it in the head. For a split second it was stunned and its strength ebbed.

John turned the gun into its face—squeezed the firing mechanism. The plasma discharge exploded into the creature. Fire sprayed across its shields; they shimmered, flickered, and dimmed.

The energy splash washed over the Master Chief; his shields drained to a quarter. The internal suit temperature spiked to critical levels.

But the Elite's shields were dead.

He didn't wait for the plasma gun to recharge. The Master Chief grabbed the creature with his left hand—his right fist struck an uppercut to the head, a hook to the throat and chest, three rapid-fire strikes with his forearm to its helmet—that cracked and hissed atmosphere.

The Master Chief pushed away and fired the pistol again. The bolt of fire caught the Elite in the face.

It writhed and clawed at nothing. The Elite shuddered . . . suspended in midair; it twitched and finally stopped moving.

The Master Chief shot it again to make sure it was dead.

Motion sensors picked up multiple targets approaching down the corridor—forty meters and closing.

The Master Chief turned and double-timed it back to Blue-One.

Linda was where he left her, shooting her targets with absolute concentration and precision.

"There are more on the way," he told her.

"Reinforcements have already arrived in the bay," she reported. "Twenty, at least. They're learning, overlapping their shields—can't get a good shot in."

Static crackled over the Master Chief's COM channel: *"Master Chief, this is Captain Keyes. Did you get the NAV database?"* The Captain sounded out of breath.

"Negative, sir. We're close."

"We're bound in-system to retrieve you. ETA is five minutes. Destroy the Circumference's *database and get out ASAP. If you cannot accomplish your mission . . . I'll have to take out the station with the* Pillar of Autumn's *weapons. We are running out of time."*

"Understood, sir."

The channel snapped off.

Captain Keyes was wrong. They weren't running out of time . . . time had already run out.

CHAPTER

THIRTY-SIX

0616 HOURS, AUGUST 30, 2552 (MILITARY CALENDAR) / UNSC *PILLAR OF AUTUMN*, EPSILON ERIDANI SYSTEM NEAR REACH STATION GAMMA

The plan started to fall apart almost the instant the *Pillar of Autumn* launched their Pelican dropships.

"Bring us about to heading two seven zero," Captain Keyes ordered Ensign Lovell.

"Aye, Captain," Lovell said.

"Lieutenant Hall, track the dropships' trajectories."

"Pelican One on target to dock with station Gamma," Lieutenant Hall reported. "Pelican Two initiating descent burn. They are five by five to land just outside FLEET HQ—"

"Captain," Cortana interrupted. "Spatial disruption behind us."

The view screen snapped to the aft. Black space bubbled with green points of light; the stars in the distance faded and stretched—a Covenant frigate appeared from nowhere.

"Lieutenant Dominique," Captain Keyes barked, "notify FLEETCOM that we have unwanted visitors in the backyard. I respectfully suggest they reorient those orbital guns ASAP. Ensign Lovell, turn this ship around and give me maximum power to the engines. Lieutenant Hikowa, prepare to fire the MAC gun and arm Archer missile pods B1 through B7."

The crew jumped to their tasks.

The *Pillar of Autumn* spun about, her engines flared, and she slowly came to a halt. The ship started back toward the new Covenant threat.

"Sir," Cortana said. "Spatial disruptions increasing exponentially."

Two more Covenant frigates appeared, flanking the first ship.

As soon as they exited Slipstream space—a white-hot line streaked across the blackness. A Super MAC gun had targeted them and fired. The Covenant ship only existed for a moment longer. Its shields flashed and the hull blasted into fragments.

"They're powered down," Captain Keyes said. "No lights, no plasma weapons charging, no lasers. What are they doing?"

"Perhaps," Cortana said, "their pinpoint jumps require all their energy reserves."

"A weakness?" Captain Keyes mused.

"Not for long," Cortana replied. "Covenant energy levels climbing."

The two remaining Covenant ships powered up—lights snapped on, engines glowed, and motes of red light appeared and streamed along their lateral lines.

"Entering optimal firing range," Lieutenant Hikowa announced. "Targeting solutions computer for both ships, Captain."

"Target the port vessel with our MAC gun," Lieutenant Hikowa. "Ready Archer missiles for the starboard target. Let's hope we can draw their fire."

Lieutenant Hikowa typed in the commands. "Ready, sir."

"Fire."

The *Pillar of Autumn*'s MAC gun fired three times. Thunder roiled up from the ventral decks. Archer missiles snaked through space toward the Covenant frigate on the starboard edge of the enemy formation.

The Covenant ships fired . . . but not at the *Pillar of Autumn*. Plasma bolts launched toward the two closest orbital guns.

The *Pillar of Autumn*'s MAC rounds struck the Covenant ship once, twice. Their shields flared, glowed, and dimmed. The third round struck clean and penetrated her hull aft—sent the ship spinning counterclockwise.

The orbital MAC guns fired again—a streak of silver and the port Covenant vessel shattered—a split second later, the starboard ship exploded, too.

But their plasma torpedoes continued toward their targets, splashing across two of the orbital defense platforms. The guns melted and collapsed into boiling molten spheres in the microgravity.

Thirteen guns left, Captain Keyes thought. Not exactly a lucky number.

"Lieutenant Dominique," he said, "request FLEETCOM to send all arriving vessels in-system to take up defense positions near our guns. The Covenant is willing to sacrifice a ship for one of our orbital guns. Advise them the Covenant ships appear to be dead in space for a few seconds after they execute a pinpoint jump."

"Got it, sir," Lieutenant Dominique said. "Message away."

"Lieutenant Hikowa," Captain Keyes said. "Send the destruction codes to those wild missiles we launched."

"Aye, sir."

"Belay that," Captain Keyes said. Something didn't feel right. "Lieutenant Hall, scan the region for anything unusual."

"Scanning, sir," she said. "There are millions of hull fragments; radar is useless. Thermal is off the charts—everything is hot out there." She paused, leaned closer, and a hank of her blond hair fell into her face, but she didn't brush it aside. "Reading motion *toward* Gamma station, sir. Landing pods."

"Lieutenant Hikowa," Keyes said. "Repurpose those Archer missiles. New targets—link with Lieutenant Hall for coordinates."

"Yes, Captain," they said in unison.

"Diversion, distraction, and deceit," Captain Keyes said. "The Covenant's tactics are almost getting predictable."

A hundred pinpoints of fire dotted the distant space as their missiles found Covenant targets.

"Picking up activity just out of the effective range of our orbital guns," Cortana said.

"Show me," Captain Keyes said.

The titanic Covenant vessel Keyes had seen before was back. It fired its brilliant blue-white beam—a lance across space—that struck the destroyer *Herodotus,* one hundred thousand kilometers distant. The beam cut clean through the ship, stem to stern, bisecting her.

"Christ," Ensign Lovell whispered.

A salvo of orbital gun rounds fired at this new target . . . but it was too far away. The ship moved out of the trajectory of the shells. They missed.

Another beam flashed from the Covenant vessel. Another ship—a carrier, the *Musashi*—was severed amidships as it moved to cover the orbital guns. The aft section of the ship continued to thrust forward, her engines still running hot.

"They're going to sniper our ships," Keyes said. "Leave us nothing to fortify Reach." He took out his pipe and tapped it in the palm of his hand. "Ensign Lovell. Plot an intercept course. Engines to maximum. We're going to take that ship out."

"Sir?" Lovell sat straighter. "Yes, sir. Plotting course now."

Cortana appeared on the holographic display. "I assume you have another brilliant navigational maneuver to evade this enemy, Captain."

"I thought I'd fly straight in, Cortana . . . and let you do the driving."

"Straight? You *are* joking." Logic symbols streamed up her body.

"I never joke when it comes to navigation," Captain Keyes said. "You will monitor the energy state of that ship. The instant you detect a buildup in their reactors, a spike of particle emissions—anything—you fire our emergency thrusters to throw off their aim."

Cortana nodded. "I'll do my best," she said. "Their weapon *does* travel at light speed. There won't be much time to—"

A bang resonated through their portside hull. Captain Keyes flew sideways. Blue-white light flashed on their port view screen.

"One shot missed," Cortana replied.

Captain Keyes stood up and straightened his uniform. "Ready MAC gun, Lieutenant Hikowa. Arm Archer missile pods C1 through E7. Give me a firing solution for missile impact on our last MAC round."

Lieutenant Hikowa arched an eyebrow. She had good reason to be dubious. They would be firing more than five hundred missiles at a single target. "Solution online, sir. Guns hot and ready."

"Distance, Lieutenant Hall?"

"Closing in on extreme range for MAC guns, sir. In four . . . three . . ."

An explosion to starboard and the *Pillar of Autumn* jumped. Keyes was braced this time.

"Fire, Lieutenant Hikowa. Send them back where they belong."

"Missiles away, sir. Waiting to coordinate MAC rounds."

Blue lightning washed out the view screen. Dull thumps sounded through the *Pillar of Autumn* like a string of firecrackers going off. The ship listed to port, and it started to roll.

"We're hit!" Lieutenant Hall said. "Decompression on Decks C, D, and E. Sections two through twenty-seven. Venting atmosphere. Reactor's damaged, sir." She listened to her headset. "Can't get a clear report of what's going on belowdecks. We're losing power."

"Seal those sections. Lieutenant Hikowa, do we have gun control?"

"Affirmative."

"Then fire at will, Lieutenant."

The *Pillar of Autumn* shuddered as its MAC gun fired. Pings and groans diffused though her damaged hull. A trio of white-hot projectiles appeared on the view screen, chasing the Archer missiles toward their intended target.

The first round struck the Covenant ship; its shields rippled. The second and third rounds struck, and more than five hundred missiles detonated along her length. Flame dotted the massive vessel, and her shields blazed solid silver. They faded and popped. A dozen missiles impacted her hull and exploded, scarring the bluish armor.

"Minimal damage to the target, sir," Lieutenant Hall reported.

"But we downed their shields," Captain Keyes said. "We can hurt them. That's all I needed to know. Lieutenant Hikowa, make ready to fire again. Identical targeting solution. Lieutenant Hall, launch our remote-piloted Longsword interceptor and arm its Shiva nuclear warhead. Cortana, take control of the single ship."

Cortana tapped her foot. "Longsword away," she said. "Where do you want me to park this thing?"

"Intercept course for the Covenant ship," he told her.

"Sir," Lieutenant Hikowa cried. "We have an insufficient charge rate to fire the MAC guns."

"Understood," Captain Keyes said. "Divert all power from the engines to regenerate gun capacitors."

"May I point out—" Cortana said and crossed her arms. "—that if you power down the engines, we will be inside the blast radius of the Shiva warhead when it reaches the Covenant ship?"

"Noted," Captain Keyes said. "Do it."

"Capacitors at seventy-five percent," Lieutenant Hikowa announced. "Eighty-five. Ninety-five. Full charge, sir. Ready to fire."

"Fire at will," Captain Keyes ordered.

"Missiles away—"

A javelin of blue-white energy from the Covenant ship slashed at the *Pillar of Autumn*. The beam struck, and cut through the hull. The *Pillar of Autumn* slid into a flat spin as the explosive decompression knocked the ship off course. As the *Autumn* spun, the Covenant energy beam carved a spiral pattern in the hull, shredding armor and puncturing deep into the ship.

The ship lurched sickeningly as the beam played across the portside Archer pods; the missiles detonated in their tubes. Keyes was nearly thrown from the command chair as the deck bucked beneath him.

He tightened his safety straps and scowled at the tactical displays. "Damage report!" he yelled, his voice competing with the dozens of hazard alarms that blared through the bridge speakers.

Cortana brought up a holographic view of the ship and flagged damaged areas in pulsing red. "Port launch and storage bays have been breached—fires on all decks, all sections. Primary fusion chamber is breached."

The *Pillar of Autumn* tumbled out of control.

"Cortana, get us straight and level. We have to fire our guns!"

"Yes, Captain." Her body became a blur of mathematical symbols. "This is an extremely chaotic trajectory," she said. "Atmosphere still venting. Hang on. There. Got it."

The *Pillar of Autumn* righted herself. The Covenant ship centered on the main view screen. This close, Captain Keyes saw how huge the ship was—three times the mass of a normal cruiser. There was a pod mounted on the top deck; it swiveled and tracked the *Pillar of Autumn*, bringing the turret to bear. It glowed electric white as it built up another lethal charge.

"Fire when ready, Lieutenant Hikowa," Captain Keyes ordered.

"Firing!" Thunder rumbled belowdecks. "MAC rounds away."

The shells struck the Covenant vessel; Archer missiles impacted . . . only a handful got though her downed shields.

"Cortana, crash-land our Longsword on that bastard. Set timer delay on the nuke for fifteen seconds."

"Afterburners on," Cortana replied. "Impact in three . . . two . . . one. She's down, sir."

The *Pillar of Autumn* sped past the Covenant ship.

"Lieutenant Hall, divert any power you can muster to the engines."

"Bringing secondary reactor back online, sir. That gives us fifteen percent."

"Aft camera on center screen," Captain Keyes ordered.

The Covenant ship slowly turned toward the *Pillar of Autumn* and its turret tracked their position. For the first time in his life, Keyes prayed that a Covenant ship's shields would hold.

The alien ship became a flash of white light; its outline blurred. Their shields held for a split second as the Shiva warhead detonated *inside* its protective aura. The shockwave rebounded off the asymmetrical shape of the shields just before their collapse. Jets of energy exploded outward at three different angles. Thunder and plasma roiled into space . . . cleanly missing the *Pillar of Autumn*.

The light faded and the Covenant flagship was gone.

Captain Keyes puffed again on his pipe and tapped it out. Maybe now they had a chance to rally what remained of the UNSC fleet and defend Reach.

"Congratulations Captain," Cortana said. "I couldn't have done better myself."

"Thank you, Cortana. Is there a planet nearby?"

"Beta Gabriel," she said. "Fourteen million kilometers. Practically next door."

"Good. Ensign Lovell, plot a course for a slingshot orbit. Reverse our trajectory back in-system."

"Sir," Lieutenant Dominique interrupted. "Incoming transmission from Reach. It's the Spartans."

"On speakers, Lieutenant."

Static hissed from the channel. A man's voice broke through. *"—bad. Reactor complex seven has been compromised. We're falling back. Might be able to save number three. Set off those charges now!"* There was a series of explosions . . . more white noise, then the man returned. *"Be advised* Pillar of Autumn, *groundside reactors are being taken. Orbital guns at risk. Nothing we can do. Too many. We will have to use the nukes—"* Static washed away the transmission.

"Captain," Cortana said. "You need to see this, sir."

She overlaid a tactical map of the system on the main view screen. Tiny triangular red markers winked on the edges: Covenant ships—dozens of them—reentered the system from Slipspace.

"Sir," she said, "when the guns around Reach go down . . ."

"There will be nothing left to stop the Covenant," he finished.

Captain Keyes turned to Lieutenant Dominique. "Get those Spartans back online," he said. "Tell them to evac ASAP. In a few minutes, it's going to get very nasty around Reach."

He took a deep breath. "Then raise the Master Chief on a secure channel. Let's hope he has some good news for us."

CHAPTER THIRTY-SEVEN

0637 HOURS, AUGUST 30, 2552 (MILITARY CALENDAR) / EPSILON ERIDANI SYSTEM, REACH STATION GAMMA

"Multiple signals on motion tracker," the Master Chief said. "They're all around us."

The passageway behind the Master Chief and Blue-One swarmed with blips. So did docking Bay Nine, ahead of them. The Master Chief saw, however, not all the blips were hostiles. Four Marine friend-or-foe tags strobed on his heads-up display: SGT. JOHNSON, PVT. O'BRIEN, PVT. BISENTI, and PVT. JENKINS.

The Master Chief opened up a COM channel to them. "Listen up, Marines. Your lines of fire are sloppy; tighten them up. Concentrate on one Jackal at a time—or you'll just waste your ammo on their shields."

"Master Chief?" Sergeant Johnson said, startled. "Sir, yes sir!"

"Blue-One," the Master Chief said. "I'm going in. We're going to open up the *Circumference* like a tin can." He nodded toward the Pelican in the adjacent bay. "Give me a few grenades over the top."

"Understood," she replied. "You're covered, sir." She primed two frag grenades, swung around the pressure doors, and threw them behind the Jackals.

The Master Chief pushed off the wall—propelled himself in the zero gee across the bay.

The grenades detonated and caught the Jackals on their

backsides. Blue blood spattered on the insides of their shields and across the deck.

The Master Chief crashed into the Pelican's hull. He pulled himself to the side hatch, opened it, and crawled in. He got into the cockpit, released the docking clamps, and tapped the maneuvering thrusters once to break free.

The Pelican lifted off the deck.

The Master Chief said over the COM channel, "Marines and Blue-One: take cover behind me." He maneuvered the Pelican into the center of the docking bay.

A dozen Jackals poured in through the passage that Blue-One had just left.

The Master Chief fired with the Pelican's autocannon—cut down their shields and peppered the aliens with hundreds of rounds. They exploded into chunks; alien blood twisted crazily in zero gravity.

"Master Chief," Linda said, "I'm picking up *thousands* of signals on the motion tracker, inbound from all directions. The entire station is crawling."

The Master Chief opened the Pelican's back hatch. "Get in," he said. Blue-One and the Marines piled inside.

The Marines did a double take at Blue-One and the Master Chief in their MJOLNIR armor.

The Master Chief turned the Pelican to face the *Circumference*. He sighted the autocannon on the ship's forward viewports—and opened fire. Thousands of rounds streamed from the chain-gun and cracked through the thick, transparent windows. He followed up with an Anvil-II missile. It blasted through the prow and peeled the craft open.

"Take the controls," he told Blue-One.

He slipped out the side hatch and jumped to the *Circumference*. The inside of the ship's cockpit was scrap metal. He accessed the computer panel in the floor deck and located the

NAV database core. It was a cube of memory crystal the size of his thumb. Such a tiny thing to cause so much trouble.

He shot it three times with his assault rifle. It shattered.

"Mission completed," he said. One small victory in all this mess. The Covenant wouldn't find Earth . . . today.

He exited the *Circumference*. Jackals appeared on the level above them in the docking bay. His motion tracker blinked with solid contacts.

He jumped back into the Pelican, strapped himself in the pilot's chair, and turned the ship to face the outer doors.

"Blue-One, signal the dockmaster AI to open the outer bay doors."

"Signal sent," she said. "No response, sir." She looked around. "There's a manual release by the outer door." She moved toward the aft hatch. "I'll get this one, sir. It's my turn. Cover me."

"Roger, Blue-One. Keep your head down. I'll draw their fire."

She launched herself out the back hatch.

The Master Chief tapped the Pelican's thrusters and the ship rose higher in the bay—up to the second level. The upper decks were the mechanic bays; the area was littered with ships that were partially disassembled in various stages of repair. It was also where a hundred Jackals and a handful of Elites were waiting for him.

They opened fire. Plasma bolts scored the hull of the Pelican.

The Master Chief fired the chain-gun and let loose a salvo of missiles. Alien shields blazed and failed. Blue and green blood splashed and flash-froze in the icy vacuum.

He hit the top thrusters and dropped down to the lower level—slammed the ship back into a berth for cover.

Blue-One crouched by the manual release. The outer doors eased open, revealing the night and stars beyond. "You're clear for exit, Master Chief. We're home free—"

A new contact on the Pelican's targeting display appeared—right behind Linda. He had to *warn* her—

A bolt of plasma struck her in the back. Another bolt of fire blazed from the upper decks and splashed across her front. She crumpled—her shields flickered and went out. Two more bolts hit her chest. A third blast smashed into her helmet.

"No!" the Master Chief said. He felt each of those plasma bolts as if they had hit him, too.

He moved the Pelican to cover her. Plasma struck the hull, melting its outer skin.

"Get her inside!" he ordered the Marines.

They jumped out, grabbed Linda and her smoldering armor, and pulled her inside the Pelican.

The Master Chief sealed the hatch, ignited the engines, and pushed them to full thrust—rocketing into space.

"Can you fly this ship?" he asked the Marine Sergeant.

"Yes, sir," Johnson replied.

"Take over."

The Master Chief went to Linda and knelt by her side. Sections of her armor had melted and adhered to her. Underneath, in patches, bits of carbonized bone showed. He accessed her vital signs on his heads-up display. They were dangerously low.

"Did you do it?" she whispered. "Get the database?"

"Yes. We got it."

"Good," she said. "We won." She clasped his hand and closed her eyes.

Her vital signs flatlined.

John squeezed her hand and let go. "Yes," he said bitterly. "We won."

"Master Chief, come in." Captain Keyes' voice sounded over the COM channel. *"The* Pillar of Autumn *will be in rendezvous position in one minute."*

"We're ready, Captain," he answered. He set Linda's hand over her chest. "*I'm* ready."

The instant the Master Chief docked the Pelican to the *Pillar of Autumn*, he felt the cruiser accelerate.

He took Linda's body double time to a cryo chamber and immediately froze her. She was clinically dead—there was no doubt of that. Still, if they could get her to a Fleet hospital, they might be able to resuscitate her. It was a long shot—but she was a Spartan.

The med techs wanted to check him out as well, but he declined and took the elevator to the bridge to report to Captain Keyes.

As he rode inside the lift he felt the ship accelerate port—then starboard. Evasive maneuvers.

The elevator doors parted and the Master Chief stepped onto the bridge.

He snapped a crisp salute to Captain Keyes. "Reporting for debriefing, sir."

Captain Keyes turned and looked surprised to see him . . . or maybe he was shocked to see the condition of his armor. It was charred, battered, and covered with alien blood.

The Captain returned the Master Chief's salute. "The NAV database was destroyed?" he asked.

"Sir, I would not have left if my mission was incomplete."

"Of course, Master Chief. Very good," Captain Keyes replied.

"Sir, may I ask that you scan for active FOF tags in the region?" The Master Chief glanced at the main view screen—saw scattered fights between Covenant and UNSC warships in the distance. "I lost a man on the station. He may be floating out there . . . somewhere."

"Lieutenant Hall?" the Captain asked.

"Scanning," she said. After a moment she looked back and shook her head.

"I see," the Master Chief replied. There could be worse deaths . . . but not for one of his Spartans. Floating helpless. Slowly suffocating and freezing—losing to an enemy that could not be fought.

"Sir," the Master Chief said, "when will the *Pillar of Autumn* rendezvous with my planetside team?"

Captain Keyes turned from the Master Chief and stared out into space. "We won't be picking them up," he said quietly. "They were overrun by Covenant forces. They never made orbit. We've lost contact with them."

The Master Chief took a step closer. "Then I would like permission to take a dropship and retrieve them, sir."

"Request denied, Master Chief. We still have a mission to perform. And we cannot remain in this system much longer. Lieutenant Dominique, aft camera on the main screen."

Covenant vessels swarmed through the Epsilon Eridani System in five-ship crescent formations. The remaining UNSC ships fled before them . . . those that could still move. Those ships too damaged to outrun the Covenant were blasted with plasma and laser fire.

The Covenant had won this battle. They were mopping up before they glassed the planet; the Master Chief had seen this happen in a dozen campaigns. This time was different, however.

This time the Covenant was glassing a planet . . . with his people still on it.

He tried to think of a way to stop them . . . to save his teammates. He couldn't.

The Captain turned and strode to the Master Chief, stood by his side. "Dr. Halsey's mission," he said, "is more important than ever now. It may be the only chance left for Earth. We have to focus on that goal."

Three dozen Covenant craft moved toward Gamma station and the now inert orbital defense platforms. They bombarded the installations—the mightiest weapons in the UNSC arsenal—with plasma. The guns melted, and boiled away.

The Master Chief clenched his hands into fists. The Captain was correct: there was nothing to do now except complete the mission they had set out to do.

Captain Keyes barked, "Ensign Lovell, give me our best acceleration. I want to enter Slipstream space as soon as possible."

Cortana said, "Excuse me, Captain. Six Covenant frigates are inbound on an intercept course."

"Continue evasive maneuvers, Cortana. Prepare the Slipspace generators and get me an appropriate randomized exit vector."

"Aye, sir." Navigation symbols flashed along the length of her holographic body.

The Master Chief continued to watch as the Covenant ships closed in on them.

Was he the only Spartan left? Better to die than live without his teammates. But he still had a mission: victory against the Covenant—and vengeance for his fallen comrades.

"Generating randomized exit vector per the Cole Protocol," Cortana said.

The Master Chief glanced at her translucent body. She looked vaguely like a younger Dr. Halsey. Tiny dots, ones, and zeros slid over her torso, arms, and legs. Her thoughts were literally worn on her sleeve; the symbols also appeared on Ensign Lovell's NAV station.

He cocked his head as the symbols and numbers scrolled across the NAV console.

The representations of Slipspace vectors and velocity curves twisted across the screen—tantalizingly familiar. He'd seen them somewhere before—but he could not make the connection.

"Something on your mind, Master Chief?" Cortana asked.

"Those symbols . . . I thought I had seen them somewhere before. It's nothing."

Cortana got a far-off look in her eyes. The marks cycling on her hologram shifted and rearranged.

The Master Chief saw the Covenant fleet gathered around planet Reach. They swarmed and circled like sharks. The first of their plasma bombardments launched toward the surface. Clouds in the fire's path boiled away.

"Jump to Slipspace, Ensign Lovell," the Captain said. "Get us the hell out of here."

John remembered Chief Mendez's words—that they had to live and fight another day. He was alive . . . and there was still plenty of fight left in him. And he would win this war—no matter what it took.

SECTION VI

HALO

EPILOGUE

0647 HOURS, AUGUST 30, 2552 (MILITARY CALENDAR) / UNSC *PILLAR OF AUTUMN*, EPSILON ERIDANI SYSTEM'S EDGE

Cortana fired the *Pillar of Autumn*'s autocannons—targeting a dozen Seraph fighters harassing them as they were accelerated out of the system. Seven Covenant frigates were now locked into the pursuit. She dodged a volley of pulse laser fire, using the ventral emergency thrusters.

She pushed the damaged secondary reactor to critical levels. They had to build up more speed before activating the Shaw-Fujikawa Translight generators or the jump to Slipstream space would fail.

She rechecked her calculations. Under the Cole Protocol, they would be jumping away from Earth . . . but it would not be a totally random heading.

The Master Chief had been right when he said that he recognized the shorthand navigation symbols on the NAV display.

Cortana accessed the Spartans' mission logs. She sifted through the data, and filed it into a secondary long-term storage buffer. When she reviewed the database of his mission reports, Cortana learned that Spartan-117 *had* seen something similar on the Covenant vessel he had boarded in 2525. And again—the symbols almost looked like those on the rock he had extracted from Covenant forces on Sigma Octanus IV. ONI reports on the symbols found in the anomalous rock had defied cryptoanalysis.

Keyes' order to plot a navigation route sparked a connection between the data; she accessed the alien symbols, and rather than compare them with alphabets or hieroglyphics, compared them to star formations.

There were some startling similarities—along with a number of differences. Cortana reanalyzed the symbols and accounted for thousands of years of stellar drift.

A tenth of a second later she had a close match on her charts—86.2 percent.

Interesting. Perhaps the markings in the rock recovered on Sigma Octanus IV were navigation symbols, albeit highly unusual and stylized ones—mathematical symbols as artistic and elegant as Chinese calligraphy.

What was there that the Covenant wanted so badly that they had launched a full offensive against Sigma Octanus IV? Whatever it was . . . Cortana was interested, too.

She compared the new NAV coordinates with her directives and was pleased with what she saw; the new course complied with the Cole Protocol. Good.

The Covenant frigates fired their plasma again. Seven bolts of fire streaked toward the *Pillar of Autumn*.

She dumped the coordinates to the NAV controls and stored the logic path that led to her deduction in her high-security buffer.

"Approaching saturation velocity," she told Captain Keyes. "Powering Shaw-Fujikawa Translight generators. New course available."

The Covenant frigates aligned with their outbound vector. They were going to try to follow the *Pillar of Autumn* through Slipspace. Damn.

The Shaw-Fujikawa Translight generators tore a hole in normal space. Light boiled around the *Pillar of Autumn* and she vanished.

Cortana had plenty of time to think on the journey. Most of the crew were frozen in cryo for the trip. Some of the engineers had elected to try to repair the main reactor. A futile gesture . . . but she lent them a few cycles to try to rebuild the convection inductor.

Had Dr. Halsey been on Reach when it fell to the Covenant? Cortana felt a pang of regret for her creator. Maybe she had gotten away. The probability was low . . . but the doctor was a survivor.

Cortana ran a self-diagnostic. Her Alpha-level commands were intact. She had not jeopardized her primary mission by following this vector. There were, unfortunately, sure to be Covenant ships when they arrived . . . wherever they arrived.

The Covenant had followed them into Slipstream space. And they had always been faster and more accurate than UNSC navigators in the elusive dimension.

Captain Keyes and the Master Chief would get their chance to disable and capture one of those vessels. Their "luck" had so far defied all probability and statistical variations. She hoped their defiance of the odds continued.

"Captain Keyes? Wake up, sir," Cortana said. "We will enter normal space in three hours."

Captain Keyes sat up in the cryo tube. He licked his lips and gagged. "I hate that stuff."

"The inhalant surfactant is highly nutritious, sir. Please regurgitate and swallow the protein complex."

Captain Keyes swung his legs out of the tube. He coughed and spat the mucus onto the deck. "You wouldn't say that, Cortana, if you ever tasted this stuff. Ship status?"

"Reactor two has been fully repaired," she replied. "Reactors one and three are inoperable. That gives us twenty percent power. Archer missile pods I and J rows serviceable. Autocannon ammunition at ten percent. Our two remaining Shiva warheads are intact." She paused and double-checked the MAC gun. "Magnetic Accelerator Gun's capacitors depolarized. We cannot fire the system, sir."

"More good news," he grumbled. "Continue."

"Hull breaches patched—but the majority of decks eleven, twelve, and thirteen are destroyed—that includes the Spartans' weapons locker."

"Are there any infantry weapons left?" Keyes asked. "We may need to repel boarders."

"Yes, Captain. A substantial number of standard Marine infantry weapons survived the engagement. Would you like an inventory?"

"Later. What about the crew?"

"All crew accounted for. Spartan-117 is in cryo sleep with the Marine and security personnel. Waking bridge officers and all essential personnel."

"And the Covenant?"

"We'll know in a moment if they were able to track us, sir."

"Very well. I'll be on the bridge in ten minutes." He eased out of the tube. "I'm getting too damn old to be frozen and shot through space at light speed," he muttered.

Cortana checked the status of the waking crew. There was a minor flutter in Lieutenant Dominique's heart, which she corrected. Otherwise, status normal.

The Captain and crew assembled on the bridge. They waited.

"Five minutes until normal space, sir," Cortana announced.

She knew they could see the countdown timer, but Cortana noticed that the crew responded well to her calm voice in stressful situations. Their reaction times generally improved by as much as 15 percent—give or take. Sometimes, human imperfection made calculations maddeningly imprecise.

She ran another check on all intact systems. The *Pillar of Autumn* had taken a tremendous beating at Reach. It was a wonder it was still in one piece.

"Entering normal space in thirty seconds," she informed Captain Keyes.

"Shut down all systems, Cortana. I want us to be dark when we hit normal space. If the Covenant did follow us—maybe we can hide."

"Aye, sir. Running dark."

The view screen filled with green light; smears of stars came into focus. A purple-hued gas giant filled a third of the screen.

Captain Keyes said, "Fire thrusters to position us in orbit around the planet, Ensign Lovell."

"Aye, sir," he replied.

The *Pillar of Autumn* glided around the gravity well of the moon.

Cortana detected a radar echo ahead, an object hidden in the shadow.

As the ship rounded the dark side of the gas giant, the object came into full view. It was a ring-shaped structure . . . gigantic.

"Cortana," Captain Keyes whispered. "What is that?"

Cortana noted a sudden spike in pulse and respiration among the bridge crew . . . particularly the Captain.

The object spun serenely in the heavens. The outer surface was gray metal, reflecting the brilliant starlight. From this distance, the surface of the object seemed to be engraved with deep, ornate geometric patterns.

"Could this be some kind of naturally occurring phenomenon?" Dominique asked.

"Unknown," Cortana replied.

She activated the ship's long-range detection gear. Cortana's holo image frowned. The *Pillar of Autumn*'s scanning systems were fine for combat . . . but for this kind of analysis it was like using stone tools. She diverted processing power away from ancillary systems and channeled it into the task.

Figures scrolled across the sensor displays.

"The ring is ten thousand kilometers in diameter," Cortana

announced, "and twenty-two point three kilometers thick. Spectroscopic analysis is inconclusive, but patterns do not match any known Covenant materials, sir."

She paused and aimed the long-range camera array at the ring. A moment later a close-up of the object snapped into focus.

Keyes let out a low whistle.

The inner surface was a mosaic of greens, blues, and browns—trackless desert; jungles; glaciers and vast oceans. Streaks of white clouds cast deep shadows upon the terrain. The ring rotated and brought a new feature into view—a tremendous hurricane forming over an unimaginably wide body of water.

Equations scrolled furiously across Cortana as she studied the ring. She checked and rechecked her numbers—the rotational speed of the object and its estimated mass. They didn't quite add up. She ran through a series of passive and active scans . . . and found something.

"Captain," Cortana said, "the object is clearly artificial. There's a gravity field that controls the ring's spin and keeps the atmosphere inside. At this range—and with this gear—I can't say with one hundred percent certainty, but it appears that the ring has an oxygen-nitrogen atmosphere and Earth-normal gravity."

"If it's artificial, who the hell built it . . . and what in God's name is it?"

Cortana processed that question for a full three seconds, then finally answered: "I don't know, sir."

Captain Keyes took out his pipe, lit it, and puffed once. He examined the curls of smoke thoughtfully. "Then we'd better find out."

ADJUNCT

OFFICE OF NAVAL INTELLIGENCE

CONFIDENTIAL: DIRECTORATE MEMORANDUM
INTERROGATION FINDINGS

UNSC Everest
28 December 2530
1230 Standard

"The Groombridge Subject"

This report was generated by AI Solipsil immediately following the interrogation of SUBJECT 386—also known as "The Groombridge Subject."

SUBJECT 386 was a biological life-form captured in Waterford, Lemuria of Groombridge-1830 on December 24, 2530, at approximately 1805 hours. This interrogation was conducted on December 25, 2530, 0240 hours. The subject was confirmed deceased at 0417 hours. The following is a series of transcription excerpts from the interrogation of SUBJECT 386, as recorded by AI Solipsil.

RECORDED TRANSCRIPTION EXCERPT:

[SOLIPSIL] Current date and time is December 25, 2530, 0240 hours standard. We are in orbit above Groombridge-1830, aboard the UNSC *Everest,* within the ship's biohazard unit R-12. This is UNSC AI Solipsil, service number SLP 0391-5. Lieutenant, please state your rank, name, and service number for the record.

[BARCLAY] First Lieutenant Richard Lionel Barclay, Office of Naval Intelligence, service number 00045-23994-RL.

[SOLIPSIL] Admiral, your rank, name, and service number for the record, please.

[COLE] Fleet Admiral Preston Jeremiah Cole, UNSC *Everest*, service number 03956-26127-PC.

[SOLIPSIL] Let the record show that SUBJECT 386 was captured from an enemy assault carrier which attempted to flee to the planetary surface during the engagement designated GB-5546. Two heavily armed tactical strike teams retrieved SUBJECT 386 from within an enclosed compartment which survived landfall. The subject is approximately 2.3 meters in height and approximately 153 kilograms in weight.

[SUBJECT 386] [unintelligible]

[SOLIPSIL] The SUBJECT 386 is restrained and Lieutenant Barclay has a weapon drawn on the subject. Lieutenant, can you verify that for the record?

[BARCLAY] The weapon is drawn and ready to fire.

[SOLIPSIL] Thank you, Lieutenant. Admiral, you can begin.

[COLE] Can you hear me?

[SOLIPSIL] Let the record show that SUBJECT 386 has made eye contact with the admiral.

[COLE] Do you understand what I'm saying?

[SUBJECT 386] [unintelligible]

[COLE] If you can hear me and understand what I am saying, nod your head.

[SOLIPSIL] SUBJECT 386 has nodded its head.

[COLE] What is your name?

[SUBJECT 386] [unintelligible]

[COLE] Solipsil, is that thing working?

[SOLIPSIL] Let the record show that the admiral is referring to TSV-442, Everest's onboard translation program. Yes, Admiral, it's working. The subject's not speaking any words recognized by our database.

[COLE] State your name.

[SUBJECT 386] [unintelligible]

[COLE] Barclay, I'm clearly confusing it. Please help me articulate.

[SOLIPSIL] The lieutenant has cocked the M6 sidearm and has placed the barrel at SUBJECT 386's right temple.

[SUBJECT 386] That will not persuade me, human.

[COLE] Your name and rank . . .

[SUBJECT 386] You are not worthy to hear it.

[COLE] You're going to die here, you know. You have absolutely nothing to lose. Give us your name and rank.

[SUBJECT 386] [laughter?]

[EXCERPT 01 ENDS] [EXCERPT 04 BEGINS]

[COLE] Why are you here? Why Groombridge?

[SUBJECT 386] It is just another human world. Like all the others.

[COLE] Just like the others? Then why the other worlds?

[SUBJECT 386] [unintelligible]

[COLE] What was that?

[SUBJECT 386] Even now, you stand without [unintelligible] or honor. You are unclean, human, and nothing can save you now.

[COLE] Unclean?

[SUBJECT 386] You are an affront to the gods, desecrating their temples by committing horrors with their consecrated [unintelligible].

[COLE] Temples? What temples? Who are these gods?

[SUBJECT 386] You are ignorant swarming maggots. You know nothing of the Great Journey or of our gods' treasures, yet you [unintelligible] intend to destroy them. We will root out every single world you possess and lay waste to them one by one until there's nowhere left for you to go.

[COLE] I seem to remember us destroying your ships yesterday. Did you think we were going to let you just waltz right in?

[SUBJECT 386] Yesterday? Three ships, human? You boast about [unintelligible] three of our vessels when you had five times that many, and lost almost all?

[COLE] We—

[SUBJECT 386] Our fleets approach from beyond the stars and they are far more vast than your [unintelligible] mind can fathom. There is no defense which you can muster. No escape.

[SOLIPSIL] Let the record show an increase in the heart rate of SUBJECT 386.

[COLE] We're not afraid of you. We'll stand and fight.

[SUBJECT 386] And you will perish. By the billions.

[COLE] We'll stop you. I promise you.

[SUBJECT 386] Your [unintelligible] is weak. Nothing more than slithering [unintelligible] to be cut away and discarded.

[SOLIPSIL] Let the record show that SUBJECT 386 is moving within its restraints. Lieutenant . . .

[BARCLAY] Stay down! Do not move or I'll blow your [EXPLETIVE] head off!

[SUBJECT 386] We are the holy and glorious inheritors.

[COLE] Why are you attacking us?

[SOLIPSIL] Subject is slipping into some kind of arrest or seizure. Medics! Let the record show that SUBJECT 386's extensive injuries and trauma have—

[SUBJECT 386] You have been judged unclean! A scourge that must be burned away! Every one of your worlds will be reduced to ash.

[SOLIPSIL] Medic! Medic! Let the record show—

[SUBJECT 386] [unintelligible] destroy you all . . .

[SOLIPSIL] Medic! Let the record show that the subject's vitals have flatlined.

[COLE] We can't let them find her.

[BARCLAY] Earth?

[COLE] Earth.

[SOLIPSIL] Let the record show that as of December 25, 2530, 0417 hours, SUBJECT 386's vitals flatlined and, lacking the necessary understanding of its anatomy, the subject was not resuscitated. Transcription terminated.

WORD FROM THE THIRD FLEET OF GLORIOUS CONSEQUENCE

TO THE HOLY CITY OF HIGH CHARITY, VICE CLERIC OF ZEAL

Excellency—

Since we last spoke, much has changed. The human world we had targeted has been laid to waste. The last cycle of purification is in its final stage—May we all walk The Path!

Unfortunately, our return will be delayed due to a local magnetic irregularity, but an early report may help to stay any concern you might have about this protracted engagement. In particular, any concern about one Major Thel 'Lodamee and the actions which placed our fleet and his entire battalion at grave risk, extending this skirmish needlessly.

Thel's devout hatred for the humans is commendable, but it feeds an unchecked and dangerous level of recklessness. He is a vicious commander and a skilled warrior, but he is incapable of self-control—even at the peril of the troops who serve under him. All were concerns which I respectfully addressed at the last assignment tribunal.

During our siege, some of the vermin attempted to escape. We destroyed each and every vessel before they could even breach their world's gravity well, but one managed to find the system's edge. It was then that Thel left his battlegroup without notice in pursuit of this single ship with a small strike force.

You already know what befell our fleet and the cost we have paid. Early estimates are somewhere near three thousand—all on the shoulders of reckless abandon.

While Thel managed to slay a human demon—something we were surprised to find here—he came to understand that its purpose was to protect a key military asset. We are not certain what this asset's significance is, only that it is, in fact, significant—it is a human, a female. So important, that the demon protector swiftly traded its life for the creature's safety. Such dedication is rather surprising.

They will follow and we will be ready for them. And then, we will continue as planned, rejoining the Fleets of Furious Retribution and Rigorous Prayer at our assigned rendezvous point.

In faith, your humble servant,
SUPREME COMMANDER LURO 'TARALUMEE, RESPLENDENT FERVOR

OFFICE OF NAVAL INTELLIGENCE
NARROW-BAND POINT-TO-POINT TRANSMISSION
CLASSIFIED TOP-SECRET // FOR YOUR EYES ONLY

RE: WARM BLANKET
FROM: VADM. BERLIN M. TURSK, UNSC HEAVY CRUISER *SWIFTSURE*
TO: CPT. LUCIUS R. JIRON, ONI PRO-49776

Lucius, my apologies for the brevity of this message. Rain check on that coffee too, we're pulling out of the system.

As you already know, yesterday the UNSC declared the colony of Miridem lost. The fight had gone on for over two weeks and we killed a mountain of those bastards, but apparently not enough.

During civilian egress, one of our evac craft [BL-9400493] carried a pseudocivilian the spooks consider Pri 1—DOCTOR CATHERINE ELIZABETH HALSEY. Not sure how the hell that went down, and usually ONI has a good eye on where she is at all times, but there she was, on Miridem's surface, just as the Covenant started their thing. Apparently her S-II bodyguard was taken out during extraction, but the ship she was on still managed to escape.

They even made it to the edge of the system safely, but a Covenant interceptor disabled the vessel before it was able to slip. Everyone on board was killed except for her, so they obviously realize they have *something*. As you know, they're not big on taking prisoners. Our continuous pings to her beacon indicate that she's still alive and still on ice.

One other complication—they're bound to have detected the short-radius M-wave bounce, which means they know they have a microtail and they're letting it follow, so they'll be expecting trouble. If we stop pinging her tracker, they may assume she's of no value to us. We're between a rock and a hard place.

For the time being, we're fairly certain that the Covenant don't fully understand the value or nature of the package they have in their possession, but we're also pretty damn sure that once they find out, they'll attempt to exploit her to the fullest extent.

For now, prep your OF92s. Admiralty's sending Spartans your way for a quick and dirty extraction.

Orders will follow shortly.

- B.

Hello Agnes,

Your probably didn't expect to hear from me, not while we're in the middle of this mess, but I know you've seen the bulletin and it's been eating away at me. You're the only person I can really talk to about it. I have no doubt my communications are being monitored, but all of this is public record, or at least, official record.

Ralph 303 is hardly anomalous in terms of what happened to his mind state and general psychological condition after his removal from the Spartan-II program, but the recent revelation regarding the *manner* of his death and the declassification of some elements of the Spartan-II program make this as good a time to talk about an uncomfortable part of our lives as any.

We have to be careful with children.

I don't mean to sound glib or preachy, you know I'm not that way, but we have a moral responsibility, even in the face of great challenges and difficulties, that we cannot ignore. If we are tasked with saving humanity, then we must, as scientists, understand what saving "humanity" actually means. If we abandon the very things that make us human to defend balls of rock, then what are we saving, precisely?

Better to take the path of least resistance offered by the "Flood" *anomaly,* or even annihilation by the Covenant, than abandon our own *human* worth. Self-preservation simply isn't a strong enough argument.

So I said I wasn't going to be preachy or glib, and I failed there, I suppose. I'm sorry. This has been eating at me since I saw the bulletin. He was a good kid. Most of them were good kids, and I feel like we let them down. Daisy handled it better than Ralph did, at least in the short term. But I think at the end of the day, Ralph's path was better. I think he lived a happier life, even if it was truncated.

I read his whole file. He led a good life.

Physiological differences can't be ignored. Although some of his gene treatments were curtailed and suppressed, some irreversible changes had occurred. He'd have been an intimidating child in school, even with a strict military upbringing. Being an alpha male in an environment replete with them hardly makes his adolescence and emergence into adulthood typical—he had some advantages.

We can assume that the lack of typical "schoolyard" competition and relative lack of stresses in those environments made some of the transitional years easier for him than if he had been, for example, a shorter, weaker child, more prone to bullying.

School reports do show some bullying tendencies on his part, but nothing particularly cruel and the reports indicate a simple and perhaps normal phase, rather than a trend or pattern. To all intents and purposes he was a fair-minded and ostensibly "good" child. The fact that he recovered from that much trauma and actually served in the Marines is a testament to his strength. We tend to use successful Spartans as a yardstick for strength, sometimes. And that's unfair. Nobody can bend that much and not break a little.

His adoptive parents understood that he was a special case and I feel, very strongly, that this kind of reset of environment was important to his recovery and his subsequent growth as a human being. Ironically, I suspect that when he did finally pass away (honorably and in action, I might add) that he was more stable and mature in his outlook than many of the Spartan "success stories."

Parental placement is important in these cases for a number of reasons. Secrecy, of course, is paramount, but we've found that the structured, disciplined lives afforded by military families help create a sense of stability and purpose for otherwise very confused children.

There are elements of the Spartan program we still can't discuss this openly, stuff Halsey didn't know about, for example, but we can speak with conviction about relative morality, because we have the luxury of hindsight. And the burden of guilt.

I guess my point is that you have to think about Ralph. I know you're working with new children. I know that doing this for years can inure you to what they are and what they mean to us. Our child never made it, and I cry every time I think about our little girl, Agnes, I really cry. And I know that's why we never made it. I will always be sorry for that and for being too weak to help you get through it.

But these new ones—they have to make it. And when you're not teaching them, not monitoring them, you have to be a mother to them. You were good at that. You always were.

Yours faithfully,
Mike

United Nations Space Command Transmission 34670J-17
Encryption Code: Red
Public Key: File / Douglas-Six-Six-Lima /
From: Captain Jacob Keyes, Commanding Officer, UNSC *Pillar of Autumn* (UNSC Service Number: 01928-19912-JK)
To: Vice Admiral Kopano N'Singile / UNSC Section Two Sub-Commander /REACH CENTCOM (UNSC Service Number: 25088-67602-KN)
Subject: READINESS
Classification: EYES-ONLY (RND Directive)

Vice Admiral,

The *Pillar of Autumn*'s refit is 98 percent complete, and if we can maintain the current pace we should meet all RED FLAG specs in seventy-two hours.

The Halcyons were always impressive but with the modifications made here this ship shows what the Hals truly could have been. My concern about the fragility of her reactor remains, but after seeing its energy output in our test sequence I can appreciate the value of the new design. Let's just hope that nothing gets loose in there.

You told me that this mission is big, and you and I have been through enough together that I believe you. While I expect I'll be the last person to know where we're sailing, I've been around long enough to be able to tell that we're going alone. I've got a who's who of engineers, scientists, and ONI "monitors" crawling all over my ship right now, and if they're all here that means every other ship in the dock is going without. Plus, we've already taken on enough ██████████ to account for every gram left at Reach if I've been reading the fleet reports correctly the last few months, so no other ship could even keep up with us if they tried.

All this, and the modifications to stow an army's worth of heavy weapons without any room for an army make it pretty clear that I'm about to get some visitors . . . and I know what kind of missions they go on.

My men know it, too.

Which leads to why I'm reporting out of schedule. You can give me all the missiles in the fleet, but I need a crew to fire them, and I need them for the duration.

The damned ONI orders not to discuss what's going on out there are a serious interference with my command. I get the briefings and the real numbers and I understand that there's not much we could do if we launched the *Autumn* directly into the heart of it, but I can't explain any of that to my men because I can't officially acknowledge that any of it is even taking place.

But you know as well as I do that these Blackout orders aren't worth a damn. Crew talks. Always have, always will. If it's not the techs or the NAVCOM ops, it's my platewelders out verifying the hull with a great big view of the show below, and there's no way that stays quiet, not with as many husbands, wives, and kids as we have down on the surface. And every day those doubts grow, and my crew is one more nightmare further away from full readiness. I can't have that if you expect me to do my job, whenever you tell me what that job is.

They need to know that Reach won't be here when we get back. There's nothing we can do about it but make this loss mean something by completing our mission to the best of our abilities. And I have to make them understand that this

MEANS STANDING DOWN ON BOARD THE *AUTUMN* WHILE EVERYTHING GOES TO HELL AROUND THEM.

I WAS LUCKY ENOUGH TO MAKE MY PEACE DOWN THERE WHILE ON OFFICIAL BUSINESS, BUT NONE OF MY CREW THOUGHT THEY WERE SHIPPING FOR THE LAST TIME AND NOW IT'S TOO LATE. I HAVE TO FOCUS THEM, TURN THEIR DOUBT INTO AN ANGER I CAN USE, AND HOPE LIKE HELL THAT THEY DON'T TURN THAT ANGER ON ME. NOT SURE I'D BLAME THEM IF THEY DID. IF SOMEBODY TOLD ME I HAD TO STAY IN ORBIT THIRTY MINUTES AWAY FROM MY LAST CHANCE TO SEE MIRANDA, WELL . . .

BUT I'M GOING TO KEEP THIS SHIP AND HER CREW READY TO FLY, SO I HAVE TO BE ABLE TO TELL THEM THE TRUTH.

THIS IS A HELL OF A WAR, THAT WE HAVE JOBS LIKE THIS.

NOW LET ME DO MY JOB.

KEYES

<\ FILE: ██████ - ███ - █████ **DATE:** ██████

<\ USER: Classified [Level █████ and above]

<\ ENTRY: 19-021/024

<\ CLEARANCE: Classified [Level █████ and above]

<\ TYPE: Post-incident investigation

<\ SUBJECT: Investigation into secure network [SecNet] message exchange between SGT. SCHICKER, Alasdair R. [GLancer] and SGT. POTEET, Joseph M. [TRIGTECH] to ascertain culpability of individuals involved, and classified information contained within, as it relates to the subsequent discovery and ultimate destruction of Reach by the Covenant.

<\ OBJECTIVE: Determine whether the details captured in the conversation contained within File No. ██████ - ███ - █████ held any relevance to the events that followed, i.e. potential enemy understanding of defensive forces and tactics present on Reach prior to and during the Covenant invasion. [MORE]

<\ FILE TYPE: Basic [For further details pertaining to this document, including participant background files, clearance-sensitive amendments, and more—click HERE]

<\ NOTE: All other entries related to File No. ██████ - ███ - █████ are under review. Full report pending completion of investigation.

<\ DATA: Begin 19-021/024 transcript . . .

GLancer: You online?
[1327, 19.07.2552]

GLancer: Trig! You on?
[1332, 19.07.2552]

TRIGTECH: [1332, 19.07.2552] Hold up

TRIGTECH: [1332, 19.07.2552] Sorry. One of our lifts is bust. We got Hogs backed up out the gate. What's up?

GLancer: [1333, 19.07.2552] Busy?

TRIGTECH: [1333, 19.07.2552] Always, but got a few. What's up?

GLancer: [1333, 19.07.2552] Not bad. I'll take yer Hogs and raise you 144s. Had three in yesterday.

TRIGTECH: [1334, 19.07.2552] What'd the 144s set you back? I can run diags on 3 Hogs in the time the flight mechs can run one bird.

GLancer: [1335, 19.07.2552] Wasn't bad. They take a helluva lot longer for sys-checks, but no glitches=not a complete cluster. Last week got one with a catch in the rotor. Bork'd the whole damn day.

TRIGTECH: [1335, 19.07.2552] That's why I stick to wheels 'n' mud.

GLancer: [1335, 19.07.2552] You stick to ground transpo cuz you hate flying.

TRIGTECH: [1336, 19.07.2552] Point?

GLancer: [1336, 19.07.2552] No point. We stick with what we know, right? You like dirt, I like clouds.

TRIGTECH: [1336, 19.07.2552] True. Not that yer toys aren't interesting, just never had much love for gravity. Must be my infantry blood—boots on the ground and all that.

GLancer: [1337, 19.07.2552] Don't know what yer missin'.

TRIGTECH: Says you.
[1337, 19.07.2552]

GLancer: HA!
[1337, 19.07.2552]

TRIGTECH: So, what's up?
[1338, 19.07.2552]

GLancer: Nothing, really.
[1339, 19.07.2552]

TRIGTECH: Just miss me? I'm touched.
[1339, 19.07.2552]

GLancer: Yeah. Something like that. Just been
[1339, 19.07.2552] awhile,thought I'd check in on the old shop.

TRIGTECH: You been out a year? Over, right? How's
[1340, 19.07.2552] field life?

GLancer: It's alright. Got four months left this
[1340, 19.07.2552] deploy,then shufflin' back to the "real" world.

TRIGTECH: Careful what you wish for. I don't know
[1341, 19.07.2552] that base life is any less a grind than a forward plot. Least not these days.

GLancer: Problems?
[1341, 19.07.2552]

TRIGTECH: Not so much problems.
[1341, 19.07.2552]
[1341, 19.07.2552] You hear things, right?

GLancer: About how it's going?
[1342, 19.07.2552]

TRIGTECH: Yeah. The war.
[1342, 19.07.2552]

GLancer: Yeah.
[1342, 19.07.2552]
[1342, 19.07.2552] It seems different don't it? Like more tense?

TRIGTECH: [1343, 19.07.2552] Yeah, I think. I know it ain't goin' great, but things've definitely gotten tighter lately.

GLancer: [1343, 19.07.2552] That's kinda why I hit you up. Wondering if you had the same vibe there as here?

TRIGTECH: [1343, 19.07.2552] Guess so, yeah. Assumed it'd be a bit more crunch-mode where yer at. I understand we're getting our asses kicked, but do you think it's gettin' worse?

GLancer: [1343, 19.07.2552] That's what I'm wondering.

TRIGTECH: [1344, 19.07.2552] Seems like. But it's a war—a BIG one—so it's not like it's suppose to be pleasant.

GLancer: [1344, 19.07.2552] Was actually hoping you'd tell me I was being paranoid. That I'm overthinking it 'cause I've been in-field too long, maybe I was getting twitchy. Guess not.

TRIGTECH: [1344, 19.07.2552] Things that bad out there?

GLancer: [1345, 19.07.2552] Not so much bad, just different. A lot of activity and a lot more personnel movements and we've been stockpiling artillery and rides when that shit usually gets allocated for deploy off-world.

TRIGTECH: [1345, 19.07.2552] Could just be there aren't that many off-worlds left to ship 'em to.

GLancer: [1345, 19.07.2552] Comforting thought.

TRIGTECH: [1345, 19.07.2552] Just jokes.

GLancer: [1346, 19.07.2552] Not so sure.

TRIGTECH: [1346, 19.07.2552]	Don't get all "end is nigh" on me.
GLancer: [1347, 19.07.2552]	I'm trying, but I'm seriously stressed. Hearing it's the same back home isn't comforting.
TRIGTECH: [1347, 19.07.2552]	I wouldn't worry too much.
GLancer: [1347, 19.07.2552]	Wouldn't or don't?
TRIGTECH: [1348, 19.07.2552]	I mean, I think about it and notice things, but I'm not gonna overanalyze anything. Ramp-ups happen. They're just keeping us primed and ready.
GLancer: [1348, 19.07.2552]	That's what I tell my paranoid self.
TRIGTECH: [1348, 19.07.2552]	Talkin' to yourself . . . there's yer problem.
GLancer: [1349, 19.07.2552]	It's not the talking I'm worried about. It's when I answer back.
TRIGTECH: [1349, 19.07.2552]	Well, if you end up crazy at least you'll have company.
GLancer: [1349, 19.07.2552]	There's a nice spin on mental illness.
TRIGTECH: [1349, 19.07.2552]	Not a doctor, but happy my expert opinion could be of some assistance.
GLancer: [1350, 19.07.2552]	Yer seriously not worried?
TRIGTECH: [1350, 19.07.2552]	Hell yes, I'm worried. Pretty sure I made that clear, but you can't dwell on shit outside yer control.
GLancer: [1350, 19.07.2552]	More sage advice?
TRIGTECH: [1351, 19.07.2552]	Not really. More like common sense.

[1351, 19.07.2552] LOOK, WE BOOST PROD ON THE HEAVY STUFF, LOAD UP ON THE SHOOTERS, AND KEEP THE GEARS GREASED, THE PUMPS PRIMED, AND THE SITUATION AIN'T GOOD, BUT WE'RE READY IF NEEDED. THAT'S OUR JOB. THAT'S THE GIG.

GLancer: I KNOW.
[1352, 19.07.2552]

TRIGTECH: I KNOW, YOU KNOW.
[1352, 19.07.2552]

GLancer: IT'S ALL KINDA STANDARD ISSUE, BUT THIS
[1352, 19.07.2552] IS DIFFERENT. YOU EVEN SAID—IT'S JUST DIFFERENT.

TRIGTECH: WE PROBABLY SAY THAT EVERY TIME THERE'S
[1353, 19.07.2552] ESCALATION. I'M SURE EVERYBODY SAYS IT EVERY TIME. JUST THE NATURE OF THE BEAST.

GLancer: MAYBE.
[1353, 19.07.2552]

[1353, 19.07.2552] TELL ME SOMETHING—SEE ANYTHING NEW THERE? NEW EQUIPMENT? NEW CREW?

TRIGTECH: NEW GUYS ROLL IN ALL THE DAMN TIME. WE
[1354, 19.07.2552] GOT THREE NEW TECHS LAST WEEK.

GLancer: NOT TECHS.
[1354, 19.07.2552]

TRIGTECH: LIKE MORE GRUNTS?
[1355, 19.07.2552]

GLancer: NOT SO MUCH INFANTRY, BUT YEAH. I MEAN
[1355, 19.07.2552] SOMETHING ELSE.

TRIGTECH: BIG DUDES?
[1356, 19.07.2552]

GLancer: BIGGER THAN NORMAL, YEAH.
[1356, 19.07.2552]

TRIGTECH: GROUP CAME THROUGH DAYS AGO.
[1356, 19.07.2552] TOUGH-LOOKING BASTARDS WITH FANCY EQUIPMENT, AND BIGGER THAN HELL. AND NOT

JUST SIZE-WISE, THEIR PRESENCE WAS BIG. LIKE, THEIR AURA OR WHATEVER, YA KNOW? BUT THEY WERE ONLY HERE AND GONE IN A DAY OR TWO.

GLancer: [1357, 19.07.2552] KNOW WHO THEY WERE?

TRIGTECH: [1357, 19.07.2552] NOT FOR SURE. YOU GOT THE SAME OUT THERE?

GLancer: [1358, 19.07.2552] YEAH. TWO SETS. BEEN HERE FOR TWO WEEKS-ISH.

TRIGTECH: [1358, 19.07.2552] WHO ARE THEY? 'BERTO SAYS SPARTANS, BUT I DON'T KNOW. NEVER ACTUALLY SEEN ONE. COULD BE.

GLancer: [1359, 19.07.2552] APPARENTLY, YUMA HAD A FEW COME THROUGH AS WELL. TALKED WITH TUPO OVER THERE AND SAME THING, HE SAW A GROUP OF BADASSES ONE DAY—BIG, MEAN-LOOKING, HARDCASES—THEN THE NEXT THEY'RE GONE. HE THOUGHT THEY MIGHT BE 'JUMPERS OR SOMETHING, BUT IF THEY WERE FROM THE SAME CLASS AS WHAT WE GOT HERE, NO WAY IN HELL.

TRIGTECH: [1359, 19.07.2552] THINK THEY'RE SPARTANS? EVER SEEN ONE?

GLancer: [1400, 19.07.2552] NOT IN PERSON, SO I CAN'T SAY, BUT PRETTY DAMN SURE THEY WERE SOMETHING SPECIAL AND THAT'S WHAT'S GOT ME FREAKED.

TRIGTECH: [1401, 19.07.2552] WHY? IF WE GOT SPARTANS ROAMING AROUND I'D LIKE TO SEE THE COVIES PICK A FIGHT, RIGHT? REACH'S ALREADY FORTIFIED LIKE THE GATES OF HEAVEN, SO ADDING SOME HIGH-END FACE-PUNCHERS TO THE MIX ONLY WORKS IN OUR FAVOR. CRISIS AVERTED.

GLancer: [1401, 19.07.2552] THAT'S THE THING.

TRIGTECH: [1401, 19.07.2552] WHAT?

GLancer: [1402, 19.07.2552] THAT'S WHY I'M WORRIED.

TRIGTECH: [1402, 19.07.2552] WHAT, THE FACT THAT YOU DON'T NEED TO WORRY?

GLancer: [1403, 19.07.2552] FUNNY. NO. THE FACT THAT TOP BRASS IS WORRIED ENOUGH TO POSITION SPARTANS HERE INSTEAD OF THE FRONT LINES.

TRIGTECH: [1403, 19.07.2552] FRONT LINES COULD ALREADY BE STOCKED UP WITH THEIR QUOTA OF SUPERSOLDIERS? THESE COULD BE RESERVES.

GLancer: [1403, 19.07.2552] OR MAYBE WE'RE ON THE FRONT DAMN LINES AND JUST DON'T KNOW IT.

TRIGTECH: [1403, 19.07.2552] THAT'S A BIT OF A LEAP.

GLancer: [1404, 19.07.2552] IS IT?

TRIGTECH: [1404, 19.07.2552] YOU JUST SAID YOU DON'T EVEN KNOW IF THEY'RE SPARTANS.

GLancer: [1404, 19.07.2552] SO DID YOU.

TRIGTECH: [1404, 19.07.2552] RIGHT. SO WE'RE MAKING ASSUMPTIONS.

GLancer: [1404, 19.07.2552] MAYBE.

TRIGTECH: [1405, 19.07.2552] MAYBE? YOU'RE JUST LOOKING FOR EXCUSES TO STRESS.

GLancer: [1405, 19.07.2552] HOPE YER RIGHT. I GOT NO PROBLEM LIVING A LONG, STRESS-FILLED LIFE COMPLETE WITH CONSPIRACY THEORIES AND IRRATIONAL FEAR, BUT WHAT IF I'M RIGHT AND YOU'RE JUST SCARED?

TRIGTECH: TELL YA WHAT. I GOT A TON ON MY PLATE,

[1407, 19.07.2552] So I'm going to go back to being a grease monkey. You can stew in yer doomsday fantasies, and we'll talk again in a week or two when we're both in the same damn place we are today—overworked, overstressed, and underpaid. In the meantime, have a beer. Have four! Just do something other than whatever the hell it is you're currently doing to yourself.

GLancer: [1408, 19.07.2552] This is just how my brain works. I get hung up on this crap and I can't help but overthink it. Thanks for listening

TRIGTECH: [1408, 19.07.2552] Don't mention it.

GLancer: [1408, 19.07.2552] We'll talk.

TRIGTECH: [1409, 19.07.2552] Sure thing. Talk to you later, and for Christ's sake, relax a little, this is Reach, we'll be fine.

\\End Transmission>>

<\Back>>

ABOVE TOP SECRET: PRI ALPHA
OFFICE OF NAVAL INTELLIGENCE
WINTER CONTINGENCY DECLARATION SUPPLEMENTAL ORDERS

1. The following numerically identified officers, Headquarters: United Nations Space Command, Reach, Epsilon Eridani System, will execute the following orders before evacuation of system according to Cole Protocol strictures.

Field Officer #345-261b
Field Officer #345-104b
Adjunct Field Officer #311-112b
Field Officer #227-112b
Special Officer #223-212a

- ORDERS FOR FIELD AGENTS FOLLOW

Redact all XNAV and ASTRONAV assets.

//ORDERS FOR FIELD AGENTS TERMINATE

BACKGROUND, HISTORY AND DETAILS FOLLOW

You are reading an evacuation order mandated by the emergence of a WINTER CONTINGENCY situation. This particular order is automated and the circumstances surrounding the specific emergence are not detailed here. Please consult EMERG/PUSH/SECURE for more current information.

FURTHER INSTRUCTIONS FOR FIELD AGENTS

All Cole Protocol mandates are in force. It cannot be stressed enough that Cole Protocol mandates include machinery, equipment, records, logs, AND personnel. Every agent on this distribution list has been through SCALED MORALITY TRAINING and should understand the responsibilities entailed.

Cole Protocol measures are useless without sterilization of all triangulation information whether it is stored digitally or *organically*. As a field agent, this single fact is the most important guideline you should follow.

BACKGROUND

All Astronavigation personnel carry a subdural pulse-coded emitter that is activated by WINTER CONTINGENCY and nullified once aboard a secure vessel or location. They are unaware of this device or its purpose.

You can exploit local GROUNDNET or utilize ONI NAVSPEC to identify and secure these assets. There is no termination date for this order. Once WINTER CONTINGENCY is declared, all assets must be secured or REDACTED until such time as Protocol-mandated rendezvous point is reached safely.

Do not be overestimate the apparent complexity of the (astronav) task. A good Astronavigator can identify and triangulate a very precise point in space using just a few known XNAV Pulsar signatures and any consumer-grade spectrometer or field kit. Our opponents are of course aware of this and have shown interest in such personnel in the past. So far hermetic measures have worked. They are not guaranteed to work forever.

UNSC HIERARCHY

Under the LIMON-NAXLA EXCEPTION you are hereby ordered to ignore or countermand all mission-contradictory orders from ranking UNSC officers below the grade of *secure-clear Captain*. ONI ranking officers may still issue contravening orders but use your judgment and common sense in applying the EXCEPTION. If the logic of the situation dictates that an advantage may be gained in your mission by following orders then do so. This is not carte blanche for intrabranch insubordination. Superior officers can and will file reports on LIMON-NAXLA EXCEPTIONS. You must also, if possible, clearly assert LIMON-NAXLA privilege to any senior officer giving excepted orders, if the situation provides an opportunity to do so. Otherwise, agent discretion is in play.

//DETAILS/DOC END

MARVEL®